SHACKLED

More Than One Life *A NOVEL*

BY *Marie Monroe*

Bloomington, IN   Milton Keynes, UK

AuthorHouse™
1663 Liberty Drive, Suite 200
Bloomington, IN 47403
www.authorhouse.com
Phone: 1-800-839-8640

AuthorHouse™ UK Ltd.
500 Avebury Boulevard
Central Milton Keynes, MK9 2BE
www.authorhouse.co.uk
Phone: 08001974150

First published by AuthorHouse 4/23/2007

ISBN: 978-1-4259-3889-5 (sc)

Library of Congress Control Number: 2006905325

Printed in the United States of America
Bloomington, Indiana

This book is printed on acid-free paper.

Cover artwork by Carol Love-Waddell.

Acknowledgements

This book is dedicated to my life extensions: James Michael, Christine Marie, Jamie Dawn, H. Curt and Branson Thomas.

Also to my husband and soul mate, Bob Smith, an everyday source of support.

My deepest appreciation goes to Genevieve Chase, my teacher and friend; my daughter, Christine, for long computer hours and good counsel; Amy Garvey for her skill and enthusiasm; Patti Patane, my client of twenty years, for the new computer; and Mike Mulkeen for technical support.

1

REMA

The eight-year-old boy twists inside the tornadic funnel of green ocean water. Trapped by the power of shimmering fury, globe-shaped bubbles from his lips rush to the empty space above. The savage water becomes more intense; the boy's head pushes downward until it rests between his skeletal knees.

For a moment, the fury is calm. Suddenly, moving from the base of the funnel, a frothing mass of greenish-yellow, effervescent water spirals upward and sucks the boyish body into the deep abyss.

Rema Swenson lunged forward to snatch her son from the water and fell forward on her knees. She opened her eyes and moaned. "Will this ever end?"

Clutching the arm of the brown leather couch, she pulled herself up from the floor of the reception room of the Arcane Studio. She inhaled deeply as though her breathing would change the intended consequence of her son's final struggle against the sea.

In her resolve to destroy the dreadful image, she watched the rays of the morning sun drift through the window and frolic across the red tile floor. When they collided with the airborne particles of dust, she watched them change into shiny pieces of floating gold.

"A sunbeam, a sunbeam," she sang in a half-spoken tone. Continuing the next line of the old Sunday school hymn, she whispered, "Jesus wants me for a sunbeam." Her voice withdrew to a soft whisper. "Emille, Emille my sunbeam."

1

The click of the minute hand on the face of the large, wood-rimmed wall clock reminded her it was 7:20 a.m. As night supervisor of the month-old Arcane Studio, she had been on duty until 7:00 this morning. She often used the serenity of the unoccupied reception room to complete the night's activity report and prepare for the 7:30 meeting with the daytime staff in the conference room. Falling asleep was not part of her plan.

Even though the brief nap interrupted her intended chore, she finished the report feeling grateful for the opportunity to work in the new state-supported rehabilitation center for wayward girls in Miami, Florida.

She realized her planets were in the right places when she got the job at Arcane Studio. It was a fortunate gift. Her social service skills were rusty. She had not worked for eight years. Her willingness to work six nights a week clinched the deal.

After one month of operation, the facility was providing quality care. Calling the facility a studio rather than a clinic or center diverted the media to find stories of interest elsewhere. The word, arcane, suggested secrecy or something that was understood only by those with special knowledge.

The local judges were taking the secrecy factor seriously. Twenty-five guests were staying in the studio and the illegal adventures and identities of young girls, particularly those from well-known families living in the counties of Broward and Dade, were protected.

The clock's minute hand clicked. Without looking up, Rema gathered the report papers, arranged them and went to the meeting.

Twenty minutes later, she returned to the reception area. Sitting at the secretary's desk, she added final comments to the staff report, signed her name and completed the form with the date, Thursday, August 21, 1970.

Preparing to go home, she paused at the front door and looked in the full-length wall mirror. Her hands pressed the wrinkles from the soft fabric of the long, floor-length skirt that nearly covered her favorite bronze leather sandals. Moving her head to one side, she adjusted the neckline ribbon of her peasant-style blouse.

The mirror reflected her impish grin. She reasoned her Gypsy-style wardrobe was not suitable for a degreed social worker and calculated it might be another week before the studio's director would advise her to wear the obligatory two-piece suit and dress shoes.

Her mischievous grin became a wide, victorious smile. She carried a lot of self-imposed guilt and had lost many battles, but when the discussion of her inappropriate clothing came about, she planned to win.

Peering closer into the mirror, she searched her face for wrinkles. The disappearance of her husband and son in the Atlantic Ocean eight months ago made grieving, at least for her, a devastating sport. She knew the grief monster would never let her win and questioned how long it would hold her in its spinney grasp.

Approaching footsteps caught her attention. It was too late to rewind her shoulder-length, black hair she had freed from its mooring. She stepped back from the mirror and wound it at the back of her head. While inserting a knitting needle in each side of the knot, she realized Marge Coverman, the day supervisor, was standing in the doorway.

"Are you going home or do you have an early morning rendezvous?" Marge asked.

"No rendezvous. Why would you think that?"

"You shouldn't be alone. Your green eyes and black hair are definitely men-catchers."

Rema smiled and added, "I'm taller than most men and I have a long nose, but I did meet someone a month ago. We're just friends."

Marge winked. "A friend is nice but a lover is better."

"I'm a grieving widow."

"You need a lover. A good loving might chase grief away."

Rema laughed and leaned over the receptionist's desk to answer the ringing telephone.

"Good morning, Arcane Studio. Yes, Judge Clare, the Bentley girl is quiet. I'll have Dr. Murdock call you after she completes her examination."

Rema wrote Judge Clare's message on a pad, placed it where the receptionist would see it, waved to Marge and exited through the side door.

By bus, it was a fifteen-minute ride to her new home in the older section of Miami. When the bus stopped in the turn-around near a public park, she went out the side door and hurried toward the trailer park.

Reaching the front of the rented mobile home, she found refuge from the hot sun under the tattered, blue canopy. She looked inside the blue, paint-crusted mailbox beside the front door. It was empty. She frowned.

Where is Felic? He didn't keep our date.

Slouching into a 1935 vintage metal lawn chair, she knew the time for a romantic venture was not in the cards. It was too late to apologize for her life. Right now, her timing was off. She grinned at her own truthfulness. Nevertheless, the memory of meeting Felic Ort was tucked inside her heart. It was early to place a label on her feelings for him. Still, her mind asked a silly question.

He stood me up. Will I see him again?

She closed her eyes and mentally revisited the first time she saw him. It was a Saturday afternoon. He came from behind the high-wire gate of the compound for the homeless into the public park, sat at a nearby table and watched her read the Tarot cards for some of the compound's residents. When the last person went away and she was alone, he walked toward her.

"You have quite a following," he said.

She reached for the cards.

"No card reading for me," he said. "Not today."

She fumbled in her knapsack for a pencil. "I can do your natal horoscope? When were you born?"

"May 3rd, 1930."

"Are you a native of Florida?"

"No, I was born in Ohio."

"What town, Columbus?"

"No, Wexlor. It's a small college town."

"Do you know the time of your birth?"

"Is that important?"

"Yes, very."

"It's odd you ask. I recently learned I was born at 6:26 p.m."

He shrugged and walked away.

"I'll have your natal horoscope next Saturday," she yelled. "Will you be here? What's your name?"

"Felic Ort."

"Is Felic spelled with an 'x'?"

He turned toward her and grinned. He was tall and erect, stomach flat, chest slightly expanded. His grin, sexy and telling, was the type that gives women chills.

"With a 'c'," he said.

Her memory was short-lived when she realized she was still sitting in the paint-peeling metal lawn chair under the trailer's canopy. She stood up and opened the trailer's door, stepped inside and tossed her knapsack on a chair.

Although domesticity was not her best talent, the trailer's cramped interior caused her to cringe. She was tall and the ceiling was low. The room resembled the inside of a closed coffin. How could she decorate a coffin with furniture selected from a second-hand store? A twelve-inch television in the corner of the living area was the only appliance saved from her marriage. It supplied evening entertainment of her favorite shows like *Gunsmoke*, *Here's Lucy* and *Marcus Welby*.

She kicked at a throw rug and scolded herself for shoplifting the past. Dragging old memories into the present defeated her state of mind. Her life was different now. During her ten years of marriage, she lived in an upscale, four-bedroom home in Miami's Kendall area.

She reached over the sofa and straightened the window curtain hanging above the noisy air conditioner. Stepping backward, she bumped into Grammy Perez's rocking chair. The chair had become her only refuge from the dreamy visions of Emille's drowning. When she sat in the chair, she was able to sleep without seeing her son consumed by ocean water.

For the rest of the day, despite the cranking noise of the air conditioner, she slept until mid-afternoon. Hoping Felic would drop off a note and apologize for missing their date, she stepped outside the front door into the August heat to look into the mailbox.

Where is your mind? Has grief and loneliness screwed you up to a point that you've developed romantic feelings for a homeless man?

Angered for allowing her romantic sensitivity to take a dominate place in her life, she went back to the living room and went to sleep in Grammy's chair.

At 9:30 p.m., a thunderstorm passed over the area. A few minutes after 10:00, Rema was ready to go to work. She locked the door and walked toward the bus stop. As usual, she arrived at the Arcane Studio to attend the staff meeting.

2

FELIC

5:00 a.m.
Monday Morning

Inside the Miami Canal Medical Clinic, Felic Ort peeked from the half-open door of treatment room #2. He swiveled his head around to be able to see if Dr. Whitetail was at the front desk. He stepped back and rubbed nervous moisture from his forehead.

After spending the past four days and nights at the renovated store-front medical clinic, he had devised a plan to leave without being noticed. The long days in the clinic were the result of last Thursday night's wild-assed experience.

On that evening, he had walked from Miami's compound for the homeless to Harding Street and into Dead Man's Alley to pick up food for the compound's residents. The alley had a notorious reputation in the 1940's as the dumping ground for the bodies of Miami's gang–related homicides.

Felic Ort savored the praise from his peers and volunteered to go into the alley. It was a danger-filled mission where no thinking man would go after sundown.

He had waited in the alley's entrance to muster up the courage to go inside. Before him stood the condemned, six-story Green Palms Hotel. The old hotel had dodged the wrecking ball for the last two years and was currently inhabited by rent-by-the-hour prostitutes and wayward alcoholics.

Sally's Restaurant was on the first floor of the hotel. This morning, a rumor spread through the compound that after ten o'clock at night Sally agreed to supply food for the homeless if the residents of the compound would discontinue annoying her customers at the restaurant's front door. She promised the food would be put in a breadbox under the window by the back door.

As he stood in the entrance amid the cluttered rain-soaked boxes and rotting garbage, he tried not to breathe the offensive odors. Adrenaline was rushing through his body urging him to move forward. He focused on a single beam of light shining under a metal-shaded lamp over the rear door.

After side-stepping puddles of muddy water, he reached up to open the breadbox but stopped at the sound of a high-pitched wail.

It's only a litter of kittens.

He raised a corner piece of a white, discarded shower curtain that lay over a wood crate, leaned over and looked inside.

"It's a baby boy!" he exclaimed. "He's naked and wet."

Without a thought, he jerked the brown knit sweater from his shoulders, wrapped it around the naked body and lifted the wailing infant from the crate. In his arms, the infant stopped crying. Felic walked between the wet boxes calling, "Lady, I have your baby. Come out! I'll get help for you."

The warmth of the newborn's body penetrating through the sweater onto Felic's arm awakened a memory. Five years ago, he had cradled his own newborn son. The child died later that day.

He continued to call to the mother, but only water dripping from the downspouts returned his calls. Frustrated by the immensity of holding a newborn, he walked around the alley looking for the child's mother. Stopping at the alley's entrance, he walked away. Outside under the flickering street lamp, he lifted the sweater from the newborn's face.

The kid's surviving. I've enough problems. I'm putting this problem back where I found him.

He returned to the alley. As he stared across the plumes of mist drifting above the hot, wet cardboard cartons, he tightened his arm around the infant. Thoughts, pro and con, rambled through his brain. To keep the baby would give him mounds of trouble. To return the infant could mean the infant might never be found. He turned and walked into the street.

Before he could decide on his next move, a flashing light atop a patrol car on Harding Street moved toward him. His thoughts were widespread, yet centered.

Anyone found on Harding Street after 8:00 p.m. already has a bad reputation. If I give this baby to the police, I could be arrested for kidnapping. I've no permanent address or a job.

He stepped against the shadows of the empty storefronts. The patrol car drove by. He stepped out away from the shadows. In the daytime, he had been in the area. Void of light it was not familiar. Walking at a fast pace, he saw a dimly lit sign hanging over the sidewalk.

A guiding light, he thought.

Walking along the empty store windows, he followed the light and stood at the front door of the Miami Canal Medical Clinic. In this moment, life stood still. He lifted his left hand to press the emergency button, but slowly withdrew it and waited. When his reluctance overpowered his determination, he thrust his left index finger hard against the emergency button and stepped back and waited.

The low-toned vibrations of the emergency bell awakened intern, Dr. George Whitetail, from a desktop nap.

Standing up, he blinked sleep from his eyes, glanced at his watch and was reminded it was Thursday, August 21, 10:20 p.m. He walked toward the front door, opened it and stepped aside hoping the man standing outside was not hiding a weapon under the brown sweater wrapped around his arm.

"Come inside," he said. "Is your arm injured?"

When Felic did not reply, Dr. Whitetail pointed down the hallway.

"Follow me. Treatment room #2 has a better lamp."

Felic followed him.

Dr. Whitetail turned on a swivel lamp.

"Let's have a look."

Felic opened the sweater.

The doctor grinned. "That is an armful."

Searching for a convincing lie, Felic stammered.

"The boy was born to a woman living in the homeless compound. I volunteered to bring him here for an exam. She's anxious to know if he's okay."

George Whitetail placed the baby on a small examining table and unfolded the sweater. "He's small, about six pounds. Does the mother plan to nurse him?"

Felic shook his head. "No, she was against that. Is there something you can feed him?"

"Yes, but I'm staffing the clinic alone over the weekend. I'll send him to the downtown hospital."

"Could you keep him here? If you send the kid downtown, the mother could get spooked and take off."

"I don't have time to feed a newborn. By the way, do you want this pink ribbon? It was tied around the bundle. What's his name? I'll put it on the birth certificate. On Monday, the receptionist will complete the form and have the information registered at the court house."

"His name is Mylowe. M-y-l-o-w-e."

Felic grabbed the pink ribbon and slid it into his pants pocket. The movement gave him time to think up another lie.

"I could stay here and care for him. I've lots of experience. I have younger brothers and sisters."

The doctor walked toward the door. "Okay, give it a try. It's not medical protocol, but nothing in this forsaken clinic sticks to rules."

Felic's four-day stay at the Canal Street Clinic had begun with telling a string of lies. He knew he was destined to tell many more.

As the days passed, Felic realized if he was to keep the baby as his own, he would need to get away from the clinic without being noticed and make sure there were no medical records of a baby treated there over the weekend.

On this fourth morning, while Dr. Whitetail was away from the front desk, Felic tied the sleeves of his brown sweater together and slung it around his neck. The body of the sweater fell waist-high and formed a hammock. Two diapers placed in the hammock made the infant a comfortable bed.

Felic stepped into the empty hallway and moved toward the front door.

"Quick Watson," he whispered. "The game is afoot!"

3

GUILT

After the Monday morning staff meeting at Arcane Studio, daytime supervisor, Marge Coverman, followed Rema into the reception room.

"Is there anything I can do? You seem perplexed."

Rema slumped down on the couch. "On the days when I feel I'm not grieving, something triggers my memories and I start all over again. Since Thursday morning, I've fretted because I didn't include my childhood hymn in the memorial service for my son and husband."

"Have you mentioned your feelings to your new male friend?"

"No, I haven't heard from him in seven days."

"Is that normal?"

"No, he's been very attentive."

Marge, wanting to offer support, sat beside her.

"I've wanted to tell you that I remember reading about your husband and son drowning in the Atlantic. Wasn't your husband an oceanographer?"

"Yes, his name was John Swenson."

"What was your son's name?"

"His name was Emille. The Miami Herald ran a headline about their disappearance but only printed a small article."

"Why?"

"There was a government investigation into the accident. I was not told the reason for the investigation, but I know the CIA was involved."

"The newspaper story said the Coast Guard found the boat?"

"Yes, they found the Mi Toi. It was John's thirty-eight foot Chris Craft. After the Coast Guard towed it in, I went to the boat yard to look at it. It was

11

weird to see the splintered hole in the bow. There was no sign of life and no bodies to bury—just the boat."

"Do you have family?"

"No, my Grammy Perez died ten years ago. My mother and father have been dead three years. I've lost contact with my four brothers. The service was held in the small ballroom at the Tide Edge Hotel in Miami Beach. Over the years, John had spent many hours there with his fishing buddy, Craig Everhart. Craig's family owned the hotel. Many city and state officials attended the service. John's colleagues were also there."

Rema stared at the yellow curtains on the reception room windows. The color reminded her of the yellow drapes at the windows in the ballroom at the hotel. The drapes in the ballroom reached from ceiling to floor and were always closed to shut out the sound of the rolling surf. On the day of the memorial service, the drapes were open.

Marge touched Rema's arm. "Are you all right?"

"Sorry, I was caught in a memory."

"Was it a good memory?"

"Yes, I was remembering Reverend Maxwell's eulogy. I still hear the ebbing tide splashing on the beach. Also, there was a rain shower as John's brother spoke of John's love for the sea."

"Those are good memories."

"Yes, Emille's third grade classmates stood at the front and recited, in unison, a farewell to him. It was sad to hear their voices chanting, 'We will miss you Emille Swenson, our classmate and friend. Now you live in our hearts.'"

Marge squeezed Rema's hand. "Do you realize this is the only time you've mentioned the accident?"

"I have a lot of guilt."

"Why?"

"John and I weren't happy. We didn't love each other."

"Why are you feeling guilty?"

"I screwed up our marriage."

"How did you do that?"

"I wasn't a partner. I took more than I gave."

Marge smiled. "We usually don't take enough."

"I've learned something. If things get good for me again, I'll be more attentive."

Marge patted Rema's hand. "Tell me why you're living in a trailer park across from the homeless compound. It's a terrible neighborhood."

"I'm broke. My husband did not include me in his will. His entire estate was bequeathed to Emille. The estate is held by the Florida court."

"Did John and the boy have life insurance?"

"Yes, but insurance benefits will be withheld until John and Emille are declared legally dead by the court."

"That's incredible. You have nothing to live on!"

"That is true. But more importantly John managed to reach me from his watery grave. I'm still under his thumb. I'm trying to shake his tyrannical authority."

"Do you really need to live in that awful trailer park? Don't you earn enough to afford better?"

"I should be able to move to a better place in a few months."

"You're very brave to live so close to all those hobos. Did you know that until the new compound was built, the homeless had been living beneath the main highway in the heart of downtown Miami? Do you feel safe among those people?"

Marge stood up before Rema could reply. "That's my bell," she said. "I'm wanted in Room 12. I'll see you tomorrow."

Rema nodded. Although Marge's concern for her was well-meaning, Rema was not ready to tell anyone the truth about the guilt she feels.

It happened three years after Emille was born, when her marriage began to teeter. To assist with the family expenses, Rema played piano in a downtown Miami hotel lounge two nights a week. On Saturdays, she played until midnight in a bar near her home.

While playing the old upright piano at the age of fourteen, in the recreation room that was open to migrant workers and their families, she discovered her updates and revisions of the melodies of Ellington, Porter, Berlin and the big bands brought applause. Before her marriage, she had numerous job offers but in the eighth year of marriage, she turned them down knowing another ten minutes at the keyboard would break up her marriage.

After her husband's drowning, she realized by being in two or three places during her marriage, she had ended up being nowhere. She had been two people and neither was a good marriage partner.

But now fate had taken over. Within a matter of minutes, she was changed from a wife and mother to that of a lonely woman of forty trudging through a quagmire of grief and learning that death never gives anything back. She had no place to go. Not even a door to run through.

4

THE CONFESSION

An hour later, when Rema walked into the old trailer park, the far-reaching odor of used-up, damp charcoal hovering over the area took her breath away. Her heart sank at the sight of the rows of old, road-weary mobile homes surrounded by knee-high, white picket fences marking each territorial piece of ground.

She wondered if the voices of laughing children and barking dogs were still imbedded within these forlorn silver masters of the roads. Surely, there were remaining memories of quiet nights parked by rippling brooks or campgrounds hidden in groves of trees beside favorite fishing streams.

Rema hurried down the sandy road between the white fences. Reaching her trailer and standing inside the living room, she hurled her knapsack across the room and sat in Grammy Perez's rocker. Her frustration was apparent. Marge Coverman had touched some sensitive subjects.

Rema knew she had made a bad move when she decided to cut expenses. A trailer wasn't for her. She leaned back and sensed Grammy Perez's spirit nearby. Grammy would say, "No problem leaves you where it found you."

A knock on the front door aroused Rema from the reverie.

Felic?

She stood up and decided not to be stuck in her depression and allow life to be unbearable. At the door, she pushed it open.

Felic stood on the bottom of the trailer's three wood steps. The sleeves of a brown sweater were tied together and hung round his neck. Part of it was across his midsection.

"You look awful," she said. "Why are you wearing a sweater?"

15

"I'm late for our date," he said.

"Are you coming in?"

Felic stared toward the street.

"Are you being followed?" Rema asked.

He shook his head, climbed the steps and walked inside. She closed the door and leaned against it. He stood in front of her and unfolded a portion of the sweater.

Rema gasped. "You've a baby in there."

"It's a boy," he said proudly. "He's nearly five days old."

"Is he a relative?"

"No, I found him in wet garbage on Thursday night."

"Where?"

"In Dead Man's Alley."

"What were you doing in that awful place after dark?"

"I was getting food for the people at the compound."

"Do you know how dangerous the alley is?"

He laid the baby on the sofa and slumped down beside him.

"Did I say something wrong?" she asked.

"No, I just forgot."

"What?"

"On Thursday night, I went to the alley to pick up food from Sally's Restaurant for the people at the compound. They'll think something terrible happened to me."

"That was Thursday night. It's Monday morning. Where have you been?"

"I took the baby to the Miami Canal Medical Clinic. A doctor allowed me to stay with the baby. I told him the baby had been born to a woman in the compound."

"Did he think you were the father?"

"I don't know."

"What time did you find the baby?"

"It was after ten o'clock. Only the doctor knows I have the baby. The medical staff was not in the clinic over the weekend. This morning, I walked away from the clinic before the medical staff arrived. I took the baby's medical record."

Felic opened his shirt and pulled out a folder. "The doctor already signed the baby's birth certificate."

"You took a medical record?"

Ignoring her question, he said, "All I need to do is complete the certificate and register the birth at the courthouse."

"How do you plan to care for a baby? You're homeless."

Felic walked into the kitchen. At the sink, he turned on the faucet and ran the water until it was warm. From his bulging trouser pockets he took two nursing bottles, a container of Similac and three diapers.

"Felic, you know you should take the baby to the police."

"I don't intend to do that. However, this morning, after I walked away from the clinic, I saw the clinic doctor get into a police car. They drove toward the homeless compound."

"What is the doctor's name?"

"Dr. Whitetail. He probably discovered I disappeared and took the medical record. The police could be at the compound looking for me. I did not give the doctor my real name."

"What name did you give him?"

"Martin."

"You gave no last name?"

"No last name."

Rema sensed from Felic's determined tone he was not going to report the baby to the authorities.

In the kitchen, he mixed Similac, poured it into nursing bottles and stood one bottle in a pan of warm water.

"Please sit down and tell me what happened in the alley," she said.

"After the rainstorm on Thursday night, I went to the rear of Sally's Restaurant in Dead Man's Alley to pick up food for the people at the compound. At the back door, I heard wailing. I assumed it was a litter of newborn kittens. When I raised a corner of a piece of an old plastic shower curtain, the baby was underneath. He was naked and cold. I wrapped him in my sweater. Walking out of the alley, I saw a police car. I thought about giving the baby to them."

"So you went to the Miami Canal Medical Clinic."

"Yes. The doctor examined the baby and pronounced him okay. He said the mother was not a drug addict. The baby's umbilical cord had been closed with a rubber band."

"Why did you stay at the clinic for nearly four days?"

"I needed time."

"Why?"

"I had to decide how to keep the baby. The doc was working alone and didn't have the time to care for the baby."

"So, he let you stay in the clinic?"

Felic nodded and took a small vial of blood from his shirt pocket.

"What are you doing with a blood sample?"

"It's the sample the doc took from the baby. I couldn't leave anything in the clinic for the police to find. I washed my fingerprints from the doors, plates, spoons, the sink and everything I touched."

"Do you think the doctor knew you were lying about the baby being born in the compound?"

"If he knew, he didn't question me. He's Apache. His ancestors escaped into the Everglades when the government was chasing Geronimo. His family still lives near there on a vegetable farm."

"I'm surprised he let you stay four days."

"He said he'd seen me before in the clinic's waiting room."

Rema picked up the baby. "Does this baby ever cry?"

Felic grinned. "When he's hungry, he whoops it up."

"So, you're not sure you escaped the clinic unnoticed. Why would you take such a risk?"

Felic began to pace. He knew this was not the time to confess everything. His reasons for keeping the baby were much too complicated. Her questions would require deeper answers than he was willing to give.

"I need to make a confession," he said.

Rema's heart raced.

He's married.

She lowered her head.

"I've misrepresented myself to you and the people at the compound," he said.

"What do you mean?"

"I'm not a vagrant. I'm Dr. Felic Ort, a Professor of Theology and Religion at Miami University."

She took a deep breath.

Maybe he isn't married.

"Why are you living at the homeless compound?" she asked.

"I'm conducting a research project. It's in the final three months. I must finish it or I'll lose my funding."

"What kind of research is it?"

"I'm studying whether homeless people, who continually face problems and conflict, use a religion for support."

Rema started to speak, but Felic put his finger to his lips.

Surprised by his finger language, she waited.

"I believe destiny has a plan for everyone," he said. "While I was in the clinic, I decided to keep this baby. I'm acting against the law, but I have reason to hate the welfare system. I believe I was chosen to care for this child."

"Chosen?"

"Yes."

"Chosen by whom?"

"By a higher authority."

The baby began to cry. Felic cradled the infant in his arms.

"No one in this country despises the welfare system more than I do," he said. "I lived in nine different foster homes in three states over nine years."

Rema gasped.

Felic continued. "There's not one redeeming grace about any welfare system. With one stroke of a pen, that organization can destroy the lives of children. I've decided to keep this child because five years ago, my son died at birth. My wife died three days later."

Rema was silent. She knew the hand of fate was stirring a magical pot in the center of her living room. Was it her destiny to be with Felic and this baby? Legally, this child's existence should be reported to the authorities. If she made a report, she would detour Felic's destiny and his opportunity to fill his empty heart with a castaway infant.

Against all she was feeling, she recognized it was a wondrous moment. She watched the strands of Felic's life and the infant being tied together so securely that neither time nor the world could tear them apart.

Rema put her questions aside, at least for the present.

"Have you named him?" she asked.

"Yes, I'm calling him Mylowe." He spelled it slowly, "M-Y-L-O-W-E."

"Mylowe Ort?" she said.

Felic smiled.

She waited for the magic to diminish. Suddenly, she said, "Tick, tock, tick, tock."

He stared at her. "What did you say?"

"Tick, tock, tick, tock, time is getting short. Where do you intend to care for this child?"

His jaw twitched. "If I had thought this through, I would not have come here." He gathered the infant close. "I can tell you're upset with me."

"What would you do if the situation were reversed?"

"I haven't given it a thought."

"You have an hour and a half. I've an appointment at two o'clock. I suggest you come up with a plan."

5

PINCHEY WILSON

Wilson's Bail Bonds did not appear to be a prosperous business. At a desk in the storefront office near the west Miami police substation, Pinchey Wilson looked up from a stack of credit journals and grinned at Rema who was standing in the doorway. He pushed a well-chewed, Havana cigar stub to one side of his mouth.

"Hi there, little lady. What do you have for me today? I hope it's something good." He clutched his right side and leaned forward. "I've a pain in my gut. God! It hurts."

Rema laid her knapsack on a nearby chair.

"What does the doctor say about your pain?"

"He keeps telling me the same bull. I'll bet a hundred bucks I have cancer."

Rema walked behind him and laid her hand softly on his shoulder. In the window, a neon sign blinked "Bail Bonds" in garish green and red letters. Despite Pinchey's annoying manner, Rema was drawn to help him even though his uncontrollable temper usually turned the freckled spots on his bald head a flushing pink.

"I almost had another stroke," he grumbled.

"When?"

He pointed at the desk calendar. "It was on the 19th. I wrote it down."

"I see you have new eyeglasses."

"Yah!"

"Do you see more than you did before?"

"Naw!"

Pinchey was stubborn and cranky. When angry, he swore in improper use of invented words that would send Webster's proofreaders scurrying to record them into a new dictionary.

She moved away to escape the sour, smoky odor of his cigar. Flakes of dandruff around the neckline of his rumpled, black, pinstripe suit caught her attention. She knew he was hiding behind Coke-bottle lenses to see only the parts of life he deemed important enough to warrant his attention. He regarded his hearing aid in the same way.

Placing a file folder on the desktop, she asked, "So, what have all your medical tests discovered?"

"The doc says they don't show nothing. He says the pain's all in my head."

Rema turned toward him. "Last week, we talked about your fear of getting cancer."

"Yah, I remember."

"Did you close your eyes and see your body healthy?"

Pinchey hunched his shoulders up and down. "I didn't try to see anything. My gut hurt too much to play a silly game."

Rema took papers from the file folder and sat on a chair close to him.

"Do you believe anything I say?"

"About that astrology junk? Yah! Maybe."

"Then, let me show you this."

She organized the papers. "I made you a storyboard."

"A storyboard? That's what my grandchildren do in Sunday school."

"This is a different board. It's a 360 degree circle usually with 30 degrees in each of 12 sections. In astrology, the sections are called houses. Now, look where I've put my finger.

"Your moon is in the sign of Aquarius 27 degrees in the 9th house. When I delineate an astrology chart for a client, for my own information, I look for cancer or tumors or any kind of growths. I also look for signs of worry and stress."

"Well, I've plenty of that."

"To find worry and stress in a chart I look for the Moon in Pisces or the planet Mercury in the sign of Virgo in a poor aspect to the Moon. The North Node of the Moon also provides important information."

"My wife says I worry too much."

"Since the storyboard shows your Moon in Aquarius, it's not likely that your body would produce any type of tumor or growth unless you are radiated by an atom bomb."

An impish grin crossed Pinchey's lips. "Do I have to worry about that, too?"

"According to your natal horoscope, you're not a person likely to get cancer because your Moon trines Neptune. That's a fortunate aspect."

Rema clutched Pinchey's hand and guided his index finger on the drawing of the Zodiac.

"Look, there's the trine. It's shaped like a pyramid and touches your Moon, Neptune and Venus. Your current health problems may not be coming from a tumor or cancer."

"My wife nags me about my smoking cigars."

"The trine is your best aspect. If a cancer is found in you, it's curable."

"Thanks a lot!" Pinchey yelled.

Rema yelled back. "Hey! You're in much better shape than a person with his Moon opposing Neptune. Nine chances in ten, his cancer will be masked and discovered too late to cure.

"Or what about the person with his Moon square Neptune who won't be too bad off if he gets regular check-ups?"

She was talking in generalities in hope it would help Pinchey think through his fears.

"Come on," she teased. "You're letting fear get the better of you. If you really want to worry about something, you should worry about theft and deceit in your financial affairs."

"That's a hell of a thing to say to a bail bondsman."

"The last time I was here, I told you there was deception and fraud in your progressed chart."

"I believe that. I get more counterfeit collateral in a week than the Catholic Church gets in a year. If the church had my track record with receivables, it would be out of business."

Pinchey's fear of losing large amounts of money was understandable. His was a risky business. Armed with a quick temper, he often used money as a wedge to gain the upper hand. It was evident that the eight years he spent in prison for fraud had not taught him anything.

"Can you come back next week?"

Rema patted him on the shoulder. "Sure," she said. "I'll be here next week at the same time."

"You're a college girl, aren't you? What did you study?"

"I'm a degreed social worker with a minor in psychology."

"Why do you bother with the astrology mumbo jumbo?"

"My Grammy Perez taught me basic astrology. I also studied astrology at the university. Grammy taught me to read the Tarot cards, understand herbal medicine, read palms and use faith healing to help my body."

"Was this stuff always handed down in your family?"

"Yes, Grammy and her mother, Arvilla, knew these things. My ancestors were from Mexico."

"It all seems eerie, but I'm feeling better now that I can see some direction in my life."

"In the hands of a skilled astrologer, a person's horoscope is an accurate tool for pointing out the various kinds of conflicts that are outside the human awareness."

"Well, your teaching is saving my sanity and my life. I want to be a better person. I didn't know where to begin."

Rema nodded and gathered her papers from the desktop.

"To dream the person you would like to be, is to waste the person you are. I'll see you next week. Is Tuesday at the same time okay?"

6

THE PROPOSAL

Leaving Pinchey's office, Rema hurried to her trailer. In the compact living room, Felic was rocking Mylowe in Grammy Perez's chair. Felic had shaved and brushed his hair. He jumped to his feet.

"I have no right to involve you in this," he said. "Am I being too premature about our feelings for each other?"

She nodded.

"You're being generous. The truth is that we barely know each other."

Rema felt mummified and spoke without expression. "Under any conditions, legal or not, if I were given the opportunity, I would fight to keep my son."

He took her hand and guided her to sit in the rocking chair. When she was settled, he began to pace around the room. After several moments, he stopped.

"Would you permit me to stay in your trailer with Mylowe while you're working at night?"

"Do you mean while the police are looking for you?"

"I don't know what to do about the police."

"Perhaps I could ask Pinchey Wilson to check the police blotter for someone named Martin. Pinchey has good connections with the police."

Felic sighed. He desperately needed her to say he could stay in her trailer at night. He stopped pacing and stared at her.

"I was thinking that during the portion of the day when you're awake, I could go to compound and work on my research project."

Her eyes widened. She sat erect. The tone of her question bordered on unfriendly. "You're asking me to baby-sit?"

"Only for three hours a day," he replied. "I would contribute to your household expenses. In three months when I've completed my research project, the three of us could move to a two-bedroom apartment near the university."

A shiver raced down her spine.

He ignored her apparent discomfort. "My wish is," he said, "that we will grow together into a comfortable, loving relationship. If it doesn't happen, we would go our separate ways."

Rema tried to move her feet but her ankles were stuck together. Her fingernails dug into the arms of the chair.

"I'm still married," she uttered. "My husband and son have been missing for eight months. They have not yet been declared dead. The court will address those issues in five years."

Before she could recover from his proposal, he kneeled before her. "I didn't know. I'm so sorry."

She nodded and walked toward the bedroom. "I need some time to think."

"I've got a hell of a nerve," he said. The tone of his voice displayed what he was about to say was important. "Would you explain the legal problems surrounding your husband's disappearance?"

She stared at him. "Without a certificate of death and power of attorney, I have no financial support from my husband's estate. His entire holdings were willed to our son. My husband's insurance companies demand proof of the deaths. When there are no bodies, death certificates are not issued. The insurance companies do not pay the beneficiary. As I said, a Florida court must issue a declaration of each death."

"You mentioned that it would be five years before your husband's estate could be distributed."

She tried not to believe he was on a fishing expedition. "Five years," she said, "that's the Florida law. At first, the insurance investigators believed my husband had run away. They checked into bank records to see if he had withdrawn a large amount or had closed an account. They didn't find anything. They also checked with John's employer and colleagues to determine if there was any evidence of a planned disappearance. They found nothing."

Felic pulled her into his arms and whispered. "I'm such a blunderer."

7

ANXIETY

Inside her closed bedroom and alone, Rema felt the room's temperature rising. She opened the door to let cool air in, kicked off her sandals and loosened the drawstring on the waist of her long skirt. The skirt dropped to the floor. The peasant blouse rolled easily over her head. Tugging at the knitting needles in her hair, a cascade of black, silky hair dropped down onto her shoulders. From the back of the bedroom door, she took a blue rayon kimono and pulled it around her. The soft material felt cool against her skin. She rubbed a tender spot on the back of her neck. She was certain it had not been there prior to Felic's proposal.

Her feelings were stymied between fear and anger; she pounded her fists into the bed pillows. Felic's proposal wasn't about love. It was an arrangement.

She knew the stories of the women who rushed into love matches because of loneliness or other reasons and later realized they were trapped in untenable relationships.

She turned on her back to lie on the cool bed sheet and thought it unfair that life was testing her about love so soon after the death of her husband.

She frowned and bit her lip.

Suppose she agreed to Felic's arrangement. Would she again experience unrequited love? Living in a marriage with a man she didn't love had been hell.

Her frown faded. Instead, the usual impish grin formed on her lips. The battle had started and she would be the winner.

On the other hand, Felic might teach her more about love than she wanted to know. Although the suggested arrangement did come about through a bizarre set of circumstances, he didn't know he had already built a fortress around her heart.

A full smile opened her lips. *Yes, she would become his lover.* The love between them might even grow into a kind of love and companionship she had never experienced. Doesn't every woman have that right?

"Okay! Okay!" she whispered to the persistent prodding of the voice from her inner-self. *In many ways, Felic is similar to John. Why am I surprised? Usually when a person selects a different love partner, the new mate is often similar in physical appearance to the previous mate.*

Living with my husband, I was a housekeeper, a servant and a concubine. I would be the same to Felic. I've done exactly what many women do. I'm attracted to Felic because he physically resembles my husband and I prefer that type of man. To be honest, I was prepared to begin a serious relationship with Felic before I knew he was a university professor.

She pounded the pillows again. "Enough," she whispered, "I'm not going to be vulnerable to the first man who is attentive to me. John was an abuser. His outbursts of harsh and scathing words taught me to stay within myself and remain aloof from the disagreements he instigated for his own enjoyment."

She sat up and slid her legs over the side of the bed.

John also taught me to give in and be the losing partner in the marriage. I learned I had to lose the arguments in order to win. By giving in to his demands, I ultimately became the winner. In a strange way, when I lost a battle, the loss allowed my soul to win the war.

She lay across the bed and looked at the ceiling.

When the student is ready, the teacher will appear. I wonder what Felic might teach me.

She smiled. *I might be the teacher. What would I teach the prideful Professor Ort?*

Still on her back, she said, "It's time to make an accounting sheet of the positive and the negative."

Waving her index finger in the air, she drew an invisible outline of a sheet of paper. In the center, she drew a vertical line. On the right side, she wrote the word, positive. On the other side, she wrote negative.

On the positive side, she concluded both men were (1) professionals; John was an oceanographer. Felic was a university professor. They were both (2) intelligent, and (3) physically attractive.

She turned to the negative. John was (1) dishonest, (2) secretive, (3) self-serving, (4) verbally abusive and (5) selfish.

Felic is (1) dishonest, (2) secretive and (3) self-serving.

The comparison faded. She sat up, folded a pillow in half, bent forward over it and rocked back and forth. Rocking gave movement to her fears. In a strange way, the movements made her feel safe. She learned her foolish fears vanished in the same way they appeared. She had rocked as a child when her father yelled abusive, drunken phrases at her mother. After her husband and son disappeared in the Atlantic Ocean, she rocked every night.

Now, eight months later, she felt a stirring inside. Felic had pushed her love button to the "on" position. Was she ready?

She didn't try to stop the tears that rolled down her cheeks. She knew tears had a way of cleansing all the main organs and tissues in the body. A good cry always made her feel better.

After a minute had passed, she wiped away the tears and visualized the magic moment when Felic Ort and Rema Perez Swenson would proclaim their true, honest feelings for each other and revel in the wondrous joy that accompanies new love.

Fearfully, she clutched the pillow. Fate had offered her a second son. Could she love Mylowe with the same intensity she had felt for Emille? She placed the pillow behind her head.

Every child needs a mother.

Once again, warm tears rolled over her cheeks and dropped upon the pillow.

8

THE HONEYCOMB

Daylight had faded when Rema awoke at 8:30 p.m. The aroma of food cooking in the kitchen drifted into the bedroom. She stood up, gathered the kimono around her and peeked into the kitchen through the half-open door. When Felic heard her footsteps, he turned around.

"I made Bedouin stew," he said. "It's tasty, but it could be better. You didn't have any goat meat in the refrigerator."

"Bedouin stew? Where did you learn to cook it?"

"Years ago, I lived as a Bedouin."

He spooned stew into a bowl and placed it on the pull-down table near a window. Rema walked over to the divan and looked at Mylowe.

"He's so peaceful," she said. "Do you have supplies for him? I could shop for you in the morning."

Felic held up both thumbs.

She stared at them and assumed she had been commissioned to do the shopping.

He pulled a chair away from the table and with a wide-sweeping movement of his right arm he guided her to sit down and lowered himself into the chair on the opposite side. He reached for her hands and held them. His energy rushed through her.

"Do you feel that?" he asked.

The gleam in his eyes made her to shiver. She knew his crooked smile would make her bend to his every wish. The gravitational pull toward him made her feel like a worker bee eager to experience the sweetness of the honeycomb.

She sensed the complexities of meeting a mate for her soul and knew they each had traveled separately through eons of time to find the other. Now, in this lifetime, as teacher and student, they were again bound together.

9

TOGETHER AGAIN

Sitting across the table from Felic, Rema stared at him. There was a familiarity about him. She knew deja'vu was only a passing fragment that occurs when an echo from a past lifetime begins to open and is often triggered by a similar situation.

"We were together in another lifetime," she blurted.

"These days, that's what everyone wants to believe."

"Our roles were reversed."

"Reversed roles?"

"Yes, you were female and I was male. In the reincarnation process, male and female roles are often reversed."

"Why?"

"So each can walk in the other's shoes and experience life from a different perspective."

He grinned impishly. "Do you think we come back into the same family?" He leaned toward her. When she hesitated, he began to speak. Imitating his use of hand language, she held up her hands to stop him.

"You're a quick study," he said.

She nodded. "We come back to live on earth again and again. Our souls push us forward until we learn enough in each lifetime to finally put it all altogether."

"You mean we reach perfection."

"We often delay our soul the growth it needs because of the stupid things we do, but we are constantly challenged to move back to our perfect level."

"So, we're perfect when we're born?"

"Yes, but coming into the human form makes us imperfect. Being human challenges us to work toward our original state of perfection."

"How do we do that?"

"Consider the problems we have. To exist we need to have money, shelter and transportation. We have parents, caregivers, spouses, children, in-laws, friends, and even enemies. We get disease and have accidents. Everything in life is problematic."

"What about fear, love, anger, guilt and jealousy?"

"Those are emotions. They are human reactions to human problems. When we're in another dimension (like heaven) we don't have a physical body and we are perfect."

Felic stood up and walked toward the front door. "You make me feel like I have no freedom to choose whether I reincarnate. Are you telling me I don't have a choice? I feel trapped and shackled. You want me to believe the earth was created so each lifetime I can advance myself and reach for perfection. What if I don't want to advance?"

Rema stared at him and wondered if she could deal with his mindset. "Do you believe you have a soul?" she asked.

"I don't know. Do I need a soul?"

"The soul's development is based on the responsible acts its human body performs. The soul's power receives growth when an individual realizes his soul actually exists."

He pulled the front door open. A warm breeze drifted in. When Rema turned to speak to him, he held up his hand. She decided his hand signals were intimidating and planted her feet firmly on the floor.

This man has more hand signs than a third base coach.

Ignoring his hand signal, she said. "I'm late. In the morning, I'll stop by Pinchey Wilson's office and ask him to check the police blotter."

Felic followed her to the bedroom and stood outside the door while she dressed. "Whether I'm wanted by the police or not," he said, "I need to go to the compound."

Holding a chopstick between her teeth before placing it in the woven knot of hair at the back of her head, she muttered, "In two days, we should have an answer from Pinchey. Sleep in here tonight. There's a good breeze. Bring Mylowe with you."

She rushed by him and stepped outside. Moving from under the swaying canopy, she stopped to look at the stars. Headlights from the approaching bus illuminated the area around her. She raced across the park.

Boarding the bus, she walked toward the side exit. The tires squealed as the bus navigated the oval turnaround and rumbled back onto the street.

Thoughts of Felic's beliefs filled her mind, but one thought blocked out the rest.

He loves me.

10

INSIGHT

The next morning, after working the night at Arcane Studio, Rema walked the six blocks to Pinchey Wilson's office. Through the window, she saw Pinchey making the morning coffee. The blinking neon sign hanging in window kept pace with her beating heart. She opened the door. Pinchey dropped the coffee scoop to the floor.

"What the hell are you doing here?" he yelled. "Is something wrong? Does my astrology chart say I'm going to die?"

"You're just fine! I need a favor."

"What can I do?"

"The police may be looking for my friend. Would you check the police blotter?"

"What's she done? Robbery? Murder? Jay-walking?"

"It's nothing too serious. His name is Martin. That's the only name he uses."

"I suppose it's one of those guys at the homeless compound." He grunted and leaned over the desk. "Whoever this guy is, I can tell you're in love with him. Don't try to deny it. I'm seldom wrong about these things."

"You might be right."

Despite the gruffness in his voice, there was amusement in his eyes. He grumbled and cleared his throat.

"When did the crime occur?"

"Monday morning, August 25th."

"Are you going to tell me anything else?"

"No."

"Okay! Okay! Stop by this afternoon."

She walked behind him and put her hand softly on his shoulder. "Thanks," she said. "I'll be here at three o'clock."

Waving a small piece of paper at her, he growled. "By the way, I've got another client for you. She's one of my wife's friends. Stop by her place. She lives one street over on Graham Street, the number is 736."

Rema tucked the paper inside her knapsack asking if all the information she would need to construct an astrology chart for the friend was enclosed. Fifteen minutes later, when the bus pulled into the end of the route turnaround, she jumped off.

In the park, she rested on a bench and remembered the notes she had made while delineating Felic's natal horoscope. The notes were in her knapsack. She was hoping the next time she mentioned the chart to him, Felic would not make another excuse to delay it.

While reading the notes, she was reminded that Felic's ascendant was Scorpio. The Scorpio ascendant creates an intensity that intimidates some people and intrigues others.

His personality was forceful and steely. Not a person to trifle with.

His Sun in Taurus in the seventh house makes him stable, slow and deliberate. But, when pushed, he could turn into a raging bull.

Rema scanned the chart for other challenging aspects. The Moon in Cancer square Uranus, Venus in Gemini square Neptune.

From the squares and the positions of the houses, it was apparent she should be cautious. She would need to deal with his independence and not be taken in by his soft emotional side. The position of Venus makes him a good sex partner. Lastly, his temper could be ignited by a large amount of energy. Once fired up, he had no discipline to stop it.

Rema gathered the papers, tossed her knapsack over her shoulder and walked toward the trailer park. She had decided not to give Felic an answer to his proposed arrangement until she combined his chart with hers and made a compatibility chart.

At the trailer, she found Felic and Mylowe in the living room.

"Did you have a quiet night?" he asked.

"It was busy."

"Did you see Pinchey?"

"Yes, he's checking with the police. I'm to be at his office by three o'clock this afternoon. How is Mylowe?"

"We were up two times during the night. He eats, burps and pees in an orderly fashion. A good guy! I made coffee. Do you want a cup?"

Rema nodded. Felic poured the steaming liquid into a waiting cup. "If I'm not wanted by the police, we may need to ask Pinchey to do another favor," he said.

"What?" she asked.

"Mylowe's birth certificate should be registered at the court house. I can't go if the cops are looking for me. The person with the certificate might be picked up and questioned."

"Okay," she said. "Wake me at two-thirty. I'll take the birth certificate to Pinchey."

Felic waved his hand.

She winced and thought. *There's the third base coach again.*

Although she needed to sleep, she was curious to see if any legal entanglement or jail time was indicated in Felic's chart. She was relieved to discover he would not be imprisoned in his lifetime.

When she lay on the bed, she was struck with a dose of reality. Her knowledge of astrology that her husband had despised was now giving her vital information to help her plan a life with Felic.

She arranged the pillow under her head and remembered an important part of her natal horoscope.

In this current life, she would be married only one time.

11

DELIBERATION

With only four hours of catch-up sleep, Rema awakened and blinked until her vision adjusted to the bright afternoon sun.

What time is it?

She looked at the clock.

Dressing quickly, she applied a touch of makeup, stuck a knitting needle on each side of the knot of hair at the back of her head and hurried from the bedroom. Rushing past Felic, she whispered, "I'm late for my meeting with Pinchey." At the turnaround, she boarded the waiting bus. It was ten minutes after three o'clock when she arrived at Pinchey's office.

"I know I'm late," she said.

"Don't make no difference. The police aren't looking for a guy named Martin. Your boyfriend's in the clear."

She tried to hide her galloping heart. Pinchey shook his head and grinned while she rummaged through her knapsack.

"Did you lose something?" he asked.

"Oh! I found it. It's in an envelope. This might be confusing," she began, while clutching her knapsack for support. "I need your help."

"What can I do?"

She pointed the small envelop at him. "Could you have this birth certificate registered at the Clerk of Courts?"

"What the hell for? Don't tell me it's your kid and this guy, Martin, is the father. Is he one of those hobos living at the compound?"

Rema bristled. "You know I try to help the homeless people. They live near my trailer and trust me. There's nothing illegal about this birth certificate. It's complete and signed by the attending physician at the Canal Street Medical Clinic."

"Well if the doc signed it, why didn't he have the clinic people take it to the courthouse?"

Rema put her hands on her hips and planted her feet firmly. "The situation is complicated. Will you have the birth certificate recorded?"

Pinchey stared at her. "Okay! Okay! I'll get it done, but you owe me."

She put two fingers to her lips and transferred a kiss to his bald head.

"Thanks," she whispered. "You're the best."

During the bus ride to the turnaround, Rema decided it was time to find out what Felic was thinking. At the trailer's front door, she smoothed her hair before going inside.

Felic was at the stove in the kitchenette sterilizing nursing bottles. He turned off the boiling water and met her at the door. "What did Pinchey say? Am I wanted by the police?"

"Pinchey said you're in the clear. He was annoyed about registering the birth. He might open the envelope. Did you put your real name on the certificate?"

"Yes."

"Who did you name as Mylowe's mother?"

"I wrote that the mother was unknown. Do you believe Pinchey has the contacts to get the birth recorded?"

"I'm certain he does. He was too upset to tell me how he would do it."

Felic rolled his eyes. "I guess we can always check at the courthouse later. But before any of this goes forward, I would like to append my proposal."

Her anger rose inside. "You mean you want to add to that business arrangement you proposed last night?"

He laughed and stifled the urge to wrestle her onto the divan. "You're in bloom again. I love it when your eyes flash dot-dit-dash messages."

To protect herself from his advances, Rema picked up baby Mylowe. "Shouldn't you go to the compound?" she said. "This situation needs more discussion. For now, I'll care for Mylowe in the daytime and you can stay in the trailer with him at night."

His eyes searched her face. "You haven't said how you feel about us."

She leaned forward and lightly touched his lips. He took Mylowe from her arms, laid him on the divan. When he turned toward her, she leaned forward into his arms. "You haven't answered my initial question."

She moved from him and tucked in her blouse.

"Can we be sensible?" she said.

"Ok! Let's see if this makes sense. I own a house in Wexlor, Ohio. It was my grandmother's. Wexlor is a small college town. It would be an ideal place for the three of us to live. I could teach at the university and continue my lecture tours. I know we can't marry right away. Maybe you won't want to."

He brushed against her and leaned over the divan to check on Mylowe. "I should go to the compound and change clothes."

He framed her face in his hands, kissed her on the forehead, on the right cheek, on the left cheek, on the right ear, on the left ear and finally pressed his lips firmly against hers.

"See you tonight," he said.

She stepped back to let him pass and stood at the door and watched him go into the compound. Her thoughts turned to his proposed move to Ohio.

By using the latitude and longitude of Wexlor, Ohio, and the date the town was founded, she would delineate a natal horoscope. By progressing the town's planetary positions to the present time, she would compare them with the current planet positions in her chart and Felic's.

Her thoughts wandered as she stood over the sleeping Mylowe and rubbed her fingers over his soft blond hair.

Emille was also a good baby.

She walked away tearfully. After a soothing shower and wearing a comfortable pair of shorts, she made a natal horoscope for Mylowe using August 21, 1970, and used his birth time as 10:00 p.m. When Mylowe awakened, she warmed a bottle, fed him and they both slept in Grammy Perez's chair.

Felic returned to the trailer at 10:30 p.m. Rema was dressed and arrived at Arcane Studio before 11:00.

The next morning in the reception room, she made the compatibility chart for her and Felic.

Felic's Sun was in a trine position to her Moon—they would be more compatible in a partnership situation than in a marriage. His Mars squared her Moon and his Mercury squared her Neptune—marriage for them could be stormy and disappointing.

Although new emotions and problems often surface when the blush of new love subsides, Rema felt her knowledge of astrology was providing good direction. Studying further, she discovered more negative challenges between her and Felic than good positive aspects.

She held her head cupped in her hands and asked a question.

If any one of my clients had a compatibility chart like this, what advice would I give?

Her reply was immediate and definite.

Do not marry.

12

MONA

The following afternoon, Rema was still struggling to put a positive spin on the information she learned after constructing the compatibility chart for her and Felic. She knew passion had brought them together and she was guilty of love in the first degree. She also believed that falling in love with Felic might be the catalyst to deepen her knowledge of the universe and find her place in it. There was always a philosophical foundation in astrology to be used when she was confused.

Still, everything seemed wrong. In her memory, she had built a shrine where she could sit and talk to Emille. But in the same memory, she had accepted the karma created while married to John. Attached to that memory bank was the gentle feeling of Grammy Perez's presence. Grammy had said, "Karma is either accepting or denying responsibility for what you have done."

As if all of these things weren't enough, there was the nagging thought that she, like ninety percent of the population, was only one paycheck away from being homeless. On the other hand, she tried to remember that small changes in life had a way of turning into something big. An obvious road had opened. Should she take it? In spite of everything, astrology was giving her direction, but fear had a way of raising its ugly head. When she allowed fear to take over, she always got what she expected—the worst.

Rema walked from the bus stop through the steamy Florida heat to 736 Graham Street. The address was a row condo inside the gated Purple Parrot community recently constructed in the older section of Miami, two streets west of the Atlantic Ocean.

After she rang the doorbell and announced that Pinchey Wilson had asked her to come, the petite blond woman who opened the door introduced herself as Mona Pierce.

"Oh! Please come in," Mona said. "Ella Wilson is such a dear. Pinchey told me you have been a tremendous help to him."

Mona pointed to the opposite side of the sitting room decorated in earth colors and Georgian furniture. "Please sit in the chair near the large rear window."

"I've not been to this part of town before," Rema said.

"It's new. The land had been neglected for years. It's so close to the ocean, it's amazing it hadn't been gobbled up by the land-hungry shopping center crazies."

Rema realized that Mona was one of the financially secure, middle-age widows living independently in Miami. She had the typical beauty shop look. Permed blond hair, nails manicured and polished, and a boutique-style, pink, silk scarf draped around the neck of an expensive, satin blouse.

"Since my husband died," Mona said, "I've been in a fog. The antidepressant drugs helped. Now I can't get through the day without them." She waved her hand in the air as if the movement might sweep away her depression.

"Ella is concerned about me. She's afraid I'm addicted to the drugs. As long as the doctor fills the prescriptions, I keep swallowing the pills."

For a moment, Rema was distracted by the diamonds on Mona's fingers and the red polish on her nails. "How long since your husband died?" she asked.

"Four months. He had a heart attack. It was a terrible shock. I thought being brave was the socially correct thing to do. Honestly, I wanted to scream how unfair it was of him to die. My pastor and my friends urged me to be strong. I tried not to cry. I wish I could understand death."

Rema stood up, stepped in front of Mona and put her hand over Mona's thin clasped hands. "Let's sit together on the sofa."

When they sat together, Rema recognized the white, jagged edges of extreme stress around the irises of Mona's eyes. "Perhaps, you should have cried. Crying is always a healthy outlet and a good cry carries away body toxins, especially after a severe emotional shock. The shock you've experienced often wreaks havoc with the immune system."

"I can't cry. It isn't as if I don't want to. I just can't."

"The drugs may be blocking your grieving process, but grieving does not have an on/off switch. I doubt if you want to live the rest of your life feeling like you do today. Do you have children?"

"Yes, we have a daughter and a son. My daughter is married and my son is a student at Florida State University."

"Are you able to talk to them about your husband?"

"No. I can't."

Rema squeezed her hand. "There is sudden loss and gradual loss. Sudden loss occurs when a loved one dies or a partner in a relationship decides to leave, getting fired from a job or experiencing the loss of a home through some catastrophe—fire, hurricane, flood."

Mona's facial expression relaxed. "I suppose gradual loss is slower. It's something you come to expect."

"While not everyone agrees, I've found there are three levels of grief. First, we retreat in disbelief. That's a natural reaction. Second, we soon find that we have to cope with our feelings whether we want to or not. While we grieve, our fear, anger, self-pity, guilt or hate all rise to the surface and one by one they consume us.

"When we lose a loved one to death, in one fleeting moment our entire life is changed. If we stay bottled up inside, we continually ask the same questions without finding any answers. I believe it's impossible for you to move in any direction."

"My whole life is afloat."

"When we allow our emotions to come to the surface and we get mad, feel sorry for ourselves, or hate what the death of our loved one has done to us, we begin to enter the third stage of the grieving process. The third stage is resolution. We have to resolve within ourselves that we are going to live even though we don't want to."

"I'm not sure I want to live."

"Many people feel as you do. However, I discovered that grief just folded into my life. There was no getting completely over it."

"Does it get easier?"

"It depends."

"On what?"

"It depends on our personality and attitude. Somewhere in the process of grieving we are able to make the memories of our loved one a part of moving ahead. When we reach this stage, we discover our memories actually help to sustain us rather than cause us despair and sadness. We begin to feel hope again and are able to be free from the overbearing emotional pain. We have advanced our spirit by learning that nothing in this life is permanent and accept change."

Rema released Mona's hands. "When you say you don't understand death, there are many explanations. Death is when the brain ceases to function and our body is no longer alive and a built-in system within our spirit automatically taps into a higher, immeasurable class of vibrations."

"What happens after that?"

"Our spirit is transported by the higher vibrations back to the dimension from where it originated within the soul. The spirit leaves but the body remains. Death is leaving our old body and being reborn into a better place."

"Is heaven another dimension?"

"I really can't say. Modern science has not measured the power of the high level vibrations. Perhaps, by the year 2000, the power level of the vibrations will be found."

"Do we have bodies when we're in another dimension?"

"I believe we have spiritual bodies and all the problems we encountered as humans are swept away. Without a body or any of the human elements, we are free from disease, health concerns, broken hearts, financial woes and stress."

"Why is death so scary?"

"In early civilizations, the Greeks represented death as a pleasing, gentle, beautiful child. Sleep and Death were twins. Death was a child holding an inverted torch and a wreath in his hand. Sleep was a child without the torch and wreath."

"That's not so bad."

"Death changed when the Greek culture changed. Greek poets and artists began painting death as scary and horrible. In the play, 'Alcestis,' Euripides introduced death in a black robe holding an instrument of iron in his hand. After that, the Romans began speaking of death as a horrible thing."

Mona turned her rings around on her fingers and adjusted the silk scarf around her neck. "I've read about people who died and returned to life."

"Yes, the 'near death' sensation is due to the sudden surge of the built-in bioenergy or vibrational thrust that lies dormant within the human spirit until death occurs. Some people describe being transported at high speeds through a long, narrow tunnel toward a bright, white light."

"How do you know about these things?"

"Eight months ago, my husband and son drowned in the Atlantic Ocean. Since then, I've learned that death is not the end of life but a part of a cycle similar to a revolving door, life to death, death to life. We should be comforted that our loved ones are safe and well on the other side."

"That is a consoling thought!" Mona said walking toward the kitchen.

Rema sat quietly and wondered if, like the Greeks, our society in twenty years would look at death differently. Medical science could become so proficient at prolonging life that people wouldn't be able to die when they should be dead. She wondered if modern medicine would treat patients like guinea pigs in order to beat death. Her thoughts were interrupted by Mona bringing iced tea. She waited until Mona was settled and they had sipped the tea before asking her what her husband's name was.

"His name was William Sanford Pierce. I called him Will."

"What did you like about him?"

"These days I try not to remember."

"Did you like his smile? Could he cook? Did he like to fish?"

Mona stared but did not reply. Instead, she took a pharmacy bottle from a table drawer and handed it to Rema.

"If I stop taking the pills, can you help me get along without them?"

"I'll be nearby to help you. First, you should ask your doctor if your prescription requires a slow withdrawal. If it does, you'll need to follow the proper timeline."

Rema walked toward the window gathering words to help Mona. "After my husband died," she said, "I discovered he was a pack-rat. He saved everything. When I prepared to move from my house, I found he had saved an entire lifetime in cardboard boxes. Did your husband save everything?"

"I don't know. I haven't gone near our bedroom or the garage since he died."

For a moment, Rema was reminded she was the counselor and Mona the client. She found herself comparing her financial misfortune with Mona's apparent good fortune and wondered if financial security influenced the length and the depth of the grieving process. One thing was evident. Mona Pierce might be financially well-situated, but she was mentally devastated.

Mona interrupted Rema's thoughts. "My husband was a proud man. He provided for me and was a good father."

"Then you were in love forever?"

Mona eyes filled with tears. Her lips quivered. A wail exploded from her throat. "Oh! Yes!" she sobbed. "He left me here all alone. I have no one to love me."

Rema stretched her arms around Mona and realized this visit was not the time to talk about the horoscope she prepared for her. There would be many other times to help Mona understand life and death. Today, they each had found a lifelong friend.

13

JUSTIN HOUSE

Ten-month-old Mylowe had been walking for several weeks on the day Felic and Rema arrived in Wexlor, Ohio, to live in Felic's boyhood home. For the last eight months, Rema's life had changed. She resigned from her position at Arcane Studio to stay in the rented apartment and care for baby Mylowe while Felic completed his research at the university.

Rema placed her hopes on the new location. Although the astrology relocation charts indicated they each were compatible with Wexlor, Ohio, she felt a shiver in her spine when they reached Wexlor's city limits. As Felic drove south through the tree-lined streets to #1 Justin Lane, she realized Wexlor was a quiet, little place. When he turned the car from the main road, he stopped and then drove between tall brick gateposts and up the circular drive at a slow pace. "Beyond this grove of maple trees, is Justin House," he said. "I want you to experience the grandeur of the old Victorian mansion."

Driving through the last row of trees, Rema felt the car surge forward and stop. Felic leaped from the car and ran onto the side lawn. He was waving his arms and yelling "What has happened to my house?" Pieces of spouting dangling from the eaves and being pushed by the wind resembled giant pendulums. High on the wood siding above the natural stone exterior, peeled strips of white paint moved in the high breeze. "The damn pigeons have pooped over the entire roof," he yelled. "They've set up housekeeping around the chimneys."

Rema watched as Felic used several keys in the front door lock before the tumbler turned and he was able to squeeze the doorknob. He was like a madman pushing all his body weight against the center of the door. Once the door opened, he returned to the car, opened her door and gathered Mylowe in his arms.

Inside the house was another world. The elegant mahogany staircase with opulent handrails and supporting posts resembled an out-of-service roller coaster. Despite the condition, the house had a soul. Rema imagined people dancing on the large, white, marble floor in the foyer. She saw beauty everywhere and elegantly-dressed ladies standing on the staircase were watching the dancers.

In the sitting room beyond the foyer, a brown water stain ambled across the high ceiling without regard for direction. Pieces of dust-covered glass from a broken front window lay scattered on the sill and floor.

Felic grabbed Mylowe's shirt and held him before the toddler could reach the broken window glass. He motioned Rema toward a large room in the back corner of the first floor.

"This is the den," Felic announced as he hurried to open the graceful, French doors that opened into the garden. "It's not just a regular den that is traditionally on the first floor off the entrance or foyer. It's a library, a reading room, a quiet place without a television."

As Felic was speaking, Mylowe ran through the open doors and down a garden path grown over with weeds. Rema dashed after the ten-month-old and reached him moments before he sat in a patch of thistles. Felic turned from the doors and walked around the den. When Rema and Mylowe returned from the garden, they found him standing on the fireplace hearth.

"Mi lady and mi lad," he said. "You see before you the highest, the widest and the most elegant fireplace in Ohio. It is made of the identical natural stone as the stone turrets and the lower area of the house exterior. The stone was dug up from the nearby fields by early farmers who cleared the land for planting. Each stone was hauled in oxen carts to this location. This fireplace was designed by a master craftsman. It stretches eighteen feet long and raises upward to connect with the ten-foot high ceiling above us."

Felic grinned, took a deep breath and bowed.

Rema laughed at his ringmaster performance. "Are there other fireplaces?"

"Indeed, yes," he replied. "There are four on the second floor and one in the kitchen." She moved toward him and sat down on the hearth holding Mylowe by the shirttail while Felic went to inspect the second floor.

His expedition upstairs was unsettling. In the six bedrooms, the plank floors were pitted from years of abuse and darkened by too much varnish. Fortunately, the ornate, carved woodwork, popular from another century, had withstood the ravages of people and time.

After walking around on the third floor, he stood at the top of the stairs and leaned over the hand railing. Looking down into the foyer, he noticed the eight-foot grandfather clock. The first owner of the giant timepiece was Felic's great grandfather, Eben Justin, who had placed it in the foyer one hundred years ago.

Felic's first thought was to walk away from the ruins and leave his precious memories behind. He walked down the stairs into the den, sat on the hearth beside Rema and lifted Mylowe over his shoulder.

"How bad is it?" Rema asked.

Felic buried his head in Mylowe's shoulder. "It's horrid! The entire house is in shambles. I don't know what to do. Renovation will cost thousands. I don't understand how a house can deteriorate in just a few years."

"Weren't you here five years ago?"

"Yes, I did notice a few repairs were needed, but the house was not in this condition. The last tenant was a good friend and my colleague. I don't understand what happened."

"There's a lot of history here?" she asked.

"Yes, I was born upstairs and lived here with my grandmother for nine years. My mother died three months after I was born. My father died when I was in the first grade. Grandpa Justin died a year later and Grandma Justin died when I was nine. There were no other living relatives. I was put in a foster home.

"On my eighteenth birthday, I was released from a fouled-up welfare system. I celebrated my birthday and my freedom by hitching rides to Wexlor. By the second day of hitching, I crossed the Indiana-Ohio line. My last hitch was in a pickup truck loaded with homegrown vegetables. Eventually, the old truck rattled down the Main Street of Wexlor. The driver stopped the truck in front of the Presbyterian Church.

"I picked up my canvas bag and walked toward the campus of Wexlor College. The old university has been the center of the community for over eighty years. At Lima Avenue, I turned right onto Justin Lane. Ahead, I saw the brick gateposts marking the entrance of Justin House. Outside of each second story window, drifting in the breeze, were black and orange crepe paper streamers, the Wexlor University colors. Young men were sitting on the wide porch that reached from the front door to the side of the house. I walked closer and saw the words 'Justin House' engraved on a plaque by the front door.

"A young student standing in the doorway asked me if I came about the kitchen job. Startled, I said yes. He said to go to the end of the hall and turn left. 'That's the kitchen,' he said. 'Our cook is Mrs. Bink.'

"I followed the clatter of pans and walked down the hall. A floorboard creaked under my feet. I rocked back and forth on it and remembered how much fun the loose boards were to jump on."

Felic stopped talking and swallowed. There was a lump in his throat and he didn't like the feel of it. Emotions weren't for him.

He paused but continued. "I took the kitchen job," he said. "A week went by before I could go into the hand-dug cellar to inspect the boxes piled on my Grandma Justin's old kitchen table. When I opened the boxes, there were family pictures and legal papers. The next morning, I told Mrs. Bink I was Emma Justin's grandson."

Felic hesitated.

"That was the best day of my life. The local lawyer had been searching for me. My Grandma Justin had deeded Justin House to me and there was an adequate supply of family investments and bonds.

"In that fall, I enrolled as a student in Wexlor University. Except for sleeping in my old bedroom on the second floor of Justin House, I honored the term of the lease between the estate lawyer and the university.

"For the next ten years, Justin House continued to be used as a dormitory. I graduated from Wexlor University with a degree in philosophy and continued to study five more years at Columbia University in New York, where I earned a Ph.D. in religion history. For the next three years, I traveled and lectured on world religions."

Felic sighed and bowed his head. "And that's all there is to tell."

"Hey, buck up!" Rema said. "Our furniture from Florida will arrive tomorrow. We'll have a bed. Mylowe will have his crib. There'll be chairs and plates to set on the table. I'll check the stove."

She hurried into the kitchen. At the sink, the faucet gave a deep groan, sputtered and spit before any water came. Three of the four burners on the electric stove glowed bright red and the oven crackled as it heated. Plugging in the refrigerator, the motor plunked and knocked but settled into a rhythmical hum. Although some of the outside finish on the refrigerator was chipped, the inside porcelain was in good condition.

Rema walked back to Felic. "The kitchen could use a cleaning."

"The entire house needs more than a cleaning," Felic said sadly.

"Happily, the appliances are all working. I flushed the downstairs toilets. It's not the Ritz, but we can get by."

"This is my fault," Felic said. "I should have come ahead to look at the house."

"If you would have come here alone, you would never have brought us here. You might have denied yourself a lifetime of comfort and pleasure."

54

"You're right, of course." He put his arms around her and asked, "Where should we begin?"

"Let's begin by fixing the broken window. I have duct tape in the car."

Before dark, they had fixed the broken window, turned on the water heater, made some tea, ate canned corned beef and crackers for dinner, fed Mylowe and laid sleeping bags in front of the fireplace.

When Mylowe was asleep, Felic held Rema in his arms.

The following day, the moving van arrived from Miami. Felic watched as each piece of furniture was placed in the rooms. Both he and Rema agreed the used furniture they lived with in Miami looked like trash inside Justin House.

"Someday," Rema said, "Justin House will be stately again."

During the days following, the open windows were an invitation to every flying creature in the county. Two sparrows sat on the molding at the top of the entrance hall until workmen escorted them outside. At night, errant mosquitoes sang tuneful arias in high-pitched whines around Felic and Rema.

For the rest of that year on any day except Sunday, the house was filled with tradesmen each performing a specific task.

The windows were replaced with new storm windows and screens. The hot water heating system was repaired and bathrooms were refurbished with new toilets, tubs, showers and fixtures.

Rema often asked Felic how they would pay for the renovations. His reply was always that he would take care of it.

By the summer of the second year, the renovation of the old mansion was nearly complete. The cleaning and staining of the second floor woodwork completed the bedrooms. Felic decided the pungent odor of varnish and turpentine was too overpowering and moved Mylowe's crib to the veranda outside the den. For two nights, he and Rema slept on lawn chairs.

In the fall of that year, before the chill of the October winds, the outdated hot water heating system was dismantled and a gas system was installed. Outside, the painting crew scrambled on high scaffolding to finish putting a final coat of white paint on the high turrets.

As the final group of the craftsmen drove away, Felic and Rema stood huddled against the cold wind in the driveway. Later, when three-year-old Mylowe was put down for the night, they drank a toast to Justin House.

14

EBEN'S TOWER

1984
Eleven Years Later

Mylowe and his friend, Chet Ashton, had amused themselves in Mylowe's bedroom most of Thursday morning until Rema went shopping. At the sound of a closing car door, they ran to the window and watched Rema's car disappear beyond the maple trees.

Racing down the stairs into the kitchen, Mylowe looked outside the rear door for the housekeeper's car. The space was empty. He grinned and motioned Chet to follow him.

The boys ran from the kitchen, across the foyer and into the den. Mylowe knelt down behind Felic's desk and pushed his fingers along the inside of the bottom drawer until he found the large key that opened the lock on the iron gate to a tower room on the second floor.

The tower room had been added three years after Felic's great grandfather built Justin House in 1866. Eben, a self-schooled astronomer, also had a transom window installed in the tower for his nighttime observations of the stars. The tower room was higher than it was wide, and loomed upward from the back roof of the house like a giant barnacle.

Although book-filled shelves lined each wall, the tower room was impersonal, without character as if no person had enjoyed being there. The odor of glue and musty paper was strong. Rema knew the soul of the house did not reside there.

The desk was old and dusty. It had been pressed into service from an out-of-the-way storage room. The desk chair was stiff and confining. On the ceiling around the transom window were circles of red and yellow stains.

On this Thursday afternoon, the fourteen-year-old boys raced up the stairs to open the gate's monster lock. The gate groaned as Mylowe pulled it aside. The knob on the wood door inside the gate turned easily. Chet hesitated in the doorway and whispered, "This place is weird."

Mylowe noticed the hand-hewn wood desk was littered with more papers than the time he had come here alone. He sat in the wood, high-backed desk chair and pulled open each desk drawer. Chet investigated the contents in a box on the desktop.

"What's in the drawers?" Chet asked.

Mylowe stretched his arm full length into each drawer. "What's this?" he said. "It's cold."

He put his fingers around the object and pulled it toward him. "What a beauty," he whispered as he held the pearl-handled handgun with both hands.

"Oh! Gee!" Chet exclaimed. "That's an old gun. What kind it is?"

Mylowe fondled the pearl handle and stroked the barrel. Although the feel of the steel on his fingers made his spine tingle, from somewhere he understood its power.

He jumped from the chair and galloped around the tower room while spinning the empty cylinder and pointing the gun at Chet.

"Pow! Pow!" he yelled. "Pow! Pow! Pow! You're dead!"

Each time he pulled the trigger, vibrations slithered through his hand and into his fingers. Crouching behind the desk he paused and wiped his moist hands on his trousers. More deliberately than before, he took aim at the transom and squeezed the trigger.

Chet held the gun and tried to twirl it in his fingers.

The drone of Rema's car motor moving in the driveway jolted the boys from their playfulness. Mylowe returned the gun to the dark corner of the desk drawer, locked the gate and hurried down the narrow stairway. Chet followed.

"We can't say anything to Rema about finding the gun," Mylowe said. "Not a word to anyone."

"If you're going up there again, can I come?"

"I'll think about it. In the meantime, don't mention it to Bo, or Charlie. It's our secret, okay?"

"Sure, I won't tell."

The boys reached the kitchen and were standing by the sink when Rema entered through the back door. After carrying the groceries from the car to the kitchen, the boys headed toward the den to put the gate key back in the desk.

Through the evening, Mylowe felt a tingling sensation inside his chest. Holding the gun had awakened a yearning he could not explain. He knew he had to feel the gun's real power.

15

GROWING UP

One Week Later

To celebrate Mylowe's fourteenth birthday Felic and Rema invited his friends and teachers to a late Tuesday afternoon gathering in the garden at Justin House.

The guests were greeted at the door by Churchill, Mylowe's six-year-old Dalmatian. Churchill had arrived at Justin House on Mylowe's eighth birthday—a gift from Felic and Rema.

For his fourteenth birthday, Felic and Rema presented Mylowe with a dozen leather-bound journals. For the last seven years, Mylowe had been recording his thoughts in spiraled notebooks. The bound journals would better serve as permanent records for his writing.

As dusk approached, Japanese lanterns hanging in trees were lit and a three-tiered birthday cake with fourteen glowing candles was pushed into the garden by Mylowe's best friends, Chet and Bo. After the cake was served, Mylowe, Chet and Bo walked downtown to the Sugar Bowl. Inside the teen hangout, the booths and tables were filled with boys and girls sipping Cokes and root beer floats while the juke box blared.

Chet grinned and bent across the table toward Mylowe. "Are you going to ask Millie Haskins to dance? All you do is look at her."

"I'm not ready to ask her."

"Well, you don't want to get any older. You should stake your claim before someone else does. It's you-r-r-r birthday. As I see it, you have a perfect excuse."

"Mylowe's a fraidy cat, Mylowe's a fraidy cat," chanted Bo.

"No I'm not!"

"Come on, I'll go to her table with you," teased Chet. "I'll bet she's waiting to dance with you."

The dance floor was full. The teens, persuaded to move to the rock and roll music, were frantically moving their bodies. Some moved at a more subdued pace.

Chet stood up and pulled Mylowe to his feet. "Come on, fraidy cat. Millie's all alone at the table."

"Okay, I'll ask her," said Mylowe. "But you guys stay here."

Mylowe walked through the maize of tables toward Millie. Barely breathing he approached her slowly and felt as if his mouth was glued shut.

"Hi! Millie. Will you dance with me? It's my birthday."

Millie Haskins took a sip of Coke and slowly raised her head to look at him. Her lips parted slowly showing a full set of silver braces. "Happy Birthday, Mylowe. I heard you were having a party at your house. Is it over?" He knew she was asking why she hadn't been invited. Mylowe stammered, "For me it's over. My parent's guests are still at the house. It was really my parent's party. Chet and Bo were my guests."

"Your parents keep you tied close to home."

"Well, they have plans for my future. Do you want to dance?"

"Okay, but make it a slow one."

Millie stood and moved close to him. It was much closer than he had anticipated. As they swayed to the music, Mylowe experienced his first sensation that he had reached puberty.

Chet and Bo watched him dance.

"Yah know," said Bo. "He's really in tight with her."

"Or she's in tight with him. That's what happens when you go for an older woman."

"What do you mean, older woman?"

"She's sixteen. I bet she has experience."

"You think she's had that kind of experience?"

"Yeah! In one night, a girl like Millie could make ol' Mylowe become a man."

16

HEARTBREAK

At 6:00 a.m. on Sunday morning, Mylowe and Churchill walked from the house. At the corner of Lincoln Avenue and Gilbert Street, they ran toward the Gilbert Street railroad crossing.

Mylowe jumped onto the crossing's macadam platform, turned west and leaped between the wooden crossties. Churchill, on a leash, ran beside him.

They had moved westward the distance of two city blocks when Churchill pulled at the leash. "You can run now," Mylowe said. Churchill ran across the tracks to a small hill on the opposite side.

Mylowe pulled the gun from his pocket. In the last several days, he learned from a book in Felic's library that the firearm was a .38 Special Smith & Wesson that had been updated in the 1950's.

With a boyish thrust, he dug deep into his trouser pocket to retrieve the five bullets he had taken from the desk drawer.

He pushed each bullet into the cylinder and stood on the center wood crosstie. Raising the gun shoulder high, he sighted down the barrel. His fingers trembled. With a slow squeeze on the trigger the gun fired. He staggered backward, laid the gun down and wiped the sweat from his hands.

A headlight beam of an approaching train twinkled in the distance. He playfully pointed the gun upward but did not shoot it. He saw Churchill was on the opposite side of the tracks.

"Come with me," Mylowe pleaded. "Here Churchy, come here."

Mylowe stepped off the tracks and called again to Churchill. The short, shrill whistle blasts from the approaching engine were coming closer.

"Here boy," he yelled. "Come here."

As a long line of freight cars rumbled by Mylowe, Churchill remained on the other side of the tracks.

Mylowe raised the gun, aimed and pulled the trigger twice at the moving freight cars. Against the deep rumble of the train's wheels, the noise from the gun shots was inaudible. The red caboose rushed by and the crossing bells stopped ringing. In the distance, Mylowe could hear the rhythmical clacking of the rumbling train wheels.

Mylowe ran up the embankment and crossed the tracks to the other side. Churchill lay on the ground. Mylowe ran to him and stooped down beside him. Blood oozed from a hole in Churchill's neck. His eyes were closed. His long, slender, bluish-pink tongue hung from the side of his mouth.

Mylowe cried in a soft boyish tone.

"Churchy, Oh! Churchy. You'll be okay, boy. Don't die! Don't die!"

The gun lay on the ground.

"No, no, Churchill. I didn't mean to do it."

Mylowe picked up Churchill in his arms and staggered to stand up straight. He carried him to the sidewalk and raised his knee to push Churchill's body upward into his arms. Mylowe's tears formed beads of water on Churchill's taunt, white-spotted coat.

A police car moved slowly along the curb. The officer stretched across the front seat to the passenger window.

"What do you have there, Mylowe?"

"My dog."

"He's heavy, isn't he?"

"Yes, sir."

"Is he hurt?"

"He's dead."

"What happened?"

"I killed him."

"How?"

"I shot him."

The officer stopped the patrol car. "Do you want a ride?" he asked.

"I guess so."

Although the officer tried to take the dog, Mylowe managed to slide into the back seat of the patrol car with Churchill still in his arms. At Justin House, the details leading up to Churchill's death unraveled like a ball of yarn tumbling down a flight of stairs.

"I didn't mean to shoot Churchill," Mylowe sobbed as Felic and Rema stood at the front in the door.

The police officer stepped forward.

"Dr. and Mrs. Ort, I'm afraid Mylowe has had an accident."

"What happened?" asked Felic.

"Well, sir, as you can see, the dog is dead. The boy accidentally shot him. We received a report from the local stationmaster that a train engineer had seen a boy shoot a handgun at moving freight cars.

"I checked the Johnson Street crossing first but found nothing. At the crossing on Gilbert Street, I searched along the grain elevator and found blood on the ground and a gun.

"When I went back to the patrol car, I saw a boy walking on the sidewalk north on Gilbert carrying something heavy. When I drove the car beside him I saw it was Mylowe."

The officer turned and walked to the patrol car and returned with a large, brown envelope. He slipped the cord from the envelope, unfolded two sides and laid the open envelope on the palms of his hands. He stepped toward Felic.

"This is the gun I found beside the tracks. Do you recognize it?"

Felic stepped forward and looked into the envelope. "It's mine," he said.

"Two initial actions will be taken," said the officer. "The railroad will charge Mylowe with discharging a firearm across railroad property. Since Mylowe is a minor, the judge will order you, as the owner of the gun, to appear at a hearing."

The officer finished writing the citation and gave it to Felic.

"Sign here, sir. A summons will be issued from the county juvenile court within ten days. I will also appear at the hearing."

"Is this a long, drawn-out legal process?" Felic inquired.

"Yes, it is, sir."

During the conversation between Felic and the officer, Rema coaxed Mylowe to sit with her on the front steps. Mylowe held Churchill across his knees. The onset of rigor mortis had stiffened Churchill's long, slender legs until they extended horizontally from the main part of his body.

As the patrol car drove away, Felic turned and looked at Mylowe. The sight of the boy holding the dog was sad, but the gun in the brown envelope angered him. Mylowe had disobeyed him. Eben's Tower was off limits. Felic bounded up the steps. Like an angry bull, he spat at Mylowe. "You have ruined my reputation." He charged past them and disappeared inside the house.

Rema had not seen such intense rage in him. Felic was not a man who would allow his reputation to be questioned. She remembered his birth chart where the planet Mars in the sign of Aries showed an incontrollable temper in the fifth house relating to children. Also, Mars conjunct Uranus indicated he had an explosive temper and a desire to have things his own way.

For months, she had been watching Felic have his way. He was spending an inordinate amount of time with one of his female students, a woman in her thirties. Since the beginning of his relationship with this younger woman, he had been in a brighter mood and less critical.

She hugged Mylowe realizing the family atmosphere in Justin House had changed to something she was unprepared to manage. She couldn't begin to count the hours and days Felic had found reasons to stay away from her and Mylowe.

17

THE QUESTION

Six Months Later

"Was man created by God or did man create God?" asked Morry Diltz, a freshman student at Wexlor College.

Professor Felic Ort leaned forward against the battered wooden lectern in the front of the classroom where thirty-five students had gathered for the ten o'clock class on Religion History.

Yeh, Gad! he thought. *Maybe I've reached at least one insipid mind.*

For over eleven years as a professor of religious studies and as an international lecturer, Felic had fielded hundreds of questions about the existence of God from many young, aspiring students.

When the outbursts occurred, he allowed them to happen. From experience with young people, he had discovered that the tirades of frustrated students usually stimulated other students to learn about different views of the religions of the world. The outbursts were often controversial and served as hypothetical forums that turned out to be invaluable to the entire class.

Although preferring just to present the lecture and go to an early lunch today, Felic recognized that the outburst from young Mr. Diltz was a welcome diversion from the constant turmoil he faced with Mylowe and Rema at Justin House.

"Mr. Diltz," said Felic, acknowledging the short, rotund young man who shared his ringlets of blond hair with Shirley Temple, "I assume from your posture you would like to use the lectern? If that is the case, I shall adjourn to my chair."

Morry strode in measured steps to the front of the room. Adjusting the necessary, thick, black-rimmed glasses, he looked accusingly at the entire class.

"Creationism, evolution or intelligent design?" he yelled. "What are we to believe? To my notion, there's a lot of fuzzy thinking going on.

"I just don't get this religion thing! It's all mixed up. I guess it's because there are so many different gods to worship.

"Does anyone know who worships the right one? How can intelligent people devote their lives to a deity they can't see?"

Morry's tone lowered as if he were about to pronounce a benediction.

"In Christianity, Judaism and many other religions, the religious leaders teach that God is a loving god. If that's the case, then why do these same religious leaders make us fear God by threatening we will go to hell if we break a commandment?

"Am I afraid to break a commandment? You bet I am. Do I fear going to a place hotter than the California desert? You bet I do.

"We justify disasters, accidents and fatalities by saying, 'It's God's will.' But, if you think about it logically, all the horrible things that happen to man begin from the actions of man.

"If you get down to all the facts, man is the cause of all the destruction of human life. Man has even affected the weather patterns so that hurricanes and tornadoes are more frequent and more violent. Man made automobiles that crash. Man made the erroneous engineering decisions that force the waters of the rivers to overflow into populated areas. Man built the buildings that crush thousands in an earthquake. It is man's neglect and self-indulgence that creates the city slums. Man makes the decision to wage wars that kill thousands of young men.

"Religious leaders tell us there is one set of laws sent from God that we are to obey. And, if the laws aren't obeyed," Morry raised this hands wriggling quotation marks with his fingers, "a loving god will arrange the punishment. Do you feel threatened?"

The classroom erupted in uncomfortable laughter, but Morry, serious and concerned, continued to speak.

"Do any of us know which of the umpteen religions is God-approved? Is it Buddhism, Hinduism, Mohammedanism, Jainism, Shintoism, Lamaism or any of the other two hundred religious sects in the world today, each one spouting its own doctrine, rules and regulations?

"There are also big corporate-based religions that are professionally developed, well-organized and profiting from a global collection system.

"Did God direct man to build magnificent gold-draped, spiraled, glass-enclosed, air-conditioned structures of worship? Or was it man's idea?

"Is paying off those large building mortgages with money collected in the name of a God the way the church was envisioned?"

Morry's manner was now abusive and undisciplined. The tone of his voice resembled that of the barker at a state fair hoochie-coochie sideshow.

"Whatever the original intentions were for man, man has screwed it up!" yelled Morry as he turned toward Dr. Ort.

"That's why I asked the question! Was man created by God? Or did man create God to have an invisible icon to rely on instead of handling matters himself? Could religion have started because man is a gregarious, social, insecure creature who needed to believe in something?

"Or is God waiting for us to perfect him? Is he letting us make mistakes until some generation understands that each individual is within himself responsible for his own actions?

"When we pray, aren't we praying to ourselves? Aren't we telling ourselves our own wants and needs?"

Felic stood up. It was a sign to Morry that time at the lectern had ran out. Taking his place at the lectern, Felic shuffled papers and waited for the class to come to order.

"For a brief moment, Mr. Diltz, I thought you were going to declare that you are an agnostic," he said. "Happily, you did show that you are still open to in-depth discussions. However, you did not touch upon pervading questions."

On most days, Felic enjoyed the thrill of teaching and took pride in stimulating young minds, but today he was weary from the anguish of Mylowe's impending trial. He spoke slowly.

"Agnostics are God fence-sitters. They do not admit that a God exists or does not exist. The agnostic refuses to accept evidence of the origins of the universe, an unseen power or a promise of a future life.

"You should note that Thomas Henry Huxley initiated the term agnostic. He said the existence of beings on a higher level than man is rather probable. And, it was quite logical that the universe was undoubtedly governed by a divine syndicate of spiritual essences."

Felic walked from behind the lectern. "I have an addendum to Mr. Diltz's questions. Although he only touched briefly on the scriptures, I believe if the members of this class would read about the Apocrypha, you would discover it was the group of books not found in Jewish or Protestant versions of the Old Testament.

"This particular group of books was included in the Septuagint and the Roman Catholic editions of the Bible. The Septuagint, translated by seventy

Jewish scholars in 1555, is the oldest Greek version of the Old Testament. The scholars who studied the Apocrypha concluded that even one word in a language could have an entirely different meaning in another language; thereby, the context of the story or subject could have changed its focus many times. Concern was also expressed that writers of the Bible may have expanded the stories by adding their own imaginative flair. Thereby, if any of you has the same probing questions as Mr. Diltz concerning the validity of information in the Bible, please reserve them for next semester."

Felic walked to the window to watch the February wind whip snowflakes against the windows. There was something soothing about a new snow.

Unlike life, he thought, *snowflakes fall gently to a final resting place.*

He turned toward the class. "Ladies and gentlemen, I bid you good day! Class is dismissed."

The students filed out of the classroom allowing Felic a moment before meeting Bruce Williams for lunch. Dr. Williams would be teaching Felic's class tomorrow morning. Tomorrow was the day Felic was scheduled to appear in court with Mylowe. In the days since the shooting, Felic had not tried to control his anger. To his way of thinking, it was a clear and devastating fact that six months ago his reputation had been sabotaged by a fourteen-year-old boy and a family keepsake, a gun.

18

VEILED INNOCENCE

In the hearing room at the Hardin County Courthouse, Rema sat in a row of seats directly behind the defendant's table where Felic and Mylowe were sitting.

Six months had passed since the Sunday morning when Mylowe had taken Felic's gun from Eben's tower, shot at a moving freight train and accidentally killed Churchill, the family dog.

Now, one hundred and eighty days had cascaded over her. Each was a nightmare. She had maintained her sanity by talking to her friend, Mona Pierce. There were long conversations via the telephone to Miami.

"If Felic is home, he refuses to talk if Mylowe is in the same room," Rema told Mona. "But, if he knows Mylowe is close by, he fills the air with loud, angry accusations that can be heard throughout the house.

"At the dinner table, Felic never utters a word. With each bite he stares at Mylowe. I don't know how Mylowe stands this treatment. The family unit is shattered. Felic only communicates with me when we're in bed."

Sitting in the small courtroom this morning, Rema sensed a small measure of peacefulness. She sighed, adjusted her coat around her shoulders and wondered if Felic's negative reaction to the tragedy would be a barrier between them for the rest of their lives. She continued to watch Felic's sensitivity to public scrutiny and wondered if he would survive. Would any of them survive?

On the other hand, it was clear that whatever punishment Mylowe received, it would be a life learning lesson for him. She knew Mylowe would adjust just as he had adjusted to Felic's abusive behavior.

Noise from the front of the room interrupted her thoughts. The bailiff was announcing The Honorable William Sobol as the presiding judge.

Peering over Benjamin Franklin spectacles at Felic and Mylowe, Judge Sobol brushed a mound of white hair from his forehead and directed his first question toward Felic.

"Sir, do you have counsel?"

Felic stood and replied, "No, your honor."

"The Pennsylvania Railroad and the State of Ohio request a preliminary hearing on the charges of a minor discharging a gun across railroad property."

A chair sliding against the wood floor disrupted the proceedings. Judge Sobol glared over the rims of his spectacles toward the sound.

"David Meyers for the plaintiff, your honor."

"What is it, Mr. Meyers?"

"The State also stipulates that the defendant's father, Felic Ort, had in his possession an unlicensed firearm and was derelict with regard to the safety of the minor."

Judge Sobol nodded and turned toward Mylowe. "How old are you, son?"

"Fourteen," Mylowe replied.

"I understand you have met with Dr. Sparta of the County Juvenile Center. His report shows you to be an exceptional young man and a student far advanced in your schoolwork. What caused you to take your father's gun from your home and shoot at a moving train?"

"I wanted to feel its power."

"What do you mean, 'feel its power?'"

"You know, judge. The shiver that runs through your body when you pull the trigger."

Judge Sobol motioned to Mylowe.

"Come to the bench."

The judge leaned forward. "How many times have you shot a gun?"

"Three times, sir."

"Did you shoot those three shots while you were at the railroad?"

"Yes, sir."

"If you only shot the gun on that day, how did you know you would shiver?"

"I didn't know for sure, but I kinda thought I would."

Footsteps were heard crossing the room. "Your honor, I'm Dr. Barry Sparta. May I approach the bench?"

"Come ahead."

"Your honor, when I evaluate young people, I often discover extenuating circumstances, and I try to bring the information to the court's attention."

"What did you find in this case?"

Dr. Sparta leaned forward and spoke in a subdued tone. "This boy's propensity toward guns stems from a past life memory."

Judge Sobol stiffened. "Dr. Sparta, are you using my court as a comedy club?"

"Not at all. A past life memory is not an unusual occurrence with children. Actually, it's really a past life echo. Children, at least until the age of ten, are far more in tune with the nature of the universe than are adults. Unfortunately, as children grow they absorb conflicting thoughts from parents or caretakers and the past life echoes are forgotten."

"Is this the basis of your dissertation, Dr. Sparta?"

"Yes, your honor. I believe this particular circumstance would be better discussed in chambers, sir."

"I'll consider your request. Have you finished?"

"Just one more point, your honor."

Judge Sobol displayed his impatience by removing his spectacles, rearranging his rotund body inside the arms of the high-back leather chair.

"You have one minute."

Dr. Sparta nodded. "Our society raises boys to be brave and strong and to hide their feelings. Caregivers teach that boys don't cry. Consider what happens to those emotions hidden away in the deep recesses of a child's mind and spirit. The emotions often turn into undetectable, invisible pain. Parents aren't aware of it until it erupts in the home, in the classroom or on the schoolyard. It's an explosion that damages all the lives around it."

"Are you finished?" asked the judge.

"Not quite. Throughout our history and in today's advanced society when adults create wars between countries, it is the brave, strong, 'no crying' boys (and girls) who are recruited to fight and bring home the flags of victory.

"By varying degrees, war exacerbates the hidden emotions of the young. In the years following wars, the remnants of war might spill from their lips in remembrance, but their actions in war reside deep within their souls.

"Large numbers of reincarnated soldiers from every war fought over the thousands of years are alive today. The echoes of their fighting experiences still reign within their souls. Many of the present-day criminal acts are a manifestation of the recessed memories of soldiers who fought in those wars. They have no compunction about using the weapons they used in past life wars to protect themselves."

Judge Sobol's impatience was evidenced in his tone. "Dr. Sparta, I assume that the rest of your information is relevant to this hearing? Shall we get on with it in my chamber?"

Dr. Sparta nodded and escorted Mylowe toward the door behind the judicial bench. Inside the judge's chamber, he directed Mylowe to be seated on his right and David Meyers on his left.

"Mylowe," said Dr. Sparta, "Tell the judge about your reincarnation memory."

Mylowe bowed his head. He didn't know if the particulars of his vision, or reincarnation memory, as Dr. Sparta called it, could help. Perhaps, it would only add to the trouble he had brought to Felic and Rema. Couldn't the memory rest? Felic would think it was a lie. Mylowe heard the judge's voice.

"Young man, we're waiting."

"Well sir, I'm with a group of boys. We live under a bridge in a big city. It is very hot, but there's an ocean nearby and we often go swimming."

"How old are you?" asked Dr. Sparta.

"About eighteen."

"What do the boys do?"

"We rob stores, steal food and grab purses from old women."

"Do you have guns?"

"Yes."

"Do you shoot them?"

"Sometimes, not often."

"Did you ever kill a person?"

"No, but I wasn't afraid to do that."

"What is your most important memory while you were with these boys?"

"I was shot. I see myself lying in an alley. I think I died."

"Did the police shoot you?"

"No, the boys did."

"Do you know why?"

"I was their leader. They didn't like me."

Dr. Sparta leaned toward Mylowe. "Tell Judge Sobol where the alley was located."

"It was in Miami, Florida."

"What is so coincidental about Miami?"

"Felic rescued me in an alley in Miami. I was less than thirty minutes old."

"What was the name of the alley?"

"Felic said it was Dead Man's Alley."

Judge Sobol shoved his eye glasses onto the top of his head. "Well, doctor, you have a strange way of making your case. Is it your intent to make me believe this young man carries a vivid past life memory of using guns and shot off his father's gun so he could feel its power again?"

Dr Sparta remained seated but spoke confidently. "The evidence does suggest that Mylowe feels comfortable with guns and gets excited when he pulls the trigger. Did you know one of the bullets killed his dog?"

"Such a tragedy. What am I to do?"

David Meyers stood, moved toward the judge and said, "In spite of Dr. Sparta's eloquent presentation, it is imperative that the boy be punished and the father held responsible."

"All right, gentlemen. I've made my decision. Shall we go back to the courtroom?"

Returning to the bench Judge Sobol inquired, "Is Officer Cassiday present?"

"Yes, sir," replied the officer.

"You found a weapon at the railroad?"

"Yes, it was a recently fired, 38 caliber Smith-Wesson revolver with three empty chambers. The revolver is tagged as evidence and I have identified it."

The judge tugged at his robe and pushed a strand of long white hair from his forehead. "This court finds the defendant, Felic Ort, guilty of harboring an unlicensed handgun and leaving it unguarded. The fine is $1,200, plus court fees.

"Mylowe Ort, a minor, I order you to serve five years probation reduced to two years with semi-monthly counseling at the Hardin County juvenile psychological facility. Court is adjourned."

Felic glared at Mylowe and walked away. Mylowe sat alone at the defendant's table. The room emptied quickly. Rema moved toward Mylowe. One nightmare was over, but the ordeal of trying to live in the same house with Felic had become a reality.

19

INDIGNATION

From the courthouse, Rema and Mylowe walked to the parking area. Felic was sitting in the car. The motor was running. He did not acknowledge them or make an effort to open the door for Rema. When they were seated, he bashed his left fist against the steering wheel.

Rema clutched the passenger's armrest to remain balanced as he drove at high speed through the city streets toward the open highway. Twenty minutes later, he drove into the driveway at Justin House. He parked the car in front of the garage, stepped into the driveway and bent forward through the back window and stared at Mylowe.

There were crimson circles around Felic's eyes. His jaw was set and his teeth clenched together. Mylowe shrank in fear. Felic kicked the car door with such force the entire car vibrated. Then, he smashed his fist against the top of the car, turned and walked down the driveway toward the mailbox. Rema hurried Mylowe into the house. In the foyer, Mylowe said, "Felic is really mad at me."

"Yes, you should go to your room now. I'll call you for lunch."

In the kitchen, Rema heard the front door close. From the sound of the footsteps, she knew Felic had gone into the den. She clutched the top of a chair. More than any other time in her fourteen years with Felic, she realized Mylowe's shooting episode and the sentencing had severely bruised Felic's self-esteem. He always upheld a high level of dignity and pride, not only within the halls of the university, but in the worldwide community of his intellectual colleagues.

Remembering that she had, years ago, identified an uncontrollable temper in his astrology natal horoscope, Rema rummaged through her briefcase files to retrieve the stored information. She scanned his natal horoscope and noted that Mars in Aries often meant a fiery, explosive temper without restraint.

She leaned against the sink, closed her eyes and mentally cast a sheath of white protective light energy around her body, hoping the energy would act as a barrier and sustain her positive energy against Felic's uncontrollable anger. Strengthened by the metaphysical covering, she walked toward the den.

Felic sat at the desk. His head was bowed. She stood over him and gently massaged his shoulders. Acknowledging her hands, he nodded placidly. "I know you're having a rough time," she whispered.

He grunted, raising his hands to rest over hers. Moments passed before he spoke.

"I was wondering how the $1,200 fine imposed by the judge on me would affect our finances for the rest of the year. I suppose I could schedule some additional lectures and bring in extra cash, but that would dash my teaching responsibilities all to hell."

Rema cradled his head in her arms. "Maybe we should discuss this in a day or two when our emotions are more settled. I'm certain the answer will come."

Felic's tone was cruel and unrelenting as he struggled away from her touch. "I do have one answer."

"What is it?"

"The boy is history," Felic hissed through clenched teeth. "He's a bladderless, disobedient, spineless, ungrateful piss ant. I don't want him around me. I'm turning him over to the welfare system."

Shocked by Felic's seething words, Rema replied cautiously. "That's strong language."

"I meant every word. I'll never know where he came from or what his gene pool is. He's probably some derelict's bastard son who will make trouble for us the rest of our lives. I'm not taking any chances."

Rema's first impulse was to disagree. She swallowed hard and pushed her thumbs deep into his shoulders.

"Ouch!" he yelled.

"Sorry, sometimes I don't know my own strength. I was thinking if we send Mylowe away we might be inviting more investigation into our private lives. The people in Wexlor aren't aware that Mylowe isn't our son. Also, your fellow workers, as well as our friends, believe we are a family."

"The family has been destroyed. Tell me, what part of this family could ever be restored?"

"There's you and I."

"Bull! We're clearly on opposite sides. You know I have other interests. You would go with Mylowe before you would stay with me."

Rema felt dizzy. Felic's anger had reached a point where he was not being sensible. She stopped rubbing his neck and sank into a nearby chair.

"There's something I've never told you," she whispered.

"Oh! I don't think this is a great time to tell me your secrets."

"It's about Mylowe. When he was a baby, I cast a natal astrology chart for him. Do you remember? I asked your permission."

"Yes, I guess I do remember. What could Mylowe's chart possibly have to do with this mess?"

Rema ignored his hissing tone and spoke softly.

"First, was I correct to cast Mylowe's chart for 10:00 p.m., August 21, 1970, in Miami, Florida?"

"That's as close as anything."

"I won't go into all the calculations, but in a past life, Mylowe was self-indulgent, greedy and took from others."

Felic slapped the desktop hard with his hand. "He's still doing it."

Rema leaned forward and looked directly into Felic's face. "He is destined to repay all of those acts in this life through a life-threatening situation."

"Good for him! Maybe he'll learn something."

"His chart shows he's a born leader. His ideas will be innovative and ahead of his time."

"Well, he has a long way to go."

"But don't you see? Mylowe needs your guidance. Disowning him will keep negative energy around him for all of his life."

Rema stepped back. "I said I wouldn't go into detail but there's an agonizing part of his chart you should know about. His Sun squares Neptune in the sign of Scorpio in the eighth house of regeneration.

"There's deception around him. A deep secret from the past could cause him to be subjected to menacing threats and possible bodily injury."

"What do you expect? He has bad genes."

Felic shuffled the papers on the desktop and began reading them as if he were alone. After an eternity, he got up from his chair and walked from the den.

The thump of his footsteps on the stairs leading to Eben's tower echoed through the den. Rema held her breath.

Tears welled in her eyes. She lowered her face into her hands and wept. She knew in her heart she could not give up a second son and vowed to save Mylowe from Felic's wrath.

20

HEARTBREAK

Mylowe squeezed out from the cubby hole behind the grandfather's clock. Felic's harsh words hovered around him. Standing in the den doorway, he asked, "Is Felic sending me to welfare?"

Rema raised her head and went to him. His shoulders quivered beneath her hands. She guided him to sit in a chair. She sat on a footstool in front of him and brushed a piece of his brown hair from his forehead.

"Oh, honey! Felic's upset. Let's give him some time to think about everything."

"He said you would be on my side and not on his."

"Well, you have to understand he is very angry."

"He thinks I'm going to be bad again, that's why he's sending me to a foster home."

"I don't believe any of the situations can be resolved for either you or Felic by sending you to a foster home. Don't you remember? As a boy, Felic lived in foster homes and despised the welfare system. When he found you in the alley, he managed to keep you away from the system. It's not likely he will send you there."

"He really wants to punish me for going into Eben's Tower and taking the gun."

"Why don't you let me talk to Felic?"

Mylowe sat back in the chair and picked at a fingernail. "Maybe Felic is right. If my past life memory is stronger than I am, I might do something bad."

"Tell me about the memory, perhaps I can help."

"I already told the judge about it."

"Didn't Dr. Sparta help you tell the judge?"

"Yes, I still don't understand why the memory makes me do bad things. I miss Churchill so much. I think about him every day."

"You'll find as you go through life you are going to experience situations that can't be changed."

"I guess so."

"Let's go in the kitchen. I'll fix a sandwich and you can tell me about your memory."

Mylowe sat at the kitchen table. "Is Felic going to stay in the tower all day?"

"Yes, he usually spends time in the tower when he's at home."

"It's such a dark, creepy place. What does he do up there?"

"I don't know. Maybe he's preparing his lectures for the upcoming tour."

Mylowe rested his elbow on the table and laid his head in his hand. Rema placed a toasted cheese sandwich in front of him.

She smiled. "You know, when I was a little girl I had an imaginary friend who stayed by me whenever I was sad."

"What was your imaginary friend's name?"

"Lucinda."

"My imaginary friend's name is Greylord. He's really old."

"Have you been friends for a long time?"

"Yes, a long time."

"Does he tell you important things?"

"Sometimes, he does. Mostly, he shows me pictures in my mind."

"Have you told Felic about the pictures?"

"No, I only told Dr. Sparta."

"Finish your sandwich," Rema said. "I'll be back in a few minutes. I need to call Mona in Miami."

In the den, Rema pushed the phone buttons, held the phone to her ear and waited. "Mona, it's Rema. There's trouble brewing with Felic. Could you come to Ohio next week? I need you to do the administrative work at the Libra Center. The astrology and tarot instructors at the center can manage the night classes, but it would help if you would be there to schedule appointments for them."

Mona recognized her friend's woeful tone. "Yes, I can make arrangements to come. What happened at the hearing today? Is Mylowe going to the reformatory?"

"Mylowe is on probation and in counseling for two years. The problem is with Felic. He's either out of his mind or his affair with the coed has gone sour."

Mona chortled playfully. "Honey, something has been going sour with him for a long time."

"It's serious. He's threatening to put Mylowe into a foster home."

Mona gasped. Although she had known Felic lived by a 'me first' attitude, in the last several years she had watched as he demanded more and more from Rema.

Mona heard herself yelling. "You're not going to let him do it?"

"No," said Rema.

"He's got his nerve. He's never supported anything you've done. Five years ago when you established the Libra Center, he did nothing to help you. Has he ever been to the center?"

"No, the Libra Center is my venture. However, in this situation, the center's house may be the solution. I can house Mylowe there with you."

"I've always wondered why you set up your business in Cira. It is twenty miles from Wexlor."

Rema sighed. "Felic would have been embarrassed if I opened a metaphysical learning center in his hometown."

"Did he think it would ruin his reputation?"

"I suppose that may have been the reason. But today, I see it was a wise move. The center could be a home for Mylowe and for me, too, if Felic keeps on this destructive path."

"Well, the center is in a well-constructed brownstone in a respectable part of Cira."

Rema frowned. "I must work something out with Felic. I hope I don't regret living with him all these years."

Mona was quick to reply. "Oh! That's right. The local people in Wexlor think you're married."

"Yes, and it's the only thing that may help me deal with Felic. At the moment, he's abject and uncaring. I can't see one sign of any feelings in him except his contrived rage against Mylowe."

Rema paused.

"What are you thinking?" Mona asked.

"He may have feelings in the bedroom."

"Oh shit! Do you still believe his anger can be controlled in the bedroom? Do you have a plan?"

"Not a specific one, but I've decided to take full responsibility for Mylowe."

"I suppose that also means financial responsibility."

"Well, yes, I'll manage."

"Okay, my friend, I'll be at the Libra Center by four o'clock tomorrow afternoon. And, don't worry. I'll handle everything there."

Rema hung up the phone and saw Mylowe standing at the den door. She motioned him inside.

"I believe I have a plan," she said. "Until I can talk with Felic, you must stay in your room. He's going on tour next week so I don't have much time to make my plan work."

Mylowe nodded.

"Can I count on you?" Rema asked.

"I'll be quiet like a mouse."

"Good boy!"

Mylowe laid a soft, boyish hand on her arm and winked. "Quiet like a mouse," he whispered.

21

VIRTUAL SURRENDER

Rema had been in bed an hour before Felic came into their bedroom. He undressed and lay beside her. She felt a silence between them, the kind that takes over following a blistering quarrel.

She turned toward him wanting to feel the warmth of his body. She dared not ask for more. On this night, she would not begin to measure her feelings for him. She remembered the intensity of their initial feelings. They had struggled through many lifetimes together. Somehow, they had to continue. They made an agreement to raise an orphan baby as their son. She vowed to keep her side of the agreement. Her hope was that Felic would allow her to do it.

By 1:50 a.m., she had not closed her eyes. Felic's breathing was steady, but she knew he was not asleep. She rubbed her hand on the long line of his slim hips. He responded almost immediately. The urgency of his manliness was all consuming.

"You're a conniving bitch," he gasped, pulling his body above hers. His thrusts came long and deep inside her. She writhed in the ecstasy of the moment.

"Still acting the part, are you?" he whispered. His tone was cold and angry. He arched his back in a catlike pose and withdrew from her prematurely.

"No, Felic, don't do this."

"Too late. Too late." The words cascaded from his scornful lips. "I know when I'm being seduced."

A flush crept over her. She turned away.

Had her intent been so revealing? Could she pierce his anger with sex? Had she truly failed?

In the morning, she barely looked at him. They ate breakfast in silence at the dining room table.

In the foyer, as he was preparing to go to the university, he said, "I really bungled it last night. I'm sorry."

"I'm sorry, too," she said.

When he opened the front door, she asked, "Can we talk tonight about Mylowe? Please don't call welfare today."

Felic looked at her contemptuously. "You really don't understand, do you?"

"I'm trying to understand, but I can't bear to lose another son."

"Okay, tonight we'll talk, but I'm not changing my mind."

His words jabbed at her heart. Fortunately, the day passed quickly. Rema shuffled Mylowe off to school, drove twenty miles to the city of Cira and counseled four clients at the Libra Center. After her final session, she checked with the Libra Center staff members about the enrollment figures for the weekend night classes.

She was grateful Mona would take over at four o'clock and manage the center. At 3:30 p.m., Rema typed Mona a note and placed it on her desk.

Mona, call me only if the place is on fire!

Use the suite upstairs.

Rema

Mylowe was in his bedroom when Rema arrived at Justin House. Maggie, the housekeeper, had prepared a casserole for dinner. Rema carried a tray for Mylowe to his room.

Hugging him, she asked, "Are you doing okay?"

"Uh huh, what's on the tray?"

"Maggie's delicious macaroni casserole. Will you be all right in here tonight? Remember our agreement."

Mylowe nodded. Rema took his hand.

"Tomorrow, we'll go to the Libra Center. You can stay there with Mona over the weekend."

The moment was interrupted when they heard Felic's car in the driveway.

"Felic's home, I've got to go," she said. "See you in the morning."

She hurried down the stairs and began to set the table when Felic came into the dining room. For a moment, he stared at her then went into the foyer.

She called to him. "Dinner's in an hour."

"Right," he muttered.

The tone of his voice made her heart freeze. "Dear God," she begged, "Give me a chance."

Within ten minutes, Felic appeared at the kitchen door dressed to go jogging.

"Are you ready?" she asked

"To eat or talk? I'd like to run, but we can talk first and eat later."

Rema turned to face him. "I thought we could talk about your plan to send Mylowe to a foster home."

"Don't tell me you agree with me?"

"I agree with the fact you can no longer live with him. I know your reputation has been damaged." She turned away to make her lie seem more sincere. "To send Mylowe away would create a scandal in this town and around the world," she said. "I don't want to put our entire lives on display."

"I've thought of that, but I don't want that little bastard around me."

"Would it work if I kept him at the Libra Center when you're working at the university?"

"That's only a hundred days a year. Where do you intend to keep him the rest of the time?"

"Would you allow him to stay at Justin House on weekends when you are on tour? I'll be here with him."

"Right now, I wouldn't trust him to be alone in the house for one minute."

Rema breathed a deep, consoling breath. "You can trust me."

His eyes narrowed. A low grunt erupted from his open lips. "I'll not support him," he hissed.

"I can manage to support him through the Libra Center."

He stood in the open door carefully picking a piece of lint from his jacket. "Why are you doing this?"

"Because I want to raise Mylowe."

"I suppose if I don't agree, you'll continually harp about my breaking the agreement?"

"No. I believe we each have free will to take any action."

"Oh! No!" he yelled. "You're not going to use that free will metaphysical bull crap on me. I suppose you'll take the little bastard to the Libra Center and make a warlock out of him."

Rema's heart pounded. He was teasing her. Although his sadistic pleasures had manifested before in their lovemaking, this was the first time he had displayed his cruelty away from the bedroom.

She hung her head apologetically.

"I'm sorry. I realize I've offended you."

"Indeed you have," he hissed. "For a woman who is pleading her case, you nearly lost it."

When Rema raised her head, she was startled by an odd look on his face. His eyes were sunken, narrow slits, deeply inset and void of color. His upper lip curled over his teeth in a sinister, devilish grin.

Was she now his discarded mistress? Had the door to his inner feelings been closed to her? Would her only access to him be in the bedroom?

Within seconds, his face returned to normal. He spoke in a modulated tone.

"Where's the little bastard now?"

"He's upstairs, in his room. When we were in the den, he heard what you said about him."

"He was probably hiding behind the clock in the foyer. When I was a kid, that's where I stood to eavesdrop on conversations."

"He's really scared. I'm taking him with me to the Libra Center in the morning."

"Good! Keep him there. Enroll him in Cira's public school and tell everyone in Wexlor he's in a private school."

Rema clutched her heart.

"I want you to understand something," he said. "This plan of yours is on probation just like the little bastard is. The first breakdown and he goes to welfare."

Rema nodded and added. "He'll be in counseling for the next two years."

"That's not my problem."

"Then having a gun in the house was not your responsibility?"

Her eyes followed him into the foyer. She stared blankly at the door. To save Mylowe she had allowed Felic to seize and plunder her entire being. She knew this would not be his final act. By agreeing to her proposal, he had managed to enslave her.

No, she had willingly enslaved herself. The only part of her life she had managed to save was Mylowe's freedom and her work at the Libra Center.

Maybe she had won a partial victory. She had based her case around Felic's ego and reputation, his most vulnerable parts. She would need to gather physical strength and build a mental fortress against his sadistic manners. She decided to survive even if it would always be on his terms.

22

CONSIDERATION

Felic returned from jogging, refused to eat dinner, thundered past Rema and went directly to Eben's Tower.

When Rema awoke the next morning, she realized Felic's side of the bed had not been slept in. Grateful for Felic's absence, she dressed and tapped on Mylowe's bedroom door. "Are you awake?" she asked.

"Yes, come in."

When she saw his face, she gathered him in her arms and held him close.

"It's going to be an uneasy time," she said. "You should stay with Mona at the Libra Center."

"How long?"

"For ten days. Until Felic goes on his lecture tour."

"Can I come home after he goes away?"

"We will decide that later. For now put some of your clothes in a bag. We must get on the road to Cira. We'll have breakfast there."

"Am I going to a foster home?"

"No, honey, you're not — not ever. Come along now, let's go."

When Rema parked in the space behind the Libra Center, Mylowe reached into the rear seat for his overnight bag.

"I don't mind living here," he said. "In many ways, this house reminds me of Justin House."

Rema nodded. "I know. That's why I bought it."

"I like the big classrooms on the second floor. Were they the bedrooms?"

"Yes, originally there were six bedrooms. We made some living space with three of them."

"I'd like to sleep on the daybed in the living room," Mylowe said.

"Yes, if you want to."

Rema moved out of the driver's seat and stood beside the car. She looked at the old brownstone house towering above a grove of young elm trees and realized the house had become the center of her life.

Mona's voice, ringing across the drive from the side door, interrupted her thoughts.

"Is everything all right?" she asked.

"We're fine," Rema whispered. "This young man could use some breakfast."

Mona motioned toward the kitchen. "It's on the table." Mylowe went into the kitchen, but didn't feel like eating. He long ago recognized Rema's immeasurable strength and decided he would follow her directions. From the living room he could hear Mona's words.

"Felic Ort is insane. Doesn't he realize he isn't the only parent in the world who has had his world turned upside down when a child makes a mistake? Parents just don't denounce their kids forever over one bad incident."

Rema slumped into chair. "It's possible that Felic could be trapped by some demonic force."

"Oh! Shit! What does that mean? Does he frighten you?"

"Yes, but only in a way I'm not explaining to you."

"Oh! I've already figured its sex. You'd better get away from him before you end up dead."

"Do you really believe Felic is dangerous?"

"First, any man who is having an affair is dangerous. He can ruin the lives of every member of his family. I worry about you, but we both know Mylowe will have a lot to contend with. So far, he's a sweet kid."

"Do you think Mylowe is a candidate for past life regression therapy?"

Mona swirled around.

"Why? Would you consider that?"

"During the court hearing we learned Mylowe had a vivid memory of one of his past lives."

"What was it about?"

Rema ignored her question. "Mylowe's memory of his past life gave Dr. Sparta important information and he used it."

"Who is Dr. Sparta?"

"He's the child psychologist at the Hardin County Counseling Center. He was able to convince the judge that Mylowe's propensity toward wanting to shoot a gun stemmed from a reincarnation life memory."

Mona bristled. "That's incredible! Could Mylowe cause more trouble? Is that why you've decided to do regression therapy?"

"My inner voice is telling me to find out if he has other memories."

"You would have a better chance of resolving this situation if you do past life regressions on Felic."

Rema's surprised facial expression answered Mona's question.

"For God's sake," Mona said, "in the fourteen years you've been with Felic, you've never thought about using past life regression therapy to find out what's chasing him. You're operating a metaphysical center to help people and you have not used your skills to help your own family."

Mona realized she had said too much. Although she felt the words were on target, she retreated to the kitchen. In several minutes, she returned with tea.

"I'm sorry for intruding," she said. "You're the best parapsychologist in the state and you're allowing the same kind of neglect to happen in your family that occurs in many physicians' families."

"You mean I'm reluctant to treat my family members."

"Right!"

"I already know Felic was connected to me in several past lives."

"Have you bothered to find out what makes Felic act the way he does? What kind of hold does he have on you?"

"If I don't stay with Felic at Justin House, he'll send Mylowe to a foster home."

"Can he do that?"

"Until I have legal advice, I'm staying at Justin House."

"I'm assuming you know where to find legal information."

"Yes, the situation with Felic deteriorated too quickly. I'll do it next week."

Mona shook her head.

Rema understood Mona's anguish and tried to speak calmly. "At the present time, I have assumed full responsibility for Mylowe."

Before taking the tea cups to the kitchen, Mona stopped and looked at Rema. "Before I left Florida, I closed my house in Miami until March. I'm staying here in the Libra Center."

"How did you know I hoped I could make arrangements for Mylowe to stay at the Libra Center and go to public school?"

Mona smiled. "I'm psychic too. I caught it from you."

"I love you," Rema said. "Until next year when Mylowe graduates from high school, I'll need to rely on you."

Mona nodded and went toward the kitchen and Rema headed down the stairs to find Mylowe. Two of the classrooms were empty. Rema found Mylowe in the astrology learning center drawing on the blackboard.

"Those are neat zodiacs you've drawn. What do you plan to do with them?"

"I'd like to learn to use them to counsel people like you do."

"Do you think you should finish high school and go to college before you venture into psychology?"

"Maybe, but how can I finish high school when I can't live at Justin House? I won't see Chet or Bo or any of my friends."

"Because of Felic's anger, this isn't a good time for you to be living in Justin House. You will need to change your education plans."

"Yes, but I don't know what to do."

"If you enroll in Cira High School, you'll graduate next year. After graduation, you could go to Focale Junior College. It's three blocks from the Libra Center."

Mylowe's lips quivered. "I'm ashamed for causing trouble between you and Felic. Even though I'm not his son or yours, I'm proud to be a part of your family."

"I know you would like to find your real parents, but frankly, I wouldn't know where to begin. After you graduate, we should go to Miami and ask some questions in the part of town where Felic found you."

"I'd like to go to Dead Man's Alley."

"You've never mentioned it before."

"From the time Felic told me about where he found me, I've known he didn't want me to go to Dead Man's Alley."

Rema hugged him and brushed a strand of his hair into place. "Okay, it's a date. After you graduate from high school, we will go to Dead Man's Alley."

Mylowe's wide grin gave her his answer. "Are you willing to enroll in Cira High School?"

"I suppose so, but what will I tell Chet?"

"You can tell him for the rest of the year you are going to Cira High in order to take some advanced subjects at Focale Junior College."

"Would that be a lie?"

"No, because you will be taking advanced courses."

"Can I tell the guys I'll be home on weekends?"

"Tell them you'll be home on some weekends. I made an agreement with Felic that you would only be at Justin House on the weekends when he was on tour. As for where you will be during the summer months, we'll need to work on a plan."

Mylowe began drawing on the blackboard again. Rema saw his disappointment, but decided to move forward and follow her inner voice. She stood beside him. "Would you allow me to take you back to a past life?"

"Why?" he asked. "Have you been regressed?"

"Yes, my Grammy Perez regressed me to several of my past lives."

"Did it help?"

"Yes, it did. Just knowing about my past lives gave me direction to study the college subjects I was best suited for."

Rema watched Mylowe's expression change. She was grateful he didn't ask for more details about her past lives. In one, she died a horrible death at a young age. There was the one where she was a field laborer in China when it was invaded by cruel soldiers. In a near past life, she was an orphan and became a famous author.

Mylowe pressed the chalk hard against the blackboard. The knowledge of having died in Dead Man's Alley in a near past life and found by Felic in the same alley wasn't giving him a good feeling. He was depressed. Maybe, past life regression therapy might show him why troubling things in his life were happening.

"Okay, I'll do it," he said. "Maybe I'll find out if Felic is going to be mad at me forever."

* * * * *

The next afternoon, Rema closed the window shades in a first floor, unoccupied classroom. Mona lit candles around the room's perimeter until a dim, twinkling haze penetrated across the area.

Mylowe lay on a cot. Rema sat beside him. "The induction to past life regression therapy is vaguely similar to guided imagery," she said. "Do you remember how we practiced imaging when you were younger?"

"I know I had to breathe lot."

As Rema prepared to the begin induction, Mona slid into a desk chair at the back of the classroom.

"Mylowe," Rema said, "you should understand that the human spirit is only one dimension apart from the memories of the soul. It is through various levels of vibrations that information from our past lives crosses from one dimension to another.

"Now, close your eyes. Inhale fully and allow your stomach to expand as if you are pushing a five-pound book upward. Next, exhale slowly. Push out every bit of air until you feel a weight on your chest. Do this twenty times and relax with the movements."

Rema watched as Mylowe breathed.

At the end of twenty breaths, she said, "Inhale once more, and as you inhale visualize a ray of white light enter your nostrils. It is the light of protection. Relax. Feel its warmth. Now, visualize the white ray of light as the color of red. See its brilliance in your mind. Let it slowly pass through you."

Once more Rema was silent.

"Breathe in the white light again. Change the color to orange. Let it pass through you."

Rema continued to move him through the colors of yellow, green and blue. As the final step, she directed him to change the blue to lilac and see his body surrounded in a cloud of lilac.

"No need to hurry," she whispered. "The lilac cloud will come gradually. You may now open your eyes if you feel threatened or do not wish to continue. If you are willing to continue, raise your hand."

Mylowe's eyes remained closed. He raised his hand.

"Good," she said. "In front of you is a pathway into a forest. See yourself stepping onto the path and walk through the trees toward a clearing. As you reach the end of the path, stop."

Rema waited. Except for a chirping bird outside the classroom window, all was quiet. She gave Mylowe further instructions. When she was satisfied he was completely relaxed, she directed him to visualize a marble stairway.

"The marble stairs go down to a platform. On my command, you will walk down the stairs. Stand with both feet on each step and follow my direction:

You are now going deeper, going deeper.

Move down to the third step.

Move down to the second step.

Move down to step number one.

Step down. You have now reached a second platform. Look down and you will see ten more steps. You are going deeper, deeper.

Stand on the tenth step and follow my directions. Step down on the first step."

Rema directed him down the additional steps. When he had reached the bottom, she asked him to look at his feet.

"What do you see?"

Mylowe lay motionless. Rema waited for his reply.

"I see the feet of a small child. The child is sitting in bushes behind a round wooden gate that opens in the center. There are black iron symbols on each side of the opening. Chinese symbols, I think."

"How old is the child?"

"One year, I think. He is Chinese. He has black hair."

"Is the child alone?"

"No, a young Chinese woman is there. She puts her fingers to her lips. She wants the child to be quiet. I believe she's the child's mother."

"Do you see the countryside?"

"Yes, there's a tall, iron fence on either side of the gate. Above is a stone mountain. I see a steeple at the top. There are steps going up toward a temple. Outside the gate on a dirt road, there are people in Chinese clothing. They are pushing carts. Others are pulling cows, goats and sheep behind them. They are frightened."

"Why are they frightened?"

"Soldiers from Mongolia are prodding them with swords."

"Why are the soldiers pushing the people?"

Mylowe did not answer immediately.

"The soldiers are throwing babies and shoving old people into ditches. It's horrible. They're yelling at the peasants. 'No babies. No old people.' The young mother leaves the child behind the gate and walks toward the soldiers."

Mylowe folds his arms across his chest and moans. "The child is me. I'm alone and sitting behind the round gate. A soldier is standing over me. His sword is drawn. He's raising it over my head. He's going to kill me! No, he doesn't kill me. He turns and walks away."

Mylowe thrashes around on the cot and waves his arms. To quiet him, Rema places her hand on his shoulder. He lies still.

In the voice of a small child, Mylowe utters one word again and again in Chinese.

Rema asks. "Are you calling to your mother? Where is your mother? Are you able to see her?"

"Yes, through the fence, I see soldiers tying her hands together. They lift her into a wood-slatted wagon. The wagon moves down the road. I am alone."

"Look ahead to the next day," Rema said.

"Yes, the soldiers are gone. I'm sitting behind the gate. A Chinese man and woman stand over me. They've come to work in the fields. The woman carries me away from the gate to a small hut. There is another small child in the hut and an old Chinese woman."

Rema pushes ahead. She is eager to learn if the young mother might be Mylowe's mother in this lifetime. "Now move ahead five years," she whispered. "When you feel ready, tell me what you see."

"I'm the same boy. I'm six years old. The Chinese woman, who took me into her family, is leading me through the round wooden gate and walking with me on the path toward the temple on the mountain. She is crying. There is nothing to eat. A famine is raging in China. Her husband has gone away. She must feed her own child and her mother. She is taking me to live in the temple on the mountain."

Rema sensed the need to surge forward. "Move ahead twenty years," she whispered and sat back to wait. After a minute, she asked Mylowe, "Do you know what year it is?"

"Yes, it's 1346. 1346 A.D."

"Are you living in the temple?"

"Yes, I work in the fields during the day and study with the monks at night."

"By what name do they call you?"

Moments passed before he replied. "Someone is calling me. My name is Chu Yuang-chang. I'm about twenty-six years old. Somehow I know the Yangtze Valley is seething with another revolt. The valley was the last province to fall to Mongolia, but this year the valley was the first to revolt against the Mongolians. I'm leaving the monastery to join the rebels."

Mylowe was silent. Rema waited. After four minutes, he said, "The revolt is over. China is a broken country. I see the devastation and ruin. I have made a decision."

"What are you doing?"

"I am forcing people to listen to my plan."

"Do they hear you?"

"Yes, I'm planning to lead a revolt against the government."

"Does your plan work?"

Rema waited.

"Yes," Mylowe replied. "China is becoming a world trade center. I'm the Master."

"What year is it?"

"1372 A.D."

Rema knew it was time to bring Mylowe back to consciousness. "Repeat after me," she said.

Slowly, during the next fifteen minutes, she brought Mylowe back to the present.

Mona snuffed out the candles around the classroom.

Mylowe opened his eyes and sat up. Rema remained seated observing him.

"What time is it?" Mylowe asked.

"It's 3:20. The therapy was long." Rema sat quietly waiting for him to speak. Finally, she said, "You told quite a story. Do you remember it?"

"I was abandoned by my mother."

"Did you have a sense who the young mother was in your past life? Could she be your mother in your present life?"

"No, but I can identify the two Chinese laborers who rescued me from behind the iron gate."

"Who were they?"

"They were you and Felic."

After a long pause, Mylowe said, "I can see a similar situation in my present life. Felic found me in the bushes in China. In my current life, he found me in Dead Man's Alley." He hunched up his shoulders.

"Tell me what else concerns you," Rema said.

"Well, Felic went away from his family in China and has gone away from his family in this life."

Rema took his hand and held it tightly. "The Chinese man could have returned to his family."

"Do you think Felic will change his mind and want to live with me again?"

"Yes, I do, but you should be patient."

"I hope it's soon."

Rema hastened to change the subject. "Tell me more about your past life."

"I grew up in a monastery. I fought in a war and later I became a leader in China."

Rema turned toward the table to make notes in a journal.

"So, what part of the past life therapy was most important?"

"It confirmed that Felic and you have been with me in a past life. In my past life, Felic went away. Your elderly mother lived in a small one-room house with dirt floors. I sensed that Mona was your elderly mother. We were starving. When I was six, you took me to the monastery because you wanted me to live."

"So, I was the elderly mother," said Mona. "I always knew Rema and I had a past life connection."

Mylowe went upstairs. Mona snuffed out the remaining candles and sat down with Rema. "You seem disappointed," she said.

"I hoped Mylowe would get a clue about who his mother is in this life."

Mona stood up and started to walk away. She stopped in the center of the room. "Well, you learned one thing from Mylowe's past life."

"What was that?"

"When life gets rough, Felic runs away."

"Male menopause," Rema said.

"Do you really believe he's going through male menopause? Is that what's ailing him?"

"Either that or there's a new woman in his life he can't control."

"Or," said Mona, "his current affair is giving him trouble."

Rema's half smile betrayed her true feelings. "Felic travels to college campuses around the country. There are young attractive women everywhere."

"He's also wacky," Mona blurted as Mylowe came into the classroom.

"Look," he said, "I found something about the Chinese dynasties in the encyclopedia. The Ming Dynasty lasted 276 years and ended in 1644 A.D."

Rema reviewed her notes and the dates Mylowe had mentioned during the past life regression therapy.

"Does the information give the name of the Master of China around 1365 A.D.?"

Mylowe read quickly through the pages. Rema saw his puzzled stare.

"What's wrong?" she asked.

"Can this be true?" he whispered.

"Read it aloud."

He moved his finger across the page.

"In 1368 A.D., a peasant, who was not a man of birth or breeding, rose to the leadership of China by his craftiness and by brute force. This undisputed leader was Chu Yuang-chang. He established the Ming Dynasty and reigned for thirty-five years."

"I've always known Mylowe was special," said Mona.

Rema looked at Mylowe. "Before you declare yourself to be a leader in China, don't you think we should do a little more research?"

"But, it's possible I was the leader," he said. "I know I was there. Upstairs in your office, I found a book on Chinese architecture that showed a round wooden gate with Chinese symbols in the center. It's called a moon gate."

"Perhaps, but you should realize the purpose of conducting past life regression therapy is to help people find some correlation between the present and past lives. We weren't all kings and queens. However, those who discover they were royalty like to brag about it."

"But what if I were Chu Yuang-chang?"

"You'll glean more useful direction by studying the life of Chu Yuang-chang and what he did for China than being concerned if you were him."

"If I study all my past lives, will I discover a reversal from one type of personality to an opposite one? Like a pauper to king, celebrity to vagrant, abused to abuser, serial killer to priest?"

Mylowe smiled. He was enjoying the moment. Past life regression therapy provided him insight into his power over people. Something he always knew about himself. Another thing he knew, whether Rema believed him or not, he still held onto the rebelliousness he had developed as Chu Yuang-chang. It surged through him like rapids swirling in a river.

23

PEDRO SWENSON

One week later

The sun-bleached splendor of Justin House loomed ahead as Felic guided his Pontiac Fiero up the circular driveway. Gusty winter winds had hoisted the falling snow flakes into the air and swirled them into waist-high drifts.

When he stepped from the car to pull open the garage door, opaque sheets of snow whirled around him. Rushing back to the car, he slid into the front seat. He decided to plan his next lecture tour in a warm climate. The Fiero's tires squealed against the ice causing the car to sway. "Damn it," he yelled. "I hate this weather."

Inside the garage, he quickly slammed the cantankerous old door to the ground and exited by the side door. Stomping toward the front door, he lowered his head and trudged forward against the howling wind.

In the entrance, the snow fell from his coat and melted into puddles around his feet. He removed his boots and angrily kicked them aside. Brushing the snow from his briefcase, he heard a low groan. "Stupid old house," he muttered. "There's always air in the water pipes."

He shook his head in disgust and wondered what damage the forceful winds were imposing. He walked toward the den fully prepared to find the French doors bulging from the pressure of the wind.

Rema was at the desk talking on the telephone.

"Are you coming down with the flu?" he asked.

"No."

"You're shaking, and your face is pale! Who was on the phone?"

"It was Pinchey Wilson in Miami."

"Why is he calling you?"

Rema leaned back in the chair and brushed stray strands of hair away from her face.

His tone was filled with anger. "Tell me right now what is going on. I don't have the patience to bother with one of your crazy secrets."

Rema took a deep breath. "Pinchey called. He has information that my son, Emille, is alive and living in Miami. Emille calls himself Pedro Swenson."

"How can Emille be in Miami? He drowned in the Atlantic Ocean sixteen years ago."

"Although Pinchey hasn't had direct contact with the person he believes to be Emille, he is almost certain Emille is living in the underground in Miami."

Felic slumped down in a chair and grunted. "We don't need Pinchey Wilson's crap in our lives. Do you think there is a remote possibility Emille could be alive?"

"I don't know."

"If your son has been alive all these years, why hasn't he contacted you?"

"How could he have found me? Only Pinchey knew I was in Ohio. Pinchey said Pedro Swenson was arrested for robbery two months ago."

"I don't like the sound of that."

"Pinchey also said a well-known Miami drug baron posted bail for Pedro. Within one month after being released, Pedro jumped bail and disappeared."

"How did Pinchey get involved in this?"

"Any bail-jumper would get Pinchey's personal attention, particularly if a drug baron was involved. Pinchey would not knowingly have any dealings with the Miami underground. When he called, I thought Pinchey was just confused. Pinchey told me he has been ill and his nephew does the day-to-day work. Pinchey still keeps his fingers on the pulse of the business. After the young man jumped bail, Pinchey began working with the police to find him."

"How are you involved?"

"By my name. The suspect's last name is Swenson."

"So-ooo? There are a lot of Swensons."

"Pinchey remembered my last name was Swenson and decided to check the young man's arrest file."

"Well, what did he find?"

"He found my name, Rema Perez Swenson. On the police file, I'm listed as the boy's mother and John Swenson is shown as his father."

Felic shook his head and held his hands over his ears as he walked out of the den across the foyer to the kitchen.

"Maggie, are you in here?" he shouted.

Maggie's answer came from the pantry.

"Yes, Mr. Felic, I'm here."

"I thought you went home. I noticed outgoing tire tracks in the snow when I came in."

"Those tire marks were made by Miss Rema's employee from the Libra Center. They've been working in the den all day."

"Could you make us some tea?"

Maggie Finch scurried to put water in the tea kettle. She had been the housekeeper at Justin House since Mylowe was two. Early in her employment, Felic had explained to her that she was the only person in the small town of Wexlor who knew he was not married to Rema and Mylowe was not their son. Over the years, Maggie remained loyal to the family and kept the secret.

Felic walked back into the den. Rema continued to explain Pinchey's call.

"The young man's name is Pedro Swenson."

"That's an unusual combination of Spanish and Swedish," Felic said. "But not uncommon for the city of Miami."

Intent on sharing all the information, Rema told Felic that Pinchey had said when he saw the name of Swenson in the young man's police record he immediately sent his investigators to find Pedro Swenson. The investigators didn't find Pedro Swenson, but discovered an Emille Perez Swenson had been born in Miami, Florida, in 1962. The mother's name on the record was listed as Rema Perez Swenson and the father's name was John A. Swenson. When the police file showed Pedro Swenson's birth place was in Cuba, everyone working on the case was confused."

Felic shifted in the chair. "You should remember that Pinchey is an old man and may be utterly confused."

"I know. However, the investigators later learned from a reliable police informant that Pedro Swenson told one of the drug dealers he had been born in Miami."

"Did the report show Pedro Swenson's age?"

"Twenty-three."

"How valid do you think Pinchey's information is?"

"Pinchey Wilson doesn't manufacture stories or look for trouble. His nephew remembered Pedro Swenson as a well-spoken young man."

"I can't see how a current description of Pedro Swenson would be any help to you in identifying Emille."

"I know. Emille didn't have all of his second teeth when he drowned."

Felic frowned at the prospect of listening to Pinchey Wilson's trumped-up story. He stood up and leaned over the back of a chair. "This sounds like a bunch of bull dreamed up by a senile old man who wants attention."

Rema sat on the edge of her chair drawing circles on a memo pad. She was apprehensive about telling Felic all she knew about Pedro Swenson. "According to Pinchey, Pedro Swenson has a police record and was on probation when he jumped bail."

"What the hell is wrong with you?" Felic yelled. "If you consider doing one blessed thing about this information, you're on your own. I want nothing to do with it. Pinchey Wilson is out of his mind. I'm going to the tower."

Felic tromped up the stairs to the tower while Rema realized the gap between her and Felic was widening.

* * * * *

After Felic had gone to Eben's Tower, Rema mentally assembled all the evidence she had gathered that unequivocally substantiated the deaths of her husband and son.

In 1975, five years after their deaths, a Florida judge legally declared both her husband and son deceased. After the declaration, she received a payment of $20,000 from John Swenson's life insurance although Emille was the beneficiary.

Later that evening, she ate alone, put the sandwich bread away, turned the lamp off in the den and walked up the winding stairway. In the upper hallway, she tried to imagine how Emille's boyish face might appear as a young man. Going to bed, she slept and dreamed about Emille. In the morning, it was 9:30 when she awoke. Felic had not been in bed. She slipped into a robe and walked into the upstairs hall. The front door closed. Felic was going to the university.

She went back into the bedroom and tried to relax. Strange thoughts raced through her brain. Commanding herself to mentally reach beyond the pounding of brain waves, she moved her mind to the same quiet, secret place she had visualized after Emille's death and questioned whether Pinchey's information was valid enough to pursue. Suddenly, in the gray light of the snowy day, the answer came. She sat up and looked out the window. White tuffs of billowy snow dropped lazily from the house eaves above to the ground.

The high wind of yesterday was gone. She dressed quickly, hurried down the stairs. In the den, she dialed Pinchey Wilson's Miami number. Pinchey's deep, raspy voice rattled in her ear.

"Hello."

"Pinchey, this is Rema."

"I've been waiting for your call. What are you going do about the kid?"

"I'm coming to Miami."

"I suppose you married that Martin guy I checked out for you at the police station."

"No, I'm not married."

"Then what are you doing in Ohio?"

She ignored his question. "I want you to tell me about the young man you believe is my son."

"Well, honey, I gotta tell ya', this bee's been buzzin' in my bonnet for the last two months. There's something rotten about Pedro Swenson. The stuff in his police file just don't ring true!"

"Is there anything more I should know?"

"Yes, before this Swenson guy jumped bail, he was reporting to a probation officer in Miami. The officer's name is Noah Mason. You should talk to Mason."

"Can I do it on the telephone?"

"You can try, but this guy doesn't give much information. I don't know how he'll react; his number is 921-3331."

"I don't know if I want to talk to him."

"That's up to you, honey girl. Let me know if the creep says anything I can use in my investigation of Pedro Swenson."

Rema hung up the phone and walked into the kitchen. Maggie was taking a pan of cookies from the oven.

"I'm making cookies for Mylowe," she said. "Will he be coming back home soon?"

Rema poured tea into a cup and turned to speak to Maggie.

"The roads will be slippery by late afternoon. You should finish here and go home."

Rema walked from the kitchen into the foyer. The grandfather clock chimed eleven o'clock. In the den, she dialed Noah Mason's number. The phone rang five times.

"Hello, this is Mason."

"My name is Rema Swenson. I'm calling from Ohio to ask you about a parolee called Pedro Swenson. Pinchey Wilson believes Pedro Swenson may be my son."

"Madame, I don't give any information over the telephone. The authorities have been looking for this guy for two months. Until he's found, the file isn't open to anyone."

To stay calm during the conversation, Rema breathed a quivering breath. "Can you tell me anything about Pedro Swenson? Perhaps you might remember a characteristic that might help me identify him."

"What would you want me to look for—a tattoo, a scar, one eye?" Mason's tone was cold and cutting. "See here lady, we're not a detective agency."

Rema ignored his sarcasm. "In 1970, my son was drowned in the Atlantic Ocean."

Mason's tone was caustic. "Lady, I can't help you."

Rema took another deep breath.

"If you'll check Pedro Swenson's file, you'll see I'm listed as his mother."

"What's your name again?"

"Rema Perez Swenson. My deceased husband, John A. Swenson, is listed as Pedro Swenson's father."

Rema could hear Noah Mason shuffling papers. "My file says Pedro Swenson was born in Cuba. Were you in Cuba? I suspect when Pedro jumped bail he left the country."

"Are you certain of your information? Pinchey Wilson's investigators talked to a police informant who said Pedro Swenson admitted he was born in Miami."

"Look, lady. I've got a case load bigger than the planet."

The deafening click on the other end of the phone startled her. Noah Mason had hung up. She thrust the receiver down. Her anger toward Noah Mason heightened with each passing minute. Without notice, she suddenly was calm. The calm was so powerful, she bowed her head. It was an omen of things to come.

She hurried to the shower, pulled on warm clothing and was in the foyer pulling on her boots when the telephone in the den rang. She rushed to answer it.

"Hello, this is Rema Swenson."

"Well, this is your friend, Mona Pierce. Are you coming to the center today?"

"Yes, I am putting on my boots."

"Is your phone out of order? I tried to call you last night, but the line was busy."

Rema nodded at the telephone. "Felic was probably using the phone."

"I suppose he's always talking to that young co-ed he's romancing."

Rema stiffened. She knew Mona's assumption was correct. "There's something other than a co-ed happening there," Mona yelled. "I can feel it in the air."

"Okay," Rema said. "I'll tell you all about it when I get to the center. See you in thirty minutes."

24

THE PLAN

Mona was at the reception desk when Rema walked in the front door of the Libra Center. Mona was in a dark mood, a mood familiar to Rema.

"I need to talk to you upstairs in the kitchen," Mona sniped. Rema nodded and followed her into the hallway. At the bottom of the stairs, Rema was stopped by Mavis Horn, a counselor at the center, who needed to meet with Rema. Mavis gave the best counsel of all the teachers working at the center and Rema liked her ideas. Calling from the top of the stairs, Mona interrupted Mavis's conversation.

"Are you coming up? The tea is brewing."

"Yes," said Rema. "I'll be right there."

Mona went back into the kitchen and muttered. "And that's not all that's brewing."

Rema came up the stairs and went into the sitting room. She kicked off her boots and curled up in the corner of the sofa. Mona brought the tea and stared at her.

"Are you ready to tell me what is going on?"

Rema pulled a sofa pillow around her mid-section and hugged it tightly. Mona heaved a sigh.

"I know when you protect your mid-section, it's something big."

Rema smiled. "Protecting my solar plexus from negative vibrations is a habit with me. But, you're right. Something queer happened in my life and it's not about Felic. Yesterday, I heard from Pinchey Wilson. He has some proof that Emille is alive and living in Miami."

Mona's cup crashed against the saucer. "Pinchey is crazy. Emille's been dead for years."

"Pinchey and his nephew have some viable information. Two months ago, a twenty-four-year-old young man with a long police record jumped bail. While Pinchey was helping the police locate the jumper, he discovered I was listed as the young man's mother and my husband, John, was shown as his father.

"The young man's name is Pedro Swenson. I talked to Noah Mason, his parole officer. He did not give me any information and was also very rude. As far as Noah Mason he is concerned, Pedro Swenson's file is off limits to everyone. I asked him if he would be more cooperative if I came to his office. He hung up.

"After he hung up, something inexplicable came over me. I have to go to Miami. But it doesn't make sense for me to go down there and go over the same ground Pinchey's investigators have already covered."

Mona stood up. "So, are you going to tell me?"

"Tell you what?"

"Your plan. The one you've already hatched up to handle the situation in Miami."

Rema took the pillow from her mid-section.

"Plan A. I'm going to ask Pinchey to have his investigators tell the police informant that Pedro Swenson's mother is visiting Miami and wants to see him. The informant will say that Pedro's mother will be at an appointed place on March 22nd. For identification, she will be wearing chopsticks in the knot of hair at the back of her head.

"March 22nd is nearly a month away. If I don't get a phone call from Pinchey's contact person, I'll drop the whole plan.

"Plan B. I'll ask Pinchey to send someone into the Eighth Street pocket of the Cuban population in Miami to purchase drugs. They'll give the same message. I have to trust the word will get around."

Mona sat down in the nearest chair.

"The second plan isn't safe. It's been a long time since you've been in Miami. Things have changed."

Rema gasped, "I'm going to be careful. I just have to hope that Pedro Swenson gets my message. If he thinks it's a police set-up to trap him, he'll never show. On the other hand, if he is Emille, he might risk it."

"So when are we leaving for Miami?" asked Mona.

"As soon as I have the date, place and time of the meeting."

"What does Felic say about Pinchey's theory?"

"Felic wants nothing to do with it."

"Good ol' Felic," Mona sneered. "You're in Miami chasing a rainbow that could change your life, and he doesn't care."

Rema retrieved a pair of her shoes from the closet and stepped into them. "I must call Pinchey now. I also promised to meet Mavis in my office in an hour."

"Are you having dinner with Mylowe and me?" asked Mona.

"I wouldn't miss it! See you then."

Rema swept past Mona.

Downstairs in her office, she fumbled through her knapsack until she found Pinchey Wilson's telephone number and dialed it.

"Bail bonds, Wilson speaking."

"Pinchey, this is Rema. I didn't have much luck with Noah Mason."

"There's something about that guy I don't like," Pinchey sniffed. "He's sneaky as hell!"

"I've decided to come to Miami, but I wanted to talk to you about a plan I've been thinking about."

"What is it?"

"My coming to Miami depends on a plan where you get the word on the street that Pedro Swenson's mother is in Miami and would like to meet him somewhere out of the city."

Pinchey was quiet. Rema could hear him breathing and imagined she could smell the smoke from his rancid cigar.

"You know, I'm cutting my own throat here," he whined. "I want this guy as badly as the police do. If I set this thing in motion, I don't want to know when or where the meeting is held. And if I set this up, the contact person will be someone I don't know. You'll have to deal directly with the contact person."

"That's all right. Give your contact my Ohio phone number and have him call me collect. I'll be by the phone every night. How long do you think it will take?"

"You should hear something by next week. Now listen to me. I want you to understand that I'm not involved in this. Don't call me until after the meeting is over. And for God's sake, stay away from my office when you're in Miami."

Rema hung up the phone and realized she may have set a plan into motion that could change her life.

* * * * *

The morning rays from the Miami sun seeped through the bedroom drapes in Mona's guest bedroom and rested on Rema's face. She squinted and pulled the bed sheet over her eyes. It had been a night filled with apprehensive thoughts based on the pre-arranged meeting with Pedro Swenson at one o'clock this afternoon. She tried to ignore the squeamish feeling in her stomach.

After coming to Miami last evening with Mona and Mylowe, she had talked about the bizarre possibility that Emille might be alive. Although she had not told Mona, she was scared. She knew the person who contacted her in Ohio and made arrangements for her to meet Pedro Swenson was a drug dealer.

During the first telephone call, a harsh male voice confirmed the contact with Pedro Swenson had been made. The second call came three days later. She was given instructions to be in front of the Main Visitor Center at Everglades National Park near Homestead, Florida, on the afternoon of March 22, at 1:00 p.m.

Rema turned over in bed to avoid the bright sunlight. It was thirty minutes after seven. Until this moment, she had not allowed herself to believe Pedro Swenson could be Emille. During the last three weeks, she convinced herself that people do not return from death, particularly after many, many years.

Her emotions raced between fear and anger. In five-and-a-half hours, she would meet a young hoodlum who was using her name. Perhaps, it was to shield him from some terrible crime or he might be her son.

She sat up and looked at a faded school photograph of eight-year-old Emille. She scrutinized every feature of his boyish face. Over the last sixteen years, she had memorized every detail of his little face. As she looked at the shape of his nose and the sparkle in his eyes, her thumb caressed the photo tenderly.

If Emille is posing as Pedro, I will see something in his face.

She tucked the photo in her purse thinking it was foolish to conjure up a miracle. Still, in spite of her foolish thoughts she had already visualized how Emille might appear at the age of twenty-three. His hair would be dark and his eyes blue. If he had his father's genes, he would be over six feet tall. Her thoughts were interrupted by a knock on the bedroom door. It was Mona.

"Good morning, did you sleep at all?"

"I'm nervous about the meeting. It's probably a waste of time, but I must go through with it."

"I'm driving you out there," Mona announced in her most commanding tone. "It's a long way to Everglades National Park."

"What will we do with Mylowe?"

"I've called Mrs. Hooper to stay with him."

"I was hoping you would decide to go with me."

"Well, I'm taking a sandwich in a bag and a book. I'm going to sit where I can see you at all times. I'll pretend to eat and read, but I'm going to be there."

Rema did not disagree. From the moment she had known of the location of the meeting, she had silently worried about going alone. There was no way she could be certain that the unidentified contact person might have been the police using her as the bait to capture Pedro Swenson.

Mona brought coffee into the bedroom and waited in the living room for Rema to shower and dress. They decided on an early lunch at the Omni in downtown Miami. From downtown, they would take Highway 1 to Homestead. Since neither woman had been to Everglades Park, they allowed time to find Highway 9336, and the Main Visitor Entrance.

Mylowe and Mrs. Hooper were playing Scrabble when Rema emerged from the bedroom attired in the same style clothes she had worn sixteen years ago. She was wearing a long flowing, dark blue skirt reaching down to sandals on her feet and a scoop-neck, hand-embroidered blouse partially covered by a tan, silk-embossed, hip-length coat.

Mona grinned at Rema's appearance. Although years had passed since Rema dressed in her normal Florida attire, Mona was pleased and told her except for a few gray hairs, she looked the same as she did sixteen years ago. "I'm delighted to have my friend back in Florida. Somehow, that heavy Ohio clothing is far too dignified."

"If Pedro Swenson is Emille, he might remember me by my bohemian attire," Rema said. "He could also identify me by the chopsticks I wear in my hair."

It was forty-eight minutes past twelve when Mona drove her car into the parking area of the Everglades Main Visitor Center. Rema sat quietly for a moment and visualized the meeting with Pedro Swenson. It was her habit to visualize the situation before going into a meeting. When she visualized ahead, she discovered the outcome of the meeting turned out favorably. Today, her vision was of a young man walking toward her. She stood up and they walked together down one of the nature paths.

Her vision was interrupted when Mona said it was one o'clock.

Rema walked from the car to the front entrance of the Visitor's Center and sat on a bench near the drinking fountain. Mona waited and found a place to sit near her.

Groups of tourists waited to board the buses. Rema glanced at her watch. It was 1:15. At 1:20, three men walked onto the concourse. Two were middle-aged and casually dressed. The third, younger and handsomely tan, wore a tailored Palm Beach suit. They stood together and watched the tourists board the buses. After the buses drove away, the tall young man moved toward Rema. He glanced at the chopsticks in her hair and walked toward her.

"Are you the mother who wanted to meet Pedro Swenson?" he asked.

Rema planted her feet firmly on the hard concrete and fought the dizziness swirling inside her.

I mustn't faint, she thought. *Dear God, not now!*

Her throbbing heart had shut off her voice. The young man's face was so hauntingly familiar for a moment she had dared to believe he was Emille. Her lips parted. She inhaled short gulps of air as she fought to find her voice.

"I want to know why you have listed me as your mother on your police records," she said.

"The records must be incorrect. My name is Pedro Nunez."

"That's very strange. According to the Miami police file, you listed your name as Pedro Swenson and I am listed as your mother and my deceased husband, John Swenson, is listed as your father."

"I know nothing about this. You see in my line of work it is necessary that I operate under many different names."

He nodded toward the two men. "My comrades filch names from courthouse records. They probably picked Swenson because it's not Cuban. I don't need a Cuban moniker hanging on me while I'm operating in this country. I'm originally from Cuba."

"You know my name is being used on your police record."

"How did you discover this?"

He motioned for her to move with him away from the park entrance. The men walked behind them.

As Rema sat down on a bench, Pedro was massaging a small object between his thumb and forefinger.

He's nervous, she thought.

She waited for him to speak and pulled her shoulder purse in front of her body accidentally hitting his hand. The object fell from his fingers.

"I'm so awkward," she said. "Let me get it."

She bent down and scooped the tiny glass object with her hand before Pedro could reach it.

Staring at the small glass object lying in her open palm, she said, "I remember this. It's the magnifying glass Emille always carried in his pocket. I bought this for him at a science fair. He was seven years old."

She turned her face upward. Their eyes met. He stepped away from her accusing glare.

"Where did you get this?"

"What do you want?"

"I want to know if you are my son."

He grimaced as Rema took his hand. Tears quelled in her eyes.

"What do you want from me?" he asked. "Do you need money?"

Before she could answer, he walked away.

She called his name and held the tiny piece of rimmed glass in her outstretched palm.

"Emille, I believe this is yours."

He hesitated and then turned around. His face was stern. His eyes were set. As he approached her, the tone of his voice was cold and detached. He took the object from her hand and slipped it into his coat pocket.

"You agreed that I should go away with my father. Why would you want to find me now?"

For support, she clung to the strap on her purse.

"Until three weeks ago, I thought you were dead!"

"Why would you think I was dead? You knew dad and I went away to keep you from being killed."

"Me, killed? What do you mean? Who would do that?"

"The mafia."

"I don't know any people in the mafia. Did your father tell you what I did to get on a mafia hit list?"

"He said you made some bad predictions and caused money problems for the mafia."

"Bad predictions. What kind of predictions?"

"You know the kind, your astrology predictions."

Confused, Rema tried to comprehend the vast tangle of circumstances and fought the blackness creeping upon her. Vowing not to lose consciousness, she gasped through her words. "The Coast Guard reported you and your father were lost at sea. The Miami Herald carried the story. I have it here in my purse. Look at it. 'Miami Oceanographer and Son Lost in the Atlantic.'"

His reply was without compassion. "Don't let anyone know you saw me. It might not be good for my health, or yours."

Rema's heart pounded. She could barely breathe. He walked away. She called his name.

"Emille, Emille." Her tone was hoarse. Her words quivered. "You have to understand. I didn't know you were going away with your father. You and I love each other so much. Why didn't you call me?"

"I tried, but dad stopped me. He said if I called you, the men who wanted to kill you would find you. By meeting you today I may have put your life in danger."

She wanted to help him untie some of his psychological knots. Compassion swept over her. Where should she begin? They had lived separate lives in separate worlds. Was it too late?

"Your father's story was a ploy to take you away," she said. "For all these years, you and I were kept apart to satisfy some desperate revenge harbored by your father against me. If he is alive, he is still manipulating you. You're his hostage."

She was speaking of a theory that had not entered her mind before this moment.

"Please tell me where you've been."

"In Cuba."

"How did you get there? The Coast Guard found your father's boat several miles out in the ocean and brought it back to Miami."

"We went on another boat," he replied as he motioned his henchmen to follow him.

"Can we meet again?" Rema shouted. "Please take my address and telephone number."

"No, it's too dangerous," he yelled, moving quickly toward the black limo waiting three yards away. "Give it to my parole officer."

He disappeared inside the limo followed by the two men. The car sped away.

Rema was numb. Mona rushed to her.

"Are you all right? Was that man Emille?"

"Yes, Pedro Swenson is Emille. He said my husband told him they had to go away to keep the mafia from killing me."

"What kind of crap is that?"

"Emille believes my life is still in danger."

"What are you going to do?"

"I'm going to give my Ohio address to Pedro Swenson's parole officer. That's what Emille told me to do."

"Why would Emille tell you to give your address to his parole officer?"

"I don't know. I believe he just wanted me to be calm."

"Do you believe he'll get in touch with you again?"

"I'm not going to count on it."

Rema turned away from Mona. She wanted her tears to be private. How she could live the rest of her life knowing her beloved Emille was alive and wanted no contact with her? His indifference had crushed her spirit. She wiped the tears from her cheeks.

Mona locked her arm inside Rema's and guided her toward the parking area. She was certain her friend had experienced the worst possible situation a mother could know. For a second time Rema was deprived of being with her son. She was the observer. It was like watching a Grade B movie unreal, and yet she was unable to shut it off.

Once inside the car, Rema pushed her head back against the car seat and closed her eyes. Her unerring insight had guided her today because she knew it was the right thing to do. If she had not come, the opportunity to see her son again would have haunted her for the rest of her life. Suddenly, she raised her head and sat erect.

Mona pulled the car out of the parking space and drove onto the main road. She glanced toward Rema. "Are you all right?"

"Yes," Rema replied, "I just had a prolific thought. This afternoon I experienced a karmic payback. If I think about what happened, John repaid me for the way I treated him. There were moments in our marriage when I believed we were soul mates. But, soul mates don't always come together to be happy. Many times soul mates journey through lifetime after lifetime searching for each other. When they finally come together, they make each other miserable. That's what happened with me and John. We were miserable. Unfortunately, there was unpaid karma between us."

Rema waved her hands in the air. "I didn't see it coming. Today I learned it's not possible for people to predict the time in their lives when a karmic payback might occur. My payback was over so quickly I was stunned." She was feeling more relaxed. Talking aloud was helping search for answers and allowing her to look for closure.

"When John took Emille from me, he knew the pain he was inflicting on my life. Emille was the only tender tie we had between us. Somehow, when Pinchey Wilson suspected Emille was alive, it was the beginning of a well-planned payback."

"How do you figure that?" asked Mona.

"John devised his plan so carefully that if I did find Emille, my son would reject me."

"So, John got you good!"

"That's the way I'm looking at it. And, I realize only the great mind in the higher order of the universe could arrange a payback of this magnitude."

Mona turned the car onto the freeway. She was anxious to say something but her close friend was hurting and she didn't know what to say. Smiling faintly, she looked at Rema. "Your belief system boggles my mind, but I've learned from you that bad things happen to good people. It's destiny!"

Rema leaned her head against the headrest. "If I had been given a choice I would have elected to have this part of my destiny upended."

25

UNCHECKED RAGE

The Next Morning

The shrill sound of the ice cream truck's calliope parked in front of Mona's house brought Rema to the kitchen window. She watched the children gather around the lavender-striped vehicle with an oversized replica of a strawberry ice cream cone centered on its top.

"That truck is a damn nuisance," Mona said. "When my children were little, they had to buy ice cream every day."

"You sound upset today."

"I am upset. This old trick knee of mine picked a fine time to go on the fritz."

"Well, you certainly know the drill by now. When your knee gives way, you are to stay off it for five days."

"Five days, shit! Let's get thumping and go back to Ohio today. Did you talk to Mylowe's probation officer in Ohio?"

"I talked to him earlier. He extended Mylowe's out-of-state privileges."

Rema pushed Mona's wheelchair across the narrow kitchen.

"After yesterday's fiasco of finding Emille, I've been studying the direction my life is taking. There's Felic's infidelity, Mylowe's court appearance and subsequent probation, Felic's personality change, finding Emille alive and all the attached emotions, the added responsibility of caring for Mylowe, and my life's work at the Libra Center."

"I'm surprised you're taking inventory," Mona quipped.

"Why not? My life is bordering on being one grand mess. Shouldn't I be taking inventory?"

"I suppose so, at least for the moment."

"Just think about it. I'm trapped in Felic's warped sense of who he is. I'm prostituting myself to keep Mylowe out of the welfare system. Yesterday the image of my eight-year-old son, whose memory I had so carefully tucked away in my mind, drastically changed."

Rema's eyes filled with tears. "I still grieve for the little boy who begged me to play with him. I can't compare that little boy to the unemotional young man I met at Everglades Park who barely acknowledged me as his mother."

Mona sighed and whirled the chair around toward the sunroom.

"I don't know how you made it through yesterday afternoon. Today, your emotions have to be off the wall because you know Emille is alive and hiding in the Miami underground."

Rema stayed in the kitchen and watched the children drift away from the ice cream vendor and was caught up in a thought that had been nagging at her since yesterday.

Why does Emille have blond hair, he doesn't have any features that look like John. And he doesn't look like my side of the family. As far as I know, there are no hazel-eyed, blond relatives on either of our family trees.

The thought passed away when she dialed Pinchey's number.

"Wilson's," answered Pinchey. "Wilson's Bail Bonds."

"Pinchey, this is Rema Swenson."

"Well, hey there little lady. What's happening?"

"I'm at Mona's in Miami."

"I heard you met with Pedro Swenson yesterday."

"How did you know?"

"Noah Mason told me."

"How did he know about the meeting?"

"I didn't question him. I just figured he was connected with the Miami underground."

Rema groaned. "Why would Pedro's parole officer know about the meeting unless Pedro told him?"

"I don't know," Pinchey said.

Rema vented her concern. "Two henchmen accompanied Pedro to the meeting. Neither man looked the type who would tell anything to a parole officer. Would your people have told Noah Mason about the meeting?"

"Hell no!" yelled Pinchey. "My people wouldn't dare do anything like that! I'd kick their asses until they wouldn't be able to walk straight."

Rema realized she had insulted him and was ready to apologize when Pinchey interrupted. "I've got to ask you, is Pedro Swenson your boy?"

"Yes, Pedro is my son, Emille."

"I'll be damned! The whole thing is like a freaking fairy tale. What are the chances of finding your boy alive after he drowned in the ocean? Hell! It's been over fifteen years."

"It wasn't a pleasant reunion. He denied he was Emille and told me to stay out of his life."

"How did you know he was your son?"

"I recognized a miniature magnifying glass he dropped on the ground. It was the same little piece of rimmed glass I had bought for Emille when he was seven years old. He didn't admit who he was, but said enough to let me know he is Emille."

Rema cleared the lump from her throat and drew a deep breath to steady her voice.

"It was not a meeting one would expect between a mother and son who had not seen each other for over fifteen years." She could not stop her voice from quivering. "He rushed away, wouldn't take my address, but told me to give it to his parole officer."

"Did you do it?"

"No."

"Something's mighty rotten. Why would a guy on the lam ask you to give your address to his parole officer?"

"That's the question. I've given it a lot of thought. Oops! I've got to hang up and help Mona. I'll call you before I go back to Ohio."

In the Florida room, Mona was teetering between the wheelchair and the edge of a door. Rema held out her arm to steady her.

"I was talking to Pinchey," Rema said.

"Something big has happened," Mona announced as she adjusted herself in the wheelchair. "I can tell from your expression that this situation with Emille isn't over. What did Pinchey tell you?"

"He knew all about my meeting with Pedro."

"Sure he would know about the meeting. Didn't one of his men set it up?"

"He didn't know who set it up. Pinchey has a lot of people working for him. I guess I will never know all of the details. But after talking to him, I've made a decision."

"And what is that?"

"I'm going to put my Ohio address and telephone number in an envelope and personally take it to Noah Mason. I have questions and I need answers. He hung up on me before our telephone conversation was over. This time I'm not giving him the chance to do it. I'm going down to the Criminal Justice Building and find him."

"You should call for an appointment," said Mona. "You could go all the way down there and he wouldn't be in."

"I don't want to give him any advance notice."

"You're really pissed at this guy. Why aren't you pissed at Felic?"

"Noah Mason is just plain rude. He knows about Pedro Swenson. I wonder what he's hiding."

"I would guess a parole officer would be tight-lipped."

"I agree with Pinchey. Noah Mason has a secret. So tomorrow is Noah Mason's big day. Tomorrow he meets Rema Swenson."

"Why?"

"Sometimes we're forced into directions we ought to have found ourselves."

Mona sighed. She knew she wouldn't change Rema's mind because she didn't have the luxury of understanding the depth of Rema's philosophical views. She reached for some iced tea and sipped it slowly. Nonchalantly, she offered some advice.

"If you're going near Flager Street and want to catch Noah Mason, you'd best go after 3:00. He might be in court most of the day."

Rema nodded and went into her bedroom. She wrote her Ohio address and telephone number on a card and put the card in an envelope, addressed it to Noah Mason, and tucked it in her knapsack.

The next afternoon, before Rema went downtown, Mona promised to stay in the wheelchair and play gin rummy with Mylowe. Once on the bus, Rema prepared a set of questions she would ask Noah Mason. When the bus stopped near the county court house, she exited through the rear door. At the front of the building, she clutched the railing, slowed her pace and reminded herself she was fifty-five years old and needed to control her emotions.

After consulting the building's directory, she walked through the maze of hallways until she was standing outside a glass-enclosed room. The door sign read "Noah Mason." Inside the room, she heard a man talking on the telephone. Through the tinted glass she saw he was sitting on a chair behind a desk. The chair was turned and he was facing a wall.

She felt dizzy. It was an eerie feeling. She turned away and began to walk back to the reception area. Behind her, a man standing in the doorway called to her. "Lady, were you looking for me?"

Rema turned and walked back toward Noah Mason's office. When she reached the office door, he was inside and walking back to his desk.

"Are you Noah Mason?" she asked.

Without turning, he replied, "Yes, I am."

"My name is Rema Swenson."

He clutched the corner of the desk, slouched into the desk chair and bent his head until it nearly touched the top of the desk. Without looking up, he pulled his arms around his head.

"Mr. Mason, are you ill?" Rema asked. "Can I call someone for you?"

He raised one arm and motioned for her to sit in a chair across from him. Rema sat down and waited. He took a deep breath and raised his head. His face came slowly into view. A familiar cut of his jaw made her gasp. She ceased to breathe when she saw the set of his eyes and the thin cruel shape of his lips.

"John?" she yelled.

He nodded and lowered his head. Her fingers fumbled to find the arms on her chair. She felt her body crumbling into a million pieces. Her anger was reaching a boiling point. She wanted to leap across the desk and clutch his throat.

Moments passed. Neither spoke. Her feet were glued to the floor. As a counselor, she knew when to talk and when to listen. This was definitely a time to listen. Talking would stifle John's response. Through her mounting emotions, she saw he was slim and fit. Although his temples were gray, he had a large mass of brown hair. His elongated face was virtually free of wrinkles. He wore glasses and a mustache.

Somehow, he had managed to shove his chair backward and walk over to close the door. She heard his footsteps behind her. His hands pressed against the back of her chair. She wondered if she should be afraid. He moved away. When he sat down again, she could feel her anger rising again. It was deep anger coming to the surface like a corpse climbing out of an unwelcome grave and clawing at the crumbling, dry earth.

"This has been quite a shock," he said. "I didn't expect to see you again."

He was searching for words. He had not considered he would be in a place and time where he would need to explain to her why he took their son away and allowed her to believe they were dead.

Gathering her strength, Rema looked at him.

"Tell me why you took my son from me! Explain why you allowed me to think you and Emille were dead."

Until this moment, he had not thought to calculate how deep her grief had been. But now, he heard it in her voice. Had he misinterpreted their love? Did she grieve for him? From stolen glances, he saw her face was as lovely as before. Over the years, he had forgotten how beautiful she was. Her body, still long and slim was crowned with naturally frosted dark hair.

He spoke slowly.

"What I am going to tell you is government classified. Early in 1969, some of my research was published in oceanographic periodicals. In my conclusions, I stated that in the oceans there are varying distributions of salinity and temperature, which give rise to a systematic distribution of the density or heaviness to the ocean waters. The variation of the density of the seawater according to the salinity and temperature is a prime factor in oceanic circulation.

"I sent the same conclusions to the Hydrographic Office in Washington, D.C., suggesting the probability that the circulation of oceanic waters, if mechanically disturbed or tampered with by an aggressive foreign government, could drastically disrupt and affect life on the entire planet."

He sighed. "I realize at this moment this may not seem important to you, but one night about six months after my publication was distributed, I had a visitor in my office. He asked if I would consider exploring my research conclusions further. He said he knew of a foreign government interested in discovering how the circulation of the ocean waters could be disrupted.

"It was one of those all expenses paid kind of proposals. The opportunity every researcher dreams about. Everything I would need for further research would be at my disposal. It was my dream coming true."

John swallowed hard. "There was just one hitch. The proposal was made by a Russian agent."

Rema adjusted herself in the chair. Her inner voice told her to listen.

He continued. "I admit I was disturbed by the agent's visit. I flew to Washington and told the people in the Hydrographic Office about the proposal. I was immediately whisked off to the Central Intelligence Agency offices where I answered a lot of questions. Three weeks later, a couple of CIA agents came to my office to tell me I was in a very dangerous and uncompromising position. It seems my research theory had raised a great amount of interest with the Russians. The agents warned me if I did not accept the Russian's proposal, I would undoubtedly be kidnapped and transported to a place where I would be forced to continue my research.

"Central Intelligence stated I would have a better chance of staying alive if I would agree to the Russian proposal. By accepting the proposal, I could dictate where I would need to work. Cuba, for example, would be an ideal location because of the warm climate and tepid ocean waters. I would enjoy a certain amount of freedom and comfort while I systematically delayed the results of further research.

"Central Intelligence promised to bring me back to the U.S. when my work was done. I was to only give enough information to keep the Russians satisfied. If the time ever came where the Russians thought the work was going too slowly and brought in additional scientists, I would have to sabotage their work in order to delay the project. Central Intelligence warned me again about the danger involved.

"I thought about the whole thing for weeks. In some ways I've always been a patriotic guy, but becoming involved with the Russians and the CIA was more than I had bargained for. I also have a natural desire to save my skin. My job was to keep the Russians from tampering with the circulation of the ocean waters. I began to see the enormity of the situation. It was certainly one I never anticipated.

"There were decisions I had to make. Leaving you behind was not as much a problem as leaving Emille. As far as I was concerned, our marriage had reached a point where we were barely friends. I knew if I didn't do this job for the Russians, you and Emille might be in danger.

"When I finally decided to accept the Russian proposal, I made the decision to take Emille with me. The Russian agent had authorized my plan to work from Cuban waters and made arrangements for living quarters in Havana. After I told them about our failing marriage, they allowed me to bring Emille with me.

"The Russians devised a plan whereby Emille and I would be lost at sea and presumed dead. Before I could get my bearings, Central Intelligence stepped in and warned me not to make any kind of financial arrangements for you. I had to leave you without any source of income. They said you would be under Russian surveillance for a long time and if you received any monetary funds from unexplained sources, it could cause suspicion.

"On the appointed Sunday afternoon, I followed the Russian agent's navigational instructions and rendezvoused with a forty-foot Hatteras at an appointed place in the Atlantic. Emille and I left my boat, the Mi Toi, and boarded the Hatteras. There were three men aboard. One had brought his young son to be with Emille during the crossing.

"While Emille's attention was being diverted on the Hatteras, a workman and I set about putting a hole in the side of the Mi Toi. He dove underneath the water and with a specially designed tool tore an opening about twelve inches in diameter near the bow. Emille was not aware that we scuttled the Mi Toi. He never knew we would be presumed dead.

"We were taken to Havana and provided a comfortable home. We had a housekeeper and a handyman. Of course, they watched our every move, but after a while we became accustomed to their prying eyes."

John's voice became softer as he spoke of Emille.

"I know you are wondering what I told Emille after we arrived in Cuba. I explained to him I was hired to work in Cuba on a secret project. It was so secret no one could know about it, not even you. I told him some men were watching you and if he tried to contact you, the men would kill you."

Even though he was searching for the words, his voice was growing stronger.

"Because Emille believed you would be killed if he contacted you, I was able to keep him from calling you. He tried to call you one night, but our housekeeper grabbed the phone before he could speak.

"It wasn't until Russia started to fall apart that the U.S. Central Intelligence contacted me. They believed my project would be ignored and Emille and I could safely return to the States. It took a year before all the arrangements were complete.

"Coming to Miami wasn't the best choice for us. Central Intelligence didn't know where you were, but they knew you didn't live in Miami. They decided I would need to change my name because of my reputation in oceanographic research. I was given this job as a parole officer. I've been here for two years.

"Emille was called little Pedro while we were in Cuba. When we returned to the States, he kept the Swenson name. I know you have discovered he has a criminal record and has jumped bail.

"It's just a setup so he can operate among drug dealers. Actually, he's an undercover narcotics agent for the U. S. government.

"When he received a message that you wanted to meet with him, he was very apprehensive. He believes you are still under Russian surveillance and doesn't want to put you in danger. I haven't told him about my connections with the Russians and the Central Intelligence Agency.

"Although our jobs in Miami were arranged by the government, we are not in a protection program. I'm up for retirement soon and will be pensioned off, but Emille will have to decide about his future. By the way, he has a law degree from Havana University and speaks three languages."

John cocked his head and waved a finger at her.

"I am curious. How did you discover Emille was alive?"

Rema let go from the arms of the chair. She was ready to confront John with all the accusations she could muster. But good sense prevailed and she recognized her words would only be lost in the futility of this bizarre situation. Her most prominent thought was that John Swenson is a liar, and he had demonstrated a form of selfishness far beyond her comprehension.

"You monster," she whispered. "What kind of man are you? You let me believe you were dead and my son had died with you. You're an insane, contemptible jerk! You're inhuman. You took an innocent little boy from his mother."

John moved toward the closed door wondering if she might attack him.

"What a cowardly story. On Thursday, when you knew Emille was going to meet me, you let him believe I would still be in danger if he talked to me. How cruel! You were willing to let me live the rest of my life without my son!"

"Yes," John replied. "Until you appeared, there had been no reason to tell Emille anything."

"Are we in danger now?" she asked.

"No."

"Weren't you feeling a little guilty when you knew he would reject me at our meeting? Why would you let that happen? Do you hate me that much? For God's sake, the boy is over twenty-one. Don't you think he should know the truth about his life?"

"I'm certain he knows part of it," said John.

"Did Emille miss me?"

"Yes. When we first arrived in Cuba, he fretted at bedtime. Up until he was in high school, he called for you in his sleep. I have often regretted causing him so much anguish."

Rema's mind reeled with thoughts of revenge against this monster. Bitter anger swelled within her. She wanted to lurch at John, snatch the glasses from his nose and dig her fingernails into his cheeks while she looked into his heartless, selfish eyes.

She gathered her thoughts. John had yet to move from the door. He leaned against the wall and waited for Rema to speak.

"As far as you know, are any of us under surveillance at this time?"

"No, we are not."

"Then tell Emille the truth."

"I don't want to lose my son."

"For Emille's emotional health, you need to set the record straight."

John reached to open the door for her and asked, "How did you find Emille?"

"The bondsman, Pinchey Wilson, called me. When Pedro Swenson jumped bond, Pinchey studied the police file and saw my name listed as his mother. His father was listed as deceased. Pinchey's investigators tracked birth records and found an Emille Swenson with Pedro's identical birthday and parents. Pinchey called me. Pinchey had one of his people put out the word that Pedro Swenson's mother wanted to see him."

"Why did you come here today?"

"Pinchey learned of my meeting with Pedro from you. I felt you were withholding some important information about Emille, particularly since you hung up on me. Also, I was curious how you knew about our meeting yesterday. I came here today to get some answers."

"Well, you certainly did get answers, didn't you?"

Rema stared at him and realized her coming to his office and catching him off guard ignited the smoldering anguish he had harbored against her for many years.

Her anger had diminished, but she wondered if John would finally tell Emille the true story. The prospect of having Emille in her life again was exhilarating.

"After you have told Emille the truth, tell him I am waiting for his call. He is always welcome in my home."

John pulled the door open and looked at her. "You realize he's working in a dangerous job. He may not think it wise to call you."

She glared at him. "The address and telephone numbers where I can be reached are in this envelope."

She could only hope that for one time John's selfishness would allow him to make a noble gesture.

26

FORGIVENESS

The next morning, Rema dialed the number of Felic's office at the university. She was uncomfortable calling him at work, but wanted him to know the outcome of her visit with Pedro Swenson.

The phone rang four times before she heard his voice. "Felic, I'm calling to say I'll be home on Friday," she said.

"Too late," he grunted.

"Has your travel schedule changed? I want to see you before you leave."

"It isn't necessary."

"I found Emille," she said. "He is Pedro Swenson and doesn't want me in his life."

Felic's tone was cruel. "Maybe you can come home now and tend to business."

She drew a deep breath. "There's one thing more. John Swenson is also alive."

"Well now, isn't that just great," he sneered. "You've got the two of them back. Isn't this going to be interesting? How are you going to play it, Rema? Will it be two against one? You will enjoy the game. You love to titillate men."

He was more belligerent than before. She wondered if he was jealous. She wanted to slam the phone against the wall. Recalling her pledge to save Mylowe, she said, "I'm going to miss seeing you."

He did not reply. The dial tone beat in her ear. She put her hands over her face.

Mona wheeled herself into the kitchen.

"I see your conversation with Felic did not go well. Let me guess, he wasn't pleased to learn that John Swenson was alive."

Rema uncovered her eyes and looked toward the window.

"I can't figure why Felic was upset."

"Well, finding John was a coincidence."

Rema bristled. "You and I know there are no coincidences. Finding John was my fate."

"Did Felic want to know if you are still married to John?"

"He didn't ask. Since you bring it up, I'd better check on Florida law."

Mona pulled her body out of the wheelchair and hobbled out of the room. She mumbled that today was the next to the last day she would use the damnable wheelchair.

From the kitchen window, Rema saw Mylowe sitting on the front porch writing in one of his journals. He was nearly six feet tall. In the last month since his parole sentencing, his brown hair had darkened and the line of his jaw had lengthened to blend with the contour of his strong broadening facial bones. When he saw her watching him, he stared at her with a look that windowed the deepest part of his being. The sadness in his eyes sent a ripple through her. She realized he was still a child in a man's body. He needed her love and attention. Since arriving in Miami, his demeanor had been mirthless. He was storing up a bundle of hurt feelings. She feared the buildup might turn into his anger and move on to depression. Opening the door leading to the porch, she stepped outside and sat down beside him.

"I know you are feeling hurt. Perhaps we should talk about how you reacted to Felic's anger."

"It wasn't so bad. I didn't want to talk to him anyway. He didn't want to know why I took his gun."

"How do you feel about Felic?"

"I love him, but I know he doesn't want me near him."

"What you're feeling could be unresolved anger."

"I don't think I'm angry."

"You may not feel angry now, but if you don't recognize your pain as anger, the anger will fester and eventually explode into guilt."

"I already feel guilty. I destroyed our family."

"Can you forgive yourself?"

"I don't know how."

"When I was a little girl I lived with my family in migrant camps. We traveled from camp to camp and worked in the onion fields in Georgia. My father's mother was a special person. Everyone called her Grammy Perez. She told me about forgiveness and said no one could hurt my feelings or cause me pain unless I gave them the power to do it."

"I'm guilty of all of Felic's accusations."

Rema realized Mylowe needed to hear more of Grammy Perez's philosophy.

* * * * *

Later that morning, Felic dialed Mona's number in Miami. When Rema answered, he said, "My lecture itinerary was altered this morning. I'm going to Columbia today and will be speaking tonight at the University of South Carolina. Tomorrow night, I'll be in Coral Gables. Can you come?"

"Of course," Rema replied. She hung up the phone as Mona hobbled into the kitchen. "I'm never going to get the hang of these blankety-blank crutches," Mona exclaimed.

"If you'll stay in the wheelchair for two more days, you can walk again."

"I'm going stir-crazy."

Rema smiled. "It's time to get reservations to go home."

"Hooray! When are we leaving?"

"How about Friday evening? Can you handle the details?"

"Sure, why should we wait until Friday?"

"Felic is speaking in Coral Gables tomorrow night. He wants me to be there."

Rema knocked on the kitchen window. "I'll tell Mylowe we're going home. We can all stay together at Justin house over the weekend."

* * * * *

Felic was being introduced as Rema sat down in the fifth row aisle seat of the Miami University auditorium. She heard the speaker saying that Dr. Ort's subject was "Should World Religions Seek Common Ground?" She was familiar with Felic's lecture. His contention was that all religions consider joining together. His suggestion was controversial, but that was the intent. Many diverse religions, active throughout the world, had been established, designed and perpetuated by men who, for various reasons, needed to gain control over a large group of people by training them to follow a specific doctrine.

Felic often recited a history of century-long disagreements among self-appointed religious leaders that often led to the religious wars. He would continue by pointing out that from the beginning of religions, men have always disagreed on religious subjects.

Religions follow believers from one country to another. When religious groups or individuals move from country to country, they take their religious beliefs with them. In the United States, there are more Muslims than Episcopalians. Over a third of the world population practices Buddhism.

As Felic continued to speak, Rema was drawn to the stress in his voice. He appeared disheveled. His hair, blown in all directions by a brisk Coral Gables wind, was not patted into place. The collar of his shirt was crinkled and the lapels on his coat curled upward.

He quietly related that religion has managed to develop some common ground. The buildings of worship are similar and the structures are named to identify each religion. Each church, cathedral, temple, mosque, pagoda, synagogue or tabernacle reflects a specific belief or doctrine. There are many religious symbols. Costumes, crosses, swastikas, crucifixes, candles, bread, water, lambs, roses, amulets, statues, and incenses all created by earlier civilizations remain as common denominators in worship services. Animal and tree worship is still practiced in some remote parts of the world.

He added that religion creates a voluntary association of people. The building becomes a center of the community. The members worship together as a family and choose friends with similar religious convictions. Members of various families often intermarry and raise their children according to their faith. A religious group is tightly knit and gives its members little opportunity to interact with people outside the group, especially if a religious school is maintained. Consequently, the religious belief becomes a way of life.

For the next half-hour, Rema didn't hear his words. Her relationship with Felic had been so strained she was concerned about the future. The sound of applause made her aware that Felic was ending the lecture.

She heard him say that tight control of the membership and minimum contact with non-group members is a way to maintain the integrity of religious sects. Many groups such as the Amish, Mormons and Hutterites have survived by keeping beliefs pure among themselves. Religion has become a way of transferring beliefs and values from one generation to another. Institutions of religion and their leadership often reinterpret social failure in spiritual terms.

The lecture ended when Felic said, "Religious wars will continue to riddle world peace until one common religion is established. There is a desperate need for world peace. Every member here tonight representing his religion should push religious leaders to search for a common inter-faith."

Applause reverberated throughout the auditorium. Rema watched Felic acknowledge the standing ovation.

After a group of autograph seekers drifted off the stage, Felic turned to gather his papers and was putting them into his briefcase when a man approached him.

"Dr Ort, do you remember me?" said the stranger. "It's been a long time."

Felic looked at the large man with a black pony tail. "Yes, I recognize you. You're Dr. Whitetail, Dr. George Whitetail."

"Yes, I am."

Whitetail moved to shake Felic's hand. "I sat through your lecture trying to remember where we had met before," he said. "I finally figured it out. It was long ago at The Miami Canal Medical Clinic. You brought a newborn to the clinic. I remember the infant boy was wrapped in your sweater. You stayed with me at the clinic for several days."

Felic walked toward a nearby chair, sat down and motioned to Whitetail to sit beside him.

"I'm low on energy today," Felic explained.

George Whitetail sat down and ran his fingers across the program brochure in his hand, creased it and put it into the breast pocket of his coat.

"I've often wondered how everything turned out for you. It was my fault that I didn't follow through to see if the baby's mother was examined at the clinic."

Felic's heart thumped. He had put the memory of finding Mylowe in Dead Man's Alley out of his mind. Now he was confronted with it. Did the doctor know about his planned get-a-way from the clinic? Could the doctor know he had stolen Mylowe's medical records and blood sample? Should he bare his soul and confess how he had lied and cheated to keep Mylowe out of the welfare system?

There was a more important question he wanted Dr. Whitetail to answer. It had nothing to do with the old storefront converted into a medical clinic, crudely partitioned, with second-hand plumbing and cast-off lighting. What he had to know was the reason a police cruiser came to the clinic on that Monday morning. Were the police looking for him?

Felic began to speak cautiously.

"I never knew why you left the clinic that Monday morning in a police car."

"Oh! Yes! That was the morning some people were stuck inside an automobile in one of the canals and were partly submerged in water. The ambulance couldn't get to the car because the only access bridge was stuck in the up position. A police cruiser picked me up at the clinic and took me a round-about route to the scene." Dr. Whitetail smiled. "I wasn't much help. When I ran down the side of a canal toward the submerged car, I broke my leg and was hospitalized. Later, I was assigned to work at the hospital and did not return to the clinic."

For the first time in fifteen years, Felic realized the police were not looking for him. They were escorting Dr. Whitetail to an accident.

"Where is the boy now?" asked Whitetail. "He must be about sixteen."

"Actually he just had a birthday; he's fifteen."

"You must be a very proud father. Although you didn't say you were the boy's father. Did the boy's mother recover?"

Felic's swallowed and adjusted his shirt collar. Except for Rema, no one except Dr. Whitetail knew he had found Mylowe in a Miami alley.

"Actually," said Felic slowly, "I'm not his father. I didn't know his mother."

Stunned, Dr. Whitetail sat back on the chair.

"I found the baby in the garbage in Dead Man's Alley," Felic said. "I was looking for food when I found him. I looked to see if his mother might have fallen into the debris, but no one was there."

"You have not turned the baby over to the authorities?"

"No, I knew what would happen to him. I was raised in foster homes."

"But how did you care for the child? Weren't you homeless?"

"I wasn't homeless. Actually, I was doing research about the homeless."

Whitetail grinned. "I always thought you were different. I just assumed you were just down on your luck."

"I took Mylowe to live with a lady friend while I completed my research. Together, we raised him. At present, we live in Wexlor, Ohio, my hometown."

"Do you teach at Wexlor University?"

"Yes, but I want to make a confession. I did some underhanded things while I stayed at the clinic on that weekend. It was to keep Mylowe out of the welfare system. On that particular Monday morning, I sneaked from the clinic and took Mylowe's medical records and blood sample."

"How did you manage that?" asked Dr. Whitetail.

"I slipped out the front door before the clinic staff came in."

"So all these years, you thought I was looking for you."

"I realized I was meant to be part of the boy's life. Recently, I've begun to see that Mylowe has a great amount of spiritual insight. Someday, he'll share his knowledge with mankind."

Whitetail stood up.

"I am so glad we met again. I would be thrilled to meet Mylowe."

"Perhaps it can be arranged. He knows about the days we spent at the clinic with you."

The two men shook hands. Whitetail gave Felic his business card and walked away. Felic finished putting papers in his briefcase and turned to see Rema walking toward him.

"Hi!" she said. "It was a great audience. You look tired."

"Nothing that a night with you won't fix."

"Who was the man you were talking to?"

"It was Dr. Whitetail."

"Wasn't he the doctor from the Miami Canal Medical Clinic who helped you with Mylowe?"

"Yes, he's the one."

"What did you say to him?"

"I told him the truth."

"How do you feel?"

"I feel like I've just bathed in heavenly energy. Telling the truth can be very cleansing. By the way, I hope your heavenly energy is strong because tonight I intend to take advantage of it."

They laughed and walked arm-in-arm from the auditorium to the hotel. Felic was his old self. Attentive and loving, he acted as if there had not been an angry word between them.

At dinner, Felic said, "I have this inherent need to possess my loved ones. Being angry with them is not pleasant. My anger is so real at times, I feel like I've lost my entire being."

Remembering Mylowe's past regression therapy, Rema replied. "Your feeling of loss could be coming from a past life echo."

"Perhaps," he conceded, "Lately I've been wondering what I did in my past lives."

"Are you feeling the loss of your family?"

"I don't want to talk about that. Let's go to the hotel."

In the hotel room, he watched her undress. Before she finished, he pushed her down on the bed kissing her full on the lips and pressing his mouth hard against hers. She gasped as his tongue engaged her tongue in a heated contention. His fingers hungrily explored the flesh under her blouse. Cupping a breast in his left hand, he slid his right arm under her waist and pulled her lower body upward to meet the steeple of his manhood.

His brute strength excited her and she slid her panties off of one leg and breathlessly welcomed him as he entered the sanctuary of her being.

She reciprocated to his thrusting until they were both subdued and satisfied. He rolled to the edge of the over-sized bed and whispered, "You're a bitch in bed."

"That's because I'm a widow for rent."

Felic turned and looked at her. "What did you say?"

I said, "I'm a widow for rent. In the many past lives when we've been together, we each had a different role. In this life that's who I am."

He seemed shocked. "That is the damnedest rendition of our relationship I've ever heard."

Rema buttoned the top of her pajamas and winked at him. "Don't knock it!"

He shook his head in disbelief. "Let's call a truce," he whispered. "I need to sleep."

Rema wondered if the truce was only for her or did it include Mylowe. She dared not ask.

The next morning Rema drove Felic to the Miami airport. In the parking garage, he pressed her against the side of the car and pulled her to him. His tone was teasing. "So you think you're a widow for rent?"

She smiled.

He nuzzled her ear. "If I had the time I'd rent a few more of your bumps and grinds. I'll need to be careful because I might not be able to afford the rent."

They smiled. A simple private joke and playful phrases had reconnected them. He grabbed his suitcase and walked away turning around one time to wave to her. She watched him until he entered the elevator. Her mind was filled with questions she could not answer. What had happened to cause him to change?

Before going back to Mona's house, she drove to the county building in Miami to get a copy of Mylowe and Emille's birth records. She felt life with Felic would be back on track and she may not need to use the inaccurate birth certificate to blackmail him into keeping welfare out of their lives. As for Emille's birth certificate, she also wanted it for her records.

Twenty minutes later when she drove into Mona's carport, Mylowe hurried to greet her.

"Did Felic ask about me?" he asked.

She put her arm around him.

"He was exhausted. We didn't talk about our troubles. He needed to rest."

"Is he ever going to want to be around me? Do you think he'll like Emille better and let him live in Justin House?"

"I believe Felic is feeling better about our family. We need to be patient."

Mylowe sat down on the top front step. "I'm glad we're going home tomorrow."

She hugged him and rustled his hair. "So am I. Come on, we must help Mona close the Florida house. You know how fussy she can be."

"I know. She's been ordering me around all day."

27

PANIC

Mona and Rema went to bed after the eleven o'clock nightly news. Rema was still awake when the phone rang. She looked at the digital numbers on the clock as she reached for the phone. It was 11:47 PM.

"Hello."

"This is Lieutenant Tibbler of the Tallahassee police. I'm calling for Rema Swenson."

"This is Rema Swenson."

"Ma'am, do you know Professor Felic Ort?"

"Yes, has something happened?"

"Well, yes ma'am. Ma'am, Dr. Professor Ort fell gravely ill and was taken the hospital. He didn't survive."

Rema fell backward on the bed with the phone to her ear.

"Are you sure it's Dr. Ort?"

"Yes, ma'am. Professor Ort gave a lecture at the university this evening and collapsed outside the auditorium. He was taken to the hospital around 10:30 p.m. I was called to the emergency room and found your name and number on an emergency card in his wallet.

"I've been calling a number in Ohio for over an hour. Finally, I noticed your name, alongside another number, on the back of an envelope that was in the breast pocket of Dr. Ort's coat. I decided to try it. I'm sorry. So very sorry."

"Just give me a minute, Lieutenant. I'm in bed. I'll need to get to the desk."

"You go right ahead, ma'am. Take your time."

135

Rema turned on the lamp and stumbled toward the desk. Opening the drawer, she took out a pad of paper, picked up a pencil from the desktop and went back to the phone.

"All right, Lt. Tibbler. What's your number? Should I come to Tallahassee? What do people do in cases like this? Please help me. I'm numb."

"Ma'am, here's my number. You get yourself straightened around and call me back. I'll be here all night."

Rema hung up the phone and went to Mona's room. She tapped on the door.

"Mona," she whispered. Opening the door, she stood in the doorway. Mona switched on the light.

"I heard the phone ring. Was it for me?"

Rema dropped to her knees beside Mona's bed and laid her face in the blanket.

"Felic's dead. The doctor's aren't sure what happened. The police called me from Tallahassee."

Mona put her arms around her.

Rema sobbed. "Last night, he was so sweet. He wanted to call a truce." She raised her head. "I don't know what I should be doing."

Mona went to the desk. "Jeff Swift is a good friend and my lawyer," she said. "I'll ask him to come over. You'll need some advice."

"Should I call Lt. Tibbler?"

Mona gave Rema a pad and pencil. "I think you should get all the information from him before Jeff arrives."

Rema dialed Lt. Tibbler's number in Tallahassee.

"Is Lt. Tibbler there?"

"One moment, please."

"Hello, this is Lt. Tibbler."

"Lieutenant, this is Rema Swenson."

"Yes, ma'am."

"I've contacted an attorney friend who will help me with arrangements for Dr. Ort. Is there anything I should be doing before he arrives?"

"How soon will that be?"

"Within two hours."

"I'll notify the hospital of the situation. What is the attorney's name?"

"Jeff Swift."

"Ma'am, just let Mr. Swift handle the arrangements."

Rema hung up the phone. She felt numb. She wanted to cry but could only think of last night as they lay in each other's arms. They had parted with deep conciliatory feelings. She wondered if the karma between them was complete. It didn't matter anymore. Destiny had prevailed.

The sound of chimes at the front door interrupted her thoughts. She moved through the hallway toward Mona's whispering voice.

"Oh! You're here," Mona said. "Rema, this is Jeff Swift."

The undersized balding man in a green jogging suit walked toward Rema. "I'm so sorry," he whispered. "We should sit down. How about some tea?"

Mona limped toward the kitchen. "Before you go to the kitchen," Rema said, "we should decide when to tell Mylowe."

Mona leaned against the doorframe looking at Jeff for advice. "I don't know what would be best."

"How old is Mylowe?" Jeff asked.

"Fifteen," replied Rema.

"He's old enough to participate in the arrangements. It could be a mistake to disregard him at a time like this."

Rema agreed. "I'll wake him."

Mona returned to the room and sat with Jeff while Rema went to Mylowe's room.

Outside Mylowe's bedroom door, Rema clung to the doorknob rehearsing the words to tell Mylowe of Felic's death.

"Mylowe," she whispered. "Can you wake up?"

"I'm awake."

Leaning against the open door Rema reached toward the table to turn on the lamp. "Cover your eyes," she said.

"Have you been dreaming?"

"Yes, I dreamed about Felic."

Rema walked around the bed and turned on another lamp so that the room was fully illuminated.

Mylowe slid out of bed and went to the bathroom. When he returned she said tearfully, "Mylowe, come sit by me."

"Something is really wrong, isn't it?"

"Yes, please hold my hand."

"Are you crying? What has happened?"

"The police in Tallahassee called about an hour ago to say that Felic collapsed after his lecture tonight and was taken to the hospital. He was very sick. He did not survive."

Mylowe plunged his head into his hands. His long youthful fingers clutched his face.

"I caused this, didn't I?"

Rema did not answer. He wouldn't hear her. She held him close.

"You and I have some decisions to make before morning. Mona's lawyer is waiting for us in the sunroom. He's going to help us give instructions to the police in Tallahassee. Will you come and help me?"

Mylowe sat erect and wiped tears from his cheeks. "I'll get my robe."

Rema stood up. "I'm so sorry," she whispered.

"I'm sorry for you, too," Mylowe whispered.

In the sunroom, Mona was serving tea to Jeff Swift. She stopped pouring and turned to Rema.

"Did you tell Mylowe?"

"Yes, he's putting on a robe. He'll be right in." She addressed her next words to Swift.

"I think it's best to begin as soon as Mylowe arrives. He understands that we have decisions to make before morning."

Jeff stood as Mylowe walked in. He extended his hand. "Hello, Mylowe," he said. "I'm Jeff Swift."

Mylowe sat on the wicker settee beside Rema and held her hand.

"The first order tonight is to give the hospital permission to release Professor Ort's body," Jeff said. "However, should you want an autopsy, the hospital can order it through the coroner's office. After the autopsy, we give permission for the body to be sent to a Tallahassee mortuary and then transported to your hometown."

Mylowe and Rema stared at each other. Neither spoke.

"You've got to decide," said Mona sternly.

"I can't bear to have him autopsied," said Rema. "I just couldn't think of it!"

"I want to know why he died," Mylowe said.

Jeff answered quickly. "If there is no other person to consult about an autopsy, I suggest you wait until morning to make the decision.

"Since it is already Friday morning, within a few hours we will need to notify personnel at the university. They will be responsible for canceling Professor Ort's lecture tour, preparing a dossier and advising the media in Wexlor and other cities around the country of his death. I'll tell Wexlor University of Dr. Ort's death. Should I anticipate that the university will ask permission to hold a memorial service on campus?"

Mylowe glanced at Rema and answered, "That's customary, isn't it?"

Rema agreed. "Do we want a private funeral service?"

Mylowe squeezed her hand and said, "A service just for us?" Rema drew a deep breath and closed her eyes.

Jeff talked in rapid phases.

"We also should call Professor Ort's physician and attorney. Do you have those numbers? Did he have a private secretary?"

"I have those numbers in my address book," Rema replied. She went to her bedroom and returned with the book. "Felic didn't have a private secretary. There's a secretarial pool at the university."

Jeff acknowledged the information and continued with arrangements. "Mona says you are flying to Ohio early this evening."

"Yes, at 5:30 p.m."

"Well, then, that is all for now. We still need to notify the police and the hospital of your decision regarding an autopsy. The police will give us names of Tallahassee mortuaries."

Mona looked at Jeff. "This is a difficult decision for them. What is the deadline to call Tallahassee?"

Jeff realized that Mona was begging for time. "I'll call Lt. Tibbler and inform him that a decision about autopsy will be made by early morning. He'll notify the hospital."

He closed his briefcase and Mona escorted him to the door. In the hallway he spoke quietly, "Call me as soon as a decision is made. I'll be at home in the morning until 9:00."

When Mona returned to the sunroom, Mylowe had gone back to his room. "He wanted to think," explained Rema. "Something occurred in his room before I got there. I believe he was dreaming, but he insisted he was awake. He said Felic had been in his room."

Mona stared at her. "Haven't you heard about dead people appearing to close family members?"

Mona didn't finish. She hobbled out of the room.

Rema was glad to be alone. Of all the logical things she knew about death, she also realized that supernatural appearances of the deceased were not uncommon. She was experiencing the clutching heavy weight of grief that grips the human spirit in a strangulation hold. She resented its power and inwardly was screaming to be left to her own feelings. Reaching for the phone, she dialed the area code for Tallahassee information to get the number of the hospital nearest the university.

"Hello, would you connect me to the emergency room?"

"Hello, this is Rema Swenson. I would like to speak with the emergency room physician who cared for Professor Ort tonight. It's very important that I talk to him."

She waited, holding the phone tight against her ear. By the sound through the earpiece, she heard someone was picking up the phone.

"Hello, Mrs. Swenson, this is Dr. Mede."

"Dr. Mede, I believe Lt. Tibbler told you that Professor Ort and I have been living together for fifteen years. Would you give me the particulars about Professor Ort's death? His son and I have some decisions to make about an autopsy."

Dr. Mede's tone was comforting.

"When Professor Ort arrived in the emergency room he was unconscious. We were able to quickly determine that for some length of time he had been experiencing trauma on the right side of his brain. His lungs filled quickly with fluid. We were not able to stabilize him before the heart monitor flat-lined. We conducted emergency treatment, but were unable to bring him back. I'm so sorry."

"Thank you for speaking to me. The professor's son and I need to make a decision about an autopsy. Would you recommend an autopsy?"

"Yes, I would recommend an autopsy."

Rema laid the phone back into its cradle and tried not to think about Felic being examined by such an extremely impersonal method. The vision consumed her. She snapped the lamp off and sat in the dark.

When the sun came up, she knocked on Mylowe's door. "Are you awake?"

Mylowe responded. "Come in."

He was sitting by the window. "All night I've thought about the autopsy."

Rema sat on the edge of the bed and spoke quietly, "I have decided that I want to know what caused Felic to die."

In silence, they looked across the room at each other. Rema moved toward the open door and turned toward Mylowe. "I'll call Jeff Swift."

28

THE MEETING

Three Weeks Later
May, 1985

Standing by French doors in the den at Justin House, Mylowe noticed how the color of the garden soil had changed over the winter. After the winter snows, it appeared lifeless and marble-hard. He sighed and wondered if the flowers would know when to bloom this spring without Felic's tender care.

Mylowe turned and sat on the floor to review some of the journals he had found lying on the carpet. He heard the doorbell and Rema's voice in the foyer and realized she was guiding the visitor into the living room. He selected a journal closest to him and was deeply engrossed in its contents.

At the front door, Rema directed the tall, robust man into the living room. She was surprised to see him again. His straight black hair, trimmed short around the contour of his brown distinctive high cheekbones, trailed over the starched collar of a dazzling, white shirt.

"I sincerely hope I'm not intruding," Dr. Whitetail said. "I was unable to attend the memorial service for Felic. Did you know I spoke with him in Coral Gables?"

"Yes, I was there. I saw you talking with him."

"It had been fifteen years," he said. "I guess we were destined to meet again. I sat through most of his lecture wondering where I had seen him before. When I approached him, he recognized me at once."

Rema smiled. "I'm not surprised. Within these walls, you have been frequently remembered. I'm certain Mylowe will be pleased to meet you. I believe he's in the den."

Rema stood up and guided Dr. Whitetail toward the den. She paused at the open door and beckoned to him to stand beside her.

"Mylowe, Dr. Whitetail is here to see you."

Mylowe jumped up as George Whitetail extended his hand and said, "I'm pleased to meet you, Mylowe. I'm sorry we meet under this sad circumstance. I was out of state when I learned of your father's death."

George Whitetail sat on the sofa and asked. "What are all those books?"

"They're my journals. I've been writing in them since I was five."

"What kind of subjects do you write about?"

"I like philosophical subjects. I was just reading something I had written when I was six about Chiron."

"Chiron?"

"In Greek Mythology, he was a teacher. Hercules drove him away from Mount Pelion. In a battle, Chiron was wounded with a poison arrow. Since he was immortal, he could not die. Finally, Zeus allowed him to die and placed him in the sky as the constellation, Sagittarius."

"Isn't Sagittarius half man and half horse?"

Rema smiled. "Explaining the origin of a half man-half horse to an inquisitive six-year-old was difficult."

"You should have heard all the 'round about' explanations she gave me."

"When did you discover the real answer?"

"When I was seven."

George Whitetail laughingly said, "My curiosity is killing me. Tell me the real answer."

"Well, Chiron's father wanted to have sex with another woman. So, in order to deceive his wife he turned himself into a horse. Chiron was the child born to the other woman."

George Whitetail said, "The half horse-half man symbol closely follows along the line of one of the symbols created by my ancestors."

Rema uncharacteristically interrupted the dialogue between them to ask Mylowe a question. "Why did you take all your journals from the shelves?"

"I didn't. They were on the floor when I came in."

Rema gave a questioning glance to Dr. Whitetail. "These books were not on the floor earlier today, I worked in here at the desk until noon." She hovered over them for a moment, moved away slowly and sat down. "Sorry for disrupting your conversation."

Sensing Rema's concern, Mylowe said, "That's okay. I'll ask Maggie if she was dusting them."

After Mylowe left the room, George Whitetail asked, "Is something happening here?"

"There have been some inexplicable incidents in the past week similar to the books on the floor. They are centered on Mylowe. A ceiling light comes on in his room in the middle of the night. The French doors in the den fly open and embers in the fireplace spring into high burning flames."

"You know what is happening, don't you?"

"I suppose I do."

"Does Mylowe believe Felic is contacting him?"

"I think he does. It's important for Mylowe to know how much Felic cared for him."

Mylowe returned from the upstairs announcing that Maggie had not been in the den. He stood poised over the journals sensing there was something important in them.

"Before I put the journals away, I'll go through them," he said.

"Good thinking," said George Whitetail as he stood up and looked at Rema. "It's been a pleasure to meet you. Felic told me how important you have been to Mylowe."

Rema stood and nodded.

George Whitetail turned toward Mylowe. "And, Mylowe, you've grown a bit since I last saw you. I hope we will not be strangers."

"No sir."

"I must go. I have an appointment at the university at four o'clock."

"Could you have dinner with us tonight?" asked Rema.

Mylowe stood beside Rema, his arm resting on her shoulder. "Could you come back?" he pleaded.

"I'd be delighted," George Whitetail replied. "I must leave for the Dayton airport at nine o'clock."

* * * * *

Mrs. Esther Quincy, Wexlor University's administrative assistant to President Matthews, opened the door to the president's mahogany-paneled office.

"Your four o'clock appointment is here," she said. "The gentlemen's name is Dr. George Whitetail. He's from the University of Miami in Coral Gables. He wants to make some inquiry concerning Dr. Ort."

"Bring him in, Mrs. Quincy," said President Matthews.

She escorted Dr. Whitetail from the outer reception area to the President's office. At the door, Dr. Whitetail thanked her and shook hands with President Matthews.

"Thank you for seeing me."

"It's my pleasure. Mrs. Quincy said you wanted to speak to me about Dr. Ort."

"That's my purpose. I visited briefly with Rema and Mylowe this afternoon."

President Matthews leaned forward over the oversized desk.

"Felic's death was untimely. It was a shock to the entire community, especially to the university. A memorial was held in our Woodmere Hall last week. Prior to that, a private graveside service was held for family members."

"Had Felic been in good health during the past year?"

"Yes, I have no reason to think otherwise. He maintained a busy schedule at the university. His lecture tours took him away about two hundred days a year. Why do you ask?"

"When I read a copy of his autopsy report I wondered how a man with such extreme brain deterioration was able to maintain a busy schedule."

President Matthews shook his head. "I had no idea he was ill."

Dr. Whitetail stared at the university president. "I met with Felic the night before he died," he said. "Although I had not seen him for nearly fifteen years, he did not appear to be in poor health."

"Were you an old friend?"

"In a way we were bound together. In 1970, when Felic found a newborn baby in a deserted alley in Miami, he brought the infant to a storefront clinic where I was an intern. I examined the baby thinking that Martin (that was the name Felic used) was the child's father. He stayed in the clinic with the baby for four nights. I did not see him again until I heard him lecture in Coral Gables three weeks ago. We had a pleasant chat. He told me about his life. Actually, he confessed to some things he said had been on his mind for a long time. He was proud of Mylowe and had such hope for his future. He gave Rema a great amount of credit for helping to raise the boy."

President Matthews gasped. "I didn't know Mylowe wasn't their son. Were Rema and Felic not married?"

Stunned by President Matthew's question, George Whitetail sat stiffly in the chair.

Sensing the doctor's embarrassment, President Matthews adjusted himself in his chair and continued to speak. "They appeared to be a close family. Of course, Rema used the Swenson name for business purposes when she established her counseling center in Cira, but no one questioned that."

Alarmed and dismayed by his poor judgment, George Whitetail began to recover. "I can see that I've truly spoken of a situation I had no right to bring into this conversation," he said. "I don't know whether I should creep away or stand up and take my punishment."

"I want you to know the subject matter of this conversation will not be repeated."

Whitetail nodded. "I thank you for that. I have many more questions about Felic's health, but some of the answers may come from Rema and Mylowe. However, I do know I have many more miles to go before I find what I'm looking for."

President Matthew nodded and stood up preparing to usher his visitor from the office. When he saw that George Whitetail remained in the chair, the university president retreated back to his desk.

Dr. Whitetail sat uncomfortably in the leather side chair. Neither man spoke. Finally, Dr. Whitetail broke the silence.

"Since I've overstepped a privacy boundary, I'm concerned what affect this private knowledge might have on Rema and Mylowe, if it were to became public."

"Precisely, why are you making inquiries?"

"When I read Dr. Ort's autopsy report, I found it inconsistent. I set out to learn about Felic's health for the last five years."

"Have you checked with Felic's local physician?"

"Yes, I met with him this morning. He had examined Dr. Ort last year and found nothing alarming in his physical condition."

"Have you talked to Rema about this?"

"No, it's too early in my investigation." Changing focus, Dr. Whitetail said, "Mylowe seems to be a bright young lad."

"Indeed, he is. I believe he will graduate from high school this year."

"At the age of fifteen?"

"Yes, he has a perfect grade average. He'll be ready for college next year. There's something else you might want to know. It's not a secret. Mylowe is on probation for two years for firing of a firearm on railroad property."

"I assume Dr. Ort was upset."

"Felic was embarrassed by the publicity."

"How long ago did that happen?"

"The court hearing was in February or March of this year."

Dr. Whitetail stood up. "We agreed this conversation was confidential," he said. "Am I correct?"

"Positively," replied Dr. Matthews.

29

CLARITY

Inside the rental car parked near the Wexlor College administration building, Dr. Whitetail sat pensively tapping his fingers on the steering wheel wondering why he had bothered to request the copy of Dr. Ort's autopsy report from the Leon County Coroner. Until three weeks ago, he did not know Felic Ort was the homeless man who, in August of 1970, brought a newborn to the Miami Canal Medical Clinic and stayed in the clinic for four days. After fifteen years, it was not coincidental that they should meet again in Coral Gables.

Feeling deep frustration, he jabbed at the steering wheel with his fist. The frustration he was experiencing began with his insatiable curiosity. The autopsy report showed a slow deterioration of Felic's brain. Did Dr. Ort's death occur as the result of a long-standing illness?

The blunder he committed in Dr. Matthew's office made him realize he was an inexperienced private investigator.

Why am I in Wexlor? Is it my fate to be here?

He turned on the ignition key and turned the Volvo toward Justin House.

Tonight's dinner with Rema and Mylowe might be the only opportunity to discover if Felic was living with a fatal disease.

At the Justin House front door, he decided not to press for information. Rema opened the door and ushered him into the den.

"Mylowe will be coming down for dinner," she said. "He spent the day reading his journals."

147

"I trust his day was successful."

"Since Felic's death, Mylowe has not been overly communicative. He should return to school, but hasn't made up his mind."

"Why is that?"

"Before Felic died, Mylowe was enrolled in the Cira Public schools. During the week, he stayed at the Libra Center with Mona Pierce, my friend from Miami. She is currently serving as the administrator of the Libra Center."

"Does Mylowe want to graduate from Cira High?"

"He hasn't said."

Mylowe came into the den just as Rema went to the kitchen to check on dinner. Dr. Whitetail stood and shook his hand. They sat facing each other in the blue velvet, winged-back chairs beside the fireplace.

"I understand you're going to college next year. Do you know the field you're going to study?"

"I've decided on psychiatry," Mylowe replied. "At Felic's graveside, I realized he had been mentally disturbed for a long time before he died. He was in agony. I want to study the brain so I can understand people's mental problems and lessen their pain."

Dr. Whitetail drew a deep breath. Mylowe had provided the first clue to Felic's brain deterioration. "Did you see signs of a mental illness?"

"Yes, Felic often lost control. For a long time, he was angry with me. I disappointed him and he felt betrayed. After the court hearing, he wouldn't talk to me. Every night after dinner, he went to Eben's Tower."

"Where's Eben's Tower?"

"It's a small observation room on the second floor at the back of the house. Felic's great grandfather, Eben Justin, built it so he could be alone and study the stars. As Felic told it, Eben had two wives and fourteen kids. With more than one wife, his lifestyle was not accepted by the local people. He became a loner."

George Whitetail pressed on. "How did Felic act before the shooting incident?"

"He was tired and grouchy."

"Was he writing a book or journal papers in Eben's Tower?"

"I don't know. Rema won't go into the tower to see what he was doing. She says the tower is a place only for the men of Justin House. She's already made it off-limits to me until I'm older."

George Whitetail drew a deep breath. It was certain that whatever project Felic had been working on, it was in Eben's Tower. If Rema wouldn't permit anyone to go to the tower, his investigation was stymied.

Rema appeared in the doorway accompanied by Mona. She guided Mona to the center of the room. "Dr. Whitetail," she said. "I am pleased to introduce to you my dearest friend, Mona Pierce."

George Whitetail stepped forward and shook Mona's hand. "Do you live in Wexlor?" he asked.

"No, my home is in Miami."

"Have you lived there a long time?"

"I was born in Delray Beach. I hadn't been north of the Mason Dixon until Rema enticed me to come to Ohio to help her with the Libra Center."

Rema could see George Whitetail was interested in Mona. His dark eyes twinkled when he questioned her about her life. Between Mona's exchange of playful remarks and George Whitetail's good-natured replies, the evening turned into a pleasant experience for everyone.

At the front door as George Whitetail was leaving, Rema clasp her hands around his.

"I feel you have questions about the way Felic died. Is there anything you can tell me?"

He shook his head. "For now, nothing more than the information in the autopsy report."

Rema turned away.

Mylowe walked George Whitetail to the rental car. "Felic would be pleased with your decision to study medicine," Whitetail said. "Here's my card. Call me George. I'll be waiting for your call. Maybe I can help."

"I haven't had much advice about college. After the court hearing, Felic was so angry he wanted to send me to a foster home."

George smiled. "Whatever your thoughts might be, Felic loved you and was enormously proud of your accomplishments."

Mylowe clasp George's business card in his hand. "I'll let you know when Rema and I make some decisions. If I'm going to graduate this year, I need to go back to school."

Mylowe stood near the front door and watched the tail lights of the Volvo disappear at the end of the drive.

In the kitchen, Mona was washing dishes as Rema walked in.

"There's one hunk of a man," Mona whispered in a low, sultry tone. "Why did he come here? Did you meet him in Coral Gables after Felic's lecture?"

"No, I didn't meet him, but I saw him talking to Felic. Felic told me who he was."

"Is he married?"

"What?" Rema yelled.

"Is he married?"

Rema grinned. "I don't know. Why didn't you ask him?"

"Don't you think it strange that he came here?"

"He feels a connection to Mylowe."

Mona handed a washed salad platter to Rema and dried her hands on a towel. "If George Whitetail has been in Wexlor all day, I'll wager he's been asking some questions."

"About what?"

"About Felic, you and Mylowe."

Rema picked up a towel and rubbed the platter until it was dry. Mona winked, put on her coat and exited via of the back door as Mylowe came into the kitchen.

"Is Mona going to the Libra Center tonight?"

"Yes, she has a 7:30 appointment in the morning. Did Dr. Whitetail get on his way?"

"Yes, he didn't have much time to catch the plane to Miami. He gave me his business card and asked me to call him George. I know I've been quiet. Can we talk?"

"What should we talk about?"

"How many brothers did you have?"

"Five. I was the only girl."

"Why did they call you Rema?"

"My parents were Robert E. and Maria A. Perez. They put their initials together and my name became REMA. My mother called me Lilly. Lilly translated means "little onion.""

"Whew!" teased Mylowe. "That was a smelly name."

"Nevertheless, I was born in an onion field near Valdosta, Georgia. My parents were migrant workers. On the day of my birth, they were planting a variety of onion called Allium A.cepa."

"What year was that?"

Rema grinned. "It was 1930, during the Great Depression. My parents and grandparents were of Mexican origin. They were part of the migrant workers who cultivated the vegetable fields throughout the southern regions of the United States.

"My mother died young. In her brief lifetime, she gave birth to six children, worked every day in the fields, cared for aging parents and endured the late night ramblings of an abusive, drunken husband. After her death, I assumed the chore of being a mother to my brothers. In 1941, when World War II was imminent, my three older brothers joined the military."

"Did your brothers go to the army to get away from the migrant life?"

"I suppose that was their motive. They were grown men and had little privacy living with other people in the sharecropper's shack. My youngest brother went to the local school when he was not working in the fields."

"Did you go to school?"

"I did, part time. I managed to graduate from high school by my nineteenth birthday. I stopped working the fields and worked in a five and dime store. Later, after I got married, I earned a college degree in Social Services."

Mylowe had always known there was something in Rema's background that made her strong yet resilient.

"Tell me about your grandmother."

Rema smiled. "Grammy Perez was an astrologer, a palmist, a fortune teller and a healer. From her I learned the healing values of medicinal herbs.

"Every spring when we arrived at the migrant camp, she would plant a garden of herbs. She always carried a burlap bag filled with dried herbs. There was echinacea and golden seal for infections and colds, Valerian root as a calming sedative, St. John's wart for nervousness, white oak bark to reduce swellings, yarrow and juniper berries for hemorrhoids, lobelia for angina, feverfew for headache, comfrey for burns, corn silk for bed wetting, apple tree bark and poke root for dizziness."

"Do you use herbs at the Libra Center?"

"I do when I believe certain herbs will improve a client's health or prevent an illness. I always suggest they consult a doctor before using herbs."

"I'll bet your Grammy didn't have her patients check with a physician before taking herbs."

Rema stood up and began wiping spots from the cupboard doors. "I was thirty years old before I realized I had the gift to help people."

"Was that the reason you opened the Libra Center?"

"Yes, I wanted to inspire others to examine their inner selves."

"Until our private service for Felic at the cemetery, I wasn't sure what I wanted to do with the rest of my life."

"What helped you make up your mind?"

"While I stood beside Felic's grave, I felt I should study medicine. During the last six months of his life, Felic was mentally off balance. I realize he had good reason not to trust me, but he acted as if he couldn't control his feelings."

Rema's eyes filled with tears. She leaned over the kitchen counter.

"I'm sure you're correct. Although the last time I was with him, he talked of reconciliation. He wanted us both back in his life."

Mylowe stood and put his arms around her. "If you agree, I think I should go back to Wexlor High. I'd like my diploma to be from Felic's hometown. I want to carry on the name of Ort in Wexlor, Ohio."

Rema put her hands on his shoulders.

"Felic was a pillar of the community. He'll be remembered for many years."

"I have a special feeling about the town. Who knows, I might be Wexlor's first psychiatrist or psychoneuroimmunologist. My dream is to build a medical clinic on the vacant hill behind Justin House."

"What is a psychoneuroimmunologist?"

"The field of psychoneuroimmunology is under the auspices of studies in psychosomatic medicine. Psychosocial stressors can cause alterations in immune function that can result in actual changes in overall health. Infectious diseases, wound healing and a range of common diseases, negative emotions such as anger, depressions, despair, stimulate the production of inflammatory disturbances."

"Stop!" cried Rema. "That's enough. Just say you're going to study the psychological state of people as it is related to their immune systems."

"Ok!" Mylowe said. "Psychosomatically we tell ourselves that something so traumatic has happened to us that it changed how we feel about ourselves. The feeling could affect immune systems, mental health, cardiovascular diseases, diabetes, arthritis, periodontal disease and many other diseases. Nothing happens in just one section of the body. Pain warns us that something is wrong somewhere."

"What about invisible pain?" Rema asked.

"Invisible pain is the worst. It seldom responds to medications. Whether we experience bad timing, large or small losses, self-manufactured trouble or plain bad luck, invisible pain sticks to us like glue."

Mylowe watched Rema hang up the dishtowels.

"What do you have planned for the rest of the evening?" he asked.

"I'm going to bed. Did you remember that Felic's attorney, Martin Walsh, is coming tomorrow to read Felic's will?"

"Do you know what is in it?"

"No, Felic didn't discuss it. Turn out the lights when you come up." She stopped in the doorway and turned toward him. "I am proud of you. I'm certain Felic would feel the same."

Mylowe followed her. He walked into the den to turn off the lamps. Standing in the dim light from the foyer, he sensed Felic's spirit with him.

30

GOOD WILL

The Next Afternoon

Martin Walsh sat quietly at the desk in the den at Justin House waiting for Rema to bring Mylowe. Martin had taken the coveted legal documents from his briefcase and arranged them on the desktop.

"I hope we haven't kept you waiting," Rema said. "Mylowe is coming down the stairs."

When Mylowe entered the room, he asked. "Is anyone else expected?"

"No," Walsh replied. "But, I must, by law, tell you this. A week before his death, Felic made an appointment with me."

"Did he mention the reason he wanted to see you?" asked Rema.

"Yes, he wanted to add a codicil to his will."

Walsh rummaged through the documents on the desktop.

"First," he said, "let me preface the reading of Felic Ort's will by saying Felic wrote the will himself in longhand. I notarized it along with two witnesses. I've known Felic for many years and it was under a great amount of protest I agreed to comply with his wishes."

Martin Walsh stood up and began to read.

"I bequeath Justin House to my son, Mylowe Frederick Ort, with the stipulation that the house or any of the contingent land cannot be sold or leased during his lifetime or during the lifetime of his descendants or any of their immediate descendants.

153

"If Mylowe Ort is not the legal age of twenty-one at the time of my death, I appoint Rema Perez Swenson as guardian of Mylowe Ort. Attorney Martin Walsh will act as trustee of my estate.

"I also stipulate that Rema Perez Swenson make Justin House her home for the rest of her life.

"Should Mylowe Ort enroll in an educational institution before his 21st year, from the established trust the trustee will pay all educational expenses, within reasonable amounts, and all health and life insurance premiums for Rema Swenson and Mylowe Ort.

"The trustee will match dollar for dollar all monies earned by Mylowe Ort until he graduates from college. Example: If he shows proof of earning $100.00, the trust will award him $100.00. The ceiling on matching his earnings is $20,000 per year.

"Each month, all household expenses for the maintenance of Justin House will be turned over to the trustee for payment.

"I further bequest to Rema Perez Swenson the completed manuscript of a non-fiction book. It is located on my desk in Eben's Tower. Should I die before it is published, I request that she be totally responsible for the publishing and distribution of the book. All funds from the initial sale of the book and from additional reprinting will go directly to Rema Perez Swenson with no other stipulations."

Martin sat down and removed his glasses.

"As you heard, there were not a lot of legal terms. Felic was clear that his wishes be carried out. Are there any questions?"

"This must be a sizable estate," Rema said.

She winced under Martin Walsh's wilting glare. "Felic Ort," he said, "was a frugal man. The large part of the current estate comes from the bequest from his mother's family bequeathed to him years ago along with Justin House and the contingent land."

"Mylowe, do you have any questions?" asked Martin.

"Felic always gave us the impression that we were living from paycheck to paycheck. Can you tell me the total amount of the estate?"

Before replying, Martin looked to Rema for permission. When she nodded, he complied.

"There are $550,000 in securities plus $475,000 which is the current appraised value of Justin House and the land around it."

Rema and Mylowe remained seated as Martin Walsh gathered the papers from the top of the desk and placed them neatly in his briefcase.

Martin raised his eyes but refrained from looking at either Rema or Mylowe. "You know how to get in touch with me," he said.

Mylowe stood, walked to the foyer with Martin and helped him with his coat. Martin grunted an inaudible word of appreciation and left through the front door.

When Mylowe walked back into the den, Rema was wiping her eyes. "I'm overwhelmed," she said. He sat beside her and whispered. "I never thought I would have to deal with Felic's death. Truthfully, I didn't want to think about it."

"People seldom do. Through eons, humans have been taught to fear death."

Mylowe looked surprised and squeezed Rema's hand. "When I was younger," he said, "I was so afraid of death, I would run past the funeral homes that were side by side on Wexlor's Main Street."

Rema smiled. "Felic told me when he was young, he always ran past those funeral homes."

Mylowe pulled Rema up from the sofa.

"Come on, let's get out of here. How about getting a hamburger at the shop on the corner?"

Rema picked up her coat from a nearby chair and walked with Mylowe into the foyer. They paused. "It's a wonderful house," she said glowingly. "Someday your children will be playing in this foyer."

"If they're like me, they'll be sliding down the banisters." He tugged at the sleeve of her coat. "Let's go eat."

31

THE RETURNEE

For six months following Felic's death, Rema was filled with feelings of guilt, anger and deep sorrow. The memory of the night in Coral Gables with Felic continually ran through her mind. There were moments when she thought of calling George Whitetail, but realized his silence meant he knew nothing other than the information in Felic's autopsy report.

Mylowe's high school graduation, when he was just sixteen, and his immediate departure for Columbia University in New York City, left empty space in her life and an empty house. Justin House was too quiet and filled with too many memories. She tried to keep busy at the Libra Center, but the days still were far too long. She scolded herself for not remembering that grieving doesn't have an on and off button.

Tonight, she vowed to take better control of her life and be more content. Tomorrow she would stay at home and relax. The desk drawers in the den needed to be rearranged and the ugly spot on the blue velvet chair beside the fireplace required a special cleaning.

She climbed the stairs to her bedroom and shoved the hangers apart in the closet until she found a pair of faded jeans to wear tomorrow on her day off. Next to her jeans she saw a pair of blue cargo pants. "These are Felic's," she gasped.

In the last two months, she had collected Felic's clothes. In Eben's Tower, she found his sweater hanging over a chair and held it lovingly in her arms. On the desktop, his eyeglasses lay open as if he had just laid them there. She packed the sweater along with other articles of his clothing, but placed the eyeglasses on the desk in the exact spot where he had laid them.

She knew that gathering Felic's clothes was part of her grieving process. Doggedly, she had carried each box to the driveway and waited for thirty minutes until the truck from the Salvation Army arrived. A crisp November breeze rattled the plastic clothing bags covering his coats and suits. She rushed over and caressed the bags, touching them for a final time as the truck came up the driveway.

The drone of bagpipes and the rhythmic drum beat of a marching band were missing as she tossed confetti into the air. Wafted by the breeze, the colored snips of paper fell downward and rested on the boxes and bags. A part of Felic was being hauled away. The confetti made it a celebration.

She stared at the cargo pants and remembered that Wexlor's postmaster, after the death of his son, hung the boy's varsity jacket in his office over a chair for three years. The boy's neck had been broken in a football game.

Rema blinked away the memory, went to the closet and hung Felic's cargo pants next to her faded jeans. She paused as if she were unsure of what to do next. Slowly, she closed the closet door.

* * * * *

In the morning Maggie ran to answer the telephone in the den. "This is Justin House," she chortled. "Yes, Mrs. Swenson is in. Would yah please tell me your name so's I can tell her who's calling?"

"I'm calling from Miami. Would you ask her to come to the phone?"

Maggie stuck her Irish tongue out at the telephone and gave the caller a third finger gesture. Turning, she walked through the French doors and goose-stepped down the garden path. At the halfway point, she yelled to Rema, "Someone's on the phone from Miami. He wants to talk to Mrs. Swenson."

Rema looked up from raking leaves. "I really want to finish raking today."

Maggie turned and hurried through French doors. When Rema entered the den Maggie whispered, "It's a man."

Rema nodded and picked up the phone. "Hello, this is Mrs. Swenson."

"This is Emille."

"Emille?"

"I called to tell you that dad died. His heart gave out. I found your telephone number in his address book."

"When did he die?"

"Three weeks ago. I'm still trying to clean up everything."

"Emille, I'm so sorry."

"It's been difficult managing his burial. At times I didn't know what to do."

"Are you still living in Miami?"

"Yes, but I'm not working. I need to find a teaching job for the coming year."

Rema sat down. "Could you come for a visit?"

"I guess I could. What is the best time for you?"

"I'm so happy to hear from you. Come right away."

Emille pushed the door open to the telephone booth on Wexlor's Main Street. His lips formed a sinister grin.

She's anxious. What would she think if she knew I was already in Wexlor?

He shoved at the door. "I don't want to impose on you," he said.

"Just tell me when you'll be here. I'll make arrangements to spend all my time with you. I should warn you if you fly to Dayton it's a two-hour drive to Wexlor."

"What is driving time from Miami?"

"An easy twenty hours."

Once again the ill-omened grin formed on his lips. "I think I'll drive. I'll need my car if I'm going to search for a teaching position. I can be there by Friday. What's the address?"

"Number 1 on Justin Lane. It's the only house on the street."

"Will it be okay with your husband?"

She didn't answer. For the first time, she realized how much she had disciplined her mind to live without Felic. She hurried into the kitchen to make arrangements with Maggie.

"Land sakes, Miss Rema," Maggie said, "you are flushed."

"The caller was my son, Emille. He'll be here on Friday. Could you help me over the weekend?"

Rema hurried to the den and dialed Mona's number.

"Emille called this morning. I invited him to visit me at Justin House. He'll be here on Friday."

"I can tell you're thrilled," said Mona.

"I don't know how I feel. Emille said John Swenson died three weeks ago."

"Did he die in Miami?"

"I didn't ask. Emille called from Miami. Do you know how long I've waited to have my son in my life again?"

"I know, but you don't need to experience the same crap he laid on you last year at the Everglades Park. Does Emille have a job? What kind of work does he do?"

"He's a teacher. He mentioned he'll be looking for a teaching job. I'll have more information after the weekend. I'll call you."

"I'll be waiting." Mona hung the phone up and decided she would check the Dade County records for the date of Noah Mason's death.

She dialed the number of Wilson's bail bonds and paced back and forth until she heard Pinchey's voice.

"Hello! Bail Bonds," Pinchey said.

"Pinchey, this is Mona Pierce."

"Hey there lady, what's up? Is there trouble in Ohio?"

"I don't know for certain. Did Rema get back to you about Noah Mason?"

"What about him?"

"She went to see him at his office in Miami and discovered Noah Mason was her husband, John Swenson."

"Why didn't she call me?"

"The man she had been living with since she left Miami died two days after she discovered Noah Mason's true identity. She really didn't have time to call you. We flew back to Ohio. There was a memorial service for Dr. Ort at the university. She's still grieving."

Pinchey was silent. Mona heard him clear his throat. "I suppose all this happened soon after she met her son."

"There was a rapid sequence of gut-wrenching events. The reason I called you is to ask you if you knew Noah Mason had died."

"Why do you ask?"

Mona ignored Pinchey's question. "What happened to Pedro Swenson?" she asked.

"You mean Rema's boy? Yeh! He was cleared of all the charges with the police. I heard he was working for the government as an undercover agent. You seem worried."

"I'm concerned. Emille is going to Ohio to see Rema on Friday. My gut tells me that something is going on and Rema may become involved."

"Is it something dangerous?"

"Maybe."

"Anything I can do?"

"Could you check to see if Pedro Swenson, I mean Emille Swenson is still in Miami? Also, could you find out if Noah Mason or a John Swenson died recently? Do you have my Miami number?"

"Yes, I'll call you as soon as I have any information."

"Thanks, you're a good friend."

Mona hung up the phone and walked to the Florida room hoping her intuition was giving her the wrong signals.

32

THE REUNION

Three Days Later

On Friday morning, Maggie watched Rema polish the furniture near the front door three times. By eleven o'clock, she watched Rema stand at the front windows a dozen times. Maggie knew Rema was waiting for Emille's car to come into the driveway. When a blue Ford turned from the street and moved between the gatehouse pillars, she watched from the kitchen window as Emille stepped out of the car.

Rema also watched the car move up the driveway. She moved behind a sheer drapery in the living room to get a better look of her son. The way he walked reminded her of the young John Swenson she had married years ago. Although the Mexican influence of her family was evident in his handsomely tanned face, his hair was lighter in color than her ancestors. His well-defined darker eyebrows were separated by a slim nose and his lips were expressive.

The doorbell stirred her from her thoughts. She lurched forward to open the door. Outside, Emille stood statue still. His compelling, crooked grin invited her to leap into his arms.

"Whoa!" he yelled removing her arms from his neck. "You'll strangle me before we've had our visit." Rema backed away and grabbed his hand. "Is this better?" He shook his head and walked beside her into the den. "This is some shack. How long have you lived here?"

"For over thirteen years. It's Felic's family home."

"What's Felic's last name?"

"It's Ort."

"What does he do? With digs like this he must be well-heeled."

"Felic died last year."

"Oh! I didn't know. Who else lives here?"

"Mylowe lives here. He's Felic's son."

"Then Mylowe is not your son?"

"No, I've been with him since he was three days old."

"So, he's like your son."

"Yes, he's away at college."

Emille walked around the den. He paused to look through the French doors and heaved an audible sigh.

"Why did you sigh?" Rema asked.

"I didn't know I did. Just a habit I guess."

"Would you like something to eat? Maggie baked chocolate cookies."

"Great! Chocolate is my favorite. I remember you always baked little chocolate medallions."

Rema paused. She had forgotten about the small medallions and wondered what other things about Emille had slipped away from her memory.

"Come into the kitchen with me," she said. "You must meet Maggie. She doesn't make medallions, but she bakes wonderful cookies."

Maggie took a pan of cookies from the oven when she heard Rema's voice in the foyer. It was good once again to hear an exhilarating tone in Rema's voice.

"Maggie," Rema said, "this is my son, Emille. He's visiting us for several days. Chocolate cookies are one of his favorites."

Maggie's eyes brightened. "I'm pleased to meet you, sir. You can just help yourself to those cookies on the counter."

Emille took two cookies and remarked that they tasted wonderful. Rema walked toward the den. Emille followed.

"Did you know I talked with your father last year?" she said.

"No, when?"

"It was two days after I met with you at Everglades Park."

"How did that come about?"

"Well, it was something you said when you were walking to your car. Do you remember?"

"No."

"You told me to give my name and address to your parole officer. I went to Noah Mason's office. Your father and I met face to face. Naturally, we were both stunned. I was so furious I could barely look at him."

"Why?"

"For fifteen years he let me think you were dead. Didn't he tell you he had seen me?"

"No."

"He promised he would bring you to see me."

"Why would he take me to see you?"

"Because he was going to tell you the truth about the circumstances leading to your twenty-year stay in Cuba."

Emille tried to suppress the grin that was lining his face. Listening to Rema rave about the details of one of John Swenson's crafty lies was exhilarating.

This is some joke, he thought. *Since this lady has no idea what the true story is, I know I can work this scam by tweaking her motherly instinct.*

In spite of his thoughts, Emille managed to look bewildered.

"My father was a stranger to the truth. He could weave a good story from some pretty flimsy material."

"Then he really wasn't working for Russia when he was in Cuba?"

"I really don't know. Maybe it was Russia, maybe the CIA."

"Did you have a good life in Cuba?"

"As good as anyone could. We were not affected by the politics of the country."

"Your father said you graduated from the University of Havana."

"Yes, I have a Ph.D. in languages."

"On the phone you said you were looking for a job."

He corrected her. "I'm looking for a position. I'd like to be situated in a small university. I plan to stop at several universities on the way back to Miami."

Changing the subject, Rema said, "What would you like to do on Saturday? We could explore Wexlor although there's not much to see. Or you can ride with me to Cira."

"Where's Cira?"

"It is twenty miles west of here. We could go to the Libra Center."

"What's the Libra Center?"

"It's a metaphysical counseling center for adults. We counsel and teach classes in astrology, meditation, reiki and self-healing. We also do past life regression therapy."

"That's heavy stuff."

"Actually, our mission is to make the heavy stuff lighter."

"You're good," he teased.

After dinner, Rema guided Emille into the garden.

"In the fall season," she said, "the garden in the nighttime is strangely peaceful. The stars begin to twinkle and the first thing you know the entire sky begins to tell the stories that have been gathered high above the earth for thousands of years."

Emille was bored with her small talk, but grateful for the darkness creeping around them. He didn't want Rema to see his face. He knew it was time to play another trump card. He stiffened in his chair. "I don't know about you," he said, "but the skeeters are biting me."

Rema smiled, "I haven't heard the word skeeter in many, many years."

"Well, that's what you taught me to call them." He stood up. "I'm going inside," he said. She followed him. Once in the den, he moved to another topic.

"When you were talking about the house, you mentioned Eben's Tower. What is Eben's Tower?"

"It's the tower room on the second floor where the men who live in Justin House spend far too many hours. Eben Justin, Felic's great grandfather, added it to the house sometime after the Civil War. He had two wives and fourteen children. Everyone assumes he built the tower as a refuge."

"Do you use it?"

"No, I've only been in the room two times. The first time was to get a manuscript for a book Felic had completed before he died. The second time to pack his personal things."

"What genre is his book?"

"Religious history. Arrangements are being formalized for publishing the book."

"Were you married to Felic?"

"No, we never married."

"Then Mylowe is Felic's only heir."

"Yes, Justin House belongs to Mylowe."

"It's a nice house. How long do you get to live here?"

"For the rest of my life," she said.

Rema stood and moved to the fireplace. "This is such a lovely old fireplace. Soon I'll be building the first fire of the season in it. Are you hungry? Would you like a cookie?"

"I'm filled to the brim."

They walked together into the foyer and were ready to climb the stairs when Emille initiated a sneeze to avoid clasping Rema's outstretched hand. The great grandfather's clock chimed eleven times.

"It's late," she said. "Tomorrow, we will do something exciting."

Emille looked at the long stretch of stairs. "Am I sleeping up there?" he asked as he picked up his knapsack from the bench in the foyer.

"Yes, I'll show you to your room. I hope you'll be comfortable."

After he went inside his bedroom and shut the door, she stood outside. Emille's visit had already changed her life. She walked slowly down the hall to her room.

In the guest bedroom, Emille stretched his arms high into the air and danced a powwow around the room. The open knapsack invited him to enjoy the stash of cocaine he had purchased in Miami. He set out the white powder in rows on the glass top of the nightstand and he kneeled down to snort. Within five minutes, his brain's alerting system produced a "high." He had purposely bought the short-lived stuff from Miami.

"Damn this stuff is weak," he whispered. "But Emille's mommy doesn't need to know about his terrible habit."

He sat placidly in a comfortable chair and closed his eyes. The inner conflicts of the day waned as he envisioned Rema's reaction if she should discover his secret.

I'd just have to tell her that cocaine comes from the coca shrub. It is cultivated by the Peruvian Indians and considered sacred.

Amused with himself, he stomped his feet hard against the floor.

I would also need to explain the scientific aspects of the stuff. I'd say, 'You take the cocaine out of the coca shrub, mix it with kerosene and let it evaporate into a free base substance. Then, you add hydrochloric acid and the substance is converted to salt and turns into a lovely, white, exhilarating powder.'

He leaned over on the arm of the chair.

I should go to bed. Tomorrow I will be the dutiful son. Now, where was I? Oh, yes, I was sharing the recipe for cocaine with the matriarch of Justin House, my mother.

He shoved his head into a bed pillow to stifle his laughter.

The Next Morning

When Rema entered the kitchen, Maggie had prepared pancakes for breakfast.

"Miss Rema, you look happy," Maggie said. "Did you and Emille have a good evening?"

"We had a wonderful time. In some ways he reminds me of his father."

Rema heard footsteps in the foyer. She turned and saw Emille in the kitchen doorway.

"Would you like some coffee?" she asked.

"Sure," he said, "I'll take it with me. Aren't we going to the Libra Center this morning?"

Rema nodded and went to the den for her purse. Emille followed her and was able to reach the den's door in time to see her take the purse from the bottom drawer. As he walked into the room, she looked at him.

"I'm ready," she announced. "I'll need a moment with Maggie when we go through the kitchen. Here are the keys to my car. You drive."

Emille took the keys and started the engine when Rema exited the kitchen door. In thirty minutes, they drove into the parking lot beside a three-story, brownstone house. Rema pointed toward a clapboard building behind the house.

"You can park over by the classroom extension," she said.

Emille parked the car and looked at the provincial architecture. "How long have you owned this house?" he asked.

"Five years."

"This extension looks new. When was it built?"

"Three years ago. Let's go in."

Rema led Emille through the hallway.

"My office is just ahead. It's the door on the left." Emille followed her into the room, walked the length of it, turned and smiled.

"What's so funny?" Rema asked.

"I was just thinking of something. No, I was thinking of someone."

"Oh, who?"

"My father was a stupid man to play such a dirty trick on you."

"You think faking your death along with his was only a dirty trick?" she asked.

"What else was it?"

"I think it was an egregious mistake by a self-centered, non-caring human being."

Emille adjusted his facial expression to sadness. "My father is with me everyday," he said remorsefully.

He moved to face her. He wanted to see her reaction to his heartfelt lies.

"I've always felt my father was the bridge that made my life possible. In death, he remains very close to me."

She stared at him. Her mind had heard his words, and she wanted to believe them. She nodded. "That's nice," she said.

Emille turned away and could not look at her. Had he gone too far with the fancy words that had been too exhausting even for him? He would not offer another emotional interpretation. It wasn't his style.

PART TWO

167

PART TWO

33

MYLOWE

February, 1991

The deafening roar of pumping air horns, screeching tires and flashing strobe lights caused Mylowe to jump up from his makeshift chair and ottoman bed. He wrestled from the folds of a rumpled, brown comforter and stumbled toward the window. Two floors below, brilliant orange and blue sparks were spiraling from under the hood of a curb-parked car. Pushing the window down to shut out the stench of burning oil and scorched metal that was drifting upward into the night air, he grabbed a corner of the comforter to cover his nose while he watched the firefighters extinguish the last of the airborne, glowing cinders.

Turning away from the window, he fell backward into the chair. Gathering the corners of the comforter around his long muscular frame, he remembered the brutal argument he had tried to avoid with his college roommate, Melody Ann Thames.

During the four years they had roomed together in the compact, third-floor apartment conveniently located two blocks from Columbia University in New York City, they had never disagreed so vehemently. While there had been, from time to time, petty quarrels between them, tonight she realized they were not moving toward a future together.

To Mylowe, it didn't make sense to be at odds with Melody Ann. He looked at her lying on the sofa bed wrapped in the down-filled, navy blue comforter they had purchased the day before. Huddled in the fetal position she appeared defenseless. Yet, as he had discovered, she had strong defenses and fought with the life and death conviction of a gladiator.

In the dim light from the street lamps, Mylowe realized the small apartment was inadequate for only one person. Looking back, he wondered how he and Melody Ann had survived in one medium-size room that had been subdivided into three sections. A Pullman setup served as a kitchen and the bathroom had a shower that had been whittled down to the size of a telephone booth making it impossible to bend over and pick up the soap from the floor.

Tonight, after they had confronted each other with such animosity, the room had lost its charm. Her angry assertions haunted him. He reached into the depth of his inner being for an answer to their differences and realized he had been uncommunicative. He now realized he was a senseless fool who had acted from a deep fear of losing the woman he loved.

The deepening pre-dawn shadows brought him memories of the first time he saw her. Four years ago, he had gone to the Night Owl Bookstore to buy Hans Holzer's book, *Born Again*, for Rema's upcoming birthday. Nearing the checkout counter, he was fascinated by a young blond woman who was wrapping customer purchases and answering their questions. As she packaged his purchase, he felt as if he had been overcome by some magical spell. He was so enchanted by her mystical power that he returned to the bookstore the next evening to see her again and purchased another book. Before paying for it, he made certain there were no other customers standing in the checkout line.

She was beautiful. Her skin was fresh and pink. Her face, perfectly formed, was framed by long, blond, silken hair. She was not petite or statuesque but a stunning combination of both. When she stood near him, he calculated the top of her head reached slightly above his shoulders. She moved gracefully with the poise of a seasoned ballerina, yet her step was firm and strong.

He had leaned forward over the cash register and invited her to the basketball game on Saturday afternoon. He assured her he could provide all the references she would need to know he was a grand person. And, as that grand person, she should know he was ecstatic at the prospect of seeing her. When she agreed to meet him at gate C of the arena at 1:30 p.m., he backed away apologizing for his tactless approach. Yet, at the same time, he felt great joy to be able to spend Saturday with her.

The memory of the first time he kissed her filled his thoughts. The kiss did not resemble, in any way, the time he kissed Millie Haskins after he had escorted her home from the Sugar Bowl the night of his fourteenth birthday party.

Melody Ann's kisses left him morally shaken. His sense of right conduct was threatened by the physical maleness that consumed him. He was grateful that Melody Ann understood his inexperience. Looking back, he realized his naivety was the basis of their relationship. Before their relationship became sexual, Melody Ann mentioned an amusing joke circulating among the campus coeds.

"What joke?" he asked.

"The girls sign up to go to the Virgin Islands each year."

"Why?"

"To be recycled."

"I don't understand."

"To be made virgins again."

"Are you going?"

"No, I don't want to be a virgin."

Remembering her remark, Mylowe moved to the sofa bed and sat on the floor beside her. As he stroked her hair, raging hormones surged through his loins. He stood and bent over her. She turned toward him. Her face was flushed. Strands of blond hair lay smashed against her head. He kissed her tenderly on the lips and moved his wandering tongue onto her curvature of her throat.

"You taste sweet and spicy," he whispered. He felt her shiver as his moving tongue circled the roundness of her breasts. She moved her body with each panting breath. His arm slid under her. He pulled her close to him. With each thrust of his being, he became more breathless until her deep moans told him he had satisfied her. He pressed himself hard against her reveling in a moment of rapturous frenzy. He did not move from her.

"Why did we have that damn argument?" he whispered. She wriggled from under him gathering the comforter around her. Her voice was low but firm.

"We argued because you refuse to communicate with me. I'm not a mind reader. I'm graduating in the spring and I want to know where I stand with you. You have your master's now and you're handling teaching responsibilities in the university lab, but you don't tell me what else you intend to do. What's the big secret?"

Mylowe slid off the bed and wrapped himself in the old comforter. He looked at her sheepishly. His tousled dark hair stuck out from the folds of the comforter. He looked like a little boy with a cold and a fever.

"Well," she said, in a confrontational tone. "What do you need to tell me that you can't seem to say?"

He swallowed hard. "I've applied to Harvard Medical School to study psychoneuroimmunology and psychiatry."

"How long ago did you apply?"

"I applied last year, before I completed my master's."

She jumped out of bed and lunged at him. The force of her naked body pushed him onto the floor. With her fists clenched she pounded the comforter around his head. He reached out from under the comforter to stop her. Every part of her nude body was attacking him. Her breasts bounced back and forth as her twisting torso wrestled from his grasp.

She sat up realizing it was unfair of her to react so violently. At last, he had told her his plans. She reached for the other comforter, wrapped it around her body and scooted toward him. They burst into loud, sustained laughter as they looked at the other. They each resembled a stuffed penguin.

"We should have a picture of us," she giggled. "It will help our loneliness on those nights when we're apart. You'll be at Harvard and I'll be in Des Moines learning my father's construction business. I was hoping you would come with me and teach at Drake University. It would have been such fun."

"I'm sorry I've disappointed you."

"Do you know you communicate with everyone but me?"

Mylowe rearranged the comforter around him.

"I just didn't want to upset us," he said. "We're so good together. Everything will work out. With your degree in architecture, you'll be able to provide a service The Thames Construction Company never visualized from a member of the Thames family."

"Yes, time will just fly by," she said sarcastically. "You'll be thirty and I'll be too old to have children." She stood up. In one defiant motion she flung her comforter wide open. The sight of her naked body against the background of the dark blue comforter excited him.

She paused just long enough to tease before jumping on him. "Just make certain," she whispered, "that I'm the only girl you'll go for."

He pulled her over him to let her feel his hardness beneath the confines of his comforter. "You mean this?" he teased.

She drew away and smiled. "That's what I mean."

He grinned. "As long as airplanes are flying we'll be together." He adjusted the comforter again, stood up and walked toward the thermostat. "It's cold in here." He pushed the control. "There, that ought to make it warmer." He sat down beside her.

"There may be a problem brewing at Justin House," he said. "Mona Pierce, Rema's good friend, believes Emille is using cocaine. I thought it was great when he took a post to teach at Wexlor University and moved into Justin House to live with Rema. In all the times I've been there, Emille and I have been very compatible. He's almost like an older brother. Rema is happy to have him with her. Years ago, Emille was taken to Cuba by her husband.

She thought they were both dead. It was a shock to discover they were alive and living in Miami.

"Since Emille has lived in Justin House, he spends hours and hours in Eben's Tower. Rema doesn't know what he does up there. When she asks, he says he is studying the stars using Eben Justin's old telescope."

"How can you confirm he's using cocaine?" she asked.

"I can't. Mona offered to watch him. She has good intuition. I trust her feelings. She also suspects Emille may be stealing money from the Libra Center."

"You must be concerned."

"I am. I regret I can only monitor the situation from a distance. But I know I can't ignore it."

"Are you telling me this so I won't be angry with you if you are needed at Justin House and are unable to see me?"

"I hadn't thought of it in that way."

Melody Ann snuggled against him. "I promise I'll not nag at you if that should come about. I'm not getting any warmer. Let's go back to bed."

Pushing her down on the bed, he whispered, "Lie down. I've got a lot of work to do before graduation."

34

BALANCE

Academically, Mylowe knew he was prepared to excel. With the guiding influence of Dr. George Whitetail, he had planned well. He had earned a bachelor's and master's degree in five-and-a-half years and had established his own reputation as a scholar of exceptional natural intellect in psychology. As the son of Dr. Felic Ort, he was extended courtesies rarely afforded most young men at the age of twenty-one.

During the months of conflict with Felic, Mylowe had pacified Felic by making concessions. Now, he was keeping those around him in check by not defining himself against authority. Everyone saw in Mylowe what they wanted to see. But when he engaged in combat, he was cunning and devious, the trait he learned from Felic.

On another level, Mylowe realized he had not yet begun to understand the intricate balance required to sustain a lasting love relationship. Today, while lunching in New York City with Dr. Whitetail, he said, "There's nothing in the human experience more exciting than the feeling of a new love."

George Whitetail stared at him. "You do realize the initial feeling doesn't last? It's not humanly possible to maintain that kind of exotic 'high' for as long as we would like. Although I assume you have had your share of exotic highs with Melody Ann."

"Yes, but we have a long way to go. I worry about the times after the exhilaration subsides. Can we hold on? We'll be living apart for long stretches of time. Rema once said my natal astrological chart indicated that women, especially my mother, would have a great influence on my life. Well, I don't have a biological mother."

"I've wondered what effect the absence of your biological mother might have on your life."

"It's like a missing piece of a giant jigsaw puzzle. No matter how fabulous my life is, or will be, the puzzle will not be complete. There's a magical power in the genetic connection."

"I understand loss. Losing my wife in an auto accident sent me down a different road. I was a third-year medical student. After she was gone, nothing was good for me. I nearly flunked out of medical school. Loneliness nearly killed me. I know for damn sure, the loneliness ruined my immune system. My NK cell level went way down. I could have developed cancer or some other debilitating disease with my natural killer cell level so low."

"I am fortunate to have Felic and Rema in my life. I will admit I'm drawn to return to Dead Man's Alley."

"Why don't you go?"

"Rema and I always talk about going to Miami. If we ever get there, we'll go to the alley where Felic found me. Rema says she would like to see the old trailer she lived in. Lately, with Emille living at Justin House, she likes to be at home."

George Whitetail signed the lunch check and paused.

"Did you know I've been taking Mona to dinner?"

"I know. She's a good companion for you."

George folded the lunch receipt and put it in the breast pocket of his jacket. "Mona is concerned about Emille living at Justin House. She doesn't trust him."

"Mona expressed her concerns to me on the telephone a week ago. She said she's hesitant to speak to Rema about Emille. She doesn't have any proof that he's using cocaine or stealing money from the Libra Center."

"Do you have any plans to talk to Rema about Emille?"

Mylowe shook his head. "No, I called our estate attorney, Martin Walsh, and asked him to offer Rema his expertise. The Libra Center has been profitable. She also has the proceeds from the original sale of Felic's book. Rema will be sixty-two in March and could retire within the next two years. Martin said he would help her hire a financial planner."

George leaned forward and whispered. "Is your strategy designed to catch a thief?"

Mylowe nodded. "If there is no thief, we will know Rema's finances are protected. If thievery is taking place, I hope it shows up soon. I feel so damn helpless. It's virtually impossible to monitor the situation from New York. If my clinical work is interrupted, I'll not be ready for Harvard Medical School in the spring."

"Mona and I have decided to spend more time with Rema. If Emille knows when we're coming to Justin House, he will be on his good behavior. However, if he is a long-time drug user, he could be at a point of believing he can snort up anytime and hide it."

"Could Rema be in danger?"

"I can't say. Each addict reacts differently. If he's been using for the last six years while living in Justin House, Rema would have noticed his unusual behavior. He may handle the cocaine better than most."

Mylowe frowned. "How can we know? Rema is so trusting. If she suspects he's using drugs, she may try to do some counseling on her own."

"Do you mean actually counsel him or get him into a program?" George stiffened and leaned away from the table. "I think I'll keep an eagle eye on the situation."

"Do you have time to do that?"

"I'll take the time."

Whitetail hesitated and shook his head.

"What's wrong?" Mylowe asked.

"Six years ago, when Emille told Rema John Swenson had died, Mona asked Pinchey Wilson to check the death records in Dade County. No death record for John Swenson or Noah Mason was found. Mona is uncomfortable that no record of John's death was located. She has checked all the mortuaries in four Florida counties. You know about Mona and her hunches. She doesn't let go until she's satisfied."

"I didn't know she was so concerned about John's death. Has she talked to Rema about it?"

"No, but we should all be aware that John Swenson's death was not recorded. At least not in Florida."

"I don't know what to do next. Are there any answers? I feel as if Felic sent you to guide me. Do you think he would have allowed me in his life again? Rema said the night before he died, he said he wanted his family back together."

George leaned back remembering the many occasions when Mylowe had expressed, in one form or another, the deep guilt he felt for shattering Felic's trust in him. George knew the time was near for him to help Mylowe overcome his guilt. He stood up from the table. "I'll tell Rema I saw you in New York. She'll ask dozens of questions."

"Tell her I really enjoy teaching in the lab and I'm still on track. I heard from Dr. Hammon at Harvard and my letter of acceptance is in the mail. By August, I'll be at Harvard."

George glanced at his watch. "I've an appointment in thirty minutes. I'll call you after I visit Justin House. It was good to see you. Give my regards to Melody Ann."

After George hurried from the restaurant, Mylowe remained at the table and decided he could do nothing about Emille until there was a problem. He was full of conflicting emotions. He truly believed family members should sacrifice for their loved ones. He questioned if he should disrupt his academic schedule and go back and live at Justin House. If Mona's instincts were correct, things were definitely out of order.

35

REVENGE

Emille Swenson pulled the collar of the winter jacket from his neck and adjusted the heat inside the car. Large, wet snowflakes were hitting the windshield. They ran down in icy streaks until the wiper blades swept them away. He lit a cigarette and peered through the side window to locate a mileage marker. Ohio highways were flat and boring. He hated the weekly two-hour drive from Wexlor to Dayton. It gave him too much time to think. Lately, keeping his thoughts organized was beginning to be a problem. He felt an internal contradiction between his thoughts and the actual condition of his body. He glanced at his watch and realized it would be thirty minutes before he reached the house at 1961 Kahler Drive.

He swerved his new Corvette through the Dayton traffic. The city streets were rapidly filling with drifts of snow. He grimaced and swore loudly at the slow moving car ahead. "Damn it, either move your ass or get out of the way."

His voice returned to a normal level as he began to talk to himself. "You're definitely ready for a fix. Maybe, the ol' man will let you be alone long enough to snort yourself into a great mood."

Thirty minutes later, the snow crackled beneath the Corvette's winter tires as Emille swung the black sports car into the driveway on Kahler Drive. Through the open driver-side car door, he pulled a duffle bag from the passenger seat. Hoisting the heavy bag into his arms, he walked through the snow drifts and went in a side door of the house.

Standing inside the kitchen, he yelled, "Why don't you take the snow off the damn sidewalks? Last week's snow was not shoveled."

179

"Aw, come on, kid. You know I don't shovel snow. I'm accustomed to a warm climate."

Muttering angrily, Emille dragged the duffle bag behind him into the living room. The man, sitting in a reclining leather chair, looked at the bag. "Are those more goodies from Justin House?"

"Yes, dad. That's the last of them. I've drained the well dry."

John Swenson leaned forward, shoved his eyeglasses on his forehead and dabbed sweat from his face.

Emille pulled the duffle bag closer to his father.

"These are the last of the rare books. I've verified each of them. This bunch should bring about twenty thousand if you find the right buyer."

John replied sternly. "It's not your job to be concerned about the buyer. I'll handle that part of it."

Emille sunk down on the sofa and lit a cigarette. Inhaling, he grinned. "I think we've taken Rema for about eighty thousand bucks."

John yelled, "Are you the banker now? Just remember, you little punk. I recognized the financial possibilities at Justin House and put this scam together. I'm the one who counted on her motherly love to make us rich."

Emille rubbed his hand over the arm of the sofa. "Is this new?"

"Yeh! You got the Corvette. I got a frigging couch."

Emille leaned forward, "Yeh! After all, it was my wonderful personality that got me into Justin House."

"Well, the pickings would have been mighty slim if we had only relied on the small amount of cash you took from her business."

Emille blew the smoke from the cigarette upward.

"You might be right," he said. "Getting the cash box became difficult when they hired a CPA to monitor the Libra Center's books."

Flashing a broad smile, Emille whispered, "But up in Eben's Tower, were all those shelves full of old, mold-covered, rare books."

"What a strike of good fortune," John said. "Over a hundred valuable books were in that tiny upstairs room waiting to be discovered by a bright, young man. Is there anything else valuable up there?"

"No, I've searched every inch of the tower. There are no false bottoms in drawers or secret passages behind the bookshelves. I broke into the safe and picked it clean."

"What happened to the royalties due to Rema from Professor Ort's book?"

"I managed to retrieve most of the royalty checks from the mail before she received them. When I learned the book might go into reprint, I changed her address with the publisher to a post office box I rented."

Emille was slurring his words. "You don't look too good," John said. "Did you pick up your medication from the clinic on your way in today? You know how wacky you act when you don't take your pills."

Emille grabbed his shaving kit from the open duffle bag. "I'm okay—just tired. I'll run over to the clinic in the morning."

Alone in the living room, John took each book from the duffle bag, laid them on the sofa and compared the book's titles to a catalog listing. "Quite a haul this time," he whispered.

36

CHRISTMAS EVE

1994

"We've arrived!" Mylowe yelled as he and Melody Ann shook snow from their coats in the front entrance of Justin House. He looked into the foyer and called out, "Hello! Is anyone home?"

Rema rushed from the kitchen wiping her hands on a towel.

"Welcome! Welcome!" she said. "I wish you both a Merry Christmas Eve." She hugged Mylowe and embraced Melody Ann. "It's wonderful to see both of you." She led them toward the den saying there was a surprise. At the doorway, they were greeted by Mona and George.

"This is wonderful," Mylowe exclaimed. "Now, it's a real family gathering, but where's Emille?"

"He's driving from Dayton today," Rema said. "I expect him within the hour."

"What's for dinner?"

"All of your favorites," she replied.

At that moment, Emille walked in. He hugged Mona, kissed Rema on the cheek, kissed the back of Melody Ann's hand and shook hands with Mylowe and George.

"Greetings," he said. "Brrr! It's a brisk Christmas Eve. There's new snow falling. It's slow driving on the highways. The snow plows are everywhere." He looked around the room and noticed the punch bowl on the table. "What's on the agenda?"

183

Rema replied. "Everyone wants to know the menu." She looked at Emille. "I presume your friend from Dayton is not coming for Christmas."

"He had made other plans for the holidays."

She turned and walked from the room.

Mylowe moved to stand beside George. "Rema seems happy," Mylowe observed. "Christmas is a tough time for her since Felic's death. The tree is in the same place in the foyer and the decorations are identical."

Mona added to Mylowe's comments. "Rema is diligent about keeping Christmas traditional."

"Well, let's celebrate," Mylowe said. "There's an inviting punch bowl on the table. Never let it be said we allowed Christmas cookies to go stale."

"Good idea!" said Emille, walking toward the door. "Although you'll have to excuse me for a moment, I've brought things for mother to use on the table tonight."

Not trusting any words coming from Emille, Mona felt a chill and gathered her sweater around her. "You guys have some punch," she said. "I'll take Melody Ann to her room." Walking upstairs with Melody Ann, Mona remembered a conversation with Rema that day when Rema firmly proclaimed that Melody Ann would not occupy Mylowe's bedroom until she married him.

"When did you turn so puritanical?" Mona had asked. "What are you going to do if Mylowe countermands your rules?"

"He won't," Rema replied. "And don't you dare suggest any alternative sleeping arrangements."

Standing outside Mylowe's room, Melody Ann's voice interrupted Mona's thoughts. "Isn't this Mylowe's room?"

"Yes."

"Mylowe said we couldn't be in the same room until we are married."

"Oh! I didn't know," said Mona as she led Melody Ann down the hall to another room.

Alone in the den, George and Mylowe filled the small glass cups with yuletide punch.

"I don't understand why Rema insists on these tiny cups," Mylowe said. "I can't get my nose in them."

George grinned, "They're to keep us sober before dinner. Before we go in to dinner, I should tell you about Emille's medical background. The clinical records in Miami indicate he is bipolar. He goes for long periods and doesn't take his meds. Like a large majority of individuals with manic depression, he self-medicates with alcohol or drugs. Three years ago, a physician from a Dayton, Ohio, clinic requested a copy of Emille's Miami medical record. Evidently, he's currently being treated in a Dayton clinic."

For privacy, George moved closer to Mylowe. "I'm not shocked to learn Emille is bipolar," Mylowe said. "Finally, we know what we are dealing with. Unfortunately, there are not good drugs to cure it."

"There's more," George whispered. "The report from the Dayton clinic showed Emille is addicted to cocaine. As of last week, according to his medical file, his condition is considered fragile."

Mylowe shook his head. "To me, fragile means don't confront or go against him in any manner. How much time do you think we have before he fully deteriorates?"

"It's hard to predict. When are you scheduled to fly back to Cambridge?"

"Tomorrow evening. I'm not going back to Cambridge. I'm flying directly into Boston. On the 27th, I'm scheduled to meet with the hospital's medical review board. On the recommendations from three of my professors at med school, I could begin my residency at Boston Memorial immediately."

George poured more punch into his cup. "Do you plan to complete all your clinical work in the next eighteen months?"

"That's my intent. However, this situation with Emille seems to be at a critical stage. I must do something before he harms someone, overdoses or turns the gas on himself."

George nodded. "We'll need to manage this guy with kid gloves. He's an exceptionally intelligent man. He's able to hide his dual disorder very well. With cocaine as his master, I just don't think we can walk away from here on Christmas Day believing that Rema or anyone in the house or at the university is safe."

"Do we tell her?" asked Mylowe.

"We should tell her about the bipolar part."

"If I know Rema, she'll want to step right in and help him."

"I agree. Is there any other way?"

"That's not likely. Rema understands what a bipolar condition is. I'll bet she has already suspected something is not right with him."

Mylowe set his cup on the table. As the master of Justin House the situation with Emille was his responsibility. He crossed to the other side of the den and stood with one foot on the hearth watching the blue and red flames dance across the logs. He bowed his head knowing that Rema must be protected from what Emille might do. The situation could also have far-reaching complications. Emille's actions could also jeopardize the safety of an entire classroom and put Wexlor University in danger.

Mylowe turned from the fireplace and walked toward George. "Toward the end of Christmas Day when all the celebration is over, you and I should tell Rema what we know about Emille."

"I'm going to ask Mona and Melody Ann to stay at Justin House with Rema until after the 27th."

"Why?"

"On the 27th, when I meet with the hospital board, I'll ask to delay my clinical work due to an unexpected family problem. I'll need to explain all the details to the board to get their full consideration."

"What will you do next?"

"I'll live here in Justin House until Emille can be put in a supervised treatment program."

There was a long silence. Each man was hoping there would be enough time to handle the situation before Emille's condition erupted.

George was the first to speak. "Rema will not want you to delay your clinical work. A delay could cost you six months. By then, there may not be a vacancy in the program."

"I've considered that, but I can't allow Rema to handle this alone. This is a time that tests the strength of family relationships. I've got to step up to the plate."

"Just don't get out at first base. We don't know how many times Emille has attempted suicide."

Melody Ann rushed into the room. "Follow me," she yelled. "Emille brought Rema a kitten for Christmas. It's cute. All white with long hair."

"Where is Rema?" Mylowe asked.

"She's upstairs. The kitten is in a cage four times larger than it is. Emille said it's trained to live in the cage."

Mylowe looked at George. "I suppose we should be there for the presentation. Where's the cage?"

"It's in the dining room beside Rema's chair. Come along. Dinner is almost ready."

Everyone was waiting to be seated when Rema entered the dining room. She saw the cage with the red bow on top and bent down to look into it.

"It's adorable," she cried. "Who did this? I haven't had a cat as a pet since I was a child."

"It's a gift from Emille," Melody Ann said.

Rema looked at Emille. "Is it a boy or a girl?"

"A girl," he said.

Rema took the kitten from the cage and cradled the small lump of white fur in her hands. "I christen you Angel," she said. "My Angel."

Watching the gift presentation from the dining room doorway, Maggie wiped tears with her apron and announced that dinner was ready.

As always, Christmas Eve dinner at Justin House was a spectacular array of delectable food. When the dessert tray was brought in, it equaled the sweet delicacies offered in the finer restaurants. As usual, Rema ate small portions, vegetables and refused to eat dessert declaring it was too much sugar for her sensitive body to manage.

After dessert, Mylowe raised his wine glass and said, "A toast. Here's to the culinary artists of Justin House."

"Hear! Hear!" they responded.

After dinner, Mona and Melody Ann helped Maggie clear the table and load the dishwasher. Mona insisted that Maggie go home and spend Christmas Eve with her family.

The family members gathered in the living room where they could have a full view of the beautifully decorated staircase and the tree. In the morning, they would be gathering around the tree to exchange gifts. But on Christmas Eve they sat on the elegant white sofas and powder blue upholstered chairs and listened to the carolers singing outside. When the carolers finished, Mylowe invited them inside for hot chocolate and Christmas cookies.

"The group was much larger than it has been in previous years," said Rema.

"All the young people between the ages of nine and fourteen compete all year long to get into the caroling group," Emille said. "It's an accomplishment for them to get inside Justin House on Christmas Eve."

"Is that really true?"

"That's the word on the street," he teased. "Some of my students who grew up in Wexlor talk about how exciting it was to get inside the 'big house' on the hill."

Mylowe noticed Emille's placid tone and quiet demeanor. Yet, he knew bipolar individuals usually act as normal as anyone except when they drink alcohol or take drugs to ease their mental pain. While observing Emille, he felt a sharp pain between his shoulders. He thought it could be the intuitive pain Felic described as 'the nudge'.

At midnight, when the family members had gone upstairs to their rooms, Mylowe turned off the lights in the foyer and stood at the bottom of the stairs. He yearned to have Melody Ann with him, but knew he had to follow Rema's house rules. Although he was tempted to tap on Melody Ann's door and say goodnight, he did not venture down the hall beyond his bedroom.

Inside his room, the uneasiness he felt in Emille's presence went away. Before preparing for bed, he picked up his old catcher's mitt, slouched comfortably in his favorite leather chair and punched his fist into the center of the glove. He chuckled when he noticed his initials on the back of the glove and remembered he had painted them on the strap with Rema's red nail polish. He had also softened the glove's leather using Felic's hemorrhoid salve.

In the bathroom while brushing his teeth, he winced when the pain between his shoulders returned. Acknowledging the pain as he envisioned Felic would have done, he whispered, "Show me what is out of order. I'll fix it."

Lying in bed, he closed his eyes. Rema described this time as the brief period before falling asleep or awakening when a flash of insight brings an original thought or idea. Mylowe trusted the thoughts that came to him during those times, but tonight his mind wandered through dozens of insignificant thoughts. None stayed longer than a second. It was 3:00 in the morning before he slept.

37

CHRISTMAS DAY

Awakened by the sound of sleigh bells outside his bedroom, Mylowe sat up. The noise reminded him of bygone Christmas mornings when Felic walked through the hallway shaking the bells. Mylowe looked at his watch. It was 8:15 a.m. He peeked through a crack in the bedroom door. Rema was in the hall draped in the leather equine harness. He closed the door and hurried to the shower. Dressing quickly, he went downstairs.

A Christmas morning breakfast table was set up in the open space of the foyer near the Christmas tree. Chairs and lounging pillows were placed nearby. The odor of brewed coffee filled the air as Mona placed a tray of warm breakfast rolls on the table.

"I overslept," Mylowe said. "The bells woke me."

Mona pointed toward the stairs. "Everyone is up and present except Emille," she said. "I tapped on his door earlier. He said he wasn't feeling well. I asked George to check on him."

"Good," Mylowe said.

George and Emille walked down the steps. George went to the kitchen to hustle the women into the foyer. Emille stood at attention, grinned sheepishly and saluted Mylowe. Mylowe tried not to show distain and returned the salute.

The day continued with the distribution of gifts and pleasant conversations. At 4:00 p.m., the buffet table was set in the dining room.

Before fixing a plate from the buffet, Mylowe went into the kitchen as Maggie was preparing to go home. He gave her a small box wrapped in white and silver paper.

"This is mighty nice," she said.

He put his arms around her. "You're still my best girl," he whispered. "Did Emille go to the tower? He hasn't been with the family for the last hour."

"Yes, he's in that awful tower. Just like Mr. Felic, he spends hours and days there."

"Will you watch Emille for me?"

"He's talking strange words just like Mr. Felic did before he died." Maggie eyes darted toward the pantry door. "Something's spooky in that tower."

Mylowe stepped back as if he had been struck by lightening when he realized the pain between his shoulders was a warning.

"Did I upset you?" she asked.

"I'm not upset with you. It's what you said about Eben's Tower and how the men act who stay up there. You may have given me the answer."

"You mean about the spooks up there?"

"Yes, if that's what it is."

"It's scary, ain't it? First, Mr. Felic gets sick and dies and now Emille is beginning to act funny." Maggie sat down at the kitchen table. "Oh! Lordy! Mr. Mylowe," she said. "Is Emille also sick in the brain?"

"It's important that I come back to live in Justin House."

"What about your schooling?"

"I'll get some time off."

"You be careful, Mr. Mylowe. Emille has a mean streak in him. I can hear the devil laughing."

Mylowe stared at her. She had confirmed his greatest fear.

"Good grief, Maggie," he said. "It's Christmas Day. You should be with your family." She nodded. He held her coat while she tied a Christmas scarf to cover her red hair. He helped her to her car. After standing at the bottom of the stairs leading to Eben's Tower wondering if he should talk to Emille, he turned and went into the den and sat beside George.

"It's time to talk to Rema," he said. "Let's meet in my bedroom."

Mona and Melody Ann were playing with the kitten and took the cat cage to the kitchen. George sat down on the sofa next to Rema. "Mylowe is ready to leave for the airport. He wants to talk with us in his bedroom." Rema stood and followed him up the stairs. Mylowe was in the doorway and guided her to a chair.

"As you know, Emille is not well. George has found some medical information concerning Emille's condition."

"Does the information state what is upsetting him?"

"Emille is bipolar. Medical records from two clinics, one in Miami and one in Dayton, indicate he goes off his medications for long periods. He self-medicates by using alcohol. The physicians at the Dayton clinic concluded that he also uses cocaine. Bipolar individuals have long periods when they are normal. Other times they're out of control."

Rema sighed. "Do you know when the bipolar behavior first appeared?"

"No," George replied. "The Miami clinic's last medical record is dated 1983, that's years ago. The Dayton clinic's records begin in 1989. His visits were not regular. In the last two years, the Dayton records show he's been treated on a more regular basis."

"He must be receiving treatment on the weekends in Dayton," Rema said.

"Why is he going to Dayton?" asked George.

"He has a friend in Dayton. I don't know the address."

"I have the Dayton address," George said.

Mylowe knelt before Rema and held her hands. "George has more information," he whispered.

"I need to know," she said.

George stood. "The Dayton clinic's most recent medical records indicate that Emille is fragile and abnormally vulnerable. The clinic's doctors classified him in the sixty percentile of bipolar individuals that have addictions during their lifetimes. The combination of alcohol or drugs or both can have disastrous results. Prison or jail is a common occurrence. There's a record in Miami of a crisis worker taking a long distance call from Emille. Emille was threatening to kill himself. I learned from his medical file at the Miami clinic that in one year he had been in jail three times. Two of those times were for theft. The third incarceration was for sexual assaulting another inmate. He jumped bail and a priest at St. Helen's Mission in Miami found him soliciting sex from other residents. Of course, in these cases, sexual behavior departs from the norm."

Rema shook her head. "The poor dear. No wonder he came to Wexlor to find a new life."

George nodded. "I spoke to Dr. Myron Hamil by phone before I left Miami. Dr. Hamil is a researcher in bipolar disorders. He said the addictions touch off psychiatric disorders rather than the other way around.

"Although some people are genetically vulnerable, a mental disorder might also be influenced by biological factors. Emille has a high IQ. He uses his exceptional intelligence to control his mental disorder. When his mind works too fast, the alcohol suppresses his thought process. The cocaine gives him more relief than the alcohol. It affords him a longer sleep pattern."

Rema took a deep breath and asked, "How long does the cocaine last once it is administered? How is he able to function as a teacher in the classroom? If the effectiveness of the drug grows shorter as his body becomes accustomed to it, where will it take him?"

Mylowe looked at her. "We don't know. What we're currently observing may be a bad episode. He might pull out of it and be normal for a time."

George sat down beside her. "My recommendation is that Mylowe should come back to live in Justin House."

Rema disagreed and shook her head. "Mylowe should not delay his residency in Boston."

Mylowe quickly replied. "If Emille should need to be hospitalized in a facility where he will get psychiatric treatment, I would be here to make the arrangements."

Rema stood up and grasped the back of a chair. "Mona suspects Emille has homosexual tendencies."

"Do you think it could be true?"

"No! I've delineated his horoscope again and again. There's no sign of a mental condition, drug use, or homosexuality in any of his charts."

Rema wanted to say more, but decided to consult Emille's birth chart one more time. Normally, the planet Mercury square Mars in Aries or any other thinking sign would indicate homosexual behavior, or at least the person would have thoughts about it without committing the act. In Emille's chart, this was not the case. She had spent hours searching through progressions and transits. There were no mental problems, drug usage or jail time indicated anywhere. Moreover, Emille's personality and questionable behavior of the last eight years did not match her astrology delineations. The man, Emille, living in Justin House was selfish, secretive, untruthful, undisciplined, but most of all he was a practiced actor.

"Could Emille's bipolar condition be genetic?" Mylowe asked.

In that terrifying moment when the reality of Emille's mental inconsistencies finally hit home, Rema would have traded her life for him. During her silence, no one moved. She realized she would need to face this day and the days to come. "What can I do?" she whispered. "I don't know anything about my husband's medical history.

"George, are you certain Mylowe should be the one to manage this situation? His medical residency will be interrupted."

"For your safety and others, Mylowe should manage what needs to be done," George replied. "As Emille's biological mother, you have the power to authorize any medical treatment and Mylowe understands how to get the job done within the medical system."

Mylowe walked with Rema to the door and asked if she would check on Emille. "If he's in the tower, ask Mona and Melody Ann to come here to my room. We need to tell them the situation."

After leaving Mylowe's room, Rema knocked on Emille's bedroom door. When there was no response, she went downstairs through the kitchen into the pantry. The sliding door leading to the tower was closed. Emille was in the tower. Going into den, she found Mona and Melody Ann warming their feet on the hearth.

"Are you cold?" Rema asked.

"I need some warm Florida sun," replied Mona. "Is Emille in the tower room? We were wondering what he does up there?"

"I wish I knew," said Rema. "Eben's Tower has magical power over the men of Justin House. Every man who lived in Justin House spent a good part of his life in that tower."

Melody Ann laughed, "Maybe that's where they read the girlie magazines."

Rema smiled. "If you two could leave the warmth of the fireplace, Mylowe wants to meet with you. He's in his bedroom. It's important!"

Without speaking, Melody Ann and Mona put on their shoes and hurried from the den. Rema went into the kitchen to stand watch at the tower door.

In the hallway upstairs, when Mona and Melody Ann tapped on Mylowe's bedroom door, he opened the door and stood aside. George stood up and offered Mona his chair. Mylowe sat by Melody Ann and held her hand. "I suppose you've noticed that Emille is more withdrawn than usual?"

"I thought he had the flu," said Melody Ann.

"It's more serious than the flu. Emille is manic-depressive. In addition, he's using cocaine."

Melody Ann squeezed Mylowe's hand. "That's a strong drug," she said.

Mylowe looked at Mona and George. "Currently, Emille is experiencing an episodically-related incident."

Mona folded her arms over her mid-section and nodded. "Is his condition worse than before?"

"It may be," Mylowe said. At that moment, he was less honest with her. He realized he had let the situation become critical.

"What are you going to do?" she asked.

"I'm going to delay the application for my medical residency until I can make arrangements for Emille to receive treatment. I'll be living in Justin House. Would it be possible for you to stay with Rema until I get back from Boston late on Tuesday night, the 27th or early morning on the 28th?"

Mona nodded.

Mylowe clutched Melody Ann's hand. "Would you stay with Mona until I return from Boston?"

"Is Emille dangerous?"

"Not unless he's confronted."

"You mean we should give him his own way."

"I don't want to sound melodramatic, but I think one of you should be with Rema at all times."

George stood again. "It's wise that one of you be at Rema's side and the other nearby to call for assistance."

Melody Ann hugged Mylowe. "We know what to do."

George took Mona's hand. "You were so right," he whispered. "You followed your intuition and forced me to check on Emille through the medical clinics."

Mona hugged Mylowe. "We'll manage until you return. I won't leave Rema alone. Melody Ann will be the third person. She will be ready to call for help."

George grinned. "Now that is melodramatic!"

Mona asked. "Where will you be in the next few days?"

"I'll be attending a medical convention in Cincinnati on Monday and Tuesday."

Mona and Melody Ann went downstairs and settled into chairs by the fireplace. They were silent. Each was appraising the role she would be taking for the next two days.

Mona used the silence to remember how Rema always managed to survive trouble and how she grieved when Emille was drowned in the ocean. And, twenty years later how bravely she endured his resentment when she learned he was alive. Lastly, her troubled life reached a peak when she discovered that John Swenson was alive. In the end, Felic's personality change and verbal abuse was the worst. After Felic's death, Rema seemed to rebound when Emille came to live with her in Justin House. In many ways, his presence, with her spiritual and emotional resiliency, filled her life. During Mona's silence, Melody thought about her future.

Mylowe and I are good together and close to marriage. We have been apart too long. He looked so tired this afternoon. His eyes told me to listen, yet his body language showed he was not anticipating an early solution to the current problem. I wonder what will happen to Emille. How will Mylowe react if Rema wants Emille treated as an outpatient? Will Mylowe control her decision? Mylowe is trying not to put his work first, but after nearly five years at Harvard, he has less than eighteen months of residency. In spite of that, he is very protective of Rema.

When Rema came into the room, Mona asked, "Do you know if Emille is in the tower? I hope you can put up with us for two more days. Melody Ann's flight was canceled because of bad weather. I'm staying until Wednesday. George is coming here from Cincinnati to drive me to the airport."

"Is he flying to Miami with you?" Rema asked.

"No, he's going to Kentucky."

Mylowe and George were standing in the doorway.

"It's time for us to go," said Mylowe. "I'll call up to the tower and tell Emille I'm leaving."

"It might be better to go up the stairs," Rema said. Mylowe understood her motive. He put his bags down, went into the pantry, opened the sliding door and raced up the stairs. The tower's heavy iron gate was open. He tapped lightly on the closed door.

"Emille, I'm leaving for the airport to go to Boston. I just wanted to say goodbye."

The door opened. Emille grinned impishly. "I lost track of time."

"Are you feeling okay?" Mylowe asked. "If it's a flu bug, George could order you an antibiotic."

"No, I'll be okay."

"Then, you have a good New Year."

Emille clung to the edge of the door as he closed it.

For a second, Mylowe hesitated outside the closed door. In the kitchen, he found Rema standing at the sink. When he held her in his arms, she laid her head on his shoulder. "Emille seems content," he whispered. "Just don't confront him. We don't want this situation to take on a life of its own." Mylowe turned toward the foyer and walked away.

From the alcove beside the grandfather's clock, Melody Ann rushed toward him. She clung to him, but did not speak.

"Let's go," Mylowe called to George.

A shiver ran down Melody Ann's spine. When she went into the den, Rema and Mona were sitting by the fireplace. Rema stoked the wood fire until orange and blue flames danced high between the logs. She lit the twelve Christmas candles on the mantle.

"Felic and I always sat here by the candles on Christmas night."

Mona, sitting close to the hearth, stretched her legs until her feet lay on the warm stones. "It's much too quiet," she said. "Something bad is about to happen."

"Don't say that," Melody Ann said. "I feel as if we're sitting on a time-bomb."

"There's nothing to fear," Rema said. "I've lived with Emille in this house for eight years."

"But his condition has changed," Mona said.

"I know."

Feeling uncomfortable about her time-bomb remark, Melody Ann lightened the mood by suggesting she brew some tea.

"I'll do it," Rema said. "While I'm in the kitchen I'll fix Emille a supper plate. Then I'm going to bed."

Rema put on her shoes and walked toward the kitchen. Mona slipped into her shoes and followed her. Melody Ann moved the blue chairs away from the fireplace, stoked the fire, put out the candles and went in the kitchen.

Rema prepared food for Emille and drew a large red arrow on the refrigerator door.

"Emille will see the arrow. He eats late."

"Are you going to wait for him?"

"No, Emille is waiting for us to go to bed."

"I'm moving into your room tonight," Mona announced. "It's not up for discussion."

"Could I sleep in Mylowe's room?" asked Melody Ann. "I'll be close by if you need me."

"We should lock our bedroom doors," Mona said.

Rema knew Mona's mind was made up.

"Okay, troops," she said. "Let's go to bed!"

38

MIDNIGHT

In Eben's Tower, Emille was asleep and awakened when his head fell backward and hit the wood headrest on Eben Justin's old desk chair. He squinted to see his watch and blinked until his eyes focused on the hands. "Oh! Lordy," he muttered, "I've been in the tower since five o'clock. Christmas is over."

He grinned as his thoughts centered on Melody Ann.

Mylowe's lady is a blond beauty. Sexy, I'll bet! Good in bed. Hmmm! Maybe I'll go check her out.

Emille stood up but staggered back into the chair, "Whoa. I'm not too steady. I need air." He stumbled toward the door and opened it. "That's better," he mumbled.

At the top of the stairs, he reached for the hand railing. "Oops!" he muttered. "My legs aren't working. Methinks I should sit down."

When a wave of nausea rolled through him, he sat down on the top stair step. Thrusting his head down between his legs, he chuckled uncontrollably at the thought of his vomit gushing down the stairs.

He sat up and pushed his head against the wall. Thirty minutes passed before he could stand. Holding onto the hand railing, he was able to walk down to the sliding door. He rested against the warm pantry wall.

Too hot!

He realized he still was wearing the heavy jacket and lined boots he always wore in the tower.

He pushed away from the wall and went into the kitchen. The light above the sink cast a dim shadow across the room. Through distorted vision, he saw the red arrow on the refrigerator door. He shook his head. "No, No, nothing to eat. Those pills from the clinic upset the ol' tummy tum tum."

Muttering, he went into the foyer. "What this place needs is an escalator. When I'm the master of Justin House, I will build one over these silly steps! By that time, the good boy Mylowe will have experienced a whole mess of trouble."

Grinning devilishly he walked the stairs by pulling himself up by the hand railing. "Shhh!" he rambled, "Don't say that again. That's a secret between me and the great one."

In the upper hallway, he leaned against the wall. He grasped the doorknob for support, turned it precisely to the right. When his bedroom door opened, he held onto the edge of the door. Gathering the last bit of physical strength, he shoved his body, inch by inch, around the door until he was able to push the door shut and close his eyes.

Minutes later, his eyes open, he dreamily calculated the distance of forward movement needed to reach the bed. Pushing his body against the door, he lunged forward and fell into the center of the bed.

The next morning at 7:30, Melody Ann and Mona opened their bedroom doors and stepped into the hallway. "I'll make coffee," said Rema.

She stopped in the kitchen doorway. The light above the sink was on. Going into the pantry, she opened the door leading to the tower. The light was on. She assumed Emille must have slept in the tower.

Melody Ann was standing on tiptoe to reach coffee mugs on the top shelf of the cupboard when Rema returned from the pantry. "Didn't you give Emille a stadium blanket for Christmas? Was that for him to use in the tower?" she asked.

Rema nodded. "There's no heat up there. I hope he has it with him."

Mona went from the kitchen across the foyer into the den. She was cold and wondered why people would elect to live in such cold weather. She crumpled sheets of newspaper, added small pieces of wood, and struck a match. Flames shot upward. She pulled her sweater close around her and went back to the kitchen. Melody Ann was pouring coffee in cups. Mona looked around and asked, "Where's Rema?"

"She went up to the tower to wake Emille."

Mona yelled, "She's not to be alone. Why didn't you stop her?"

"I tried to go with her."

Mona rushed toward the tower door and met Rema in the pantry.

"Emille isn't in the tower," Rema said. "The gate is standing wide open. I wonder if he ate the food I put in the refrigerator."

Trying not to appear anxious, Rema fed the kitten. "There's your din-din, my Angel. Would you like to get out of that big, old cage? Come with me, little darling."

Rema ran to answer the telephone in the den. "Yes, we're having breakfast. No, we haven't seen Emille since yesterday afternoon. I just checked the tower room. The door was open. I was about to go to his room but decided not to wake him so early. Yes, Mona's right here."

Rema motioned to Mona. "It's George. He wants to talk to you."

Rema ran into the foyer after the kitten. "Come back. I know there are plenty of places to hide in this big house, but today is not the day for you to find them."

Mona whispered into the phone. "George, we could have a situation brewing here. Call back around noon. I know Rema is going upstairs to wake Emille."

In the lobby of a Cincinnati hotel, George Whitetail closed the door of the telephone booth to shut out the noise.

"Mona," he said, "just follow your intuition and don't let things get out of hand. If you need emergency help, call 9-1-1. The police always arrive with the medics."

Rema ran into the den holding Angel. "Angel and I had a bit of exercise, but it's time for her to go into the cage." Breathless, she sat down and exclaimed, "I'm out of shape."

Mona grinned. "The whole world is out of shape. Why don't you convert one of the upstairs bedrooms to a workout room?"

"Emille mentioned setting up a workout room. He also thought an escalator should be installed for my old age."

Mona frowned. "Your old age?"

"I told him we should talk to Mylowe about an exercise room. Mylowe and Melody Ann might have other plans for the extra second floor rooms."

Mona noticed it was nine o'clock. "While we're waiting for Emille to come down, we should take a food inventory. There's too much food left over from Christmas."

"I could call the thrift center," Rema replied. "They usually distribute food and clothing to the needy during holidays. When I walked through the pantry this morning, I noticed there is an unusually large supply of canned goods on the shelves. We don't keep anything in the walk-down cellar during the winter, but there's frozen beef and turkeys in the freezer in the garage."

Mona wanted to keep Rema occupied and away from Emille's bedroom.

"We should load the canned goods, staples and meat in the car and take them to the thrift center. What time do they open?"

"We don't need to drive there," Rema said. "I'll call and ask them to send their truck."

As they were packing the food, Mona realized her plan to delay Rema from going to Emille's room had only been a partial success. By noon, eight boxes of food were stacked at one side of the kitchen. The truck from the thrift center was due to arrive at one o'clock.

Melody Ann finished putting tape on a small box of pastries and discovered she was alone in the kitchen. She walked into the foyer and looked inside the den.

Where are Rema and Mona? I thought we were to stay together.

She moved to the bottom of the staircase and walked up the stairs. Mona was standing outside the door to Emille's room. She heard Emille's voice. "Stay there," Mona whispered to Melody Ann. "You may need to call 9-1-1."

Mona then pushed the door open to get a better look inside Emille's room. Rema was standing beside Emille. He was sitting in a large chair dressed in a gray and red jacket with the hood pulled over his head. Rema was tucking a green comforter around his waist. He was wearing black boots. She watched as Rema leaned over him.

"Are you still cold. Could I bring you a hot water bottle?"

Emille shook his head and pointed toward the bed.

"I threw up. Will you call the great one and tell him I won't be coming today. There isn't enough mustard for all the sandwiches. I don't know what to do. The troops have eaten sandwiches before without mustard. Mother, do you have some mustard I could take to the troops?"

Rema's heart froze. She turned toward Mona and shook her head. Emille peered at her from beneath the hood.

"You're a spirit keeper, aren't you, Mommy? You keep all our spirits locked away in a great big room at the Libra Center and let them out when I'm good. Isn't that right? You've got my spirit all locked up and I can't get to it. I know that's where it is. You've got it all locked up!

"You're not my Mommy. Did you know that? My father is not my father. I don't know when my Mommy went away. I've always been alone—a poor lost little boy always looking for his mommy."

He began to cry. Tears ran down his cheeks and mucus dripped from his nose. Rema went to the night table to get a Kleenex. She stopped abruptly. The glass on the night table was covered with thin, horizontal streaks of white granules. She put her hand to her ear and motioned to Mona to call for help.

She returned to Emille. "Are you having trouble breathing?"

"I don't think so. The snake around my neck is heavy, but I can still get my breath."

"Are you uncomfortable in any other place?"

"Only on the tip of my finger. Do you see it glowing? It's a giant lightning bug. I have to keep my evil eye open or the skeeters will attack." His lips twisted into a wicked sneer. Rema stepped away and bent down to look at his face under the hood. His lips were curled.

"The skeeter story convinced you that I was your little boy. I fooled you with the skeeters." Emille's nostrils flared. His lips parted as he pushed his tongue in and out of his mouth. "See how I catch those skeeters."

Mona rushed to Melody Ann. "Call 9-1-1." Back inside Emille's doorway, Mona saw that Rema had filled a hot water bottle. It was on Emille's lap. He began to talk.

"You know, Mrs. Swenson, you run a mighty fine boarding house. Oh! Don't look so shocked. That's how you treat me. I'm just a boarder. But the great one's plan will change all that. First, the great one will get rid of your favorite son, Mylowe. When Mylowe is no longer the master of the house, you'll feel better about me. We will grow old together. When you take your last breath, I will be master of Justin House."

"Do you feel warm now?" she asked, daring to stand beside him. He did not move or reply. She walked to the bedroom door.

"I don't know what to do for him. Have the emergency people arrived?"

"They're due in five minutes. Melody Ann is waiting at the front door."

Rema looked at Emille. "He's very weak. I don't think he can stand. When they get here, give them the particulars of what we know and give me a sign so I can tell him that people are coming into the room."

"Is he dangerous?"

"The emergency crew has arrived," Mona whispered.

"Meet them in the hallway and explain what has been happening. Give the details of Emille's condition. I'll tell him the people are coming."

Mona hurried to the top of the stairs. Two men in heavy brown jackets and a police officer were coming up the stairs. The EMT's carried a sheet-covered gurney. Mona walked beside them.

"Emille Swenson is thirty-two years old," she said. "He's bipolar and being treated at a medical center in Dayton. He used cocaine. He's weak and incoherent. His mother is with him. They are in the room on the right."

Hearing the movement in the hall, Rema leaned over Emille's hood-draped head. "Emille, the troops are here. Are you ready to go with them?"

"Did you get enough mustard for the sandwiches?"

"Yes, you don't need to be concerned."

"They won't like the snake around my neck. Snakes are against regulations."

"If you don't move, they won't see the snake."

"Then I'll be okay."

"Yes, you'll be perfect."

When the emergency crew entered the room, they approached cautiously. Rema bent over Emille and whispered.

"Emille, the troop commander tells me they need to check you out before you can join them. Is that okay?"

Emille grasped the neck of her sweater and pulled her face close to his. "What about the snake?"

"The commander has the answer."

Mona stood in the doorway with the police officer while he completed a standard information form for police records when an EMT yelled, "Gun! Get down! The guy's got a gun!"

Three shots flew around the room. Both members of the medical team tackled Emille. They wrestled him to the floor.

"We've got him."

The police officer drew his gun and ran toward Emille. "Tie him down," he yelled. "Do you have a jacket with you?"

"The patient is secured," they replied. "Check out his mother. She may have fainted."

The police officer kneeled beside Rema. "She's been shot!"

Mona sat on the floor beside Rema while one EMT examined her. "The bullet hit her right shoulder," he said. He opened Rema's sweater and blouse and pressed sterile pads over the wounds.

"Get the wheelchair from the truck. We'll strap the guy in the chair and put her on the gurney. Let's get moving!"

Rema mumbled, "What happened?"

"Emille had a gun under his jacket," Mona said. "You've been wounded in the shoulder. They're driving you to the hospital in Cira. They're taking Emille, too."

Melody Ann ran into the room. "What was that noise?"

"Emille had a gun under his jacket," Mona said. "Rema was hit with two bullets. She's losing a lot of blood. What are they doing with Emille?"

"They sedated him. The police officer brought a straight jacket. The EMT is strapping Emille into a wheelchair."

Mona moved aside as an oxygen mask was put on Rema. "Is she critical?" Mona asked.

"Do you know her blood type?"

"It's in her billfold." Mona looked at Melody Ann. "Get her purse. It's in her bedroom."

When Melody Ann returned with Rema's purse, Mona was preparing to ride in the ambulance with Rema and gave Rema's blood type information to the EMT. Leaving Rema's side she went to Melody Ann.

"Could you call George in Cincinnati? Here's the telephone number. Have him paged and tell him what has happened. Also give him the number at Cira Memorial. Do you know if Mylowe is coming back from Boston tonight?"

"He's to arrive at the Dayton airport by five o'clock today."

An EMT stood over them. "It's time to move the lady," he said.

"When Mylowe arrives, have me paged at the hospital. Here are the keys to Rema's car. Remember to feed the kitten."

Rema was wheeled on a gurney from Emille's bedroom and carried down the winding staircase. Mona followed the gurney. In the foyer, Melody Ann stood with two Wexlor police officers and one officer from the sheriff's office.

Mona put on her coat and boots. When a police officer opened the front door, a path through the snow had been shoveled to the back door of the ambulance. While walking to the rear of the ambulance, she leaned on the arm of the officer who helped her step inside.

The officer also entered the back of the ambulance and sat on a stool beside Emille. Mona found an empty space on a narrow bench across from the gurney where Rema was being treated. Emille was strapped in the wheelchair. His head was bowed. The hood of his jacket covered his face. The black boots were still on his feet.

Five people were riding in a space designed for two.

"How is she?" Mona asked.

"She's not conscious. We're ready to move. The hospital is waiting for us."

He stepped toward the officer and whispered, "We're about ready." He motioned toward Emille. "Watch this fellow. He may not like the movement when we begin to move. These vehicles ride like trucks. The driver will use the siren when we're inside the city."

In the cab of the vehicle, the driver had dialed the telephone and was waiting for the hospital's emergency room doctor.

"Forty-one this is Dr. Wellman. Do you need to speak to me?"

"This is forty-one. We're transporting a gunshot victim and a psychiatric patient. The psychiatric patient is manic depressive and using a chemical substance. The nurse supervisor said she didn't have staff to manage him at Cira Memorial. Shall we take him down the road?"

"No, bring him to the emergency room. Later on, if necessary, I'll make arrangements to have him transported to the psychiatric facility. Come on in. I'll be waiting for you. In the meantime, I'll speak to the nursing supervisor."

"We'll arrive in twenty minutes."

From her cramped seat against the van's supply cupboards, Mona was angry. "Damn it," she whispered, "George and Mylowe waited too long."

The ambulance reached the highway and picked up speed. Mona held on to the edge of the bench. The supplies in the cupboards rattled and tumbled from the shelves. The medic steadied himself by holding on to a rod overhead. He reached down, adjusted the oxygen mask on Rema's face and held the IV feed line steady. From time to time, he glanced over at Emille. The police officer was holding onto the arm of the wheelchair to stop it from moving across the floor.

With all the movement, Mona could only see Rema if she peered around the medic. The ambulance's siren began to rotate a loud, jet air sound. They were inside the city limits. She was jolted sideways as the ambulance lurched over the rough driveway at the hospital entrance. The medic ignored her plight while he prepared Rema for transport. The ambulance swerved around a short circle. Before she regained an upright position, Mona was jerked backward and pushed forward.

The rear doors were pulled open and a four-member medical team boarded the ambulance to move Rema directly to surgery. A second three-member team lifted Emille's wheelchair through the open doors. The police officer helped Mona from the ambulance.

Inside the emergency entrance, Mona was approached by a newspaper reporter. "We understand Rema Swenson, the owner of the Libra Center, has been shot by her son. Can you confirm this?"

Mona shook her head, "No, I can't."

The reporter walked beside her. "Is her son mentally disturbed? How old is he? How badly is Mrs. Swenson hurt? Was it a family squabble? Are you a family member? Where's Mylowe Ort?"

Mona stopped and looked at him. "How do you know Mylowe?"

"We were in the same grade at Cira Public School. I've been to Justin House in Wexlor at a party and met Mrs. Swenson. I often went to the Libra Center after school with Mylowe. Aren't you Mona?"

She stared at him. "Yes, I am. Mylowe is in Harvard Medical School. He was home for Christmas. I'll see that you get the facts when I know them. If I were you, I'd be very careful about poisoning the water around here with false information. Cira people and the people in Wexlor who read your newspaper want stories that are accurate."

"I won't argue with that."

"What's your name?"

"Tim Collins."

"Mylowe will be here later tonight. I'll tell him you would like to write the correct story for your newspaper."

Tim Collins nodded and leaned against the wall outside the admissions office after Mona had gone inside. He concluded that problems usually occur when mental illness strikes a member of a family. He shook his head and decided to sit in the hospital lobby near the front door to wait for Mylowe.

At the admission's desk, Mona provided the information requirements. A teenage candy-striper, wearing the customary pink and white apron, waited to take Mona to the surgery waiting room on the fifth floor.

"Who will tell me about Mrs. Swenson's condition?" Mona asked.

"There's a mobile nurse in surgery who will keep you informed," replied the admission's clerk.

"I need to know about Emille Swenson's condition," Mona said, looking at her watch. "A family member is arriving from Boston."

The clerk did not reply, but dialed her phone. "Hi!" she said. "It's Darla in the Admissions Office. A member of Emille Swenson's family will be in the surgical waiting room. She would like to know about his condition."

The clerk hung up the phone and turned toward Mona, "You'll have a report on Mr. Swenson in about an hour. Doctor Wellman will come to the surgical floor and speak to you."

The candy-striper guided Mona into the elevator and pushed the button for the fifth floor. When the elevator door opened, she followed the young lady down the hall and realized there weren't any patients' rooms on the floor. The entire floor consisted of operating rooms, laboratories, conference rooms, and surgeons' offices. The waiting room was a small, green room at the end of the hall. Mona sat on a tan leather couch while the candy-striper made her a cup of tea.

"There are books on the shelf if you care to read," said the candy-striper. "I'll tell the mobile surgical nurse you're in the waiting room." Before Mona could reply, the candy-striper darted from the room. Mona sipped the tea and heaved a sigh. The releasing of her own breath startled her. She wondered why there was so much conflict lurking behind the relationship between Rema and Emille. Although mother and son had lived in the same house for the past eight years, there was something strange between them. Was shooting Rema really an accident or was Emille acting from some hidden motive? Will

Rema survive? Would Emille be institutionalized—for how long? Can Rema's metaphysical belief system get her through this?

The candy-striper appeared in the doorway. "Mrs. Pierce," she said, "Dr. Wellman wants to see you immediately. I can take you to the ER."

Mona picked up her purse and checked the contents inside to be sure Rema's billfold was still there. "Let's go," she said.

At the elevator, they squeezed in beside an aide and a patient on a gurney. The elevator stopped on the third floor and the patient was wheeled into the hall. On the first floor when the door opened, a nurse was waiting to take Mona to Emille's room.

"Mr. Swenson needs to talk to you," she said.

Mona stopped outside the closed door to Emille's room. "Is he lucid?" she asked.

The nurse understood. "He asked to see his mother. When he learned she was in surgery, he asked to speak to you."

Mona paused by the closed door, "I don't want to be alone with him."

The nurse nodded. "I'll go in with you."

At Emille's bedside, Mona looked at him. His heavy clothing had been removed. He looked thin and pale lying between the aqua hospital sheets.

"Emille," she whispered. "It's Mona. Did you want to see me?"

Emille turned his head to look at her. His voice was weak. He spoke haltingly.

"Take __a__ message __to__ mother. Tell__ her__ I've__ tried__ on__ other___ people's lives, but__ they didn't__ fit. I'm still__ the__ envious__ creature__ I was when I came__ to__ town. Being __human__ only runs in__ one direction—that's death. Tell__ Rema I'm in the__ final__ stages__ of Satan's__ service."

Emille gulped air and gasped. The nurse went to his bedside to study the monitors. Emille's eyes turned toward Mona.

"Tell her, I've seen__ Satan. He's not__ like the__ pictures—no horns or red__ beady__ eyes. He has__ controlled me__ for a long time. You'll tell her I'm so__ sorry, so__ very sorry. Tell__ her__ I__ love__ her."

Mona put her hand on his shoulder. The sharpness of his protruding shoulder bone startled her. "I'll tell her," she whispered.

"We should go now," said the nurse. "I was able to write down his message." She handed the notepaper to Mona. "It's for Mrs. Swenson after she has convalesced."

Mona took the pages and looked down at Emille knowing she had witnessed a different part of him. She shook her head sadly. He had struggled against overwhelming personal contradictions.

As they walked from the room, Mona turned and looked at Emille. The nurse was waiting for her in the hall. "Dr. Wellman is in his office. You can go right in," she said.

In Dr. Wellman's waiting room, the nurse tapped on an inside door. "Come in," said Dr. Wellman.

"Mrs. Pierce," he said, "please be seated." Mona sat in an armchair at his right and the nurse stood behind her. "Mrs. Pierce, I just had a report from the operating room. Mrs. Swenson is still in surgery, but the repair to her shoulder is progressing. The two bullets that penetrated the shoulder have been removed."

Mona gasped. She wanted to ask more questions but realized she would not receive any additional information for now.

"How is Emille doing?" she asked.

"Frankly, we're confused. While the effects of the psychotic condition and the substance usage are trouble enough, there is also brain cell deterioration accompanied by pulmonary edema."

"He was barely able to speak to me."

Dr. Wellman nodded. "That's our main concern. His condition requires assisted breathing. Do you have the authority to order that for him?"

"No," she said, looking at her watch, "Emille's closest relative, next to his mother, is Mylowe Ort. He'll be here later today. I could speak to him by telephone. Would it be helpful?"

"Yes, you may use the phone in my waiting room."

Mona thanked Dr. Wellman and dialed Justin House.

39

FEELINGS

At 5:20 p.m., Mylowe arrived at Justin House from Boston and listened without comment to Melody Ann's account of the shooting. He called Cira Memorial Hospital.

"Hello, this is Dr. Ort. Please page Mona Pierce."

"Wait!" said Melody Ann, "Rema's business telephone is ringing. Mona must be calling me."

Mylowe picked up the business line. "Hello," he said.

"Mylowe, is that you? It's Mona. Thank God, you're back from Boston."

"I managed to change my meeting with the medical board to this morning. Melody Ann just told me about the shooting. How are Rema and Emille?"

"Two bullets have been extracted from Rema's shoulder. She's still in surgery."

"How is Emille?"

"I'm calling from Dr. Wellman's office. Emille needs life support. As a member of the family, you'll need to sign the order."

"Is Dr. Wellman there?"

"Yes, he's in his office. I'll get him."

Mylowe looked at Melody Ann. "They've extracted two bullets from Rema's shoulder. Emille's condition is not good."

Mylowe turned away and spoke into the phone. "Hello, Dr. Wellman, this is Dr. Mylowe Ort. I am Emille Swenson's brother. What is his condition?"

"His brain cells have deteriorated and the edema in the pulmonary region is causing his body to shut down. He's critical. We need to get him on life support."

"I authorize you to go ahead. I'll be there in twenty minutes. Have the consent forms prepared."

"I'll be in my office."

Mylowe squeezed Melody Ann's hand and hung up the business phone. She motioned that the house phone was ringing. Mylowe picked it up. "Dr. Ort, Mrs. Pierce is on the line."

"Hello, Mylowe. Is something wrong?" asked Mona.

"It was just a telephone mix up. I was dialing the hospital when you called on the business phone. Melody Ann and I are leaving this minute for the hospital."

"Has Melody Ann heard from George?"

"She talked with George earlier."

"Then George knows about the shooting?"

"Yes, he'll be at the hospital tonight by eight o'clock."

Mylowe hung up the phone and grabbed Melody Ann's hand. "Let's get going. We'll take Rema's car." On the way to the hospital, Melody Ann repeated the details of the shooting. At the hospital's entrance, Mylowe guided the car into the parking lot.

"I'm meeting Dr. Wellman in his office," he said. "Will you find Mona? She'll be in a waiting room somewhere, possibly near the surgical wing."

Melody Ann snuggled against him as they walked from Rema's Buick through the snow to the emergency entrance. Inside, Mylowe kissed her on the cheek and said, "See you soon."

At Dr. Wellman's office, Mylowe stepped inside. "Are you Dr. Ort?" asked the secretary.

Mylowe nodded.

"Dr. Wellman wanted you to go directly to Mr. Swenson's room. It's around the corner to your right and down the hall, # 128."

Mylowe hurried toward the room. Once inside, he introduced himself to the three physicians standing by Emille's bed.

"Dr. Wellman," he said, "I'm Dr. Ort."

One of the doctors leaned on a cane and moved toward him. Mylowe noticed how skillfully the doctor guided his muscular body around the foot of the bed. By the cut of his jaw, Mylowe could see this man was not disturbed by his restricted mobility.

"I'm Dr. Wellman," he said. "We're losing him."

Mylowe leaned over Emille. "How long has he been comatose?"

"About thirty minutes."

Dr. Wellman nodded toward the other two white-coated physicians who had stepped away from the bed. "I called these gentlemen in as consultants. They are from Fillaman Psychiatric Hospital. This is Dr. Mayberry and Dr. Horstner."

Dr. Horstner moved toward Mylowe. "We're puzzled by the extent of the brain cell damage," he said. "The condition of this man's lungs is of an old man."

Mylowe noticed Dr. Horstner stood on one foot as he spoke. His posture was the mark of a professional and a self-starter, one who always stands prepared to be the first in line at the starting gate.

Dr. Mayberry stood across the room. His voice was robust, yet kindly.

"In my experience, cocaine does damage the lungs and the brain. When you see the MRI results, you'll understand why we are perplexed."

Mylowe said, "It's too late for supportive breathing, isn't it?"

"It was too late months ago," said Dr. Horstner. "How did this man keep going? When we arrived, he was having irregular breathing cycles."

"Cheyne-Stokes," Mylowe whispered. He squeezed Emille's bony shoulder. Emille's face showed the torture his body had succumbed to. Mylowe touched his skeletal cheek.

Dr. Horstner pressed Mylowe's shoulder. "We're very sorry. If you need information about our diagnosis, please let us know."

Placing his hand on Emille's emaciated fingers, Mylowe bowed over him. "Emille's depleted physical condition is a shock. My family will have questions."

As Dr. Horstner and Dr. Mayberry walked from the room, Dr. Wellman moved beside Mylowe.

"Dr. Ort, the hospice nurse has arrived. This is Mrs. Derrie," he said. "She will attend to your brother. I'll be in my office getting an update on your mother's condition. I hope I return with good news."

Mrs. Derrie's professional manner was obvious. Looking away from Mylowe, she took Emille's vital signs and adjusted his oxygen cannula. There was nothing more to be done. She moved away from her patient and spoke above a whisper.

"I was with Mr. Swenson earlier today when he conveyed his thoughts to Mrs. Pierce. It was a message to your mother. I wrote it down for Mrs. Pierce."

Although Mylowe wanted to know the content of Emille's message, he managed to put his curiosity aside.

"Do I have time to go to the surgery floor to find Mrs. Pierce?" he asked.

"Don't be long," she whispered. "The surgical rooms are on the fifth floor."

Mylowe paused at the door and said, "A family friend, Dr. Whitetail, is due to arrive. Have him wait here for me."

He hurried to the fifth floor. The hustle and noise of an area that is normally filled with patients was nonexistent. The placard on a metal stand affirmed that the blue arrows led to the waiting room. The arrows, yellow and red, pointed to surgery rooms, labs and the doctors' lounge. As he entered the waiting room, Mona rushed toward him.

"Oh! Mylowe," she cried tearfully, "we waited too long to protect Rema."

Mylowe embraced her. "Do you have any information about mother?"

"The mobile nurse was just here. The surgeon is repairing the damage to Rema's shoulder. There are complications."

Mylowe put his arm around Mona. Melody Ann jumped up and embraced both of them. "I must go to Emille," he said. "Earlier, Emille experienced Cheyne-Stokes Respiration and slipped into a coma. He won't survive."

Both women clung to him.

"What is Cheyne-Stokes Respiration?" asked Melody Ann.

"It's an irregular cycle of slow then rapid breathing. It usually occurs in the last moments of life." Mylowe hugged them and whispered. "I must go back to Emille."

George Whitetail was at Emille's bedside when Mylowe entered Emille's room.

"Hello, George," Mylowe said. "Did Nurse Derrie give you the prognosis?"

George shook his head. "What a pity!"

"Baffling, isn't it?"

George motioned to Mylowe. "Come around to this side of the bed."

Mylowe leaned over Emille and listened to the pulse points. He cupped Emille's face in his hands. Mrs. Derrie recorded Emille's death as 8:20 p.m., December 26, 1994. She hurried from the room and returned with Dr. Wellman who examined the body. When he finished, Mylowe guided George to meet Dr. Wellman. After the introduction, Dr. Wellman walked toward the door. George Whitetail followed him. The two men stood together in the hallway.

"This is the second death in this family," George said. "Both deaths were primarily associated with sudden respiratory failure and deteriorated brain cells."

"You must be concerned," replied Dr. Wellman.

"I'm very concerned."

"Is there anything I can do?"

"If you have a conscientious medical examiner, I would like to meet him."

"Of course. I'll arrange it."

In Emille's room, Mylowe removed the oxygen cannula from Emille's face and had pulled the sheet over Emille's head.

"Where are Mona and Melody Ann?" asked George. "Do they know about Emille?"

"I told them Emille's death was imminent. They're on the fifth floor in the surgical waiting room. Go on up there. I'll manage things here."

"You're going to order an autopsy, aren't you?"

"Of course. I know mother would agree."

"Good! I brought a copy of Felic's autopsy with me. We need to give it to the medical examiner."

"Are you insisting on a comprehensive study of the similarities of Felic's and Emille's deaths? Felic died nearly eight years ago. Where is the connection?"

"I've thought of two connections. Both men lived in Justin House and were teachers at Wexlor University. Let's not ignore this opportunity to find out what is killing the men of Justin House. It may be our last chance." George paused at the open doorway. "I'll be upstairs with Mona and Melody Ann."

Mrs. Derrie returned to Emille's room. "Orderlies will be here to prepare the body for transport to the morgue in the basement," she said. "Are you requesting an autopsy?"

"Yes," said Mylowe. "Before the procedure is performed, Dr. Whitetail has some specific instructions for the doctor in charge of the forensic team."

"Dr. Patterson is our medical examiner. I'll arrange for you and Dr. Whitetail to meet him."

Mylowe nodded. "I have some arrangements to make on Emille's behalf, but first I want to get some information about my mother's condition."

"Dr. Wellman has not received an update in the last fifteen minutes," replied Mrs. Derrie. "The last report was that Mrs. Swenson is still in surgery and is in stable condition."

Mylowe nodded, "Thank you again for your assistance. I'll remain here with Emille until they remove him to the morgue. After that, I'll be on the fifth floor."

Mrs. Derrie left the room to prepare forms for Mylowe's signature. There was a noise at the doorway. Mylowe turned around. Two orderlies, dressed in hospital blues, pushed an empty gurney into the room. They bathed Emille's body using large sponges dipped in water and alcohol. The opening of the zipper on the plastic body bag gave Mylowe goose bumps. He stood against the wall as they lifted Emille onto the gurney. He clenched his jaw when the zipper closed. His entire body felt numb as the orderlies pushed the gurney into the hall.

Until this moment, Mylowe's encounter with death at Boston Memorial had been on an impersonal plane. He stood alone listening to the soft turning of gurney's wheels. There was a loud noise at the elevator as the gurney was shoved inside. A hollow scraping followed as the doors closed causing the floor to vibrate under his feet. Mylowe put his head in his hands and cried. He had waited much too long.

40

DESPAIR

From the #3 surgery pavilion, Chief Surgeon Dr. Arton Granger had walked a long hallway and pushed through two sets of wide swinging doors before reaching the door to the fifth floor waiting room. At the same moment, Mylowe had entered the waiting room from another hallway. George Whitetail was sitting in the family waiting room with Mona and Melody Ann. He stood as Dr. Granger and Mylowe walked through opposite doors.

Once inside the room, Dr. Granger paused, leaned against a sturdy wood table and motioned to Dr. Whitetail and Mylowe to be seated. He was dressed in maroon-tinted scrubs covered with a white mid-calf length coat. From beneath a surgical cap, bushy white sideburns trailed down the full length of his cheeks. He was noticeably as wide as he was tall. Around his knees were wide elastic braces. The braces, made firmer with strategically placed flat-bone stays, were held together with black Velcro bands. Before he spoke, he crossed his arms over his chest and wobbled his head from side to side.

"I'm Dr. Granger," he said, "I'd sit down but these supports do not allow my knees to do much bending." He heaved a sigh and stared directly at the four people sitting across the room. Waving his hand in the direction of the surgical pavilion, he said, "It was a long haul in there today. When my surgical nurse, Miss Camden, told me the members of Mrs. Swenson's family were in the waiting room, she described the younger man as Mrs. Swenson's son and the ladies and a distinguished man as close family friends."

A sincere grin formed on his lips.

"I hope you don't mind. Miss Camden provides insider information and interesting tidbits about my patients and their families." Pausing briefly, he stared curiously at the four people sitting before him. "Most surgical assistants," he added, "shy away from telling their supervisors additional information about patients, but Cira Memorial is a small facility."

Mylowe and George stood and stepped toward Dr. Granger. Mylowe extended his hand, "I am Dr. Mylowe Ort, Mrs. Swenson's son." He turned toward Mona and Melody Ann. Gesturing toward Mona, he said, "I am pleased to introduce Mona Pierce, Mrs. Swenson's closest friend and this is my dearest companion, Melody Ann Thames." He turned toward Dr. Whitetail. "This distinguished gentleman is Dr. George Whitetail."

Dr. Granger pushed himself away from the table, nodded graciously toward the ladies and shook hands with the men. He repositioned his body against the table and paused. The weighty surgeon was about to give some shattering news.

"The wounds in Mrs. Swenson's shoulder were deep," explained Dr. Granger. "Two Nyclad-tipped bullets pierced the head of the humerus, the anterior deltoid muscle, separated the tendon biceps brachi and shattered the head of the lateral cord nerves stemming from the brachial plexus. As a result of all that damage, Mrs. Swenson might be permanently paralyzed on most of her left upper body. On a more positive note, I am hopeful only her left arm would succumb to permanent damage. If that should be the case, physical therapy will provide her with a bit of mobility in the left arm."

"Are you saying she might be able to raise her arm?" asked Mylowe.

"Yes, but only as high as her midsection. Her mobility might be comparable to the United States Senator, Bob Dole, whose right shoulder was torn apart in World War II. If you've seen him on TV, you've noticed he uses his good arm to help position his injured arm near his midsection."

"Will Mrs. Swenson experience chronic pain?" asked Dr. Whitetail.

"I can't say because I don't know. It's much too early. I repaired the muscles and pinned the shoulder bone together. Recuperation, in her case, may be slow. Her age is a factor."

Mylowe rubbed his brow as he asked another question. "You mentioned Nyclad-tipped bullets. Were you familiar with the type of ammunition before today?"

"Yes, I've extracted many Nyclad-tipped bullets. Years ago, those bullets were used by most police departments. The bullets were lead-tipped, had hollow points and were colored with royal blue Teflon coating on the tips. When the gangsters discovered the effectiveness of the Nyclad bullets, they began using them against the police. The bullets penetrated the policemen's protective vests. Additional shields had to be installed in the vests. Finally, for personal safety, the police stopped using the Nyclad bullets. I'm certain ballistics will show the gun used to shoot Mrs. Swenson was a Smith & Wesson .38-Special."

Color drained from Mylowe's face.

"Is that particular gun nicknamed the Saturday Night Special?" he asked.

Dr. Granger, noting Mylowe's reaction, continued to speak.

"I'm optimistic about your mother's condition. She'll be in the recovery room until ten o'clock tonight. I suggest only you visit her. Tomorrow, depending upon her condition, other visitors will be welcome."

Using the table as support, Dr. Granger pushed himself forward and lumbered toward the entrance. In the doorway, he slid the surgical cap from his head. A rush of wavy white hair fell from the cap stopping two inches above his shoulders. Mylowe followed him into the hallway.

Dr. Granger turned toward Mylowe. "I know you're concerned about infection. The Nyclads do present a possibility of infection. We're taking all the precautions. Within four days, we'll know if we've done a good job."

"Thank you," said Mylowe.

Dr. Granger shook Mylowe's hand. "Miss Camden also told me about the death of your brother. I'm so sorry. The entire situation is truly a tragedy. I'll keep a close watch over your mother." Dr. Granger then moved clumsily down the hall toward the doctors' lounge.

Back inside the waiting room, Mylowe exclaimed, "Rema was shot with Felic's gun. Felic told us he dismantled that gun."

"Before you jump to conclusions, you should check with the police about the gun," said Dr. Whitetail. "If it is Felic's gun, you'll recognize it. Until then, you have enough on your mind."

Still angry, Mylowe stepped away from Dr. Whitetail and stared out of the window. "You heard the prognosis," he said. "It's going to be a long night. You should go back to Justin House. Have some dinner on the way home."

Mylowe put his arm around Melody Ann. "In the morning, I'll notify President Matthews of Emille's death. I also will give him an updated report on Rema's condition."

Mylowe's next sentence was interrupted when the waiting room door opened.

"Dr. Ort, I'm Dr. Patterson. Mrs. Derrie asked me to conference with you and Dr. Whitetail concerning Emille Swenson."

Mylowe turned toward the door. The tall, slim doctor, who stooped to avoid hitting his head on the top of the door, clutched a clipboard in his hand.

Mylowe moved toward him. "I'm Dr. Ort," he said. "This is Dr. Whitetail. Is there a room nearby where we can talk?"

"There's a small conference room next door."

"Good! We'll just need a few minutes." Mylowe looked at Mona and Melody Ann. "We won't be long."

Inside the small conference room, Dr. Whitetail explained to Dr. Patterson the apparent similarities of the medical diagnoses in the sudden deaths of Felic Ort and Emille Swenson.

"We have questions about the unexplained brain cell deterioration in each man," he said. "Also, we should know in what area of the lungs did the pulmonary distress originate? Was it in the larynx, trachea, bronchi or the bronchioles? I have a copy of Felic Ort's autopsy report and have questioned the findings for over eight years. Now, with Emille's sudden demise, the real reason for the unexplained sudden deaths of these two men may be forthcoming. I realize that DNA tests are not, as yet, a procedure considered standard, but I suggest you extract samples from Emille for future examination."

Dr. Patterson leaned back and clasped his hands behind his head. "Did these two men live together in the same environment?"

"No, Felic died months before Emille lived in Justin House," Mylowe replied.

"They had nothing in common?" questioned Dr. Patterson.

"Nothing except both men lived in Justin House at different times and worked as teachers at Wexlor University."

"Who lived in the house with them?"

"My mother, Rema Swenson. She lived in the house with Felic over sixteen years. After Felic died, she lived there with Emille for eight years. Emille was my mother's son by birth. Rema raised me from the time I was three days old."

"Has there been domestic help in the house during those years?"

"Only Maggie. She has been in our household since I was able to walk."

Dr. Patterson turned in his chair and stretched his long legs under the table as he read Felic's autopsy report.

When he finished he said, "If Mr. Swenson's autopsy resembles Felic Ort's report in the slightest manner, I would want your permission to confer with some of my colleagues. Should the toxicology report come back with questionable aspects, it will certainly be a challenge to find the common denominator."

"Do you suspect poison?" asked Mylowe.

"I won't be able to say until we finish the autopsy. If poison was involved, it must have had a long reaction time. Most poisons have short reaction times from fifteen minutes to eight hours. I will need the body of Emille Swenson in the lab for a minimum of three days."

Mylowe nodded. "If your initial findings are inconclusive, you may keep Emille's body for a week."

Mylowe and Dr. Whitetail stood and shook hands with Dr. Patterson.

"We'll be waiting for your conclusions," Mylowe said.

When Dr. Patterson had gone from the room, Dr. Whitetail sighed and moved toward the door. "Well," he said, "the fat is in the fire. I hope we get some answers."

Mylowe seemed hesitant to go back to the waiting room. Noting his reluctance, Dr. Whitetail sat with him.

"I've been thinking about Rema and her recuperative powers," Mylowe said.

"You mean her faith."

Mylowe leaned forward. "I realize in times of trouble, members of the human race have always called upon an invisible force for comfort. Sometimes they turn to an icon, an intermediate or a special kind of invincible energy. I'm not just thinking of Rema's wounds and the physical stress on her body. The finality brought about by Emille's death may cause her added emotional stress. Her grief for him will be deeper than before."

George echoed Mylowe's words. "Rema has always survived."

"That's true, but how many times must she lose her son? This is the third time."

"The third time?"

"Yes, Emille was eight years old when he was lost in the Atlantic Ocean along with Rema's husband. Nearly twenty years later, she discovered Emille was alive. When she met him in a public park in Miami, he told her he didn't want her in his life."

"But she survived."

"Yes, but this time Emille is really dead. We both can testify to that."

George shifted in his chair.

"If you're wondering if she has the physical stamina to become strong again, I would say she has the strength to do it. I've learned there's a difference between curing and healing. Doctors can instigate a cure but the healing must come from deep within the patient. Rema has that healing power."

Mylowe leaned his head back and closed his eyes. "As medical people, we have an enormous job before us."

"What is that?"

"Our job is to show our patients how to tap into their personal belief systems."

"You mean as a companion to our traditional health care?"

"Has a patient asked you to pray with him because he thought your energy would contribute to his healing?"

"No, but I do know that some of my patients use meditation, prayer or white light energy. Those things act as a healing balm. I would pray with a patient if I'm asked."

"Then you've not suggested to a patient that you pray with them?"

"No."

"Did you know there's been talk about forming a Harvard-affiliated Mind/Body Medical Institute with a curriculum designed for health care professionals? The purpose would be to prepare physicians to simply interact with their patients by encouraging the patients to express their religious beliefs."

George smiled. "I came into medicine hoping to exercise my native spiritual beliefs. I found it was difficult to introduce them unless I offered a scientific basis. Of course, my American Indian spirituality is not something I can use daily, but I do listen to my patients."

Mylowe shifted in his chair. "As physicians," he said, "we need to take this step forward."

"Is prayer and white light healing going to be part of the curriculum at Harvard?"

"It's possible. Right now, there's resistance to research on energy healing. As soon as the AMA forms a metaphysical think tank and figures how to make money from energy healing, they will get involved. The forces of the mind and spirit are as real as atomic power. Yet, we can't see this mysterious energy. Like insurance, it's intangible until you need it. I plan to include a healing protocol in the program at my clinic."

"Ah! Yes," said George, "one purpose of your new clinic is to improve doctor/patient relationships. To improve that will take a great amount of energy healing."

Mylowe noted that George's lack of interest in the medical protocols planned for the new clinic was apparent.

"We'd better go back to the waiting room," Mylowe said. "I'll help escort Mona and Melody Ann to your car and I'll call you in the morning. Would you please feed the kitten when you get to Justin House? Mother will ask about Angel."

41

GRIEF

When Mylowe and George entered the waiting room, the task of telling Rema of Emille's death was lined on Mylowe's face. He insisted on escorting Melody Ann to the parking lot. She didn't want to go and pleaded to stay. "I can't sleep knowing you are alone tonight," she said. "Isn't our relationship about being together not only in the good times but in the stressful ones, too?"

He looked into her anxious eyes and smiled. "Do you think Mona and George Whitetail can be trusted to stay the night together in Justin House?"

She burst into laughter. "You have a mischievous mind. I doubt if either one of them remembers what to do."

In the parking lot, Mona handed Mylowe the piece of notebook paper. "Written on this paper are Emille's last words to Rema," she said. "The nurse had the presence of mind to write them down."

Mylowe hugged her, put the paper in his coat pocket and whispered, "Thank you. You've been very brave."

She leaned away from him and looked into his eyes.

"Right now, I don't feel as if Emille's words will give Rema much comfort. She will be destroyed when she learns of his death. This time he's really dead. How much more sadness will she be made to endure?"

Mylowe patted the paper in his pocket. "I'll keep this for her until a more appropriate time."

Mona started to walk toward George's rental car.

Turning around, she said. "Oh! Your classmate from Cira High School has been waiting in the lobby to talk to you. He's a newspaper reporter and wants to write about the shooting. His name is Tim Collins."

Mylowe nodded. "Yes, we were friends at Cira High. Some of the other guys were less than friendly."

Mona looked surprised. "I didn't know you had problems with kids at school. Why didn't you mention it?"

"It was something I had to handle. Don't be upset. I learned to negotiate with my enemies. Tim learned that, too."

Mona again turned toward the car. "George is waiting. Are you coming, Melody Ann?"

With an entreating gaze, Melody Ann turned toward Mylowe. "I'm going to stay with Mylowe. In the morning, I can help make some telephone calls."

Mona opened the car door and moved inside. "Okay, we'll wait for your call in the morning."

Mylowe and Melody Ann stood in the parking lot as George maneuvered the car into the street. Melody Ann grinned impishly.

"Mona didn't put up much resistance about being alone all night with George."

"Now you're being mischievous. You're conjuring up something that isn't possible."

"You're a dunce, Dr. Ort," Melody Ann said. "Sex between sexagenarians is indeed possible. I wish I were a little mouse."

"What would you do?"

"I'd watch."

"If you wanted to watch you should have gone with them." Mylowe locked his arm in hers and guided her toward the emergency entrance.

"Okay," he whispered. "Since you've elected to stay with me tonight, I suggest your hormones simmer down." He leaned over and kissed her firmly on the lips.

Melody Ann put her arms around his neck. "And, since we aren't allowed to exercise our hormones in Justin House, we could go down the street to that cute little motel."

Mylowe kissed her lightly on the lips. "Go have some coffee and cool off while I talk to Tim Collins. I'll meet you in the cafeteria."

Melody Ann pursed her lips into a playful pout and walked toward the cafeteria. From a corner of the lobby, reporter Tim Collins got up slowly from a chair and walked toward Mylowe.

"Hi!" Tim said softly. "I heard about Emille. I'm so sorry."

"It's a tough break," Mylowe replied.

"How is your mother?"

"We won't know about her condition for forty-eight hours. Mrs. Pierce said you wanted some information for the newspaper."

"The rumors in the hospital are unconfirmed. I want to write the facts."

"I appreciate that. The truth is my brother hid his illness from the family. This morning he was too weak to get out of a chair. My mother dialed 9-1-1. When the EMT's arrived, Emille took a gun from beneath his jacket and began shooting around the room. Two of the bullets hit mother in the left shoulder. She was in surgery for over four hours. Her condition is guarded."

"There was no disagreement between Mrs. Swenson and her son?"

"No, none at all. They had lived together in Justin House for eight years."

"What did Emille do for a living?"

"He taught language at Wexlor University."

"Is there anything else I should know?"

"No, except I need to know when this story will appear in the paper."

"Tomorrow morning's edition will carry the story."

Mylowe turned toward Tim. "I trust you'll write the story as I described it. It was nothing more than an accidental shooting. Emille's physical condition deteriorated quickly."

"Was he on drugs?"

"We have reasons to think that he used drugs. Although we can't be certain the length of time Emille had been using."

"Was he using drugs to help his medical problem?"

"We assume that to be the case." Mylowe started to turn away. "If you'll excuse me, I'm to meet my girlfriend in the cafeteria. I will be allowed to see my mother in about two hours. Tim, it's so good to see you again. Remember those exciting verbal matches we had at school with the members of the Oz Gang? It's a miracle we weren't attacked."

"We weren't attacked because of your negotiating skills. I wrote their term papers for them and you told them about life and gave them hope."

"I wonder if anyone from that gang is still living in Cira," Mylowe said.

"No, they have moved away. From all the advice you gave them on how they could better themselves they undoubtedly became lawyers or gamblers."

"Or mobsters," Mylowe said.

The two friends laughed and clasped their palms together in the Cira High handshake. Tim headed toward the telephone and Mylowe went to the cafeteria. Each man instinctively knew the shooting would be blown out of proportion in the media.

Mylowe hurried to the cafeteria and found Melody Ann sitting near the entrance. "Sit down," she said. "I'll bring you macaroni and cheese."

Mylowe leaned forward. "I need to call President Matthews tonight at his home. According to Tim Collins, the story about the shooting will be in the morning edition."

"Oh! Darn! I hoped you could make calls in the morning."

"This can't wait until morning. The university should know about Emille's death before the papers come out. It's nearly nine o'clock."

"Eat the macaroni and cheese."

"Okay, okay."

* * * * *

On nights during the week, the great room inside the President's residence on the Wexlor campus was the congregating place for students preparing for master's degrees. By 8:30, the students had returned to their living quarters. President Matthews was sitting by the fireplace when the telephone rang. He rose slowly, crossed the room and picked up the phone. "Hello," he said.

"Dr. Matthews, this is Mylowe Ort."

"Are you still at Justin House?"

"Yes, I'm calling to tell you some sad news. Emille Swenson died tonight in Cira Memorial Hospital."

President Matthews sat down on a chair. "What happened?"

"This is what we know. You can decide how to handle the information. In the morning, the Cira Journal will release the story. I will tell you exactly what I told them. I don't know what they will print, but here's the truth. Emille has been battling a mental illness for some time. He was very strong and kept it controlled with cocaine. The family learned of his condition on Christmas Day. This morning he couldn't control it. Rema found him in a chair. He was not able to move and was incoherent. She called 9-1-1. When the EMT's arrived, Emille took a gun from his jacket and began shooting around the room. Two bullets hit Rema in the shoulder."

"How is she?"

"She's critical but expected to survive, although she may be paralyzed on the left side. The better news is that she may be paralyzed only in the left arm. She's in the recovery room. I expect to see her in thirty minutes."

"I'm shocked to learn about Emille. He was extremely competent and well regarded. What can I do?"

"You can relay the facts to the university's personnel and the local citizenry. It would be best coming from you. I'll call you in the morning to see how you handle it. I don't know what arrangements mother may want to make for funeral services. She doesn't know of Emille's death. I'll appreciate your help with the gossip."

Mylowe hung up the phone and leaned against the inside of the telephone booth. The reality of Emille's death and Rema's injury had finally reached him. He looked through the glass at Melody Ann sitting at the table in the cafeteria and wondered how he was going to tell Rema about Emille, and at some point, relay the truth to her about her injury. He knew he must be prepared to answer all her questions. As always, he knew she will expect the truth from him and nothing but the truth will do.

42

SORROW

Rema was conscious when Mylowe entered the hospital room. "Who goes there?" she whispered.

"Mylowe goes here," he said softly. "I'm here to watch over you."

"Maybe now I'll find out if you're really a good doctor."

"Do you have any pain?"

"Not much. There's so much pain killer dripping out of that bag hanging up there, I doubt I'll feel anything again. What's all the hardware and plaster around my shoulder?"

Mylowe pulled a chair close to the bed and sat down. "The cast is to protect the surgery procedure. You should rest now. I'll stay here."

"How is Emille? The last time I saw him he was being strapped into a wheelchair."

"When he arrived at the hospital, he was in critical condition."

"He looked so pitiful. I've failed him."

"None of his suffering was your fault. He had fought his mental condition for a long time. The monster drug finally overtook him."

"Where is he? Did they take him to the mental ward?"

"Two psychiatrists came from the mental hospital to examine him, but before they arrived he slipped into a coma. The MRI showed extensive brain cell deterioration and pulmonary distress."

"Then he cannot live."

Mylowe took her hand, "No, he cannot survive."

Mylowe wiped a tear from her cheek. She closed her eyes. Each time she opened her eyes, he squeezed her hand.

Before midnight, Mrs. Derrie walked quietly through the hall leading to Rema's room. She clutched the hospital forms relating to Emille Swenson's death. She was feeling the emotions of the day and was eager to go home. As a private nurse, there were times when it seemed her days went on forever. The hall was dimly lit. It was an ordinary procedure after 11:30 p.m. At the door of Mrs. Swenson's room, she saw a young woman sitting on a straight, metal chair.

"Are you waiting for Dr. Ort?" she whispered.

"Yes," replied Melody Ann.

"I'm Mrs. Derrie, Emille Swenson's nurse. Let me arrange for a more comfortable place for you."

Before Melody Ann could react, Mrs. Derrie had hurried down the hall toward the central station. Within minutes she returned. A nurse was hurrying down the corridor.

"There's an empty room next to Mrs. Swenson's room," she said. "Nurse Abbott will get you settled in. I'll tell Dr. Ort you're resting in the next room." Melody Ann nodded and followed Nurse Abbott into the empty room.

When Mrs. Derrie entered Rema's room, Mylowe stood and met her in the doorway. "Would you sign these forms?" she whispered. Gathering the signed papers together, Mrs. Derrie told Mylowe that Melody Ann was settled comfortably in the next room.

"Thank you," he said.

Rema slept quietly and stirred only when the nurse took her vital signs and checked the IV drip. At dawn, Mylowe stood at the window. The rays of the rising sun cast mysterious shadows on the tops of the trees as if a higher intelligence was trying to reach him. So far in his life, he had felt like a chicken embryo biding time before being called to burst forth.

Although Rema's tutelage in the juxtaposition of the planets had captivated him, there were moments when his feelings were so hard to pin down he couldn't begin to know the extent of them. When man revolts against his will, he is miserable. In that moment evil is king. Still in his twenties, he realized the uncertainty he was feeling happens to most people. He wondered how Emille's death would affect the family. Would the emotional stress from Emille's sudden death defeat Rema's zeal to recuperate?

His questions were unanswered when Rema sighed and opened her eyes. "Good morning," he whispered. "You look better today."

"This isn't a day I'm fully prepared to face," she said.

"But you've faced a day like this before."

"I know and I hated it."

"Is Emille with us today?"

"No, Emille is in heaven."

"Emille came to me in my dreams. He said to remember that sorrow and strength are drawn from the same well."

In the yellow dawn, Mylowe had already decided to tell Rema only what was necessary. He would wait until she was stronger. He knew by the end of the day, her questions would continue until she had all the answers. He decided to try it his way.

Rema lay still. Her eyes were closed and her jaw tight. Mylowe knew the pain medication was not totally effective. For now, he would not intrude on her private moment. He backed out of the room and went to the next room.

Melody Ann, covered with a blue blanket, was sitting by the window. She did not get up. "Rema knows about Emille, doesn't she?"

Mylowe sat beside her. "Last night I told her his condition was critical. She knew he couldn't live. This morning she told me Emille came to her in a dream."

"Does she know about her own medical prognosis?"

"She didn't ask. I'm only passing information as needed. She has a lot of pain, but isn't complaining. The nurses have been very attentive. For now, she's sleeping."

"I'll go to the cafeteria and get you some breakfast," she said.

"I'll just have coffee. I need to call Mona and President Matthews. The story of the shooting incident will be in the morning papers. I'm curious to see what has been reported."

Melody Ann tossed the blanket aside and straightened her clothes. "I'll be right back," she whispered. Mylowe stretched his legs and laid his head against the back of the chair. He was asleep when Melody Ann returned with hot coffee. She did not wake him.

By 10:00 a.m., Mylowe awoke and was sitting in Mrs. Derrie's office dialing the number at Justin House.

"Hello, Mona," he said. "Mother knows about Emille's death. The pain medication is keeping her quiet. How are you? I don't know if she can have visitors today. I'll let you know. Okay, I'll tell her you're caring for the kitten."

Hanging up the phone, Mylowe looked in the directory for President Matthews' office at the university. He dialed the number. President Matthews answered.

"Mother is conscious," Mylowe said. "What stories have appeared in the morning news?"

"The Cira morning paper carried the story about the shooting," President Matthews reported. "Justin House, as you know, is the local landmark. The paper ran a short biography about Emille. From what I've been able to gather, there is a wide range of sympathy for your family. I've had calls from people living in the county seat. Many of your friends and colleagues have called. If anyone is asking a lot of questions, only the media people are asking them. You know how they are."

"I hope you're right."

"My staff is asking about a memorial service."

"I'll get back to you about the memorial service. Confidentially, there's going to be an extensive autopsy. It could take a week."

"I understand," said President Matthews.

"For your information, Mona Pierce is staying at Justin House," Mylowe said. "If you wish to check on Rema's condition, you may call her."

Mylowe put down the phone. Once again, he searched the directory for the mortuary. After speaking with the owner, he made an appointment for the next day.

Melody Ann put her arm around him and kissed him on the cheek.

"That's the last of the calls," he said.

After fourteen days in the hospital, Rema returned to Justin House. This afternoon, comfortably seated in the den in her favorite blue velvet chair, she pleaded to Mona Pierce for mercy.

"Will you stop fussing over me? I need time to settle in. Notice, I'm able to drape this afghan around my shoulders with my other hand."

Mona walked toward the door. "I'll give Mrs. Do-It-Yourself some time to settle in."

"Oh! Come back," she murmured. "I just need to get accustomed to living outside the hospital environment. Please tell me about Emille's memorial service."

"I gave you the details when you were in the hospital."

"I want to hear them again."

"Well, after the service, Mylowe resumed his internship. George Whitetail and Melody Ann went to the airport."

Mona returned to the desk. "I know how much you wanted to be at the memorial service, but it wasn't possible. The service was held in Lambert Hall on the university campus. The Wexlor University String Quartet played while people were seated. All the chairs were filled. The faculty and Dr. Matthews sat on the raised platform at the front. Mylowe, Melody Ann, George and I sat in the first row. Emille's students sat behind us. Dr. Matthews and Pastor Morris Diltz conducted the service."

Rema interrupted Mona, "Morris Diltz, I've heard that name before."

"Mylowe told me Morris Diltz was one of Felic's students."

Rema's eyes filled with tears, "Felic thought the young man was an agnostic. He must have given up sitting on the fence. I wonder if Felic's teaching influenced the boy to become a minister."

Mona shook her head. "He gave a thoughtful message. Mylowe asked him to send you a copy of his sermon."

"Everyone has been so wonderful. Do you know if George contacted Emille's friend in Dayton to tell him of Emille's death?"

"No, but George gave me the address. Should you want to call Emille's friend, perhaps I could get the number from the operator."

"I don't want to call him. When I'm stronger, I'll go to Dayton and tell him about Emille's death. I can take him a memorial folder. After I go through Emille's possessions, I may take something of Emille's to him. Emille was making weekly trips to Dayton. It's odd that we haven't heard from his friend. You're certain there were no messages while you were at the hospital?"

"I'm positive," said Mona. "I checked the answering machine each night. He didn't call."

Rema gathered the afghan around her shoulders. "Have you told me about all of the memorial service?"

"Well," said Mona, "two of Emille's students retold the stories Emille had told them."

"Do you remember them?" Rema asked.

"Of course, their stories were prophetic and not easily forgotten. I have the copies in a folder." Mona found the folder on the desk and began to read.

"A student read, Buddha said, 'You can search throughout the universe for someone who is more deserving of your love and approval and that someone will not be found. You yourself as much as anyone deserve your love. Imagine how different your life would be today if you would have known how to love yourself before you loved another.'

"The student continued. 'It was man who invented the emotion of self-approval. He long ago learned that approving of oneself was vital to survival. Seldom do any of us extend the love word far enough to yell it from the rooftop and say, I love myself and I love life. But don't be disturbed if you've not done it. We remember all the things wrong with us and forget the good. Isn't having life better than not having it?'"

Rema closed her eyes and whispered, "Emille was an old, old soul reincarnated many times. In his current life, he was repaying a lot of bad karma."

Mona shook her head. "You're fortunate you only had to give an arm to help him repay his karma. It could have been an arm and a leg."

"You're being ridiculous. Just read me the second story."

Mona shuffled the papers in the folder and read aloud.

"In the 7th Century on the road to Damascus, the Black Plague met a Philistine. 'Where are you going?' asked the Philistine. 'To Damascus,' replied the Black Plague, 'to kill five thousand people.'

"A year later, returning from Damascus, the Philistine met the Black Plague. 'Aha!' said the Philistine, 'I hear fifty thousand died.'

"'Alas!' replied the Black Plague. 'That is true. Ten thousand died from the plague and forty thousand died from fear.'"

Mona leaned over the desk to answer the telephone.

"Yes, Pastor Diltz. Mrs. Swenson came home today. Yes, I'm certain she would welcome your visit on Friday afternoon. Thank you for calling."

Mona returned to her chair. "Pastor Morris Diltz is coming to see you on Friday afternoon at two o'clock."

"I don't feel like a pastoral visit. I just want to hide out for a while."

"And pity yourself?"

"I'm giving myself permission to feel. Feeling is part of life. I want to rest and restore. I let my son leave this world without me telling him how much I loved him. Don't tell me I'm going to recover from that in a short time."

"You're right. You do have an attitude."

"I owe it to myself to cry and heal. I intend to do it my way. Tears are healing. Each tear is a drop of remembrance."

Mona sighed and put the students' stories on the desk.

On Friday afternoon, Rema was apprehensive about Pastor Diltz's afternoon visit. She had been careful not to expose her guilt of failing Emille. She realized she had not provided him physical and emotional counseling. When she finally arrived to help him, it was too late.

Pastor Diltz came into the den.

"Good afternoon, Mrs. Swenson," he said. "I hope I'm not intruding. Mylowe asked me to bring you a copy of my remarks from Emille's memorial service. I did not visit you at the hospital because I was recovering from the flu."

Rema drew herself up and leaned forward in the chair. "Thank you for coming today," she whispered.

"Mrs. Pierce tells me you are coping with the decreased mobility in your left arm."

"Yes, the burden of it or the thought that it could become a burden is exasperating. When I think of my son and the burden he carried, I feel terrible guilt."

"You shouldn't blame yourself. Emille lost touch. His life was out of control. He was not physically or mentally able to ask for your help."

She bowed her head. "It's difficult to be a survivor. I've survived loss in the past. I just don't like the way it makes me feel."

Pastor Diltz smiled. "Professor Ort told me about guilt. He said no matter how guilty I might feel or how I know my guilty feelings make other people feel, I own those feelings. They're mine to experience. And, it's all right. But if you only live with what was, you miss the moments of what is. It's human to miss what you have had. Sometimes our memories of loss are not pleasant and the unpleasantness keeps rising to the surface. Even when we push them away, the unpleasant memories punish us."

"Before you came, I told Mona I had given myself permission to feel bad. Actually, I've discovered that my memory of Emille is of happy times. We shared life. Each troubling moment was offset with an enjoyable moment."

Pastor Diltz stood and held her hand. "Grieving must be taken a step at time."

"I know," she said.

He nodded knowingly, pressed his hand on her paralyzed arm and walked from the room.

43

CONSTERNATION

The voice on the public address system resounded around the walls of the doctors' lounge at Boston Memorial Hospital. Mylowe was studying a medical text book.

"Dr. Ort, Dr. Mylowe Ort," said the voice, "please dial extension 9103." He stood and dialed 9103 on the wall telephone. "This is Dr. Ort."

"Sir, Dr. Whitetail is calling from Miami."

"Please transfer the call to the doctors' lounge on 4B—extension 9146." Mylowe leaned against the wall until the telephone rang.

"Hi! George. What's up?"

"I received Emille's autopsy report from Dr. Patterson. Dr. Patterson's medical consults have also examined the tissues. They all agree. Emille was poisoned."

"Did they identify the poison?"

"No, they think it was administered by a small amount over a long period of time. They concluded it took five years or more to create the damage to the cells and tissue they found in Emille's body. They're stymied. The poison was not arsenic, cyanide or strychnine. They ruled out all household poisons, poisonous plants, fungi, snakes, spiders or other living things as well as medical and industrial poisons. They also tested for street drugs other than cocaine."

"Emille's autopsy has confirmed your initial suspicion about how Felic died," Mylowe said. "Dr. Patterson assumed the poison was administered by someone living in Justin House."

"In the autopsy narrative, Dr. Patterson stated his suspicions," replied George. "He's not giving up on his theory."

"Do we have any recourse to stop him from going on with his research? Are Rema and Maggie the primary suspects?"

"I think we have to bide our time."

"I agree. Rema is too fragile to cope with a coroner's inquiry."

"What about Maggie?"

"Maggie did not lace our food with poison or contaminate our water. If she were administrating poison, we'd all be dead. We always ate our meals family style. Our food was served from a common platter or bowl."

"Then I suggest we let Dr. Patterson find out the type of poison that was used and hope he doesn't instigate an inquest."

"Are you going to tell Mona about the autopsy?"

"Yes, but I won't mention the similarities between Emille's and Felic's autopsy reports."

"Then I'll only tell Rema about Emille's autopsy," Mylowe said.

"Are you coming to see me in Miami during your spring break?"

"Could you come to Justin House? I have a three-day break and I'd like to go to Des Moines to see Melody Ann. If Rema weren't so darn puritanical, Melody Ann and I could stay in my room at Justin House and I could spend more time there."

Thinking about his next words, George Whitetail grinned.

"Why don't you marry the girl? I'll stand up with you. The ceremony will take fifteen minutes and you can sleep together in Justin House or anywhere else. I'll bet if you asked Melody Ann, she'd be all for it."

"She wouldn't go for it."

"Why?"

"Melody Ann's heart is set on a big wedding."

George replied sternly. "I'm advising you to ask her."

Mylowe hung up the phone. For the last two months, he had been thinking about marrying Melody Ann. Now he had to reconsider his plan because of the probability of a coroner's inquest involving Rema and Maggie. The coming spring was not an appropriate time to have a wedding.

There was another problem. It was something he had not verbalized. Was it practical to marry? He knew nothing about his genetic pool. There might be unknown elements lurking in his body that would be passed on to his children.

Felic had vehemently discouraged him from delving into his background. After his high school graduation, Rema had promised to go with him to Miami and visit Dead Man's Alley, but it didn't happen.

In the middle of these thoughts, he realized he was being paged. He answered the page and rushed from the lounge to the Psychiatric Division.

At the same hour as Rema looked down from the upper hallway into the foyer of Justin House, Eben Justin's pendulum clock was chiming ten o'clock. She clutched the hand railing and thought of Emille. In the house in the Kendall area in Miami when Emille was two years old, he would run in circles when the clock chimed. She smiled remembering how Emille flapped his arms.

"I'm a burd," he yelled. "A burd wiff big whings."

The memory of his boyish voice brought tears. "Emille," Rema whispered. "Dear, sweet Emille. I'm so sorry." Struggling to control her emotions, she hoped Emille would forgive her for not rescuing him from his torturous lifestyle.

Still, Emille's personality differed from his natal horoscope. Over the years while he was living with her in Justin House, she delineated the positions of the planets many times looking for her miscalculation. Why didn't his charts show he was bipolar, a drug addict and self-centered? Was it her error?

She dreaded the oncoming painful, tiresome months of physical therapy. When Dr. Granger forecast there was a remote possibility she would regain only partial use of her left arm, she had decided to accept the prognosis and go on with her life. She had insisted Mona return to Miami to help her daughter with a new baby.

"I'll be fine," she said. "Dr. Matthews suggested I consider employing a student from the university to be my companion and help me around the house. He said her name is Eve Potter."

For all the reasons she could think of, Mona did not want to leave Rema. "What do you know about Eve Potter?" she asked.

"I know she was a student in Emille's language class. She's from Adrian, Michigan, and the youngest of six children. Her father is a watchmaker and her mother a church organist."

"Are you sure you want to hire a stranger to live with you? You really need me to stay."

"I'm a fighter," Rema had replied. "One of these days, I'm going to arise up from this pile of ashes and be stronger than before."

"Okay," Mona said. "I'll go back to Miami, but if Eve Potter isn't able to stay with you, I hope you don't suffocate in those ashes."

Rema hugged her. "If I need you, I'll call. You have my solemn promise."

Remembering how she had convinced Mona to go home, Rema turned away from the upstairs railing and walked down the stairs to answer the doorbell.

"Hello, Mrs. Swenson, I'm Eve Potter."

"Yes, Dr. Matthews called to say you were coming today. Please come in."

Rema guided Eve toward the den. When they were settled into the blue velvet chairs in front of the fireplace, Eve said, "You seem surprised. Didn't Dr. Matthews tell you I was not a young co-ed?"

"No, your age was not mentioned. I did assume you were younger. Dr. Matthews said you were living in one of the dormitories on campus."

"Well, I don't fit in the dorm very well. My frown lines and wrinkles are proof of that."

"Dr. Matthews said you were a musician. You play the piano."

"Yes, after my divorce three years ago, I decided to get an education and teach music."

"You knew my son, Emille?"

"Yes, I was in his French class."

"As you can see, Justin House is too large for one person. These days I'm the one person living here. I assume you know about my injury. As you can imagine, there are many things I cannot do. I'm unable to drive, or put wood on the fire, catch my cat when she's being rambunctious, open my mail, be productive at the computer, cook or wash dishes. That sums it all up. I have six months of physical therapy coming up at Cira Memorial and my business to run."

Behind sea green eyes that reminded Rema of the tantalizing hue of the water in the Gulf Stream, Eve Potter nodded knowingly. Rema saw an aura of pale blue emanating around Eve's body that intensified to a deeper blue around her neck and head. Her handsome face was pink except for deep black, meticulously arched brows. From the brows, Rema knew Eve Potter took extreme care about small details.

"Do you have children?" Rema asked.

"One daughter. She died five years ago."

"I'm sorry. Was she ill?"

"She had epilepsy from birth. She lived five years. Dr. Matthews said you have a piano."

Rema reacted quickly and understood Eve's effort to move the conversation to another subject. "Yes, it's in the living room near the front door. How many hours do you practice each day?"

"One hour. Mostly I compose tunes and write lyrics for children."

"What a wonderful endeavor." Rema walked toward the desk. Eve's eyes followed her.

"Would you like to see the rest of the house?"

Eve nodded and followed Rema into the foyer. In the next thirty minutes as they toured the house, Rema was aware that Dr. Matthews had selected Eve Potter with great care. Eve, like Rema, was her own person. Giving the impression that no task would go uncompleted, she was queenly, yet her personality was divinely understated.

In the living room, Eve sat at the small baby grand and played Dvorak's Humoresque. Rema listened with great interest.

"You have exceptional technique. I would like to hear one of your compositions." Rema noted a twinkle in Eve's eyes and realized Eve was passionate about becoming a composer.

They returned to the den. Neither woman was questioning their compatibility. "Could you be my companion?" Rema asked.

"I'd like to try. My schedule will fit in with your requirements. It's such a lovely house."

"When can you begin?"

"It will take me a day or two to cart all my things from the dorm."

"You're welcome to invite your friends here," Rema said. "If we write out a weekly schedule, it will keep us aware of our projects."

Eve nodded. "I don't have many close friends at the university. My friends are in Adrian, Michigan."

44

DISCOVERY

After three weeks, Rema was grateful for Eve's companionship. With her encouragement, Rema carried her arm in a more supportive sling and for three days a week she went to work at the Libra Center. On those days, she also went to Cira Memorial for therapy.

One afternoon when Rema was at home and Eve was playing the piano, Maggie, talking to herself, trudged up the circular stairs to Rema's bedroom. "That woman can really play that piana," she said. "It's good to have some music floating around the house."

On the second floor, Maggie looked for Rema inside her bedroom.

"Where are you, Miss Rema?" Maggie hollered. "I'm going home now. Lordy! Lordy! You've been upstairs all day."

"I'm in Emille's room," Rema said. "I've been sorting through his papers."

Maggie stood at Emille's bedroom door.

"Miss Mona wants you to call her."

"Thank you, Maggie. I'll call her from my sitting room."

Rema went into her room and began to dial the telephone when the receiver fell to the floor. "Dumbo," she whispered. "You must learn to use the telephone with one hand. First, you take the receiver from the cradle, lay it on the table, dial the number and then pick up the receiver. There, now wasn't that simple?"

"What did you say?" Mona shouted into her telephone.

"I was just talking to myself," replied Rema.

"What are you doing? Maggie said she hadn't seen you all day."

"I've been in Emille's room sorting through his belongings. I found something very strange."

"Strange, what kind of strange?"

"Tucked inside his backpack, there was a notebook where Emille had listed the titles of twenty-three books. All were rare or first editions. There was also a manual with information about first editions."

"What kind of information?"

"The title of the rare book, the author, the year it was published, the publisher and its current value. Emille must have been collecting first editions and rare books."

"Did you find any of those books in his room or office?"

"No, the university delivered the contents from his office yesterday. I've been through all the boxes. There weren't any rare books."

"Did Emille have a will?"

"I haven't found a will among his papers."

"Did you have his power of attorney?"

"No, there are no legal papers or checkbook."

"How did he pay his bills?"

"I don't know."

"Could his legal papers be in Dayton at his friend's house?"

"I know he used the Dayton address to get medication from the Dayton clinic. But, let me tell you more about the list of books. I recognized some of the authors: James Fenimore Cooper, Dickens, Mark Twain, Thoreau and a signed copy of Atlas Shrugged by Ayn Rand dated 1957. It was the 10th anniversary edition valued at $850. Emille has added the total value of the twenty-three first editions at $31,230."

"What are some of the other titles?"

"Life on the Mississippi dated 1883 by Mark Twain, The Prince and the Pauper dated 1882 valued at $1,050, The Life and Adventures of Nicholas Nickleby by Dickens dated 1839 valued at $900, and The Main Woods dated 1864 by Henry David Thoreau valued at $1,750."

"Some of those are first editions. Are the owners' names listed in the manual?"

"I'll look," said Rema. Seconds later, she groaned.

"What have you found?"

"Eben Justin is listed as the owner of Thoreau's books valued at $1,750."

"Do you know what this means?"

"Could the books on Emille's list belong to Eben Justin? Where are they?"

Together, they yelled, "In Eben's Tower."

"Oh! My God," Mona yelled. "Emille found Eben Justin's rare books. Rema, you have to go up to Eben's Tower and find those books."

"I've only been in the tower two times."

"Were there books there?"

"Yes, the shelves around all the walls were filled with books. Books were stacked on the floor. The room smelled like a mortuary—sweet, rancid and dead."

"Did Felic tell you there were valuable books in the tower?"

"No, maybe he didn't know. Do you remember when I told you about Felic's estate?"

"Yes, you said Felic had written the will himself."

"I asked the lawyer about the total dollar amount of the estate because I thought the total was higher than the assets. Felic always acted as if we were living from paycheck to paycheck. Before he died, he had made an appointment to see his lawyer."

"Did the lawyer give you a list of Felic's assets?"

Rema shivered. "I didn't ask for a listing of assets. The will stated that Mylowe was the beneficiary. Until Mylowe was twenty-one, the estate was controlled by the lawyer."

Mona's curiosity pressured her to ask more questions.

"When Felic was making a second will, wasn't he angry with Mylowe? Hadn't he threatened to send Mylowe away?"

Another shiver ran through Rema.

"Do you suppose he was writing Mylowe out of his will and died before he could meet with the lawyer?"

"You won't know unless you find the second will. Where did Felic keep his important papers?"

"I've been through the entire house and the papers from his office at the university. I didn't find it."

Rema hung up the telephone and studied Emille's list of rare books. There were notations in pencil and different colored ink pens indicating the list had been compiled at various times. Although her only recourse was to find Felic's new will, if he had written one, she could not divert her attention from the list of rare books.

Why would Emille make a list of Eben Justin's books? If Emille's consumption of a drug required more money than his salary, he would have looked for another source of money. On the other hand, he had recently purchased a new Corvette.

She shook her head to clear her thoughts. She hated the thought of going to Eben's Tower. Inside her bedroom closet as she pushed the clothing away, the hangers parted at a pair of Felic's blue cargo pants. She stared at them.

Eight years ago, when she sent Felic's clothing to the Salvation Army, she had not included the cargo pants. Stooping down to look under the hanging clothing, she saw a leather case in the back corner.

What is it? How did it get in the closet? Who had put it there?

She grabbed a wire clothes hanger, dropped to her knees and pulled the case toward her. Sitting beside it, she tried the locks. All the top locks were locked. In a fit of anger, she shoved the case on its side. Until now, what was a bad day had turned into a monster. After finding Emille's list of rare books and now having to deal with the locked briefcase, she cradled her useless arm and yelled, "Damn, Damn, Damn."

She sat quietly before pushing her body across the floor toward Felic's night table. Behind notepads and scarves, she found a ring of keys and selected the smallest key. Nodding with the feeling that her search was about to end, she waddled on her knees across the room, sat the briefcase upright and put the tiny key in the locks. The locks opened.

Inside were six folders. Labeled in Felic's handwriting on three of the folders were: 7/8/86, North Carolina; 7/9/86, Coral Gables; 7/10/86, Tallahassee. The dates were from his final lecture tour. The labels on other folders were typewritten: Additional Remarks, Expense Vouchers and Personal.

Inside the personal folder were three sealed envelopes. In Felic's handwriting, one was addressed to Martin Walsh, the attorney. The other was addressed to Mylowe. She opened the third envelope, read one page, returned it to the envelope and put it aside.

Then she read the note Felic had written to Martin Walsh.

Martin,

As you requested, enclosed is the list of the rare books currently in my possession. They are valued at $51,223. Please note that the value of these books is included in the asset section of my Last Will and Testimony. Please include this list in my file.

Felic

Rema counted forty seven books on the list and was relieved to know Felic had not written a new will. She slumped wearily in a bedroom chair and opened the second envelope entitled "Mylowe."

Inside a page of folded paper was a long pink ribbon streaked with dirt. On the paper in Felic's handwriting was Mylowe's birth date, August 21, 1970. Her heart raced. Why would Felic keep a piece of dirty ribbon in his briefcase? Had he put the briefcase in the bedroom closet? Had he lied to her about how he found Mylowe? Did Felic know Mylowe's mother? Was Felic Mylowe's biological father?

She leaned her head against the back of the chair. The three envelopes in Felic's briefcase had flooded her mind with questions. Could the mystery of the whereabouts of the rare books be solved? To whom did the dirt-covered pink ribbon belong? She needed to know.

Finding the list of rare books in Emille's room and then discovering the contents in Felic's briefcase had paralyzed Rema's emotions. Not only had the day been ruined, the enthusiasm she had experienced before breakfast was completely gone away. She went downstairs to wait in the den until Eve came back from an afternoon class. When she heard Eve's key in the front door, she called to her.

"Eve, I'm in the den. Would you please come in?"

Shivering from the cold, Eve appeared in the doorway and moved across the den to stand by the fireplace. "The March wind goes right through me," Eve said. "I hope spring comes early."

Rema leaned forward in her chair. "What are your plans for the rest of the day?"

"Not too much. A little tune for some lyrics I've written has been buzzing around in my head. I'd like to spend some time with it."

"Would you go with me to Eben's Tower?"

"Yes, of course. Why are you sounding so mysterious?"

"I didn't realize that I was. It's just that I despise going near the tower. A situation came up while I was going through Emille's things. I need to find out if there are some rare books stored in the tower."

Eve looked at her watch. "It's three o'clock. We should go to the tower before it gets dark."

"Good thought. I'll get the key to the gate."

Eve watched Rema take a key from the desk drawer. "Wow!" she whispered, "that key is the kind used in horror movies."

Rema grinned. "Eben Justin was totally rigid. The large iron gate to guard the entrance to his tower and this oversize key matched his character. After all, he was known to have had two wives and fourteen children."

"I believe you're saying Eben was so detailed in his approach to things, he was a pain in the ass."

"Exactly. I think if we're going to find any rare books in Eben's Tower, we should begin to think like Eben."

"Okay. Then the books would be under lock and key in a fireproof vault. Well, let's go for it."

Rema folded the list of rare books from Felic's briefcase, put it in her jacket pocket and followed Eve across the foyer. The late afternoon sun, shimmering through the grove of maple trees, cast long, quivering shadows over the foyer floor.

The women entered the pantry together. "Is the tower a scary place?" Eve asked.

"I wouldn't say it's scary, but it's not my favorite room in the house. Strangely enough, every man who has ever lived in Justin House has spent hours in the tower. I guess they considered the tower a refuge."

Eve opened the doors to the narrow stairway leading to the tower and stepped aside to allow Rema to begin the climb. Rema pulled herself by grasping the hand railing. At the top of the stairs, she shoved the flat black key into the gate's lock. When she turned it, the key grated against the metal tumbler.

"That lock could use some WD-40," Eve said.

Rema pulled the heavy iron gate aside and turned the doorknob on the tower door. As the door opened, they stood side by side in the open doorway peering into the dusky, dark tower. There was a somber ray of light perched on the edge of the small glass transom in the ceiling.

"This place would make a great set for a horror movie," Eve whispered. "It smells as if nothing alive was ever in here."

"It has a strange energy," Rema replied. "Without any natural light, it seems to have a magnetic pull that draws the men in Justin House to stay here for hours."

"I certainly don't feel drawn to the room, do you? It's not much bigger than a large dog house." Eve laughed at her assessment. "Oops!" she joked, "maybe it was the family dog house."

Rema waved her hand at the shelved walls filled with books. "Dogs don't read," she replied.

Eve touched the lamp on the desk. "This is a weird lamp."

"It operates by batteries And is the most modern updated item in this room. I assume Eben Justin used a kerosene lamp."

Rema reached under the shade and snapped the lamp on. It was an ugly piece of metal, painted the same shade of green as a well-know farm tractor. The stem was short and attached to an oblong base.

When Rema sat down on the desk chair, the metal shade was as high as her shoulder. She leaned to look under the shade and saw that the lamp was devouring the light.

She stared at the desk. It was old and made of hand-hewn vintage mahogany. She moved her hands along its edge and leaned down to look under it. Below were intricately-carved legs that ended on huge eagle talons that hungrily grasped oversized glass balls.

She sat up and pulled the drawers open.

"Whew! These drawers smell terrible. Come look. Do you see any folders inside?"

Eve squatted to peer into the back corners of the drawers.

"Are you looking for some documents?"

"I was hoping to find a notebook. I believe there are forty-seven rare books somewhere in this room."

Eve walked to the other side of the room and began pulling books aside and tapping her knuckles against the back of the shelves.

"If we find a safe, we'll still need to find a key to open it."

She took two books from the shelf.

"These are interesting books. Listen to the titles. <u>A Treatise on Gonorrhea Virlulenta and Lues Venera</u> published in 1795, and <u>Narrative of a Journey from Herant to Khiva, Moscow and St. Petersburg during the last Russian Invasion of Khiva</u> published in 1843. Are these titles on the list?"

"No," Rema said, knocking on another small strip of wood on the wall. "Maybe there's a secret panel?"

"Hey!" Eve yelled. "There's loose wood on the wall over here. It's behind this fence post."

"A fence post?"

"Well, it looks like some kind of post. It's planted in volcanic ash."

"Be careful. There may be spiders behind the wood wall."

Eve's shrieked. "I found something! There's a black metal cabinet behind this wall. The lock is dangling on the latch. The lock has been cut."

Rema hurried to the wall and lifted the broken lock from the latch. The door swung open. The cabinet was empty except for three manuals on the lower shelf. Stepping back, Rema's bandaged arm nudged against the fence post.

"Ouch!" she whispered.

Eve tried to push the large urn holding the fence post out of the way.

"The urn is stuck to the floor. This thing looks like a sawed-off telephone pole."

"It is strange. But remember, Eben Justice was strange."

"The post is covered with goo," Eve whispered.

"Maybe it's painted with creosote."

"Whatever," Eve exclaimed. "This must be one of Eben Justin's queer inventions."

Rema swiped her finger along the post. "This stuff feels like a gummy sap."

Eve bent over it. "It doesn't have an odor. How could anything live in this room?"

Rema shook her head and turned to examine the door on the metal cabinet. "This cabinet was built by MetalSmith in Chicago, Illinois. Our assumptions were correct. It is fireproof."

"Why is the cabinet empty?"

Rema shook her head. "The rare books could have been stored in the cabinet."

"Maybe the rare books were moved from the fireproof case and put on the shelves after the lock was broken."

Rema shook her head. "I don't think that's what happened."

Eve moved toward the door.

"We could use some light. Is there a flashlight downstairs?"

"There's a flashlight in the middle drawer left of the kitchen sink. Bring some matches and two of those scented candles from the pantry."

After Eve had gone, Rema took the manuals from the bottom shelf of the fireproof cabinet. They were covered with mold. She wiped her hand on her jeans and dismissed the thought that the manuals might give a clue to the disappearances of the rare books. She replaced the manuals when a stream of light filtered from the stairway into the room. Eve entered clutching candleholders and candles.

After lighting the candles, Rema gave Eve Felic's list. "These are the rare books we're searching for."

Eve read the list. "You use the flashlight," she said. "I'll carry a candle."

Eve tapped on the walls behind the entire collection of books. After an hour without finding a rare book, Rema called off the search. They snuffed out the candles, turned off the monster green lamp, locked the iron gate and pointed the flashlight down the stair steps.

By the kitchen clock, it was 7:30 p.m. Rema was exhausted. It was the kind of fatigue that attacks the inner senses of the heart when suspicion overwhelms logic. She didn't want to eat and suggested that Eve fix dinner for herself. She went to her room and collapsed on the bed.

The next morning she dialed Mona's number.

"Where in the hell have you been?" Mona yelled. "I've been waiting since yesterday afternoon to hear from you. Did you find the rare books in Eben's Tower?"

Rema leaned back on the chaise lounge and reminded herself that, Mona, petite and physically fragile, invoked the vocabulary of a truck driver. She paused before replying, and then told Mona about finding the list of rare books and the dirty pink hair ribbon in Felic's briefcase. She described the search of Eben's Tower as futile and mentioned the broken lock hanging on the fireproof cabinet.

Mona listened without commenting.

"Have you decided to tell Mylowe about the pink ribbon? It might be a clue to his genetic background."

"It would be a very slim clue."

"Yes, but Mylowe is really intense about finding his biological parents."

"Is that the reason he hasn't married Melody Ann?" Rema asked.

"It must be. But let's talk about Emille. What do you think happened to the rare books?"

"My worst suspicion is that Emille sold them for drug money."

Mona held her lips closed. This wasn't the time to tell Rema she also suspected Emille had taken cash from the Libra Center. Instead she asked, "Are you managing to get through all of this?"

"I'm holding up. Surviving Emille's death is making me feel old. Grief has a way of holding me in its ugly grip."

Rema realized after the discoveries she made the day before, she had to confront her suspicions concerning Emille and the disappearance of the rare books.

A recurring thought trounced about in Rema's brain.

When Emille lived with me at Justin House for eight years, why didn't his personality reflect or match more accurately to his natal horoscope, progressions or transits?

Finding the pink ribbon in Felic's old briefcase had turned into another extraordinary mystery. She knew more discussions and speculations would increase her fears.

"Are you still there?" Mona asked. "I thought you hung up."

"I'm still here."

"What are you going to do about the pink ribbon?"

"I'm wondering if Felic knew Mylowe's mother. Is the boy I raised Felic's biological son?"

"Whoa!" Mona yelled. "You'd better shut down the question machine. Those questions will drive you crazy."

"I know. But every situation within itself harbors the seeds of its own solution. I've decided to look for the seeds."

"Where are you going to begin?"

"In Dayton, Ohio."

"Are you going to the clinic where Emille was treated?"

"Yes, but I also plan to visit Emille's good friend in Dayton."

45

THE QUEST

Mona's questions about Emille's integrity convinced Rema it was important to visit Emille's friend in Dayton. From this friend she would get enough information to put aside her suspicions about Emille's theft of the rare books.

Rema looked wistfully at Emille's photograph. The grieving process was deeper than before. Since Felic's death, the thrill of life had gone from her. Along with the grief she felt for Emille, she grieved the loss of her sensitivity and the boundless enthusiasm that gave it meaning. It wasn't smart to grow dull and lose the excitement of living. Instead, she should allow her wisdom to come alive and push away the emptiness surrounding her.

The telephone rang. It was Mylowe.

"Hi!" he began. "I had a few minutes this morning. How are you?"

"I'm improving," she replied. "I've been scolding myself for taking so long to heal. Why are you calling so early?"

"You must realize how short our family grapevine is. I'm calling to ask you about what happened yesterday. Mona told George about Emille and the missing rare books. She said something else happened, but wouldn't explain it."

Rema knew the grapevine was always in good working order. However, Mona had not told George about the pink ribbon. When she was silent, Mylowe said, "Whatever it is, you can tell me."

Rema wasn't prepared to tell Mylowe there were two lists of old books. Mylowe only knew about the disappearance of twenty-three books on Emille's list, but on Felic's list, there were twenty-four additional rare books. Was it time to admit to Mylowe she was the reason Emille was living in Justin House and therefore she was responsible for the loss of a portion of his heritance?

She replied quietly. "After discovering Emille's list, I found another list of rare books in Felic's briefcase. It was in an envelope addressed to Felic's attorney, Martin Walsh."

"Did you take it to the attorney?"

"No, I opened the envelope. Replying to the lawyer's request, Felic had listed forty-seven rare books and stated the list was to verify the assets stated in his will."

"Mona said you did not find the books in the tower."

"The books are not there. The lock on a fireproof cabinet had been cut. The cabinet was empty. Eve and I searched through all the shelves in the tower."

"Do you believe Emille sold them to buy cocaine?"

"Before I'll swear to that, Eve and I are going to Dayton to visit Emille's friend."

"Do you have the address in Dayton?"

"Yes."

"When are you going?"

"On Saturday. I also found a second sealed envelope in the briefcase. Inside was a dirty pink hair ribbon folded in a sheet of paper. Felic had written August 21, 1970, beside it."

"That's my birthday. What does a ribbon have to do with my birthday?"

"It makes me think Felic might have known your mother. The ribbon is stained with streaks of dirt. I suspect it was used to tie up a woman's hair."

"Why would Felic keep my mother's identity a secret?"

"I'm certain he had his reasons."

"It wasn't fair to me no matter how it might have affected him. Do you think the ribbon might be a clue to find my mother?"

"Where would you begin?"

"I'd go to Miami to Dead Man's Alley."

"The area might be renovated or gone. It's been twenty-five years."

Mylowe paused. "Sorry," he said, "I'm being paged. I have to go. I hope your trip to Dayton is successful."

Rema hung up the phone and lay back to rest. Each hour had presented a new set of problems. She found it difficult to carry the spirit of a child into old-age. The drain-off of natural energy in her physical body and the dashed hopes and disappointments had all conspired to steal her zeal for life.

Emille's death made her realize that foreordained events take precedent over any prediction she could postulate from studying the positions of the planets. Although her knowledge of astrology gave her special insight into people, she was continually frustrated with her inability to match Emille's natal horoscope to his personality.

She took a quantum leap when she decided to delve into the reasons it was important to meet Emille's friend in Dayton. Would life give her another set of tests? Her life was already similar to the Greek tragedies. Those tragedies were all versions of the same tragedy. She wiped tears from her eyes and told herself it was a new morning, with new challenges and a new set of choices.

46

DAYTON, OHIO

On Saturday morning at 10:15 a.m., Rema and Eve arrived at the city limits of Dayton, Ohio. Eve had made overnight accommodations at a Holiday Inn for that evening. Today, they would visit Emille's friend. Tomorrow, before driving back to Wexlor, they would meet with the director of the Rehabilitation Clinic on Water Street. Using a city map, Rema directed Eve to 1961 Kahler Drive. Eve turned the car in the narrow driveway.

The houses on Kahler Drive were small and constructed of cement blocks. The small porches at the front of the houses were aligned and resembled in rows like reinforced concrete bunkers. There were no garages. Motorcycles, motor homes and small boats on trailers were parked in driveways and on the crew-cut lawns. Automobiles lined the curbs on both sides of the street. It was apparent the area once was World War II housing developed for Air Force personnel stationed at Wright-Patterson Field.

Standing near the front door of the house numbered 1961, Rema noticed parts of the concrete walk were missing. Tall, leftover summer weeds, bent and frozen, covered the sloping front door steps. Broken sprigs of neglected ornamental shrubbery hung helplessly waiting for the warmth of the spring sun. A vine of ivy, rigid from the cold wind, clung vicariously to a sagging drainpipe.

The front of the house was devoid of paint. The gray cement of the original block construction was streaked with portraits of black mold. The storm door was broken, the metal screen kicked in by an angry boot.

Eve knocked three times before a woman's voice from inside advised them to come to the side door. Rema and Eve looked inquiringly at each other as they walked up the driveway. They were met by a woman, an inch short of six feet tall with generous hips and 44D floppy breasts. She was wearing hospital blue scrubs.

"I'm sorry to make you walk through the snow," she said in a low voice. "I had to shovel a path this morning to get into the house. I can't get the front door open. Are you relatives of my patient?"

Rema nodded. The woman led them into a small bedroom.

"I'll leave you alone with him," she whispered. "He's not very good today. He has a lot of pain. This often happens when life is coming to the end. He's not overly sedated. He should enjoy visitors. You're the first. I'll be in the kitchen."

The man in the hospital bed motioned to Rema. She hesitated to walk to the bedside. Was her presence intruding on the life of a dying man? Could she live the rest of her life without answers to her suspicions about Emille?

As she moved toward the bed, he whispered, "You should always ask yourself what is the right thing to do. If what you do isn't the right thing for you, then it is the wrong thing. Nothing wrong ever turns out right."

She gasped, "My husband always said that."

"I know," he said.

She studied his thin yellow face.

"John?" she whispered.

"Yes," he said. "I thought you'd be too late."

Eve pushed a chair toward Rema and helped her sit down. Rema sunk into the chair as if wounded by an invisible weapon. She held onto the bed railing like a drowning swimmer in a tidal wave.

"Emille told me you were dead," she whispered. "He said you died of a heart attack in Miami. That was eight years ago."

"I told him to tell you that story."

"Why?"

"Because I didn't want to be Noah Mason, the parole officer, anymore. I wanted to be John Swenson. I wanted everyone to think Noah Mason was dead and gone."

Rema sat quietly remembering the day eight years ago when she discovered Noah Mason was her husband, John Swenson, a man who had been pronounced dead by a Miami court nearly twenty years before.

He ignored her reaction and spoke haltingly. "I began to think that Noah Mason was fundamentally an unlovable person. I didn't want to fade away into old age longing for things I couldn't bring myself to define. I kept remembering those years with you. Have you thought about our house in Miami? In those years, after I came home from the war, nothing went well. You and I were married but we lived together as strangers. Our son was more your son than my son. I admit I was jealous. Actually I was insanely jealous."

She turned away not wanting to look at his deep-set unblinking eyes.

He's a beast, she thought. *Bad behavior, calloused actions, thoughtless remarks and betrayal, he's done them all. Emille said John never told the truth. It's not likely he'll tell me the truth on his deathbed.*

She closed her eyes. When she opened them, his eyes were still staring at her.

"You're so beautiful," he whispered, and raised his hand. "I want to touch your hair again. I've dreamed of touching your hair."

Rema leaned forward. Although weakened and angry, she closed her eyes as he stroked her hair. He didn't seem to care that her hair was streaked with gray. She only knew he was memorizing the moment.

"How's your shoulder?" he asked. "The newspaper said you were wounded."

"You know about the shooting?"

"Yes, I know."

"Then you know Emille is dead."

"I only know that our Emille, the son carrying our genes, drowned in Cuba two years after I took him from Miami. His death was my punishment for stealing him from you."

Rema clutched the bed railing and gasped. Eve put her hand on Rema's shoulder and knew any words she could offer would be superfluous. For the moment, her job was to help Rema get through this crazed man's personal vendetta.

Rema rallied and leaned toward him silently vowing not to leave his bedside until all her questions were answered.

Shaking the bed railing, she said, "You're a liar."

He winked at her. "I wanted you to finally feel the pain and suffering I felt when you took my son away from me."

"I didn't take your son from you. He was a growing boy and was nurtured by both of us."

"You stole his love. I took him from you so he would only love me."

Rema felt she had no more tears to shed, but a warm liquid was dropping on her cheeks. She drew a deep breath.

"You're telling me it wasn't our Emille who lived in my house for eight years? You planned it? Why would you want to arrange something so cruel?"

Eve squeezed Rema's shoulder. Rema nodded to let Eve know she was coping with the situation.

"Who was that man? What was his name?"

John raised his head from the pillow. His unblinking yellow eyes stared at her.

"His name was Paul Moore, a well-educated thief with a police record. He was a beggar on horseback willing to do anything for money. When I read the reports of his death in the newspaper, I knew you would find me."

John's body shook violently.

Eve ran to the kitchen and returned with the nurse. Rema and Eve went into the living room and waited. "This is unbelievable," Eve said. "Do you think we ought to go?"

Rema wiped her eyes and shook her head.

"I'm not going until he answers all my questions."

"I don't know how you are able to take all this," said Eve. "Look! I'm shaking and I'm not involved."

"I know it will take stamina and endurance if I am to survive my karma with this terrible man. Maybe I won't survive his vengeance, but at this moment, I'm very angry. The dying man in the next room has taken the last pound of flesh from me."

Eve took Rema's hand and looked into her eyes. "I think you should be cautious. Until he answers your questions, he's holding all the cards. There's devil in his eyes. He's enjoying your reaction much too much."

Rema knew Eve was correct in assuming there was more evil to come.

John's nurse came into the room. "He's better now. He wants you to go back in."

The two women stood up. As Rema passed in front of her, Eve whispered, "Be renewed in the spirit of your mind; Ephesians 4:23."

Rema resumed her place by John's bedside exploring all her emotions of death and a past love. Was this a dream or a horrible nightmare dredged up from the deep recess of her subconscious? She wanted it to end.

John spoke first.

"Sorry about the shaking spell. I've not had enough medication today. All's well now. Where were we? Oh, yes, you were about to ask me how I found Paul Moore to impersonate Emille. Well, for three years after I returned from Cuba, I tried to find you, but your trail was cold." He looked at the ceiling and grinned. "Then I received some heavenly help."

Eve recognized John's grin was more sinister than before. She stepped closer to Rema and again squeezed her shoulder. Rema watched his eyes and realized he was having fun with her. Rema touched Eve's hand to let her know she understood his motives.

John continued to speak.

"One afternoon, I attended a conference in Coral Gables and during lunch heard a bail bondsman from Miami talking about an astrologer who he believed had saved his life. The bondsman's name was Woodrow Wilson. Everyone called him Pinchey. I took time to learn the astrologer's name. It was Rema Swenson.

"Later in that year, when I met Paul Moore and became his parole officer, the idea was born. Paul was the age Emille would have been if Emille lived. His features were similar to Emille's. I changed Paul's records and named him Pedro Swenson. When I listed you as his mother, the trap was set."

John began to choke, but caught his breath. "It was a divine plan, straight from wherever great plans are created. Old, nosey Pinchey Wilson did just what he was supposed to do. He called you." John choked again.

Rema continued the story. "Pinchey did not know where I was. He found me through a friend in Miami. Pinchey had seen our names listed on Pedro Swenson's police record and called to say he believed Emille was alive and living in Miami."

"Good ol' Pinchey. I knew he'd set up the meeting with Emille. I counted on your motherly love to bring you back to Miami."

Rema's tone was belligerent and explosive. "Pinchey only made the initial underground contact. He was emphatic about staying out of the meeting arrangements."

Remembering the arranged meeting, Rema paused. "So," she exclaimed, "at the meeting with Emille in Everglades Park when he dropped the pocket size magnifying glass, I suppose that was a part of the plan."

"Yes, I had found you. My search was over. All I had to do was to wait for the perfect time."

"A perfect time for what?"

"To make you suffer. For years, I had been searching for a way to get back at you. I wanted you to feel the loss of your son. Did you feel the loss?"

Rema lowered her head.

His voice was weak.

"One day the divine took over again. I read in the newspaper that Felic Ort, your professor, had died suddenly in Tallahassee. I got a second chance. It was time for Emille to go home to be with his grieving mother."

John choked again. Rema closed her eyes and waited until he was able to breathe again.

"I suppose you coached Paul to tell me about my special chocolate cookies and remind me that I called mosquitoes 'skeeters.'"

"More than those things, Paul contrived his own scam while he was your dutiful son."

"A scam?"

"He managed to lighten the cash box at the Libra Center until your midget friend, Mona Pierce, took control of it. But before she caught on to his scam, he had gleaned a hefty $5,000."

"Was stealing money a part of your vindictiveness against me?"

"No, I hadn't thought of taking money. That was part of Paul's scam."

Eve watched Rema's face turn pink, not quite crimson, but just a medium shade of red. She decided Rema was swallowing her angry words instead of spitting them out. She needed to do something, but it wasn't her place to offer unsolicited advice such as driving a stake through John's heart.

"You're being quiet," John said.

"I was thinking how evil you are," Rema said. "If I were stronger and had two hands, I'd hit you in the gut."

Eve put her hand on Rema's shoulder. Rema shrugged her hand away.

"You're angry," he said. "I wanted you to be devastated, full of grief and crying your eyes out. I was looking forward to telling you about Paul Moore."

"Sadly, I went through all those emotions the first time you took Emille away. The second time when Emille walked away from me at Everglades Park, I was hurt but I survived. And yes, I've been grieving for Emille, I mean Paul. After all, he lived in my home as my son. He was a tormented soul. Someday I would like to know what caused him to go so far off center."

John turned his head choking and gasping to breathe. Rema sat statue still and waited. When he was able to speak he said, "I have more to tell you."

"Is it about the rare books Paul Moore took from Eben's Tower?" she asked.

"You know about the books? You're taking away all my fun."

"Yes, I found a list of them in Emille's room. I know you're going to tell me he took them and sold them to buy cocaine."

"You're partly right. I sold twenty-three of them. The other twenty-four are in my closet. The cancer eating my liver took over before I could find buyers for them."

"Were you planning to return those books to me?"

"I hadn't decided until I saw you today."

"Well, are you giving them back? They don't belong to me. They belong to Mylowe Ort. They are part of his estate."

"Sure, go ahead and take them. Paul and I planned to take you for $80,000. But what the hell, neither Paul nor I need money anymore. He's dead and I'll be dead in a week."

"What did you get for the books?"

"$42,000. I gave Paul two-thirds. He bought a Corvette and cocaine with his share."

Rema ignored his comment and walked to the half-open closet door.

"Are all the books in these two duffle bags?"

"There's twenty-three. You'll have to trust me on that."

Rema shook her head. "I don't trust anything you say." She turned to Eve. "Make sure you count them. Can you drag them to the car?"

Eve nodded, put on her coat and waffled the two bags back and forth through the doorway. Rema waited until she heard Eve talking to the nurse. When the back door closed, she returned to John's bedside.

Anger was overtaking her. She looked around for something to throw at the wall above his head. She wanted to throw something that would be loud enough to make him cringe.

She considered throwing the pitcher of water sitting on the night stand but decided not to give in to her anger. She forced herself to look at him. His unblinking eyes watched her hating him. She turned and walked from the room.

47

ACCEPTANCE

Eve stopped at a payphone and canceled the overnight reservations at Holiday Inn and drove directly to Justin House. After parking the car at the back entrance to Justin House, she pulled the duffle bags holding the rare books into the kitchen. She hurried into the den and started a fire in the fireplace, put the kettle on, scrounged through the pantry for something nutritional for dinner and helped Rema clean the cat box.

"Why don't you get into a warm robe and slippers?" she said to Rema. "We'll have tea around the fireplace. I'll put together something to eat. I think there's a casserole of scalloped chicken in the freezer. It will be delicious with a warm roll."

Rema went upstairs, stood in Emille's room and knew her grief had not gone away. She turned and went to her room. There was finality in her movements. She had survived the dark emotions of grief, fear and despair. Her heart ached. Her eyes, too. But darkness has it own light and she knew it would lead her to understand peaceful thoughts that would take her to a new level of spiritual wellness.

After tea and dinner by the fireplace, she went to bed. The next morning she stayed in her room until noon. At ten o'clock, Eve brought hot coffee and toast and announced she was on her way to the eleven o'clock church service. When Eve returned from church, Rema was downstairs in the den dangling a feather toy in front of Angel. The kitten leaped high into the air hoping to catch the flying feathers.

Smiling at the kitten's playful antics, Rema looked up at Eve.

"I should call Mylowe and tell him about our trip to Dayton. His schedule is so hectic."

Eve sat down beside her. "Yesterday, you regained your freedom. John Swenson's psychotic vendetta against you is over. What else could he do to you?"

Rema looked troubled. "I've been asking myself that question. He'll probably try to reach out from the grave to finish me off. How will I know when he's dead?"

Eve slumped in her chair as if she wanted to be invisible. She swallowed several times before blurting out, "You'll know when he's dead because I gave his nurse our phone number and told her to call us collect."

Rema drank the coffee and ate the toast. She realized everything in life has its cycle. When it runs down and the cycle is complete, it's the making of a new day.

48

THE RIBBON

The March evening rainstorm moved over Coral Gables catching George Whitetail in the downpour as he rushed into his condo to answer the telephone. Hearing Mylowe's voice, he pulled a stool away from the bar and sat down.

"How do I rate a seven o'clock call? I thought you reserved your evening calls for Melody Ann."

Slouching in a chair in the doctors' lounge, Mylowe turned off his pager and loosened his tie. "Tonight, you rate the call because of the developing situation after Rema found Felic's briefcase."

"Yes, I know. I'm the one who told you about the rare books."

"Did Mona tell you there were two envelopes in the briefcase?"

"No, are you going to tell me about it?"

"Do you remember a pink ribbon the night you examined me at the clinic?"

"You're asking me to remember back twenty-five years."

"Did Felic mention a woman giving birth?"

"Yes, I believe he said a woman at the compound had just given birth. She asked him to bring the infant to the clinic."

"Felic told me he stayed overnight at the clinic."

"It was not protocol but I was the only medic on duty that weekend."

"He also said he told you his name was Martin."

"That's correct. I remember he had you wrapped in a sweater."

"Did you unwrap the baby from the sweater?"

"Yes, I guess I would have done that. Why are you asking these questions?"

"Did Felic say he was my father?"

"No, but when Felic and I met again in Coral Gables, I told him I believed he was your father."

"What was his answer?"

"He said he found you in Dead Man's Alley and had searched the alley to find your mother. He also told me how he sneaked out of the clinic with you and stole your medical records including your birth certificate. His confession took a lot of guilt off his mind. What do you want to know?"

"In Felic's briefcase along with a list of rare books, there was a pink hair ribbon folded inside a sheet of paper. Felic had written my birth date on the paper. Rema now believes Felic knew my mother. She thinks I may have been Felic's child."

"I see the implications."

Mylowe swallowed and cleared his voice. "For years, Felic knew I wanted to find my parents. Why wouldn't he tell me the truth?"

"I don't know. I do know he loved you."

"The pink ribbon has opened a door."

George sighed. "It's natural you would want to know your genetic disposition, but a hair ribbon is not much of a clue."

"If I weren't a physician, I might not be so adamant about finding my mother. To me, it's downright dangerous to marry without knowing medical information about the people who created me. Was Felic my father? Did my parents love each other? Was I an accident? Was I born to a victim of a rape?"

"Are you coming to Miami during spring break?"

"Yes. I'm meeting Melody Ann there. Together we'll begin to search for my roots."

Monday Morning

"That low-down son of a bitch," Mona yelled. "How many lives does John Swenson have? What are you going to do?"

Rema, still in bed, leaned against the headboard. She had estimated the depth of Mona's anger prior to dialing Mona's number in Miami. "I have no plan," she replied.

"Can't you take him to court?"

"On what charge?"

"How about pretending to be dead and sending you an imposter to steal from you?"

"I don't have the energy or the inclination to get involved in a lawsuit. Paul Moore is dead and John will be dead shortly."

"The only good thing is that you recovered part of Mylowe's inheritance."

"That's not much consolation."

"Well, get some rest," Mona said. "I'll call you tonight."

Concerned that Rema did not have a well of reserved emotional strength, Mona dialed George Whitetail's office to tell him about Rema's trip to Dayton.

"Hello, George. I'm going to give you the short version of Rema's visit to meet Emille's friend in Dayton."

"Was it bad?"

"It was terrible. Emille's friend in Dayton was John Swenson. John has liver cancer and will be dead by the end of the week. Emille, who lived at Justin House for eight years as Rema's son, was an imposter hired by John. John said Emille Swenson died in Cuba when he was ten years old. The imposter's name was Paul Moore, a thug who would do anything for money. He stole $5,000 from the Libra Center. He also stole the rare books from Eben's Tower. John Swenson sold twenty-three of the books and split the $42,000 with Paul Moore. He took ill before he could sell the rest of the books. Rema took twenty-four books back to Justin House."

"That's incredible."

"Rema hasn't yet told Mylowe she was able to retrieve twenty-four books."

"Why did John Swenson do those things?"

"He wanted Rema to suffer as he had suffered."

"Why?"

"He said Rema stole their son from him. No, he meant that Rema stole Emille's love from him. He admitted he was insanely jealous and wanted her to know the pain of losing her son."

George's concern for Rema was obvious. "Does Rema think she should have foreseen all these things in the stars?"

"She hasn't said. Her demeanor causes me to think that she believes she has lost her touch."

"Should I go to Justin House?"

"Would you? My daughter's baby is due in two days. I must stay in Miami."

"I'll make arrangements to fly out tonight. I hope I get to her before she talks to Mylowe. When he learns of this, he'll want to go home to be with her."

Mona's lips quivered. She burst into tears.

George made night flight reservations to Dayton for two, and dialed Dr. Drench Martin's telephone number.

"Drench, this is George Whitetail."

"Hey there, Big Chief, what's up?"

"Since you're enjoying retirement, I thought you'd like to take an overnight trip to Dayton with me."

"What's in Dayton?"

"We'd really be going to Wexlor, a little place two hours from Dayton. A good friend is going through the same trauma you've experienced. She could use your help."

"Hell! Why not? I'm just sitting here not enjoying my retirement."

"Good! I'll send my car for you at four o'clock. We'll have dinner before the flight."

Dr. Drench Martin was famous for his work in the field of psychiatry. Several months ago, he realized he did not relish keeping up with the pace of the academic world. He moved from Coral Cables and hung his shingle in Homestead, a small community near Miami. He now lives alone.

Ten years ago, his wife of thirty years, his nineteen-year-old, adopted twin daughters and his mother died in a house fire. The fire was started by one of his patients, a schizophrenic who had gone off medications and listened to the voices in his head. When the young man was interrogated, he said the voices commanded him to kill all the evil women in Dr. Martin's family.

George Whitetail began gathering papers from his desk and putting them in his briefcase. He realized taking Drench to meet Rema was the best approach. At least Mylowe would not feel so guilty for not being there. Of all the people he knew in the medical profession, Drench understood first hand the ruinous damage that occurs to a victim of revenge. He closed his briefcase, instructed his secretary to order a rental car in Dayton and to hold his calls for three days.

* * * * *

George Whitetail and Drench Martin arrived in Dayton thirty minutes after midnight and retired for the rest of the night at the Holiday Inn. In the morning, they had breakfast in the dining room and waited for the rental car to be delivered. By 9:00 a.m., they were driving to Wexlor.

"How did you meet Rema Swenson?" asked Drench.

"Through Professor Felic Ort," said George. "I told you about my first meeting with Felic."

"He's the man who found a baby and raised him as his son. You also speak of Mylowe, Emille and Mona. It seems you have a very close relationship."

"It was a gradual evolution of six people coming together with each person following their predetermined destiny. We became a special family not related by blood, but the caring between us is so tender and our ties are so strong even heaven will be challenged to separate us."

"How did it begin?"

"I met Felic Ort when I was a medical resident working at the Miami Canal Medical Clinic in Miami. That was in 1970. One night, Felic brought a newborn to the clinic. I'll always remember the surprised look on his face when I opened the door. I must have been an awesome sight; a big Indian warrior in a white coat. He came inside. After I examined the infant, I suggested the child stay in the clinic for several days. Felic agreed, but asked to stay with the infant."

"Did you let him stay?" asked Drench.

"Yes, I had seen him in the clinic before. I assumed he was living at the homeless compound near the clinic."

"Was he homeless?"

"Yes, but he was an unusual man. At the time, I thought he was a guy down on his luck. Years later, I attended a program in the Miami University auditorium and recognized him as the speaker. After the program, I had the opportunity to speak to him privately and learned he had been living at the compound to study the homeless.

"He was adamant about reviewing the time he spent with me at the clinic. He confessed he had lied about the newborn and spoke like a man who had harbored deep guilt for many years. When I inquired about the boy, he said a lady had helped him raise the boy."

"Was Rema the friend?"

"Yes, but I didn't meet her until after Felic died. In Felic's final months, he had turned his back on the family. The boy got in some trouble and was put on probation. Felic threaten to disown him and abused Rema for sticking with the boy.

"During this time, Rema learned her own son, who twenty years prior had disappeared with his father in the Atlantic Ocean, was alive and living in Miami. She went to Miami to meet the young man and ran headlong into a masterful, vengeful plan staged by her husband."

"But you said her husband was dead."

"Yes, both he and the boy had been declared dead by a Florida judge. However, they had been living in Cuba for twenty years. When the husband returned to Miami he began to search for her."

"What did he want?"

"He wanted to make her suffer for taking his son's love from him."

"Was he crazy? He took the son with him."

"He was jealous of Rema's relationship with the boy."

"When he learned Felic had died, he hired an impostor, a look-alike, to act as Rema's son. The man lived with her at Justin House for eight years."

"What kind of a guy was he?"

"An intelligent thug."

"What did he do?"

"He taught languages at Wexlor University. Several months ago, I discovered he was bipolar and using cocaine."

"I'll bet that's a long story."

"He went ballistic and shot Rema in the shoulder. He died in the hospital a day later. The bottom line is that he stole $42,000 of rare books from her house. Last Saturday, Rema went to Dayton to see her son's friend. Can you guess who the friend turned out to be?"

"Her husband?"

"Exactly! He was dying from liver cancer, not expected to live another week. He told Rema her natural son had drowned in Cuba. The boy was ten."

"Bless her," said Drench.

"I've really been brief about Rema's life. I'll let her tell you the rest. I told her I was bringing you to Justin House."

"How much does she know about me?"

"She knows it all."

Drench laid his head against the headrest and slept until they reached Wexlor's city limits.

At Justin House, Eve and Maggie dusted and swept the guest rooms in preparation for the arrival of George Whitetail and Drench Martin.

Rema had awakened early. After a leisurely shower, she decided to wear a gray pantsuit with exquisite lines tailored to perfection. She managed to secure diamond-studded earrings into her ear lobes, and snapped on a gold bracelet Felic had given her for Valentine's Day.

She stood before the mahogany-framed, full-length mirror and turned from side to side. To be free of the unsightly confining shoulder cast was a relief, but to continually hold her left arm tucked against her side was burdensome.

Eve's tap on the door sidetracked her gloom. "You look fantastic," exclaimed Eve.

Rema smiled. "I'm just the same old horse with a new blanket."

Eve smoothed the lapel of Rema's jacket and whispered, "Dr. Whitetail and Dr. Martin are in the den. Maggie can serve brunch when you're ready."

"How can anything go wrong with two shrinks in the house?"

Eve laughed and followed Rema down the stairs.

They entered the den. George Whitetail began the introductions. Drench wrenched his well-fed, sixty-year-old buttocks free from the narrow chair and greeted each lady with a chivalrous bow.

George announced he had a two o'clock appointment at Wexlor University and hoped the timing would not interfere with the arrangements for lunch. Rema responded by saying lunch would be served immediately. Eve hurried to the kitchen to tell Maggie.

Luncheon conversation among the four people was light and enjoyable. After Maggie served apple strudel with hazelnut-flavored coffee, George Whitetail hurried to his appointment and Eve went to the kitchen to help Maggie.

Rema placed her napkin on the table. "Dr. Martin," she said. "Perhaps, we would be more comfortable by the fire."

Drench stood and assisted Rema from her chair. In the den, the fire was glowing. They sat before the large fireplace in the formidable, matching blue velvet, high-back chairs.

"This must be your favorite room," said Drench.

"Indeed, it is. There are many memories floating around in this room."

From Drench's first comforting words, Rema surmised he knew the details of John Swenson's vendetta.

"Can I possibly survive the inner turmoil created by a bitter vendetta against me that has lasted over thirty-three years?" she asked.

"You can, but you can't absorb all of your husband's negative garbage and then refuse to regurgitate it."

His words slapped at her face. She was surprised. "That's a striking analogy," she whispered. "Is that what I'm doing?"

"If you're normal, you are."

"I've absorbed a lot of John's garbage."

"Indeed, you have. He's unloaded a lot of it. John Swenson knew exactly how to do it. He dealt it one load at a time."

"I'm stunned. Why haven't I seen this?"

"Don't punish yourself. Just decide to let it go."

"If I can do that, my only concern is the loss of part of Mylowe's inheritance. Do I tell Mylowe how foolish I've been?"

"Is telling Mylowe about the loss of his inheritance your main concern? It truly can't be. From what I know about Mylowe, he is a forgiving man. He loves you."

"He's the only man in my life who didn't kick me in the stomach."

"Is that what you're afraid of?"

"I'm not afraid. I'm angry at myself for allowing it."

"Angry?" asked Drench. "Isn't it fear of the unknown rather than anger?"

"Perhaps, it is more than just telling Mylowe about the inheritance. I truly have come to dread the unknown. I'm a caseworker. I should feel differently."

Drench shook his head. "Like a physician who fails to recognize his disease, a counselor can't always deal with personal emotions. You can't take a pill."

Rema nodded. "Buddhism teaches that negative emotions can be controlled by meditation," she said. "Negative emotions can be lessened or eliminated by visualization and the releasing of self-reflection. I guess I've forgotten how to do that."

"I also believe you have a real need to know something about the man who impersonated your son. Do you know his name?"

"Yes, his name was Paul Moore." She paused and tightly gripped her hands together. "I need to know if my son drowned in Cuba when he was ten years old."

"Is this what your husband told you?"

"Yes, but he's such a liar. I've been a terrible fool where he's concerned. I was blinded by my need to satisfy the lonely part of myself."

"Let's go back to your initial question about being a survivor of someone's revengeful nature. Did you know ten percent of the world's population is made up of cruel, vengeful people? Twenty percent are good people, and the rest can go either way depending on the circumstances. Although I hear people in my profession exclaim there are no victims, I believe eighty percent of the 'fence-sitters' are caught up in revenge and are likely to become victims."

"I've tried not to think of myself as a victim."

"Do you realize you have a great need to relax your soul? The soul gets weary when emotions are too heavy to bear."

Rema looked at Drench through tear-filled eyes. "I've lost my way."

"A vendetta robbed you of your sanity." Drench bowed his head and whispered, "Now I lay me down to sleep. I pray the Lord my soul to keep."

He raised his head and said, "Long ago that simple prayer got me out of a jam. In those dark days, I wasn't able to come up with a prayer of my own."

Drench took her hand. "Will you allow me to try to get some information about your son's death? I have a contact in Cuba."

"Would you do that?"

"Of course. I know you'll also feel better if we could find out who Paul Moore was. I'm willing to take on the research."

"Thank you," she whispered.

"Here's a little something I want to share with you. In my teachings, I've always taught that one's truth is the place from where we render all our lifetime decisions. My homework assignment to my patients is that in their minds they build a 'Truth House.' I tell them they should imagine the house to be a secluded tree house they never had, the whittling corner in the old milk shed or the small think cottage by a lake.

"Within their 'Truth House' they will continuously evaluate what they believe. Beliefs and convictions will vary according to how they are used. The data base will vary and change. They can discard what they don't need and add what they do. But they must realize that sometimes the house gets trashed when a block of knowledge goes bad."

Rema stiffened. "What is your advice when the data base goes on overload?"

"Build a new house."

Eve's footsteps hurried toward the front door. Moments later, George came into the den.

"Well, you two look cozy."

"We are," Rema replied. "Do you think tonight would be a good time to call Mylowe? I'm ready to tell him about the Dayton trip."

George stoked the fire and put on a piece of wood. "Let's put in a conference call and include Eve. She may have some invaluable input about the Dayton trip. After all, she was there with you."

"A grand idea," said Drench.

49

THE SEARCH

Three Weeks Later

It was early April when Mylowe arranged a four-day sabbatical away from Boston General Hospital to meet Melody Ann in Miami. Together they would begin searching for clues to his origin. If his quest were preordained, as he believed it to be, the clues would guide him to find his mother. Whether it was his mother's subconscious wish or not, she had put a pink hair ribbon beside her newborn infant after putting him in a box of garbage in Dead Man's Alley.

Before Mylowe dialed Rema's number to tell her of his plans, he considered what he would say and recalled the words of Ambrose Bierce.

Destiny is a tyrant's authority for crime and a fool's excuse for failure.

Since listening to Rema's anguished account of John Swenson's vendetta against her, Mylowe realized one's destiny is not a solo run. It's intertwined with the destinies of others. In this lifetime, John Swenson had definitely acted out the role of a tyrant, but how many times had he failed?

Mylowe did not want to fail. He was certain the pink hair ribbon was a part of his destiny. He dialed Rema's number.

"Hi!" he said. "I called to let you know I'm going to Miami during my spring break to search for my origin."

"Are you going alone?" Rema asked.

"I'm meeting Melody Ann at the airport. We'll begin the search together. Please don't be too disappointed."

"I do understand," she said.

When he hung up the phone, he realized he was mentally exhausted and physically beat up. The hours at the hospital had been long and grueling. He picked up his travel bag and hailed a cab at the hospital entrance. Thirty minutes later in the airport, he boarded the flight to Miami and slept until the plane landed. In the Miami terminal, he caught his luggage from the turntable and went outside to pick up a rental car. When he returned in the rental car, Melody Ann was standing on the curb outside the American Airline section.

His heart raced like a thoroughbred at the starting gate. Without prodding or whipping, he jumped from the car, wrapped his arms around her and savored the veiled fragrance that oozed from her. Her golden hair was piled high on her head. The sight of her peach-tinted cheeks and rosebud lips sent a thrill through his body. He kissed her tenderly and ignored the security patrolman motioning to him to move the car.

Driving to the hotel, Mylowe gave her a map of Miami.

"When you open it," he said, "the red circle is Dead Man's Alley. The blue is the homeless shelter where Felic lived. Rema's trailer is circled in yellow. The Miami Canal Medical Clinic is in black."

"After twenty-five years, do any of these places exist today?" she asked.

"I don't know."

It was four o'clock when they settled into a room. As Melody Ann closed the drapes, Mylowe stood behind her and pulled her close. Picking her up in his arms, he carried her to the bed and leaned over her. They embraced. The moment came when they were one.

Melody Ann disengaged from his arms and rolled to her side of the bed. Mylowe sat up and gathered three pillows behind his head.

"Are you okay?" he asked.

"I'm fine."

"Did I tell you Rema gave me a copy of my birth certificate?" he said.

"Why did she have it?"

"Years ago, when Felic threatened to send me to welfare, she got it from the Dade County Recorder's Office."

"Why?"

"Rema thought my birth certificate might be something she could use against him. Are you sure you're okay?"

She frowned and pulled her hair away from her face. "I'm fine," she said coldly.

"Do you want some dinner?"

"I'll be ready in ten minutes," she said.

During dinner Melody Ann asked, "On your birth certificate, is Felic listed as your father?"

"Yes."

"Is your mother shown?"

"No."

"If Felic and Rema had not reconciled, how would your birth certificate have been important?"

"Rema would have used it to show the authorities that Felic was my father."

"Would he really have tried to put you in a foster home?"

"I don't know. Felic couldn't deal with notoriety. If Rema would have threatened to expose the information on the certificate, he might have backed down."

Melody Ann stood up and grabbed her purse. "Let's find Dead Man's Alley," she said.

Mylowe followed her to the hotel garage. Settled inside the rental car, his hand tightened on hers. "Are you sure you want to go? You seem on edge."

"I'm okay. Start the engine."

Leaving the garage, Mylowe drove across a bridge over the Miami River. Four blocks south, he turned right and drove on Harding Street. The street was lined with empty storefronts. Large red and black placards in the windows boasted that the empty spaces were available for lease. In the next block, several stores were occupied. Mylowe parked and went inside one of the stores.

"May I help you?" asked a matronly woman wearing a white linen jacket embroidered with pink flamingos.

Pointing to the red line on his map, Mylowe said, "I'm looking for Dead Man's Alley. It should be nearby."

The woman smiled. "The alley's entrance is next door. It's not really an alley anymore. The old hotel was torn down five years ago and a new restaurant was built on part of the ground."

"Is the Miami Canal Medical Clinic on this street?"

"No, the entire block burned to the ground. There's a used car lot there now."

"How long ago did it burn down?"

"Nearly ten years."

"Where is the homeless compound?"

"Two blocks to the north and turn left. Did you live in this area?"

"I was born here and lived in a trailer across from the homeless compound."

"Dead Man's Alley used to be a frightful place. It was full of garbage and rats. A lot of scary things went on there. After the old hotel was torn down and a new restaurant built on the site, the alley's reputation changed."

"Is it possible to walk through the alley now?"

"Yes, I go through it every day to have lunch."

Mylowe rushed back to Melody Ann.

"The lady in the store said the entrance to Dead Man's Alley is next door. There's a restaurant on the other side. We can walk through the alley."

Swinging her legs out the open door, Melody Ann took his hand. "Let's go," she said.

At the alley's entrance, they paused and watched the orange sun move below the horizon. Moving inside, Mylowe shrugged away the pressure of a familiar nudge between his shoulders.

"Is something wrong?" she asked.

"Just some pressure in my shoulders."

"Is it the nudge you're always talking about?"

"Yes, this must be the place where Felic found me."

At the rear door of the new restaurant, Mylowe stopped.

"Felic said I was in a box of decayed lettuce by the rear door."

Melody Ann tugged at his hand. "There's a sidewalk here. Let's walk around to the front door."

"Give me a minute."

Melody Ann turned from him. "Okay, I'll be at the front."

Mylowe pressed his hand along the wall beside the rear door and wondered why fate had selected this area as the place where he was to begin his life. He wondered how this place was connected to his mother and father.

He moved along the wall and followed the sidewalk around Sally's Restaurant. At the front, Melody Ann held onto his arm. They went inside.

At the counter, a waitress asked, "What will you have?"

"Is the owner here?" Mylowe asked.

"I'll send him out."

A man came from the kitchen. "Did you want to see me?" he asked. "I'm Art Bradley."

"My name is Mylowe Ort. I'm searching for information. My mother left me in a crate of garbage at the back door of this restaurant."

"The Dead Man's Alley has a long history."

"I was found by a homeless man looking for food."

Art Bradley looked puzzled. "How long ago?" he asked.

"Twenty-five years."

"Sally's Restaurant was originally on the first floor of the Green Palms Hotel. Sally's my aunt. She's retired."

"Would your aunt be able to tell me about the people who lived in the hotel around 1970?"

"All the hotel residents were alcoholics and prostitutes."

"Could we visit your aunt?"

"I guess it would be okay. She lives down the street. I was going to take her dinner. If you can wait, I'll sack it up."

Melody Ann grabbed Mylowe's hand and smiled while they waited at the front door. A minute later, Art Bradley came from behind the counter carrying two plastic bags.

"Aunt Sally spends her days gardening," he said. "She's healthy and has a good memory."

They walked a block and a half before Art stopped at a house with a white fence around it. "Before we go in, give me time to tell Aunt Sally why you're here."

Mylowe nodded and moistened his dry lips.

Art returned and they were ushered into the living room. Loud music was coming from a television program. Art grabbed the control and turned it off.

"That's better," he said. "Aunt Sally will be here in a minute. She's putting the food in the refrigerator. I explained to her why I brought you here. Please sit down."

Melody Ann and Mylowe sat close together on the blue flowered couch. After several moments of noise from the kitchen, they heard the muffled sound of footsteps. Aunt Sally entered the room.

From her flaming Clairol red hair, thin and straight, to pockets of crumpled skin that sagged from her elbows and knees like wet brown paper bags, to the orange tassels on the top of purple velvet house slippers, she looked as if she had been posing for a stop-smoking poster.

"Aunt Sally," said Art, "this young man says when he was a baby, he was found in a box of garbage at the back door of the restaurant in 1970."

Mylowe walked toward Aunt Sally. "I know I was born on August 21, 1970, in this neighborhood."

"Ah! The alley hides many secrets," she said as she blew cigarette smoke toward the ceiling. "1970, huh? That makes you about twenty-five."

"A homeless man found me. When I was eight years old, he told me you had agreed to put out food in a window box if the homeless would stop begging at your front door."

"Yeah! I remember that summer. It was so hot you could fry an egg on the sidewalk."

"Did you know a lady customer who was pregnant?"

279

"There were no pregnant ladies in my place. My women customers were prostitutes. I remember a little girl who was knocked up by a guy hired by her old man to take care of her. The old drunk wouldn't let her out of the hotel room, so I took food to her at lunchtime when he was away."

"Did she have the baby?"

"I don't know. For a time, Art took food to her." Sally looked at Art. "Do you remember that little girl?"

Art leaned forward. "I do remember her. She was about twelve and couldn't talk."

Mylowe's heart pounded. "Did she have the baby?"

"I guess she did. For some time when I took her food, she didn't answer the door. I stopped going to the room."

Melody Ann turned to Sally. "Did you know the girl's name?"

"It was Ruthie. She was a sweet little thing. Too damn young to be in the family way."

"Who was the guy she lived with?"

"His name was Arnie. He was a full-time alcoholic. I didn't know his last name."

"Where was their room?" asked Melody Ann.

"It was on the second floor at the back of the hotel over the restaurant."

Mylowe asked, "Is there a bar around here where the alcoholics buy liquor?"

"Yeh! The Anchor Bar is four blocks north on the Miami Canal."

Mylowe bent down and pressed Sally's hand. "You and Art have been most cooperative."

Sally nodded half-heartedly, reached for the remote and turned on the television. Mylowe and Melody Ann went outside. Art followed them.

"Do you think the little girl could be your mother?"

"I don't know."

Art pointed toward the street corner. "If you don't want to walk through Dead Man's Alley in the dark, you'd better walk around the block."

Melody Ann grabbed Mylowe's arm and winked. "We'll walk through the alley," she said.

The next morning before driving to the homeless shelter, Mylowe parked at the entrance to Dead Man's Alley. He walked into alley and pictured the area as Felic had described it. The dilapidated Green Palms Hotel inhabited by drunks and prostitutes and the alley-smart, four-footed creatures waiting to devour each other. Mylowe tried to imagine a teen-age girl wandering through the rubble looking for a place to lay her newborn baby.

The glare of the morning sun caused the vision to retreat to the corner of his mind. With the vision gone, he walked toward the restaurant's back door. Was he imagining a scene that didn't happen? He turned and walked out the alley's entrance.

"Something happens to me when I'm in there," he said to Melody Ann. She did not reply.

"Are you feeling okay?" he asked. "You seem distracted."

"I'm a little tired."

Mylowe drove two blocks north, turned left and stopped at the gate of the ten-foot, high-wire fence.

"This must be the homeless compound," he said. "There's no sign. It's not what I imagined."

He got out of the car and looked through the fence's metal framework.

"I expected to see people cooking over open fires."

"Things change over twenty-five years," replied Melody Ann. "I don't see a trailer park."

"You're right, things do change. Let's find the Anchor Bar." His arm encircled her waist. They walked to the car.

He drove two more blocks toward the Miami Canal. After driving into three dead-end streets, he found the Anchor Bar. It was in an old two-story building that formed a wedge where two streets met. The building had recently been painted. On one side, an original Schenley Whiskey advertisement had been preserved. The streets near the building were lined with small, three-room tenant houses with clapboard siding that the paint had long ago been stripped away by the oppressive salt air.

Melody Ann grasped Mylowe's hand as they walked inside the Anchor Bar. The bright, late morning light from the opened door distracted the patrons from their self-imposed stupors. Some raised their heads and squinted. Others bemoaned the intrusion of light. Mylowe quickly shut the door and leaned against the doorframe while his eyes adjusted to the darkness.

"Wha d'yuh have?" grumbled a voice from the end of the bar.

"A draft and a ginger ale," Mylowe replied.

"Are you folks vistin' round here?"

"I think my family lived in this neighborhood. I understand this bar has been in this location for a long time."

"Where d'yuh hear that?"

"I talked to the woman who once owned Sally's Restaurant in the old Green Palms Hotel."

In the dim light, a figure stepped out of the darkness, glared at them and set a beer and a ginger ale on the bar.

"You ain't really from around here, are yuh?"

"No, but I believe I was born in the area around the Green Palms Hotel. I'm looking for information."

"I can tell you don't work for a livin'. Your hands are too clean."

Mylowe grinned and unconsciously folded his hands together.

"How long ago did your family live around here?"

"Twenty-five years."

"There's no one around here that could remember far back except ol' Grover. He's sittin' back in the corner."

"Do you think he would answer some questions?"

"He's a real motor-mouth."

Grasping Melody Ann's hand, Mylowe slid off the bar stool, The bartender grinned at the visitors and wiped his wide-knuckled hands on the front of his sleeveless, black shirt.

Mylowe and Melody Ann approached the white-haired man. "The bartender said your name is Grover," said Mylowe. "My name is Dr. Ort. Do you have time to talk with us?"

"Can you buy me a beer?"

"Yes, of course." Mylowe motioned to the bartender.

"How many?" the bartender asked.

"Two," replied Mylowe. "Keep them coming."

"Is this your lady?" asked Grover.

"Yes."

"Mighty pretty, she is."

"I think so."

"What's your name, pretty lady?"

"Melody Ann."

Grover brushed a piece of white hair from his forehead. "I had a lady once. She was pretty, too. She died."

Mylowe pushed a full glass of beer in front of Grover. "I'm sorry," he said.

"I'm sorry, too," Grover said. "I've been sittin' here ever since."

Mylowe tried not to be anxious, but his heart was racing. He pulled his chair close to Grover.

"Perhaps," he said, "you knew my mother."

"Did she come in here?"

"It's possible. I learned my mother was a young girl who was the ward of a man called Arnie. I believe Arnie came to this bar. Do you remember a man called Arnie?"

"Well, let's see now,'" said Grover. "I knew only one Arnie. He was a relative or just a friend of a Coast Guard sailor who used to come in here when he was off duty. Arnie and the sailor were real good buddies. They'd get all beered up. The sailor would put on a big act about his imbecile daughter who couldn't talk. His antics always made everyone laugh. He was a real actor."

Mylowe's body stiffened.

"What's the matter, Doc? Are you sick?"

Melody Ann replied, "He's okay. You just confirmed the story we heard yesterday about the young girl who didn't speak. Did the sailor live in this neighborhood?" she asked.

"Yah! Just around the corner. He had a wife. Years ago in the fifties there was a rumor about her and the sailor. Seems like she had a baby boy and the sailor didn't think the child was his. He made her give the baby to a convent downtown for adoption."

"Do you remember the sailor's name?"

"Give me a little time for my mind to catch up."

Grover looked at Mylowe. "Are you better now, Doc? I thought you were going to pass out."

Mylowe leaned forward. "Looking for my mother is traumatic."

"I just told the young lady I'd try to remember the sailor's name."

Melody Ann turned to Mylowe and repeated Grover's information.

"The sailor in the Coast Guard had a wife. They lived near here. The wife had a baby boy that the sailor said wasn't his. He made her take the baby to a convent in downtown Miami."

Grover tossed his head back and sucked the foam from the bottom of the mug. "I've been in this neighborhood all my life," he said. "I never had reason to go anywhere. Where are you people from?"

"Ohio," replied Mylowe, "May I order another beer?"

Grover nodded and stared at the ceiling. "The sailor's name was Dunston. Hmmm! Dunston, no it was Durston. They called him Dave. Yes, that rascal's name was Dave Durston. His wife's name was Evelyn."

"You have a good memory," exclaimed Mylowe. "What do you know about the man called Arnie?"

"Well, he was an ugly guy and real mean. He had a wife. She was a big, strong woman. Many times, I saw her push him through that door calling him names. The bar-sitters teased Arnie about Maggie and her coming to get him. Yep! They called her Mag, Her name was Margaret Tuttle."

"Then Arnie's last name was Tuttle." Mylowe said.

"Yep! Arnold Tuttle. When Dave Durston's wife died, I heard the little girl went to live with Margaret and Arnie Tuttle."

"Did they live in this neighborhood?"

"Don't know. When Mrs. Durston died, a neighbor found the daughter sitting by her mother's bedside. She'd been there all night. The girl was a pretty little thing with blond curls but couldn't speak."

Mylowe sipped his beer and leaned back in the chair. The air was stale and damp. The room needed sunlight. He realized the morning patrons like Grover couldn't hide their fears and remorse in the light of the sun.

Grover drank his beer and chuckled, "Say, Doc, what you gonna do now?"

"I don't know. I'm going to follow up on what you have told me."

"Well, I hope I helped yuh."

"You have helped me. I'm forever grateful. I won't forget you."

Melody Ann stood and walked toward the door. Mylowe followed and stopped to ask the bartender if there was anything he could do for Grover.

"You could buy him a keg of beer," said the bartender. "He sweeps up in here at night to make beer money."

Mylowe laid three twenties on the bar. "See that he gets his beer."

"Okay, Doc," exclaimed the bartender.

"I won't forget what you and Grover have done for me today," Mylowe said.

He joined Melody Ann at the door. Outside, they discovered a late morning rain had dampened the street. They welcomed a breath of fresh air although it was hot and humid.

"What a smelly place," whispered Melody Ann. "What do we do now?"

"Check the Coast Guard records for Dave Durston and the county records for Arnold and Margaret Tuttle."

"What about the young girl?"

"If she is my mother, she'd be nearly forty years old. If she is incapable of speaking, she might be in an institution."

Melody Ann realized Mylowe wasn't going to stop searching. She wondered if he knew how she felt.

"Are you going to the downtown Miami convent to look for the baby boy named Durston?" she asked.

Mylowe started the car's engine. "Let's go back to the hotel and find the addresses and telephone numbers for the Coast Guard, the County Recorder and the downtown convents."

"Okay," she said, "I should call home. My mother wasn't feeling well. Since daddy died last year, her health has been failing."

"Is it something serious?"

"She's #2 diabetic. There are lesions on her feet that won't heal."

"Why didn't you tell me? We could get her a specialist or take her to Mayo Clinic."

"She's stubborn."

Mylowe drove slowly through the unfamiliar streets. At the hotel, he parked outside. They hurried to the room.

From the local Coast Guard office Mylowe learned how to trace Dave Durston. He called the Dade County Recorder's office and placed a verbal order for the death certificate of Arnold Tuttle to be sent to Justin House.

"That's as much as I can do," he said as he hung up the phone. When I get back to Boston, I'll search Coast Guard records for Dave Durston."

The Sisters of St. Angeline's Convent was the only convent listed in downtown Miami. Mylowe dialed the number.

"This is Dr. Mylowe Ort. I'm in Miami for two days from Ohio and would like an appointment with the Reverend Mother. It's an urgent matter."

"The Reverend Mother is at lunch," replied a young woman. "She would be able to see you at two o'clock."

Feeling every human emotion that men bring on themselves, Mylowe hung up the phone and leaned back knowing his anxiety had affected his breathing. He wondered why the information about Ruthie Durston had come about so easily. It was scary. He pictured a young tormented girl with straggling blond hair—a victim of adolescence abuse and pregnant. Could Felic have known the girl or her family?

Through his reverie, he could hear Melody Ann talking to her mother and begging her to stay off her feet. In the next moment, Melody Ann was standing over him saying something about her mother's condition. When he asked her to repeat it, she snarled.

"You were miles away."

"I'm sorry. I was in the midst of sub-consciously understanding the plight of the young girl called Ruthie."

"You're feeling a connection to her, aren't you?"

"Perhaps, I am. I don't know. I sensed something in Dead Man's Alley."

"Let's have some lunch," said Melody Ann.

50

QUESTIONS WITHOUT ANSWERS

At 1:30 p.m., the rain over Miami had started again. Driven by a wind with hurricane force, water splashed against the rental car's windshield obstructing Mylowe's view of the street.

Melody Ann was studying the city map and calling the names of the streets to Mylowe.

"Turn left at the next intersection," she advised. "The convent should be at the end of the street."

Mylowe guided the car to the gate of St Angeline's Convent and parked beside the eight-foot, tan stucco, vine-covered wall. Rain was still falling but the swift winds had stopped. Melody Ann opened an umbrella she found on the rear seat and Mylowe stooped to stand under it. At the arched, gated doorway, Mylowe pressed a button. Twenty-five feet ahead, the door to the main building opened. A young novice under a black umbrella hurried toward the iron gate.

"Do you have an appointment?"

"Yes."

"Your name, please."

"Dr. Mylowe Ort."

The novice unlocked the gate and motioned them to follow her into the building. Through a dark corridor inside, she guided them to the second door on the right. The Reverend Mother sat behind a small desk. The room, scantily furnished, was dim and quiet. Mylowe noticed the entire building was devoid of noise.

After introductions, Mylowe told the Reverend Mother that he was abandoned as a newborn infant in Dead Man's Alley and rescued by Felic Ort. He added the information he had recently learned from Sally Bradley and Grover.

"I believe my mother is Ruthie Durston," Mylowe said. "Her father and mother were Dave and Evelyn Durston. I've come to The Sisters of St. Angeline because Grover at the Anchor Bar said Dave and Evelyn Durston had taken their first child, a son, to a downtown Miami Convent for adoption. Grover also said the Durston's had a second child, a girl."

The Reverend Mother leaned forward with renewed interest. "What is your age, Dr. Ort?"

"I am twenty-five."

"The young girl must have been twelve or thirteen years old when she gave birth to you. The year of her birth must be 1957. If your information is correct, the baby boy was probably born to the Durston's three or four years earlier. That would make the boy's birth year 1953 or 1954."

"What is your policy on giving information about adoption records?"

"Rather lenient if we have positive proof of the relationship. Before adoption, we have the adoptive parents agree to certain regulations."

"If your calculations are correct, the Durston boy would be nearly forty-two years old. Is it possible to contact him?" asked Mylowe.

"We follow our protocol. As a first step, I'm willing to look for the Durston file. It will take several hours."

"I understand," Mylowe said. Before they left the room, he gave her his card with the hotel's telephone number on the back.

When they were settled in the car Melody Ann asked why he had not been more assertive. Mylowe said he felt that without proof that Ruthie Durston was his mother or the Durston's were his relatives, the Reverend Mother was following the convent's rules.

Melody Ann realized the key to Mylowe's dilemma was to find Ruthie Durston. If Ruthie Durston was incapable of speaking, Mylowe would delve into all her records to find the cause of her condition. It would be another hurdle to clear. Just knowing the name of the Durston baby's adoptive parents would not solve his problem.

"If, if, if," she whispered. "There are a lot of ifs. For the moment, they're unanswerable."

Mylowe was catching his breath and looking at his watch. "I'm running out of time," he said.

"I know," she said. "If the parents' names on the Durston's baby adoption record turn out to be identical with the information from Grover, what's the next step?"

"I don't know."

She knew he was impatient. "Will you go to another convent if the adoption record is not at Saint Angeline's?" she asked.

Mylowe slammed his hand against the arm of the steering wheel. "They have to have the record. I realize it's only the tip of the iceberg, but without a birth record or a death certificate on Ruthie Durston, I have nothing."

Two Hours Later

When the telephone rang in the hotel room near the chair where Mylowe was sleeping, he sat up. Dazed and not fully awake, he stammered into the mouthpiece. "This is Dr. Ort."

"Dr. Ort, this is the Reverend Mother at the Sisters of St. Angeline. We do have a file on a baby boy Durston. The notes in the file show the two-week-old baby was brought to the Sisters of St. Angeline on January 12, 1953. The father was a sailor who claimed he was not the boy's father. He claimed he would never support the child and would divorce his wife if she did not consent to the adoption. The note, written by my predecessor, the Reverend Mother Cecelia, also stated Mrs. Durston's health was very frail."

"Is there a copy of a birth certificate?"

"Yes, the baby boy was named Francis Durston, born on January 10, 1953, in Miami, Florida, County of Dade. The father is David Avis Durston. The mother is Evelyn May Perry Durston."

Mylowe sank into a chair. "Thank you for your efforts," he said.

"My blessing goes with you, Dr. Ort."

Mylowe turned to hang up the phone, but yelled into it. "Reverend Mother," he shouted, "Are you still on the line?"

"Yes, I'm here."

"Does the file contain the names of the adoptive parents?"

"Yes, it does."

Mylowe hung up the telephone and recited the birth information to Melody Ann.

"Let's go to the County Recorder's Office," he yelled. "We have our first clue."

Four Months Later

Mylowe was working in Eben's Tower at Justin House when a fax from the Navy Department arrived and confirmed that David Avis Durston had died on August 14, 1994, in the Veteran's Affairs Medical Center in Miami at the age of sixty-nine.

After completing his residency at Boston Memorial last month, Mylowe was living at Justin House. Last week, he had electricity installed in Eben's Tower and added a telephone, a computer and a fax machine. He stored the twenty-three rare books reclaimed by Rema from John Swenson in a bank vault. Following the habits of his male predecessors who had lived in Justin House, Mylowe was spending many solitary hours in Eben's Tower.

Taking the document from the fax machine, Mylowe went down to the kitchen and sat at the table with Rema. Before he could speak, Rema asked, "What's wrong?"

"I just received the document from the Navy. It confirms what I wanted to know."

"About what?"

"About Dave Durston."

"Is he Ruthie Durston's father?"

"Yes, The document shows he died in 1994 in a VA Hospital. He was sixty-nine."

Mylowe leaned backward and balanced his body on the back legs of the chair.

"I now know that Arnold Tuttle died in 1993 and Evelyn May Perry Durston, Ruthie's mother, died January 14, 1968."

"There's still hope that you might find Ruthie Durston, isn't there?"

"No, In Dade County, there's no birth or death record for Ruthie May Durston. I'm having a private investigator check records in other Florida counties."

"If you find her, she may not be the woman who gave birth to you."

Mylowe pushed the kitchen chair upright and leaned over the table. He realized he was feeding an obsession and was weakened by his aggressiveness. Marriage to Melody Ann was not possible until he knew more about his biological background.

Rema sat quietly with him at the table and recalled the questions Maggie had asked earlier in the day.

"What can Mylowe be doing up in that awful tower?" Maggie had asked.

She replied that he was asking people and organizations to donate money to help him build a psychoneuroimmunology medicine clinic on the knoll behind Justin House.

"You mean there'll be a bunch of insane people living back there?"

To calm Maggie's fear she had said that a psychoneuroimmunologist treats the central nervous system, the immune system, the endocrine system and the emotions. Many physical aliments are influenced by the mind, but the patients will not be insane.

For the one month Mylowe had been living in Justin House, Rema had hesitated to ask him about his plans to marry Melody Ann. Melody Ann's mother had died two weeks after Melody Ann had been in Miami with him. Mylowe had flown to Des Moines to be with her but returned to Boston two days after the funeral. When Rema questioned him about his sudden return, he did not give her a plausible answer. Whatever had happened between them, Rema knew the relationship was not in good order.

The ringing of the telephone in Eben's Tower cancelled her thoughts as Mylowe bumped into the table and raced from the kitchen.

Taking two steps at a time, Mylowe ran up the stairs and grabbed the phone. "Hello," he said. "How are you today, Dr. Whitetail?"

George laughed, "I'm fine. How did you know I was calling? I suppose you were using vibrational cogitation."

"I've already proven to you it's possible to communicate with another person by using mental contemplation."

"So far, your 'thought talking' or mental contemplation only works from your end. I've been sending you mental messages all morning. And, since you have not answered my mental messages, I decided to use the telephone."

"You need to contemplate deeper," said Mylowe. "Of course, you could be a better receiver than a sender."

"So far, I'm neither, but I've found e-mail is useful. I'm calling to convince you to come to Miami to consult. I have three patients who could use your kind of therapy."

"You realize I'm working on the financial arrangements for my clinic."

"I realize you're busy scrounging for money, but doing the consult will give you an opportunity to use the stuff you learned in Boston."

"Okay, I'll be at your condo tomorrow afternoon. Leave the key under the doormat."

Mylowe grinned at George's reluctance to use the mental method of communicating. He knew for eons humans have been mentally communicating and calling it intuition. How many times had they thought of someone and the next minute the person calls on the phone?

He pushed himself away from the computer and hurried down through the pantry into the kitchen. Rema was still sitting at the table.

"The call was from George," Mylowe said. "He wants me to do a consult in Miami. I'll make plane reservations from the computer upstairs."

"How long will you be gone?"

"At least a month. I'll be staying at George's condo."

He was in the foyer before she could reply. A chill ran through her as the sound of his footsteps faded. She thought about the abandoned infant she had cradled and nurtured to manhood. She scolded herself for being so protective. She drew a deep breath and surrendered him to the waiting world.

51

THE CONSULT

Mylowe had been in Miami for three weeks doing consultations for George Whitetail. This morning in George's office, he was giving progress reports on two patients, Vinnie Rutledge and Barry Waldon.

"I see Vinnie Rutledge has improved," said George.

Mylowe nodded. "The clozapine prescribed for him blocked the serotonin, but he doesn't tolerate the drug for very long. I think he's been misdiagnosed."

George grinned widely, "I see."

Mylowe tilted his head. "Your funny grin tells me you've been waiting for me to come to that conclusion. The misdiagnosis probably occurred early in Vinnie's life. Unfortunately, he believed the diagnoses. His anger against his parents is very deep. In his case, I've decided to use guided self-imagery."

"What about Barry Waldon? Is there any chance of upgrading him into an outside housing program?"

"Barry requires more personal psychotherapy. The group therapy programs aren't doing the job. You know only fifteen to forty percent of all patients achieve an average level of adjustment after milieu therapy."

George Whitetail agreed. "I have another patient for you," he said. "She could be moved into a group home as an advisor. She's worked in the hospital laundry for the last twenty years."

"When should I see her?"

"I'll arrange it."

"How is Melody Ann?"

Mylowe hesitated, and leaned forward.

"Something has happened between us. At first, I thought it was because of her mother's death that made her uncomfortable being with me. After the funeral, I knew she wanted me to go away. I went back to Boston much earlier than I had planned."

"Don't you think she is tired of waiting for you to get over your genetic obsession?"

"I don't have a time-table," Mylowe said

"Have you followed all the leads to find your birth mother?"

"Yes."

"Do you realize she is not going to wait much longer?"

Mylowe bowed his head and whispered, "I know. I know."

The Next Day

Twenty-nine-year-old Vinnie Rutledge, one of Mylowe's patients, knew he wanted to die and had decided to do it himself. He believed his life was over. On every branch of his family tree hung a genetic biological mental disease. In addition, drugs made him feel like he was on a Ferris wheel. The therapy had not made a difference. He was losing the battle. The prescribed medications had turned his physical body into a walking toxic waste.

His life's ambition was to study medicine and become a doctor. Funny, in an odd way, he was studying medicine, but from a patient's point of view. For half of his life, he had been in group therapy.

He had stopped worrying whether his parents would react to his suicide. For him, getting out of life had passed the point of being negotiable. His parents had birthed him into a family of chronically depressed people. He was doomed to be mentally sick. His parents wanted a cute, smart, little kid. Instead, they got a vocational school dropout who raised pigeons.

Earlier this morning, peering through the barred hospital windows, Vinnie whispered, "When is a prison not a prison?"

"You talkin' to me?" asked Barry Waldon, Vinnie's friend from therapy. They also worked together. Every morning, they carted supplies from the storeroom to the various hospital departments.

"Nah! I was thinking about the new shrink," Vinnie said.

"Yeah, has the new doc been checking you out?" asked Barry.

"Dr. Ort is cool. How long have you been seeing him?"

"Three weeks," Barry replied.

"Are yuh seeing him today?"

"Yeah! This afternoon."

"I like him," Vinnie said.

"Me too."

Barry looked out the window. He was remembering his second meeting with Dr. Ort when the doctor asked him about his family and his life at home.

"That's a laugh!" Barry had snarled. "My ol' man was sixty-two when I was born. The first time we played peek-a-boo he had a stroke. How's that for trauma! When I was twelve and acting strange because of the singing in my head, my mother had a doctor probe my ears for wax. The shrinks have been circling around me like sharks ever since."

"Come on, Barry. Stop daydreaming," yelled Vinnie. "We've got to get these supplies out of here and into the wards."

"Okay," Barry mumbled while pushing the heavy steel cart into the hallway. "Let's push'em out," he yelled. "It's another day living in the loony bin."

At 2:00 p.m. on the same afternoon, Vinnie was waiting outside treatment room #14 for his appointment with Mylowe. Mylowe was two minutes late and rushed down the hall toward him "Have you been waiting long?" Mylowe asked.

"Nah, but why was the door locked? I hate locked doors."

"It's regulation. Treatment rooms are locked when empty."

Mylowe unlocked the door and Vinnie shuffled toward a white metal chair and sat down.

"Let's stand by the window today," said Mylowe. "Tell me what's on your mind."

"I've been thinking about your line."

"What line?"

"The one you reel out and hook us mentally deranged bastards into thinking the way you want us to think."

"For example?"

"The imagination stuff you've been talking about."

"You mean self-imagery?"

"Yeah. I know you want me to try it."

"It might help your migraines."

Folding his arms, Mylowe leaned against the wall. Early in his college days, he agreed with Carl Jung's theory that most mental problems were spiritual in origin. Actually, mental illness is a failure to satisfy the human spirit. When people cannot find a way to satisfy their spirit, they usually manage to get from life what they want. But getting what they want doesn't always give meaning in their lives. Mylowe walked away from the window and sat down.

"Would you want to try a waking dream?" asked Mylowe.

"What's that?"

"I guide your imagination."

"Why?"

"To help you feel on a different level so you can understand your inner spirit."

"Uh huh," Vinnie joked, "I had a nasty concussion once. My inner spirit really got a jolt from that."

"How old were you?"

"About twelve."

"Do you think your migraines are related to your emotions?" Mylowe asked. "You should realize your spirit is a reservoir of talent and resilience, but sometimes people lose touch with their internal guidance system."

"Well, my system is long gone."

"Rest your head on the back of the treatment chair and close your eyes."

"You're not going to shoot me up with drugs, are you?"

"You have my word. I will not administer a drug."

"I don't know about this."

"Just close your eyes and imagine you are walking down a narrow street. You're not in a hurry. You are looking at the many things on display in the store windows."

Mylowe spoke softly and initiated a five-minute hypnotic technique to relax Vinnie.

"In the windows, you see jewelry, the latest fashions, toys and furniture. It begins to rain and you step inside the nearest store. You discover that this store is a magic shop filled with all the things you have wished for.

"From a shelf, you may select one item, but you must leave something in its place. Take time to look around."

Mylowe waited for ten minutes before speaking. "When you've made your selection, walk from the shop and open your eyes."

Blinking, Vinnie said, "Something strange happened when I came out of the magic shop. I didn't have a body. What does that mean?"

"It could mean you don't recognize yourself."

"Are you going to ask me what I took from the shop?" Vinnie didn't pause long enough for Mylowe to reply. "I took a scroll. It's a medical degree with my name on it."

"Did you leave something in its place?"

"You're going to love this one. When I put my anger on the shelf, I thought, you're a stupid ass. How could you be a good doctor and be so angry at life?"

Mylowe knew that children before the age of six thrive on imagination. When a child's imagination is inundated by careless talk and misdirected gossip by the adults around him, the child is affected forever.

Mylowe knew Vinnie's dream of becoming a physician was beyond Vinnie's mental capacity. He could be shown that his life-long body pains were psychosomatic. Would it be in Vinnie's best interest to tell him the severity of his mental condition had been misdiagnosed? Could Vinnie understand his extraordinary imagination about his mental illness had been ignited and fueled by stories from his mentally disturbed relatives?

Vinnie walked to the door.

"Okay, Doc, how did I do?"

"You did fine. Tomorrow we'll try something a little bit different. In a few days, I'm going to prescribe an MRI."

"Why?"

"Didn't you tell me you had a concussion when you were twelve?"

"Yes."

"As a precaution I want to check it out."

"Does the MRI hurt?"

"Not at all."

As Vinnie opened the door, Barry Waldon brushed by him and sat in the treatment chair. After Vinnie had closed the door, Barry said, "Yuh know, Doc, those pills you've been dropping on me are working."

Mylowe examined Barry's eyes and turned away.

"The drug therapy will help."

Mylowe was pleased that Barry was willing to take the drugs. "If you stay on your medication, you'll be able to move from your parents' home into a support house."

"Wow! When can I go?"

"Sometime next month. I'll speak to your parents and make some housing arrangements. You understand your physical and mental condition will be monitored at the support house. If you do well, the supervisors in the home will help you find a different job. Someday in the future, you might live in your own apartment. It depends on you. If you stay on the meds, in a year you may be able to get along without them."

"I've been waiting for this kind of freedom for fifteen years." Barry bounded from the room and yelled, "Thanks, Doc."

Three Weeks Later

Mylowe kept his promise to Barry and made the necessary arrangements to move him into a supervised home. Mylowe knew Barry would do well and planned to monitor his progress.

Vinnie's invasive medications were gradually discontinued and Mylowe prescribed a short-term, low-dose Valium. Through a local high school coordinator, Mylowe made arrangements for Vinnie to be academically tested. If he tested well, he could begin attending daytime classes to get a GED. For the present, Vinnie was content to stay in his parents' home and continue working at the hospital.

Mylowe decided to go back to Justin House and mentioned it to George Whitetail during dinner at the neighborhood bar.

"Why can't you stay in Miami?" George asked. "You can work on financing your clinic in Miami instead of sitting in that smelly Eben's Tower. Before you go there's another patient I want you to see, a woman."

"Why haven't you sent her to me before now?"

"It slipped my mind. It's the woman I told you about who works in the hospital laundry. I'll arrange an appointment with her in the morning."

George quickly changed the subject. "This situation between Drench Martin and Rema worries me," he said. "Drench did not find information about Emille drowning in Cuba. Rema is in for another disappointment. Is she working at the Libra Center these days?"

"One day a week. I agree with you. A negative report from Drench might push her over the edge."

George nodded. "I'll speak to Drench. I'm certain he won't give her bad news."

"What can he do about it if it's bad news?"

George tapped the table with the handle of his fork. "In his way, he'll tell her."

52

HELLO AGAIN

Two days later, Mylowe waited in treatment room #14 for the secretary from the hospital's psychiatric division to bring him the medical file on the woman George had referred to him for psychiatric evaluation. The patient's name was May Ferry. When Mylowe opened May's file, it was blank except for some scanty notations made by a clinic intern in January, 1971.

There were no entries in the woman's file for the last twenty-four years except George's recent evaluation of her physical and mental condition. Disgusted that the health of an employee, who had worked in the hospital laundry for twenty years, had been lost or ignored, Mylowe flung the file on the desktop.

In that moment, the treatment room door opened. A woman in her late thirties clutched the doorknob. Mylowe noticed she was barely five-feet tall and small. "Come in, May," he said. "My name is Dr. Ort."

With childlike enthusiasm as if she had recently learned a new social skill, she vigorously shook his hand. Despite his assistance, she lingered in the doorway. Finally, and with one quick movement, she slid into a chair beside the door.

Mylowe pulled a white metal stool from beside the desk and sat down near her.

"Dr. Whitetail asked me to meet you," he said.

"I'm not insane," she whispered.

"Of course, you're not insane. Do you have a family doctor?"

"The nurses take care of me," she whispered.

"Where do they do this?"

299

"In the nurses' home. They are my friends."

"Do you live in the student nurses' building?"

"Yes."

"How do the nurses help you?"

"They fix my hair and take me shopping. When I have a cold, they give me medicine."

"Was 1971 the last time you saw a doctor? Do you remember what the doctor told you?"

"He asked me about my baby. My baby died when it was born."

Mylowe studied her face and sensed that she had survived a traumatic episode. Undoubtedly the trauma was severe enough to cause her to spiritually detach from life. Could it have been because she lost her child? Physically she seemed strong. Spiritually she was fragile.

After his initial examination, Mylowe determined the best therapy would be a visit to the magic shop. He turned down the overhead lights, and told her she could remain in the chair near the door.

"Close your eyes," he said.

Using a low-level hypnotic suggestion, he guided her to imagine a street lined with stores and directed her to enter the magic shop.

"On the shelves in the magic shop," he said, "is everything in the universe. You may take one new item from the shop. It should be something that you feel will change your life. In its place, you must discard something you want to throw away."

She sat so still in the chair Mylowe hesitated to disturb her. Finally, he initiated the suggestion to return from the shop.

"You're coming back now, three, two, one," he counted. "You may open your eyes."

When she was comfortable, Mylowe asked, "What did you leave in the magic shop?"

She bowed her head. "My shame."

"Why did you leave your shame?"

"I don't want to feel it anymore."

"What did you take from the shop?"

"I took happy people around me."

Mylowe sat beside her and held her hand. Her small fingers latched around his.

"You're smiling," he said.

She lowered her eyes. He pressed her hand reassuringly. "Don't be shy," he whispered. "Please come see me again."

She stood up and walked toward the door. Mylowe began to make notes in her file. He stopped, laid the pen on the desktop and stared at the empty doorway. There was something mysterious about the petite blond woman. May Ferry, so modest and unassuming, was confronting life and demanding something from it.

That evening, Mylowe and George ate dinner at their favorite neighborhood bar. Later, they returned to George's condo to watch the Phillies and the Mets on television. Comfortably settled during the seventh inning stretch, George asked, "Did you treat my female patient today?"

"Yes, May Ferry is a sweet lady. What do you know about her?"

"Only the nurses have that information. What you see is what she is."

"Her medical file was almost empty except for a 1971 exam. Do I dare ask why she was not advised to go to the clinic for basic health care?"

"I don't know. As far as anyone knows, she does not have a family."

"She's intriguing."

"I knew she would arouse your curiosity. You have a deep drive to perfect the human race."

George grinned, put on his glasses, opened a book and settled back. He had enjoyed a rare moment when he could confront Mylowe's compulsive nature.

Two Weeks Later

May Ferry kept the next appointment with Mylowe. While reviewing her status with George, Mylowe said that May Ferry was making progress.

"She has Social Anxiety Disorder," Mylowe related. "You already knew her problem. Why didn't you write it in her medical file?"

"I was leaving that up to you. I know you prefer to make your own diagnoses."

"May's spirit is fractured."

"That's not a medical diagnosis."

"For crap sake, George. Psychoanalysis is not a mystery. If done thoroughly, it pumps out all the hidden desires. It also provides the basis to help patients know what desires in their internal emotional field they have hidden away under lock and key."

"So, what's she hiding?"

"Shame."

"Shame? What did she do?"

"I believe it's because her baby was born dead. One thing I do know. When she finally connects with her internal emotional field, she has the stamina to reconstruct her life along new lines. I predict, in time, she will have a true feeling of self-worth."

Mylowe laid two more medical reports on Whitetail's desk and walked away.

"What are these?" he yelled.

"Those are detailed reports on Vinnie Rutledge and Barry Waldron. Vinnie's in night school studying for his GED and Barry is living in a supervised home."

"Why are you giving these to me?"

"I've decided to return to Justin House. These two patients should be assigned to a case worker."

"When are you leaving?"

"As soon as May Ferry agrees to live in a group home."

"Does she want to move from the nurses' complex?"

"I haven't asked her. She did say she wants to live around people. She'd do well in a group home."

From George's office, Mylowe hurried through the first-floor corridors to treatment room # 14. May Ferry's appointment was at 2:00 p.m. She was waiting. Her long hair, the color of a hay stack in late August, hugged her face and was tied in a pony tail with a white satin ribbon. The change in hair style accentuated the pearl tone of her skin. She walked into the room and sat in the white metal treatment chair next to Mylowe's desk.

"Would you agree to do some mind traveling today?" he asked.

Too shy to reply, she hunched her shoulders.

"Do you trust me?" he whispered.

She smiled.

He guided her across the room to the treatment couch.

"You may sit on the edge of the couch until you feel comfortable," he said. "Mind traveling is similar to visiting the magic shop. In mind travel, you'll feel as if you're dreaming."

It was five minutes before she leaned her head back and pulled her legs onto the couch. She reached out and grasped Mylowe's hand. Using a semi-heavy induction technique, Mylowe moved May's mind into an altered state.

"Look around, May. What do you see?" he asked.

She did not respond.

"May, where are you?"

She spoke softly. "I'm hiding beside a round wood gate in a bunch of weeds. My little baby boy is whimpering. I want him to be quiet. The soldiers are coming."

"Look around. What other things do you see?"

"There is a big stone building on the hill above me. It has a strange roof."

"What is strange about the roof?"

"It's a China roof. One part is on top of another part."

Mylowe gently squeezes May's hand. "You said you were the baby's mother. Are you young?"

"Yes, I'm seventeen." She began to breathe heavily.

Mylowe squeezed her hand. "What are you doing?"

"I'm running into the middle of a dirt road so the soldiers will see me. I'm screaming so they won't hear my baby crying. I'm saying, 'Take me. Take me.'"

"Why are you screaming?"

"I want the soldiers away from my child."

"What are the soldiers doing to you?"

"They're tying my arms behind me and dragging me down a dirt road. They throw me into a wooden wagon."

May screams. Mylowe squeezes her hand and whisperers, "Your fear will pass."

She whimpers. "One of the soldiers is walking toward the gate where my child is sitting."

"What is he doing?"

Tears run down May's cheeks. She did not speak.

Mylowe asks, "Tell me about the soldier by the round gate?"

"He's looking down into the weeds. He raises his sword. He strikes my baby."

"Are you still in the wagon?"

"Yes, there are peasants walking near me. They push carts filled with their belongings. The soldiers push the tips of their swords into their backs."

"Who are these soldiers?"

"I think they are Mongolians. They've invaded our country."

"Do you live in China?"

"Yes." Gasping for breath, May whispered, "The soldiers have taken me to their camp. They rape me again and again. I want my baby. They laugh. I die."

Mylowe felt her pain. It was not unusual for him to sense the timelessness of his patients. The details of May's past life haunted him.

He started the process to bring May from the altered state. When she awakened, she continued to sob. He held her until she was quiet. She took a deep breath and looked at him.

"I ran away from my baby boy and the soldiers killed him."

Mylowe wiped the tears from her cheeks. The details of her past life had revealed the deep shame she had expressed to him earlier. Her grief for the baby she had abandoned in China had come with her into this life. Mylowe sensed her deep distress increased when the baby in her current life was born dead.

Mylowe studied her tear-stained face. "You dreamed one of your past lives."

"It was sad."

"I'm truly sorry. But knowing about that particular lifetime may help you."

"How can it help me? I ran away from my baby. I did the same thing in this life."

"You didn't abandon your infant. He was not alive."

"Yes, I did abandon him. You just don't know what really happened."

Mylowe brushed the stray hairs away from her face. "Past lives stay close to us when we come back again. The details come through to us like echoes."

She shook her head. "I don't know what you mean. Can I go now?"

She blew her nose and stood up. Mylowe did not try to stop her. He walked with her to the door.

When he was alone, he began to write in her file. He described her journey to one of her past lives. Tossing his pen on the desktop, he dialed George's office.

"George, the strangest thing just happened. When I regressed May Ferry to a past life, she was able to describe her past life in great detail."

"Is that strange?"

"Here's what's strange. May Ferry's past life was in China. It was the same place as my past life. It was identical to what I experienced years ago when Rema used past life regression therapy on me."

"What are you telling me?"

"I suspect May Ferry and I were together in a past life."

"So, what does that prove?"

"She was my mother."

"I still don't understand."

"It's a matter of reincarnation. We usually reincarnate back into the same family unit. We relive our past life relationships over and over again with the same people. If she were my mother in a past life, couldn't she be my mother in this life?"

Dr. Whitetail sighed. "You're really going overboard in this search for your biological mother. You've almost alienated Melody Ann because of your obsession and I'm beginning to worry about your mental state."

Mylowe pounded the desk. "Listen to me, George. I'm not nuts. Rema will verify the details of my past life."

It didn't matter that Mylowe had lost his perspective. George wanted Mylowe's search for his birth mother to end.

"I have a different approach," he said.

"What?" Mylowe asked.

"Regress me."

"Why?"

"To see if you and I were together in some past lifetime."

"How would that help?"

"I don't know."

"You're playing with me, George."

"Maybe, maybe not. Can we do it tonight?"

"Okay, okay, tonight."

53

GOING BACK

Dr. George Whitetail was a total skeptic concerning matters of past life regression therapy and refused to consider that any part of life would be enhanced with regression therapy. He knew Mylowe was trained to utilize both traditional and alternative therapies, but his Native American Indian upbringing had convinced him there were inexplicable natural inconsistencies. Perhaps it was because he had not been able to distinguish between extrasensory perception and true incarnation memories. He usually did not take his psychic abilities seriously.

Mylowe, aware of George's doubts, knew he had to be cautious when investigating reincarnation memories. In George's case, it might be a problem to decide what is a true incarnation memory or merely a case of mediumship.

That evening in George's family room, Mylowe induced George's mind into an altered state.

"What is your name?" asked Mylowe.

"Nei."

"Where do you live?"

"Mongolia."

"How old are you?"

"Twenty-two."

"What is your occupation?"

"I'm a soldier."

"Describe where you are."

"The army is putting down a rebellion in China."

"What year is it?"

"Early in the 14th century."

"Tell me what you are doing."

"With the tip of my sword, I'm pushing peasants down a dirt road. There's a disturbance ahead."

"Do you see what is happening?"

"A woman runs from behind a large round wood gate. She is screaming."

"Why is she afraid?"

"Our soldiers are throwing babies and old people in water-filled ditches beside the road. My commander tells me to search behind the big round gate that leads to the temple above."

"Do you investigate?"

"Yes, I find a Chinese child sitting in the bushes."

"How old is the child?"

"One year. The child is a boy. I stand over him and raise my sword to kill him."

"Do you strike him with your sword?"

"I try to follow the order from my commander, but I cannot strike the child. I look at the temple on the hill above me."

"Do you take the child to the temple?"

"No, the commander is yelling at the soldiers to move along. I turn away from the child and walk down the road."

"Where did you go?"

"I walk to my tent in the base camp and throw myself on the floor."

"Are you tired?"

"No, I have disobeyed my commander's orders. I am weak. I cannot kill a child. I don't deserve to live."

"How long did you stay in the tent?"

"I hear the woman screaming. The soldiers are raping her. She screams until dawn. It is silent now. I'm certain they have killed her."

"What happens next?"

"In the early light, I walk to the wood gate. I am brave now and will kill the child, but the child is not there. I search everywhere. I must kill the child."

The distress in George's voice was an indication to discontinue the regression. Mylowe began the procedure to bring George back to consciousness.

"What kind of story was that?" asked George.

"Do you remember it?" asked Mylowe.

"It was so real."

"What are you doing this weekend?"

"Why?"

"Let's fly to Justin House so you can tell Rema the details of your past life and compare the details of May Ferry's past life to yours and my past life."

"Okay, I'd like to get this settled."

"Great!" said Mylowe. "I'll call Rema and tell her we're coming."

Driving the rental car from Dayton to Wexlor, Mylowe didn't mention May Ferry. George took several short naps and commented about the beauty of the Ohio countryside. There were wide stretches of green grasses, acres of newly-plowed fields and budding trees were enhanced by the bright yellow flowers on the forsythia bushes. It was spring.

They arrived at Justin House. Rema was in the den waiting for them. She noticed George's stoic behavior and assumed he was concerned about Mylowe.

She turned to Mylowe.

"Tell me about this particular patient's past life," she said. "How is George involved?"

"Recently, George permitted me to regress him."

"Will you be witness to the fact that George did not know any details of my past life regression?"

She looked at George. "Mona was present during Mylowe's regression. Did she tell you the contents of Mylowe's regression?"

"Not the contents. She said she was an old lady in Mylowe's past life."

"Did you know any details such as the date, location or circumstances?" She glanced toward Mylowe. "What are you trying to prove?"

"I've been treating my patient, May Ferry, for Social Anxiety Disorder. Yesterday, my treatment was past life regression therapy. During the session, she described a past lifetime similar in setting and circumstances as the past life I described to you."

"Are you referring to the regression I did for you when you were in high school?"

"Yes."

"What's the problem?"

"Before I answer you, do you remember the details of my regression?"

"Yes, I believe I do."

"In my absence, would you tell George the details of my past life? When I return, I'll relate the details of May Ferry's past life regression. We then can decide if there are similarities."

George nodded and jokingly handed Rema a paperweight from the desktop. "Since you are the judge, take the gavel."

Mylowe glared at him and walked from the room.

"What is going on?" Rema asked.

George folded his arms and sat down. "I'm not permitted to tell you until we've compared our past lives."

Rema stared at him and shook her head wondering if this was a game. "Mylowe's regression began in the 14th century," she said. "He was a small child sitting behind a moon gate that led to a temple on a mountaintop in China."

"What is a moon gate?"

"In Chinese architecture it's a circular gate in a wall."

"Sorry to interrupt. Please continue."

"The child watched from the bushes as his young mother was carted away by Mongolian soldiers. He was rescued by a peasant couple the next morning when they opened the gate to work in the fields. Mylowe has always been positive that the peasants were Felic and me.

"When the child was six years old, a famine beset China and he was returned to the temple by the woman who found him. Her husband had deserted his family and there was not food enough to feed her own child and the young boy.

"At the temple, the boy studied and grew to manhood. He became a monk, but later joined the rebels and fought for his country. At the age of twenty-eight he became the first non-royal man to rule China. During his thirty-five year reign, he established the Ming Dynasty."

George nodded. "Well, in my past life regression, I was a Mongolian soldier. The Mongolians were putting down a rebellion in China in the 14th Century.

"While the soldiers were herding peasants down a road, a young woman ran from behind a round gate. She was yelling that she would go with them and begged the soldiers to take her instead of an older woman who carried a child. The young woman was pushed into a wooden cart and taken away. The soldiers were killing all the babies and old people but her actions saved the older woman's child. After the commotion, my commander stared at the oval gate and ordered me to kill the people behind it

"I obeyed. Behind the gate, I discovered a child about one year old. He was sitting on a straw mat near the stone wall. The boy had black hair and a round face. He was Chinese. I drew my sword to kill him. When he looked at me, I couldn't do it. I don't know why because I was trained to kill. I walked away and went back to the base camp prepared to end my life for disobeying my commander.

"In a nearby tent, a woman was screaming. She was being raped. Her screams stopped at dawn. I knew she was dead.

"Summoning my resolve to be a good soldier, I returned to the stone wall with the intent to kill the child. He was gone. I went back to my tent and fell on my sword."

Rema stared at George. "Ask Mylowe to come in. I want to hear about May Ferry's past life."

Mylowe entered the den and explained the details of May Ferry's past life from the perspective of the young mother in China during a rebellion. Rema withheld her questions until Mylowe had finished. Before she could speak, George asked, "In your experience with past life regression therapy, have you witnessed close relationships before?"

Rema sat quietly before answering. "Yes, I've seen soul mates come together. I also have known friends that reincarnated and were together again. In some cases, even their enemies reappeared to work out karmic debts.

"Although I'm certain it has happened, I've not tried to regress a person in order for them to obtain particular details from a past life.

"Past lives are echoes. They pass through to us on a specific type of energy when we're ready to know the details about a past life. Many people can sense their past lives without being regressed."

"Is it possible that May Ferry might be my mother?" asked Mylowe.

"Is that what you came to ask me?"

"Yes ma'am."

"Have you asked May Ferry if her name was Ruthie May Durston?"

"No, not yet. There's still the matter of a DNA test."

Rema glared at him. "Was May Ferry able to speak? The old man in the Anchor Bar said Ruthie Durston didn't speak."

George stood and poured another drink. "Mylowe is anxious to show May Ferry the pink ribbon you found in Felic's briefcase."

"If May Ferry identifies the pink hair ribbon, we might learn more about her and why the ribbon was in Felic's possession."

Trying to drive away unresolved questions, George waved his hand in the air. "The ribbon could have dropped from a sack of trash. Maybe it doesn't belong to anyone."

"That may be. But since Mylowe feels he is risking his future with Melody Ann, I think he should ask every question and follow every clue."

"If you believe the six of us have come together as a makeshift family in this life to work out the karma we created in one past life in China, are we permitted to disagree?" George asked.

"Certainly, we're here to learn from each other," Rema replied.

"Understanding this, if each of us were questioned, could we explain what we have learned in these relationships?"

"Can you do it?" Mylowe asked.

"Yes, although I didn't kill you when you were the child in China sitting by moon gate, I did return the next day prepared to do it. I had killing in my heart. I hope in some way I've repaid to you that portion of my karma."

"You have been my mentor."

George replied quickly. "I am often reminded that my medical practice does not include children. I've been denied a relationship with children in every part of my life."

Rema interrupted him. "Let's get back to our initial discussion. Under past life regression therapy, Mylowe recognized Felic and me as the Chinese laborers who found him behind a moon gate. Mylowe also identified Mona as the old woman who lived with us.

"In her regression, May Ferry described the moon gate and a similar situation except her experience was the young mother's point of view. George's was the soldier's experience and Mylowe's was from the small child's perspective. I'm certain Mylowe's research during the coming years will provide much more information on past life regression therapy."

Mylowe frowned. "I hope to do more. Perhaps, I'll prove that large groups of people return together to help improve societies. On the negative side, I might discover that criminals held together in prisons come back in groups to corrupt society."

* * * *

On Sunday evening, Mylowe and George went back to Miami. They had rested from the daily pressures of work and enjoyed waking up in Justin House on a Sunday morning to the fresh aroma of the coming of spring in Ohio.

Arriving at the Miami airport in the early morning, a fast hot shower was their only wake-up call before hurrying to the clinic. At four o'clock in the afternoon, Mylowe called George's office.

"I have the pink hair ribbon in my pocket. Will you go with me to visit May Ferry?"

"To do what?"

"To see if May recognizes the ribbon."

"You're crazy and I'm tired. I'm ready to pack it in for today."

"George, just go with me. Meet me in the lobby of the nurses' complex."

George Whitetail swung his chair away from his desk. Facing the wall, he closed his eyes and imagined the forthcoming consequences with Mylowe and May Ferry. He shook his head at the images floating through his brain and knew there was nothing that would stop Mylowe from questioning her. He pulled himself up from the chair, took off his lab coat and grabbed his jacket from the coat rack. Closing the office door, he leaned against it. Listening to the commands from the little voice in his mind, he nodded and walked from the clinic building toward the student nurses' complex.

The lobby of the nurses' building was dimly lit. As Mylowe paced across the highly polished floor, his image was reflected in the wide clear windows. George arrived and stopped Mylowe's pacing by saying in a low voice, "Sit down."

Mylowe exhaled and sat down on a window seat.

"Have you considered the extent of psychological injury you could stimulate in this woman with your questions?" George asked.

"Yes, I've thought of it."

Mylowe grabbed George's elbow. "Let's go," he said. "The elevator is across the hallway."

George remained seated and pushed Mylowe's hand away. "Do you know where her room is? I'm not going up there and run into a half-dressed nurse on her way from the shower."

Mylowe laughed. "I checked with the janitor. May Ferry lives in the transients' wing. It's okay for us to visit there."

When the elevator door opened, Mylowe ushered George inside and pushed the button. When the door opened on the fourth floor, George reluctantly stepped into the hallway.

At May Ferry's door, the noise of Mylowe's knuckles hitting the door resounded throughout the length of the hall.

The click of an inside door lock was followed by a small opening at the door edge.

"May," said Mylowe, "This is Dr. Ort and Dr. Whitetail. We'd like to speak with you. Could we come in?"

The door opened slowly. The two men stepped into the room and noticed the white crocheted doilies on the backs of the sofa and chair. On a table by the door was a stack of colorful hand-crocheted afghans.

"These are beautiful," Mylowe said. "Do you sell them?"

"No," May replied shyly. "They go to elderly and the needy."

"You must spend hours doing this."

"Yes, I work on them at night after I get home from the laundry."

313

Mylowe guided her to sit on the sofa beside him. "May, I have something to show you."

George Whitetail settled into a nearby chair and watched Mylowe take the pink hair ribbon from his pocket.

"When you were a girl," Mylowe asked, "do you remember wearing a pink hair ribbon like this one?"

May took the ribbon from him and let it drop full length. Slowly, she ran her fingers along each edge.

"My mother made this ribbon. Where did you get it?"

"How can you be certain this is your ribbon?"

"Mother always crocheted the edge on each side of my hair ribbons. She was very sick. Sometimes, she missed hooking the thread into the next loop."

Placing the ribbon across her open hand, May pointed to the open loops.

"Do you recall the dream you had in the treatment room today?" Mylowe asked.

"Yes, it made me feel sad."

"You told me your baby was born dead."

"Yes."

"Were you living in a hotel near the Miami Canal?"

"Yes, how did you know that? I was sick for a long time before the baby came. When the baby came I was alone."

"Did someone live with you in the hotel room?"

"Yes, my daddy's friend."

"What was her name?"

George Whitetail raised his eyebrows at Mylowe's deceptive question.

May replied, "Daddy's friend was a man. His name was Arnie."

When she mentioned Arnie's name, Mylowe felt a strange sensation run through his body. He motioned to George to continue with the questions.

At that moment, George realized the trauma he had expected to happen to May Ferry had happened to Mylowe.

"What was your daddy's name?" asked George.

"Dave Durston."

Mylowe's face was pale.

George continued. "You said you were alone when the baby was born. Where was your daddy?"

"In the Coast Guard."

"Where was Arnie?"

"Out drinking. He used my daddy's money to buy drinks."

"Tell me about the day the baby was born."

"My baby came at night. I had hurt all day. When I went to the toilet, the baby boy came out and dropped into the toilet."

"What did you do?"

"I took him out of the water. He didn't cry. He was dead."

"What happened to the baby?"

"I wrapped him in newspaper and threw him out the hotel window."

"Why did you throw him away?"

"Because Arnie said when the baby came he was going to sell it. I knew Arnie would be awful mad if he found out the baby had come and was dead."

"Was there an alley beneath the hotel window?"

"Yes."

"Did the alley have a name?"

"Yes, people called it Dead Man's Alley."

When George saw that Mylowe had regained his composure, he leaned back and nodded to Mylowe to continue the questions.

"Do you remember the name of the hotel you lived in?" Mylowe asked.

"Yes, it was the Green Palms Hotel."

"Where was your room?"

"The second floor."

"Was it over Sally's Restaurant?"

"Yes, Sally brought me food."

Mylowe didn't know what else to ask. He gave George a quizzical look. George shot a quick glance back at him that said, "Let's go!"

Mylowe stood and asked, "May, what did your mother call you?"

"Ruthie, Ruthie May."

"Then your real name is Ruthie May Durston?"

"Yes."

"Why are you called May Ferry?"

"My mother's maiden name was Perry. After the baby came, I ran away from Arnie and my name was changed to May Perry."

"Where did you go?"

"To the homeless compound near the hotel. The people there were nice to me. Later, I went to live in a foster home."

"When did you go to work in the hospital laundry?"

"I was seventeen."

George frowned and mouthed the words, "Let's go!"

Once in the hallway, George watched as Mylowe's leaned against the wall. "Before you go completely overboard, there's one more step before you can safely declare that May Ferry is your mother."

"I know," Mylowe whispered. "I need to order a DNA test."

"That's correct. So far, the evidence you have is circumstantial."

"But it's so close."

"That may be, but May Ferry only confirmed what the old guy in the run-down bar room knew about her family from gossip. Her dead baby could have been hauled away in the garbage days before Felic went to the alley. You didn't ask the date of the baby's birth."

Mylowe glared at George.

"If you're playing the devil's advocate, you're doing a damn good job. Tomorrow, I'm collecting May's DNA and my DNA and sending them to the lab."

Believing there are no coincidences, George nudged Mylowe's elbow. "Did you catch it when she said she changed her name to May Perry?"

"Yes, her last name was changed from Perry to Ferry. I assume it was a clerical error at the hospital."

George nodded and sat down on the window seat in the lobby. "This night has been too much for this old warrior. I need a drink."

At the local hangout, Mylowe announced he had decided to stay in Miami until the DNA results came back.

"That's three or four weeks away," George reminded. "Why don't you go visit Melody Ann?"

Mylowe shook his head. "I want to wait until I get the DNA report. Meanwhile, I want to learn more from May Ferry."

"You'll question her until she throws you out."

Mylowe knew George was correct. He wasn't certain how to go about questioning May Ferry without exposing who he really was. She had a quiet nature. Her responses to his queries could cause her trauma.

Specifically, he needed to ask her the date of her baby's birth. Next, he wanted to know about her relationship with Arnie Tuttle. Was Arnie his father? Was May Ferry ever incapable of speech? From other resources, he would find how Dave Durston died. Did her father have Navy benefits and insurance?

As Dave Durston's daughter, was Ruthie May Durston listed as his beneficiary? How did Evelyn Perry Durston die? What is the Durston family's medical history? Is Arnie Tuttle's wife, Margaret, still living? If so, what could she tell him about Arnie? Did Arnie have specific medical problems?

Added to these questions Mylowe wanted to find the other Durston child, baby boy Durston, the infant put up for adoption by The Sisters of St. Angeline Convent forty-two years ago.

Question upon question flooded Mylowe's brain until he jokingly announced to George he was going back to the condo and sleep for the next three weeks until the DNA report arrived.

George interrupted Mylowe's thoughts. "Are you calling Rema tonight?"

"Why?"

"To tell her the pink hair ribbon was Ruthie May Durston's. Do you realize how stressed out Rema has been since she found the ribbon in Felic's briefcase?"

"I know. Rema thinks Felic might have been involved with my mother."

"Aren't her feelings important?"

Mylowe's guilt was evident in the tone of his next words.

"Damn, when will I learn to think about other people?"

George slapped the tabletop. "That's the one flaw in your character I've been preaching about."

Three-and-a-half Weeks Later

Mylowe was in George's office when a secretary rushed into the office carrying a white cardboard envelope.

"Dr. Ort, the package you've been waiting for arrived a few minutes ago."

Panic almost closed his throat. He knew the contents of the package represented an important item in the search for his family roots. Like a convict walking toward the gas chamber, he was certain, one way or the other, this would be the end.

"Well," asked George, "Aren't you going to open it?"

Mylowe wasn't seeing clearly. He blinked as he pulled the string. The package lay open in his hand.

"Before I open this," he said, "I want to say something."

"What?"

"When there are five million sperm rushing around during intercourse and one sperm makes life happen, that's an accomplishment. Therefore from this day, I am who I was meant to be!"

George wanted to say, "Or who you're not!" but decided not to add a wisecrack to the moment.

Mylowe leaned forward over the table. "The DNA results are positive," he said. "May Ferry (Ruthie May Durston) is my mother."

George smiled. "What are you going to do now?"

"I'm going to Des Moines to tell Melody Ann. I want to surprise her. We can begin to plan our wedding."

"How are you going to tell Ruthie May Durston?"

Mylowe did not answer. Intuitively he knew what he was going to do. After he told Melody Ann, he would return to Miami and prove to May Ferry that he is the baby she threw from the hotel window twenty-five years ago.

Somehow, with such information in his hands, he felt strangely disconnected. The search for his birth mother had added a yearning deep in his being. How was it possible that this same woman abandoned him centuries ago in China and again in this life? What was the karma between them that caused them so much pain? Would he ever know?

His first step before flying to Des Moines would be to deliver the DNA report to the Reverend Mother at The Sisters of St. Angeline Convent.

Next he would call Rema and relay the results of the DNA. He wasn't prepared to discuss his wedding plans with her and slowly dialed her number. When she answered, he clenched his teeth.

"Oh! Mylowe, I know how much this means to you and Melody Ann," she said.

"I'm leaving for Des Moines to tell her. I'll call you from there."

"Have you told Ruthie May Durston that she is your mother?"

"No, I want more time to prepare her. She has been alone for nearly forty years. It's rather sudden to tell her I'm her son and she has a brother."

"I realize that. So, have a great time in Des Moines with Melody Ann and let me know how she reacts to the news."

54

SURPRISE!

When Mylowe boarded the plane to Des Moines at the Miami airport, he realized the wheel of fortune had spun in his favor. In just two hours, he would be with Melody Ann again. He yearned to make love to her. Afterward, with her soft body lying next to his, he would describe the outcome of the clues that further substantiated his initial feeling that May Ferry was actually Ruthie May Durston.

He would explain that psychiatry sometimes uses past life regression therapy as an adjunct procedure in the attempt to help the mind rise above. Patients are directed to reach an Alpha level of consciousness. This is the level passed through each morning as we awaken and each night as we fall asleep. On the Alpha plateau, the conscious mind is held in reserve. The altered consciousness is then open to exploration of the echoes (or reverberations) of past lives.

While in an altered state, May Ferry described herself as a young Chinese woman who surrendered to the Mongolian soldiers in order to save her small son. Her description of a large oval gate at the entrance to a temple in the China countryside and the situation with the Mongolian soldiers was an exact replica of Mylowe's past life regression.

He would further explain that years earlier, when Rema had regressed him, he had seen the identical situation as May Ferry experienced. Although, Mylowe's perspective of that lifetime was that of a small child whose mother had hidden him in an area overgrown with bushes behind a round wood gate was different from May Ferry's, Melody Ann would understand the events that followed further substantiated the past life relationship.

319

He would also need to tell how Rema discovered a pink ribbon in Felic's old briefcase and May Ferry identified the edges on the pink hair ribbon.

Mylowe shuffled his feet and changed the position level of the passenger seat that was much too short for persons with long legs.

He closed his eyes and envisioned Melody Ann walking down a church aisle in a flowing white dress holding a bouquet and moving toward him. At the altar, she smiled. After the marriage ceremony, they were driven away in a horse-drawn carriage. At last, they would be together.

Again, he adjusted the slant of the airline seat, stretched his legs under the seat in front and closed his eyes. Drifting off, Melody Ann was the center of his dream.

It was nearly midnight when he parked the rental car in front of Melody Ann's family home in suburban Des Moines. The house was dark. He opened the front door with his key, turned on the hall light and put his briefcase and travel bag on the hallway bench.

In the kitchen, he drank some water and walked quietly up the rear stairs to Melody Ann's bedroom. Wanting to slip into bed beside her, he nudged the door open. The room was dark.

At the bedside, he undressed and slipped under the bedcovers. Turning on his side, he put his right arm over her. His arm lay on her arm.

Something was wrong. Her arm was wrapped around another body. He was leaning against the bare back of a second body. He leaped from the bed and switched on a table lamp.

"What the hell!" he yelled as Melody Ann and a man sat up in the bed.

They squinted until their eyes adjusted to the bright light. Although he was naked, he couldn't move.

Melody Ann's bare nipples were staring at him. He wanted to look at her eyes, but he couldn't shift his glance away from the sensual round pink centers of her bosomy exterior. As the moment passed, his glare was able to focus on the man sitting beside her.

For an interminable moment, no one moved. Mylowe finally found movement in his arms, scooped up his clothes and stumbled toward the door. He turned to glare at Melody Ann. She covered her breasts.

Adrenalin surged through his body. His face, hot and flushed, was in contrast to the chill he felt. Stepping sideways through the open door while attempting to maintain an imposing regal stature, he became aware of his nakedness.

Reaching the bottom of the stairs, he realized he should put on some clothes. The rumble of bare feet from the floor above suggested he should get out of the house.

The clothing fell from his arms. From inside the heap, he saw his shorts and tee shirt. Stooping, he picked them up and tugged them onto his body. Fumbling with his trousers until he found the leg openings, he pulled them up and managed to pull on the shirt. Leaving it unbuttoned, he wrapped his shoes in his suit coat.

At the front door, he picked up his luggage from the hallway, opened the door and wrestled the luggage and clothes down the front steps.

Digging into trouser pockets for car keys, he opened the door and threw everything on the passenger side. Sitting on the cold leather seat was a shock. He started the engine.

He drove through the dark narrow streets without purpose or direction. Each time his bare feet touched the brake he was reminded he should find a hotel. Instinctively, he turned toward the freeway that would take him to a local, downtown hotel.

Inside the hotel's parking garage, he finished dressing. After registering at the front desk, he rode the elevator to a room on the third floor.

Inside the room, he flung himself across the bed. His head throbbed. The sight of Melody Ann in bed with a man ran through his mind like a cheap movie. He wondered if he had acted noble or stupid. When the telephone rang, he let it ring. When it continued to ring, he knew Melody Ann had tracked him. He rolled over and answered it.

"Hello."

"I must see you," she said sternly.

"Why?"

"Because I want you to understand."

"Understand what?"

"I'm coming over there."

He turned off the lamp and lay on the bed. Muffled voices in the hallway and the distant ding of the elevator bell did not divert his mind from the earlier picture of Melody Ann with her bedroom lover.

It was thirty minutes before there was a knock on the door. He turned on the lamp and sat up. He felt wretched. It was as if the running knot of a hangman's noose was tightening around his throat. He walked toward the door and opened it. Melody Ann stepped inside. He looked down at her remembering his first glimpse of her at the Night Owl Bookstore. She was lovely and appealing.

Now in a dreary hotel room, paralysis had entered every part of him. She moved close to him and whispered.

"I didn't want you to find out this way."

"Why?"

"I've made a real mess of your life. I'm pregnant."

"Am I the father?"

"I don't know."

"Can we at least find out who the father is?"

"No. I'm going to marry Bart Knowles."

"The man in your bed?"

"Yes, Bart Knowles has been in love with me since the fifth grade."

"Does he believe the baby is his?"

"Yes."

"Does he know about me?"

"Yes."

Mylowe bowed his head. "What have I done?"

She looked into his eyes.

"Listen to me. When I discovered I was pregnant, I knew you would insist on marrying me. I also knew without knowing the status of your biological genes an unplanned child would, in time, have driven a wedge between us."

"Why?"

"Because of your obsession."

"My obsession?"

"Your obsession to find your birth mother."

"Did I really cause you to sleep with another man because I wanted to be certain that I pass good genes on to our children?"

"Maybe, I can't explain it. I was alone and distraught over my mother's death and Bart was there."

"I was here to be with you, but you didn't want me to stay."

Mylowe eyed the phone on the night table. The thought of calling the airport crossed his mind. Melody Ann noticed his distraction and backed away.

"Do you love him?" he asked.

She turned and nodded. She had answered his question. The door closed. She was gone.

He looked at the closed door and felt a deficit in himself. It was a sadness he didn't know existed. His life had just been sucked away by the swish of a hotel door.

After all those years of loving her, she was locked in his heart. She had named the thief that had taken her away from him. It was his obsession. He felt the noose tighten around his throat. He started to cry and buried his face deep in a pillow.

He slept, but was tormented by a series of dreams. In one dream, his hair was long and someone was cutting it. He was distressed over losing his hair and raced down a dusty road. As he ran, he turned into an old man. His hair was white. He had a white beard that grew longer each time he took a step.

322

In another dream, he watched ten goldfish swim upstream in dark muddy water. He was immediately turned into a boy running along the canal waving to barge passengers.

He awoke with a jerk. His body was writhing across the bed. A patch of cold air wafted across his face. He pushed up and rested on his elbow to look for the open window. The windows were closed. Under the warmth of the blanket, he wondered if the cold wind had been a sign from Felic. For the rest of the night, he relived his life with Melody Ann. He was still awake when the sun came up.

The next afternoon he was back in Miami in George's condo and spent the early part of evening alone. He had called George earlier to let him know he was back from Des Moines.

In the condo's great room, he paced back and forth. To change the direction of his thoughts, he focused on the Native American Indian memorabilia George had hung on the walls. There were smartly whittled peace pipes, spears of odd sizes and brilliant colors, a feathered war bonnet, beaded moccasins and arrowheads. An open blanket, a necklace and a colorful picture of tepees in a campground hung above the fireplace.

For the first time, Mylowe realized the articles were not only symbolic, but displaying them was the way George anchored himself to his ancestors. It was his way of holding on to his legacy.

He tried to erase from his mind the sight of Melody Ann in bed with the man she called Bart. It happened because of his selfishness and his relentless search to find his mother.

Not knowing what to do, he raised his arms toward the ceiling in a silent thankful prayer for being awarded his life-long wish. He slowly bowed his head and realized his wish was fulfilled when he found his mother but he lost Melody Ann.

After a dinner meeting, George arrived at the condo. It was after nine o'clock.

"That was a short trip," he said. "Hadn't you planned to stay with Melody Ann the entire week?"

"Yes, circumstances have changed."

"Oh! Are you married?"

"No."

"Well?"

Mylowe bowed his head. "I'm going to tell you what happened but until I get Ruthie May situated at Justin House, I don't want Rema and Mona to know the particulars of my visit to Des Moines."

George braced himself for bad news displayed on Mylowe's face.

"Okay," he said, "what happened?"

Mylowe took a deep breath. "It was nearly midnight when I arrived at Melody Ann's house. I let myself in and went up to her bedroom."

"Was she there?"

"Yes, she was in bed with a man."

"Did she know you were coming?"

"No, I wanted to surprise her with my good news. I'm the one who got the surprise. I left immediately and checked in at one of the local hotels. She found me and came to the hotel."

Although George believed he knew the answer to his next question he asked. "You talked to her, didn't you?"

"She's pregnant. Not sure who the father is. She's going to marry the other guy."

George leaned forward. "Why would she marry the other guy?"

"She said it was because of my obsession about not marrying her until I got information about my genetic background."

"Damn! I was afraid this would happen. Did you tell her you had positive proof about your birth mother?"

Mylowe sighed. "I didn't have a chance. She had made up her mind."

George went to the kitchen and returned carrying two beers. "Do you have any way to work this out with Melody Ann? You belong to each other. I've always seen her in your eyes and you in hers."

"No, I've got to go on without her. I don't know if I can."

George pressed on. "Couldn't you arrange to have the child tested for DNA?"

"No."

"Does she love the other guy?"

"I guess she does. I know I'm totally responsible for this mess. I need to find the guts to go on with my life. I have Ruthie May to take care of. She's going to need me. The whole process will take time."

"What are you planning for Ruthie May?"

"I'll take my time convincing her I'm her son. I also plan to find her brother. I must be careful not to put this to her all at one time."

The next morning over coffee, George told Mylowe that Drench Martin had followed up on his promise to Rema to get information about her son's death in Cuba and a dossier on Paul Moore.

"Did he find any information in Cuba that substantiated Emille's death? Did Emille drown at the age of ten?" asked Mylowe.

George paused. "There is no record of Emille's death in Cuba," he whispered. "Not even a grave site. Perhaps, Emille's body was never recovered from the sea."

Mylowe shook his head. "The terrible thing about learning this is that Rema has grieved so many times for him."

"I told Drench we were concerned about Rema's reaction."

"Did Drench find Paul Moore's background?"

"Yes, he has a dossier on him. It's not pretty," said George.

"Damn! What should we do? Should we withhold the information about Emille from Rema or just have Drench show her the papers on Paul Moore?"

"When are you going to tell Rema about you and Melody Ann?" asked George.

"In light of all this, I think I'll sidestep the subject of Melody Ann for as long as possible. I've decided to tell May Ferry that I'm the baby she threw out of the hotel window twenty-five years ago."

"Will she accept your explanation?"

"In time, I believe she will. First, I'll begin to call her Ruthie and take her back to Dead Man's Alley. Maybe, I'll take her to see Sally."

"Is that the woman who owned the restaurant in the Green Palms Hotel?"

"Yes."

"What's next?" asked George.

"After she has time to digest my story, Ruthie and I will see the Reverend Mother. She is the person to explain to Ruthie May about baby boy Durston, her brother. It's not time for that meeting yet."

"Good thought! It will help Ruthie May to be involved in the search for her brother."

"Also, if I can locate Margaret Tuttle, I think any information she could provide about Arnie Tuttle would be helpful," said Mylowe.

"Helpful to Ruthie May or you? Maybe Margaret Tuttle never knew Ruthie was pregnant."

"That could be, but she could tell us more about Arnold Tuttle. As far as I can determine, he was my father."

"How long will this take? What is your time frame—six days, six weeks or six months?"

"More like three weeks. If Ruthie May reacts favorably, I expect to take her to live in Justin House by the first part of June. Why do you ask?"

"Because I have an agenda of my own," George said.

"What is it?"

"I want you to be available to be my best man. I'm planning to ask Mona to marry me."

Mylowe sank into a chair and smiled. "I thought you would never ask her."

"I'm hoping she'll agree. We enjoy each other's company. We're also very good friends and we are both celebrating our sixtieth birthdays this summer."

"I'll be pleased to stand as your best man. When do you anticipate the marriage will take place?"

"Sometime in August. I hope Mona will think it's a grand idea to have our wedding at Justin House."

55

REMORSE

The next morning, Mylowe awoke realizing the most meaningful part of his life had been swept away during the night. He couldn't think about Melody Ann any longer. His body was a torture chamber. Every muscle throbbed. Emotionally, he was devoid of feeling. He pushed up from the center of the bed.

An excruciating pain over his brow shoved him back against the pillows. George stood over him. Mylowe looked at him through half-closed eyes.

"Did you get the license plate number?" George asked.

Mylowe grunted. "What license number?"

"You know. Didn't you get the license number of the truck that ran over you in Des Moines?"

"That truck didn't have a number. It had a name."

"Aha! I'll guess its name was Melody Ann?"

Mylowe moaned and pushed himself to sit upright on the edge of the bed. Struggling to look alive, he stared at George. "Sarcasm is wasted on me this morning," he said. "But, before you go, would you wipe out the swarm of fireflies around me?"

George grinned. Then his face changed to a scowl. He walked away and turned around. "You do realize you created this."

"Yeah, I know."

"I'm sorry."

Mylowe clenched his fingers into a fist and punched at the air. "Damn it," he hissed.

"Are you going to get up?"

"Yes, when I figure out how to live the rest of my life."

"Well, it's obvious. You've got to move on. Have you forgotten? You were given a wonderful gift when you found your mother."

"Is that how it works? We only get one gift per lifetime?"

"You know that isn't true."

"But that's what has happened."

George left the room without acknowledging Mylowe's remark.

Mylowe stood up and shifted his weight until he felt steady on his feet.

His mind oscillated between the scene in Melody Ann's bedroom and the Des Moines hotel room where she uttered the words that would haunt him for the rest of his life. *I'm pregnant. I don't know who the father is. I'm going to marry Bart.*

In the shower, the pressure of the cascading water pumped her words through his brain. "I'm pregnant. I'm pregnant," the pounding water shouted. "I don't know who the father is!"

He hammered the tops of the faucets until the water stopped, fell to his knees and wept. The warm vapor covered him. Finally, it condensed and drops of cool water dripped on his back. He turned and sat down remembering that Rema had described blame as a burning flame and forgiveness as a cooling peace.

Could he forgive himself? If he examined his feelings, he would be the judge and jury. That would be too easy! But, if he sat in the witness box condemning himself for the rest of his life, he might be jumping into water without knowing its depth.

Although gifted in his present life, he knew he had lived many past lifetimes. Most of them had been difficult. Now, he realized those difficult times had been brought about by his unyielding nature.

Sloughing the water from his face and shoulders, he stood and pulled on a terry cloth robe. It was noon when he finished dressing. Reaching for the telephone, he dialed the St. Angeline Convent and made an appointment to meet with the Reverend Mother on Thursday afternoon.

Next, he called Roy Farrell, the private investigator he hired to find Ruthie May Durston.

"Roy, this is Mylowe Ort. I found Ruthie May Durston."

Roy paused. "How did you manage that? The Durston woman's trail was cold."

"I'll tell you about it another time. I have another job for you."

"Who are you looking for now?"

"Margaret Tuttle. I need to know if she's still living."

"Do you know anything about her?" asked Roy.

"I have the death certificate for Arnold Tuttle, her husband. He died in 1993 in Miami. There could be a marriage license on file or divorce decree."

"I'll get right on it. Is there any other way I can help?"

"Yes, find out if there are unpaid benefits from Dave Durston's service life insurance. He was Ruthie May Durston's father and retired from the Coast Guard. I have a copy of his death certificate. He died in 1994 at the Veterans Medical Center in Miami."

"I'll do my best."

"I'll leave a copy of the certificate at the receptionist desk. If it turns out that Ruthie May Durston is the beneficiary on Dave Durston's service life insurance, it could help her to know she had been included in his estate. She truly needs to know people cared about her."

Before calling Rema, he decided how he would tell her about his breakup with Melody Ann. When Eve Porter answered the phone at Justin House, he was relieved.

"Is Rema at the Libra Center?" he asked.

"No, she's sitting in the garden. I told her it was too cool to sit outside but she ignored me."

"Has she been to the Libra Center this week?"

"We were there only on Saturday morning. We were back home by one o'clock. Honestly, she doesn't have much stamina. Also, Maggie is quitting at the end of this month."

"Is she ill?"

"I believe so, but she won't say."

"Is Rema interviewing for a new housekeeper?"

"Maggie's daughter-in-law wants the job. What do you think?"

"I think we should interview other applicants. I plan to be home to stay in three weeks. We can do it then. Can you continue to stay on at the house through the summer?"

"Yes, I would be happy to stay."

"Good, we'll talk later. Would you ask Rema to call me? I'm at my office."

"We thought you had gone to Des Moines to see Melody Ann."

Mylowe took a deep breath. Telling a lie wasn't easy, but for now it was necessary. "I was called back to Miami," he said meekly.

Eve's voice trailed away from the phone. "Here's Rema. She just came in from the garden. I'll talk to you later."

Eve gave the phone to Rema and whispered, "It's Mylowe."

"Are you enjoying your time with Melody Ann?" Rema asked.

"I'm in Miami. I was called back yesterday."

"Did you set a date for the wedding?"

Mylowe did not reply. Sidestepping Rema's enthusiasm, he changed the subject. "I need to help Ruthie May get accustomed to the idea that I'm her son."

Rema nodded passively.

"I plan to be home in three weeks. I'd like to bring Ruthie May with me."

"She's forever welcome at Justin House."

"I knew you'd agree."

"Did Eve tell you Maggie is quitting?"

"Yes, I'll be home to stay before Maggie leaves. We'll find someone to replace her. I think you'll find Ruthie May will be helpful around the house. I don't know if she can cook."

"You can't be serious?"

"About what?"

"Expecting her to cook."

"I didn't mean she should be our cook."

"Of course you didn't. I was just teasing. I'm so looking forward to having you and Ruthie May here in the house."

"Have you talked to Drench Martin lately?"

"No, I have a feeling his search is not progressing."

"Would you call me when you hear from him?"

"Indeed, I will."

Mylowe breathed deeply. "Good," he said, "I love you. Stay happy. Bye."

He hung up the phone and looked at his appointment book. Ruthie May was scheduled for one o'clock. He gathered some papers, tossed them in his briefcase and hurried to the treatment room.

When Ruthie May appeared in the open doorway, Mylowe walked toward her and put his arm gently around her narrow shoulders. She looked up at him and smiled. He guided her to sit beside him on the leather couch and reached for her hand.

"May I hold your hand?"

She nodded and looked away.

He touched his fingers under her chin and turned her face toward him. "Do you remember what happened in our last session? It was like a dream."

"Yes, it made me feel sad."

"You were sad because in the dream you ran away from your baby boy. But you saved his life."

"No, the soldier killed him."

"You can't be sure of that. I believe the soldier allowed the baby to live."

"How will I know the baby lived?"

"Trust me, you'll know. Can you tell me about the baby boy that was born to you in the Green Palms Hotel? What year was your baby born?"

"1970."

"What month?"

"August, on the twenty-first day."

"You told me it was nighttime. Do you remember what time your baby was born?"

"Around ten o'clock."

"Did you look at a clock?"

"No, minutes after the baby came, Arnie pounded on the door. He always returned from the bar at ten o'clock—always too drunk to use his key. Before I opened the door, I wrapped the baby in newspaper and tossed him out the window. After I opened the door, Arnie cursed because the bathroom floor was bloody. He wanted me to clean it, but I didn't."

"Why not?"

"I didn't want him to know the baby had come. If I had walked to the bathroom, he would have seen my shape was different. I wanted him to go to sleep."

"Did he go to sleep?"

"Yes."

"What happened?"

"I took money from his pocket. It wasn't stealing. The money was from my father."

"What did you do with the money?"

"I went to the homeless compound."

"How long did you stay there?"

"Three days. When Arnie came to the compound looking for me, the women hid me. When he was gone, they took me to the welfare office and I went to live with a foster family."

"When did you leave the foster home?"

"I was seventeen. My foster father helped me get a job in the laundry at the hospital."

Mylowe examined her face. "Do you remember the night in your apartment when I showed you the pink ribbon?"

"Yes, I remember."

"Was that ribbon the same one you tied around your baby?"

Ruthie May nodded.

"Have you wondered why I had your hair ribbon?"

"Yes."

"Do you want to hear the story?"

"Yes."

"In Miami in 1970, a homeless man searching for food in Dead Man's Alley heard a baby crying. He took the baby to the Miami Canal Medical Clinic. The baby was healthy. Next, he took the baby to a friend and asked her to help him raise the baby."

"Did he become the baby's father?"

"Yes, would you like to know about the man?"

"Yes."

"He was Dr. Felic Ort. He was not homeless. He was really a college professor."

Ruthie May grabbed Mylowe's hand. "But you're Dr. Ort."

"Yes, that's true. Dr. Felic Ort named me Mylowe Ort. I was the newborn baby he found in Dead Man's Alley. He saved the pink hair ribbon that was wrapped around the baby. We know now that hair ribbon was yours. When you identified the ribbon, I knew you were my mother. I am the baby you threw out the hotel window."

Ruthie May stared at him. "How could my baby be alive? When he was born, he was dead."

"It's only a guess, but the jolt of landing in a box of soft garbage made me take a breath and cry. The jolt was similar to slapping a newborn on the butt."

Her eyes studied his face. "My baby was dead," she whispered.

"You did the only thing you knew to do. If you hadn't tossed me into the alley, I would have not taken my first deep breath."

He held her hand.

"I've needed you all my life."

"I was very young. There was no one to help me."

She leaned against the leather couch. It felt cool on her back. For several minutes, she tugged at a long strand of disheveled yellow hair.

"Can I call you Mylowe?"

"Yes."

"Mylowe," she whispered, "My son is Dr. Mylowe Ort."

Although the reality that Mylowe was her son had not yet settled into her brain, the thought had created an exhilarating feeling. While she had not considered she would ever again be a mother, the death of her baby son left an empty place in her heart. Her eyes were fixed on his face. Was it true? Was this young man the baby she threw away?

"You should be twenty-five years old," she whispered. Mylowe nodded and squeezed her hand.

"I am twenty-five. I celebrate my birthday on August 21st."

She leaned her head against the back of the sofa remembering the hot, humid room in the Green Palms Hotel. She shivered. Arnie Tuttle's drunken tirades and grotesque sexual advances were her private hell.

"Is Arnie Tuttle my father?" asked Mylowe.

"Yes."

"Do I resemble him?"

"No, you look like my father."

Mylowe smiled and whispered. "I'm happy to be a member of your family."

His hands locked over hers as he pulled her up from the couch. "Since I'm your best beau," he teased, "I'm going to walk with you to the nurses' complex."

"I should go back to the laundry."

"Why?"

"It's my job."

"But you don't need to work there anymore."

"Who will do my job?"

"The manager will find someone."

He put his arm around her slim waist and drew her close. Bending down, he kissed the top of her head. She leaned against him as they walked toward the laundry.

* * * * * *

Until recently, seventy-five-year-old psychiatrist, Dr. Drench Martin, had enjoyed his retirement. On this day, he could not dodge the responsibility of calling Rema Swenson to arrange a time to see her. Flying to Dayton, Ohio, and subsequently arriving in Wexlor might indicate he was the harbinger of discouraging news.

During their first meeting, he had inadvertently overstepped the line when he offered to get information about her son's death from a fellow colleague, who was in Cuba. Much to his chagrin, getting information out of Cuba had become a political football. In addition, he had stuck his neck out when he offered to track down information on Paul Moore, Emille's impersonator.

Drench bent his rotund body over the desktop and reached for the telephone. He dialed Dr. Whitetail's office and left a message. For a brief period of time until he could speak to George, he was relieved of the chore of making flight arrangements to Ohio. He hung up the telephone and sighed.

The Same Day in Miami

Mylowe and Ruthie May walked from the medical building to the laundry while he explained Rema's role in his life. He also described Justin House.

"Your house has eight bathrooms and six bedrooms?" she asked.

"Yes. When I was young, the house was a fraternity house."

She shook her head. "Are you rich?" she asked.

"No, I am not."

He looked down at her. "I don't know what you're thinking. I want us to be happy together. I'll call you Ruthie May if it makes you feel more comfortable."

She looked up at him. "Why are you sad?"

"I'm very happy," he said.

"You are very sad."

"My sadness has nothing to do with you and me."

"A girl, perhaps?"

"Yes."

She put her hand on his cheek. "My sad little boy."

He managed to grin. "Tomorrow morning," he said, "I'd like you to go with me to Dead Man's Alley."

"Why should we go there?"

"To see how we feel being there together. Months ago when I visited there, I was able to speak with Sally."

"I remember Sally. She brought me food every day."

"Sally remembered you, too. She said when you lived in the hotel you weren't able to speak."

"I didn't speak until after my baby was born."

"Why didn't you speak?"

"I was afraid."

"Of what?"

"I had discovered it was easier to live with my parents if I didn't talk."

"Did you learn to sign?"

"No."

"Did you go to school?"

"Yes, almost through the eighth grade."

"How did you get along in school?"

"I was okay. I wrote down everything I needed to say. Ten years ago I went back to school and earned a GED."

Mylowe did not question her further. He opened the door for her. As she stepped inside, he asked, "Will I see you tomorrow afternoon?"

"Yes, after I get off work."

"I'll be here by the door at 3:30."

She nodded and went inside. He stood by the closed door knowing he would need to be patient. It would be a long time before he had all the answers to his questions.

56

ANSWERED QUESTIONS

The next day, Mylowe met Ruthie May outside the laundry door and was driving her to Dead Man's Alley. Full of questions, he asked, "Why didn't you talk when you were young?"

"I was afraid. I watched my father beat my mother with his belt. I was only two years old but I knew my life depended on my silence."

"Did your mother know you could talk?" Mylowe asked.

"I don't know. My mother never pressured me to speak."

"She certainly must have known you could speak."

"She knew if she had tried to make me talk, my father would have considered it interference. In a strange way, he took pleasure in my silence."

"Do you feel you were a victim?"

Ruthie May stared at him. "I suppose I allowed it. Perhaps if I had used my voice during the crisis points of my childhood, my words might have changed the outcome. I really don't know."

"So when you began to speak, you put the past behind you. How did you do it?"

She stared at him. "One day I'll tell you how it happened. For now, what is making you so unhappy?"

"I made a grave mistake. I thought only about myself and what I needed."

"And the woman, what did she need?"

"She needed me. She wanted me."

"Is it too late?"

Mylowe moaned. "She has someone else. I allowed my selfishness to throw away the best part of my life."

Mylowe parked across from the entrance of Dead Man's Alley and pointed. "We can walk through that small space between the buildings."

Ruthie's pulse quickened. She hesitated as Mylowe held the car door open. The memory of the months she had spent looking down into the garbage-filled alley from a second floor hotel room was not a time she wanted to recall. However, she did not want to disappoint Mylowe.

They walked hand-in-hand into the alley. "See," he said, "when I was here before, a lady in the store next door told me that the alley had been cleaned up several years ago."

As they stood at the back of Sally's new restaurant, Mylowe stepped off three paces and looked up.

"When you dropped the baby from the hotel window, it must have landed several feet from the restaurant's rear door."

Tears filled her eyes when she realized the guilt she had hidden for many years had come alive. "I feel so guilty," she whispered.

"Feeling guilty is not a sin," Mylowe whispered. "Guilt is a burden none of us should bear alone."

She continued to stare up at the open space that once was the Green Palms Hotel.

"Most often," he said, pressing her hand with his, "we are compelled to confess and unburden our guilt. It's usually easier to tell it to strangers."

A shiver ran through her body. He was not a stranger. He was her son.

Mylowe squeezed her hand as they walked to the front of the restaurant and went inside. Art Bradley recognized Mylowe and hurried to greet him.

"It's good to see you again, Dr. Ort. How is your search going?"

Holding Ruthie May's elbow, Mylowe guided her toward Art.

"Art, this is Ruthie May Durston, my mother."

"I'll be damned. You actually found her."

Mylowe turned to Ruthie May. "This is Art Bradley."

She stared at Art. "I remember you," she said. "You were kind to me."

"You can talk," Art exclaimed. "Sally's in the kitchen. She'll be glad to see you."

Mylowe glanced at Ruthie May. "Are you able to meet another person from the past?"

Art came from the kitchen followed by Sally. "My gad," Sally cried, "how did you find her?"

"It was a miracle, but you and Art helped."

"Hot damn! What did we do?"

"After Melody Ann and I visited with you and Art, we went to the Anchor Bar. An old man called Grover gave us more information. Some other things occurred and here we are."

"This is a strange story," Sally snorted. "What are you going to do now?"

"Our plans are unsettled," Mylowe replied. "We're getting acquainted. Ruthie May still has her job at the hospital. When she decides to work less hours, we'll make future plans."

Sally looked at Ruthie May. "Surely you realize how lucky you are."

Ruthie May nodded. "I know."

"Well, my advice to you, girlie, is not to make any decisions you can't live with. But I gotta ask how did your baby get into Dead Man's Alley?"

Ruthie May looked at Mylowe. "When my baby was born, I thought he was dead. I wrapped the baby in newspaper and threw him out the hotel window. I was afraid of Arnie."

Mylowe answered the rest of Sally's question.

"According to the man who found me, the bundle must have fallen from the hotel window into a box of garbage near the restaurant's back door. The landing forced oxygen into my lungs and I began to cry. The man was in the alley searching for food disguised as a vagrant. Actually, he was a college professor researching the religious habits of the homeless."

Ruthie May proudly announced, "The man was Dr. Felic Ort. He lived in Ohio and named my baby, Mylowe. Dr. Ort was a good father."

"Yes, I agree," said Mylowe.

"That's quite a story," Sally said, pushing her oversize body away from the table. "I wish you luck."

Mylowe, delighted with Ruthie May's participation in the conversation, announced it was time to go back to the hospital. In the car, Mylowe asked, "Would you like to go to dinner tonight with me and Dr. Whitetail? We usually eat at a local bar near his condo."

She shook her head. "The nurses are cutting my hair tonight."

"Okay, we'll do it another time."

That night at dinner, George told Mylowe about the telephone call he received from Dr. Drench Martin.

Mylowe shuddered. Although Drench's efforts to find any information about Emille had failed, Mylowe felt Drench should go see Rema immediately.

There was some good news. Drench's inquiries into the background of Emille's impersonator, Paul Moore, had uncovered the whereabouts of Paul's mother.

"When are you and Ruthie May going to Justin House?"

Mylowe drew circles on a napkin as he explained the areas where Ruthie's development had progressed. "Her cultural conditioning is changing, but it's slow," he said. "She is communicating and exhibiting a remarkable intuition. Her personality is quiet. She's in control of her behavior. To date, she has not opposed any of my suggested changes."

He crumpled the napkin and stared at George. "In another two weeks, we'll be on our way to visit Justin House."

"Just a visit?"

"I'm calling it a visit. I'm taking a step at a time."

Mylowe did not tell George he had decided to take Ruthie May to see Margaret Tuttle if Roy Farrell's investigative efforts to find Margaret were successful. He felt that Ruthie May needed to confront her past and feel good about it. She had harbored an abundance of ego-busting feelings and guilt for too long.

On Thursday morning, Mylowe kept his appointment with the Reverend Mother at St. Angeline's Convent. He carried the positive DNA report in his jacket pocket and parked George's Mercedes convertible by the convent's yellow stucco wall. At the wall, he remembered that Melody Ann had been with him during his last visit. For a moment, his heart fluttered. The thought of her was ever with him. He breathed deeply and quickly returned the thought to the place in his brain he had willed it to stay.

Inside the convent, he was escorted to the Reverend Mother's office by a novice and told to wait. He sat quietly trying not to think about Melody Ann. The Reverend Mother appeared in the doorway carrying a brown file folder.

Mylowe opened the death certificates of Dave and Evelyn Durston and laid them on the Reverend Mother's desk.

"There's no record of Ruthie May Durston's birth," he said. "I suspect she was born at home without medical assistance."

"Are you able to ask her?"

"Yes, but I've asked so many questions recently, I thought I would ask about her birth at a later time."

"I understand."

"I made a copy of the DNA report for you."

She nodded. "I'll begin the process of locating Ruthie May's brother. Will you be in Miami long?"

"For another two weeks."

"Have you told Ruthie May about her brother?"

340

"No, she's still processing the fact that I'm her son."

"When you were here before, you mentioned she was unable to speak."

"Yes, that was my initial information. But, I have since learned it was fear of her father that kept her from speaking."

"She's now able to communicate?"

"Yes, she said she began to speak after I was born."

"I hope you will bring her to see me."

"I'll arrange it."

"For the present, you must be patient. I'll call you as soon as I have any information about Ruthie May's brother."

"I've learned to be patient."

Mylowe drove to the condo and parked George's car in the underground garage. Walking the two blocks to the medical building, he arrived in time to see a secretary put a pink telephone slip on his desk.

Mylowe read the information on the pink paper and dialed Roy Farrell's number.

"I got lucky," Roy said. "I've located Margaret Tuttle. She's living with two women in an apartment near Delray Beach."

"You're certain she was married to Arnold Tuttle?"

"Yes, I found her through Social Security records. She's collecting a monthly sum from Arnie's Social Security. Wait a minute. I'll get her address. I also got her telephone number. She's not listed in the directory."

Mylowe wrote down Margaret's address and telephone number and thanked Roy Farrell for good investigating. He dialed the number and asked for Margaret Tuttle. When she came to the phone, he introduced himself.

"Mrs. Tuttle, my name is Dr. Mylowe Ort."

"Who?"

"Dr. Mylowe Ort. I'm calling from Miami."

"I don't know you."

"Please don't hang up. Let me explain why I'm calling."

"Okay, what do you want?"

"Do you remember Ruthie May Durston, the little girl who lived with you and Arnie?"

When she did not reply, Mylowe asked again. "Do you remember her?"

"Yes," she replied.

"I'm her son."

"Ruthie has a son?"

"Yes."

Mylowe knew from Margaret's response that she knew nothing about Arnold impregnating Ruthie May. This was a something he had not anticipated. He realized it would be cruel to disturb this seventy-year-old woman with information that he was Arnold Tuttle's son. What good would it do? He decided to lie about his intentions.

"Mrs. Tuttle, my mother has often spoken of you. On her behalf, I wanted to call and see if you and Arnie are well."

"Arnie's dead," she replied.

"I'm sorry. Was he ill for a long time?"

"He had cancer of the liver. His drinking caught up with him. We weren't living together when he died."

"My mother mentioned his drinking, but said he had a strong constitution."

"Tougher than nails and just as tough to live with."

"You're saying outside of the drinking he was a healthy man. My mother would also want to know if you are well."

"As good as I can expect. I don't work anymore. I'm living on a fixed income and bunking with two other women. We're all in the same boat. What did you say your name was?"

"Dr. Mylowe Ort."

"Tell little Ruthie I said she did okay having a doctor for a son."

"I know she'll appreciate your message. Thank you for speaking with me. I enjoyed our conversation very much."

Mylowe hung up quickly and bowed his head. George Whitetail had always teased him about his obsessive behavior. Today while talking to Margaret Tuttle, he realized he had told a blatant lie to get her to confirm the information he already knew from Arnie's death certificate. Arnold Tuttle had died from cancer of the liver.

Mylowe pushed his fingers through his hair knowing George's observations about his obsessive behavior were true. He scolded himself for lying, but was relieved to know Arnie had been relatively healthy during his lifetime.

That evening alone in the condo, his thoughts were about Melody Ann. He microwaved a prepackaged dinner, but did not eat it.

The same night

Dr. George Whitetail arrived at the door of Mona's row condo at seven minutes after eight. He had made dinner reservations for 8:30 p.m. at the Doral Hotel on Miami Beach. He took a deep breath and paused before pushing the doorbell. Mona opened the door and exclaimed. "You're late!"

He smiled and stepped inside.

"You're beautiful," he said. "Shall we go? Our dinner reservations are in twenty minutes."

Mona picked up her purse. "I'm ready." When he stood beside her, he envisioned himself as a strong, Indian warrior romancing the captured, petite girl with blond hair.

"Ohio," he whispered. "Of all the places in the world, you walked into my life in Ohio."

She searched his face.

"Are you all right?" she asked.

"At this moment, I am."

"What were you saying?"

"I was having a fantasy about you."

"Me?"

He grinned and escorted her to the waiting limo.

"Why the limo?" she asked. "Is tonight special?"

"I hope it is."

"Do you have to rush to the airport after dinner?"

"No, I'm not going out of town tonight."

Her mind was full of questions when the limo drove up to the front door of Doral. She decided the dinner tonight was with one of George's medical organizations.

The doorman opened the limo door and motioned for an escort. From the lobby, they were guided to a private, ocean-side dining room. In one corner, opposite the bar with four stools, was a conversation setting of barrel-back chairs and a coffee table. The setting, near a bay window, offered a magnificent view of the ocean. Near another bay window, a table, draped in a white cloth, was set for two.

George pointed toward the chairs.

"Let's have champagne and look at the ocean," he whispered.

"I feel like a princess," Mona said.

"You are."

She looked at him. His good looks made her heart beat faster than normal. The crop of thick, black hair slightly tinged with gray around the temples gave him an unfair advantage over men of his age. She adored his dark skin and piercing brown eyes. She idolized him. She knew he was someone she could count on.

The surround music was stimulating. She sipped champagne and felt his hand touch her shoulder. He stood beside her and guided her toward a small dance floor. His strong arms encircled her small waist as he guided her around the floor. She followed his movements feeling the energy igniting between them. She felt safe.

343

The waiter announced dinner. They sat in the opulent splendor of the room during the five-course meal.

When the music played the popular song, "You Were Meant For Me," George leaned forward and took her hand.

"I love you," he said. "Will you be my wife?"

"Yes," she replied. "Yes, I will marry you. I hope it's soon."

He stood and pulled her to him. His kiss was long and gentle. They walked to the dance floor. He took her hand and slipped a ring on her finger.

"You were meant for me," he said.

The following morning in her bedroom in Justin House, Rema answered the telephone.

"Hello," she whispered.

"I know it's only 7:30 in the morning, but I have a dilemma."

"Mona, is that you?"

"Yes, but it's the new Mona."

"The new Mona? What's your dilemma?"

"I want to get married in Justin House."

"Married?"

"Last night, George proposed to me."

Rema leaned back against a pillow. "George asked you to marry him last night?"

"You sound surprised."

"I'm not surprised."

"I want to marry George in front of the fireplace at Justin House," Mona said.

"I think it's a wonderful idea. What's your dilemma?"

"I feel I would be putting a burden on you. I promise I'll handle all the arrangements. Would the fifth of August be okay?"

"Does Mylowe know about the wedding?"

"Why do you ask?"

"You could make it a double wedding. Mylowe will be home to stay in another week. He's bringing Ruthie May."

"For a visit?"

"He's hoping she'll stay permanently."

"When is Melody Ann coming?"

"Mylowe hasn't said."

For a moment, Mona was silent. She had not considered a double wedding ceremony. Over the last several days, she had formed her own conclusion that Mylowe's love life was currently at a tumultuous level. It wasn't anything

George had said. It was his glib replies that gave her the clue. With such flimsy information she decided not to mention her suspicions to Rema.

Rema tapped the receiver. "Mona, are you still there?"

"Yes, I just bent over to pick up my pencil from the floor." Bending over was a lie. She needed a moment to organize her thoughts. "I'll talk to George about a double ceremony and call you later."

"Okay! I'll not suggest a double wedding to Mylowe until I hear from you."

Mona slammed down the phone. Her frustration wasn't directed at any one person or the telephone. She knew Rema was about to find out that Melody Ann and Mylowe were not getting married. Remembering George's proposal, she held her left hand up to the light. The large, faceted diamond glittered in the early morning light.

Last night in the limo, they had agreed to have a small wedding at Justin House with Rema and Mylowe as witnesses and a reception for the their friends in Wexlor. Following the honeymoon, there would be an open house in Miami to celebrate their union with Mona's son and daughter, George's brother and sister, and his Miami friends and colleagues.

She quickly dialed George's office.

"Are you busy?"

"I'm taking a breather and thinking about you."

"I have been thinking about you, too."

"What's wrong? You sound upset. What did I do?"

"I just talked to Rema. She thought having our wedding at Justin House was a grand idea."

"Good!"

"Rema wants us to consider having a double ceremony with Mylowe and Melody Ann."

"Gad! What have we done?"

"George, you've got to be up front with me. Tell me how much damage our impending wedding has created."

"Melody Ann is pregnant and going to marry her childhood sweetheart. She doesn't know who the father is."

"How did that happen?"

"It happened because Mylowe was obsessed with finding his mother and getting information about his gene pool."

"How's he doing?"

"He's on his feet. That's about all."

"Melody Ann must have hated his obsession."

George replied. "Mylowe noticed she had pulled away from him when he went to her mother's funeral. He was too involved in searching for his biological mother to see what was happening between them."

"So he traded Melody Ann away in order to find his mother."

"If his destiny could be foretold, I think we would discover that Mylowe's every thought and event in his life had been predetermined so he would be reunited with his biological mother."

"I knew his motives were strong."

"Since the reunion with Ruthie May, Mylowe understands how the choices he made were perfectly timed to find his mother."

"Can Mylowe explain his actions to Rema?"

"I believe he will."

"What has Drench Martin learned about Emille's death?"

"His contact in Cuba could not find any information about John Swenson or the death of Emille. There is no record of a drowning. But remember, John Swenson was in Cuba working undercover for the CIA. The CIA wouldn't want to involve the Cuban government by recording the boy's death."

"I never believed John's story that he lived in Cuba for twenty years."

"Maybe Emille died somewhere other than Cuba? If he is really dead."

"Oh! George!" Mona sighed, "Is Emille still alive?"

"Let's not get into that. There's something else I should tell you."

"What is that?"

"Dr. Patterson is threatening to hold a coroner's inquest on Emille's death."

"A coroner's inquest? Why?"

"He's certain Emille's death was caused by poison. From lab reports, we know both Felic and Emille died of the same slow-acting poison."

"But it wasn't Emille who died. It was Paul Moore."

"I realize that. The coroner's report shows an unidentified poison as the cause of Paul's death."

"Who is the prime suspect?"

"Right now it is Rema and Maggie."

"If Rema knew she was suspected of administering a poison to Felic and Paul Moore, she would die."

"I know."

"Okay, what else do I need to know?"

"Drench Martin has located Paul Moore's mother. Drench and I have been debating whether to tell Rema. If Paul's mother is available, Rema would want to meet her."

"I can't believe I had to promise to marry you to finally get all this information."

George was stunned. "I'm sorry. Don't be angry. I didn't know if I should carry tales about Rema to you."

"You're a doctor, aren't you? You ought to know how much bad news Rema can tolerate."

"I wanted her to be physically stronger before she heard any of this. It's the kind of stuff that would devastate even a healthy woman."

"I think you should come to dinner tonight and bring Mylowe. We need to make some decisions."

"I agree. I'll bring him at 7:00."

Mona hung up and decided she would call Rema after dinner.

When George called Mylowe's office, he learned that Mylowe had gone shopping. An hour passed before Mylowe returned George's call.

"Mylowe, Mona and I made a blunder. It involves you."

"Oh?"

"Last night, I proposed to Mona."

"Is that the reason I had to eat alone?"

"Don't be a joker. You knew I had made reservations at the Doral."

"I'm just kidding."

"When Mona called Rema to ask if we could have our wedding ceremony at Justin House next month, Rema suggested a double ceremony."

"With me and Melody Ann?"

"That's right!"

"Whoa! Now I understand why you feel you created a blunder."

"This morning, I told Mona the truth about everything."

"What do you mean by everything?"

"I told her how you and I have been sidetracking all the problems until Rema was stronger."

"What did Mona say?"

"She thinks Rema should know about the existing situations."

"All of them?"

"Yes, even the coroner's inquest. Mona invited us for dinner tonight to talk it over. She'll give us a woman's point of view. And that's not all bad. By the way, where have you been this afternoon?"

"I took Ruthie May shopping."

"What for?"

"Clothes."

"I would say Ruthie May is moving into a new life," George said.

"She's awakening from a Rip Van Winkle sleep."

"And you're the person who doesn't believe there are any victims."

"I didn't until recently."

"So, Ruthie May is emerging from the cocoon?"

"George, she's beautiful. By cutting her honey-colored hair, her facial features were softened. A personal fashion consultant chose pastel colors for her new wardrobe."

"Does she know she has a brother?"

"I plan to tell her as soon as the Reverend Mother gives me positive feedback about the adoptive parents."

"Mona and I are really disturbed. We never intended to focus Rema's attention on your wedding plans."

"I need to tell Rema that Melody Ann and I are not getting married."

"We're so sorry. Rema should have been the first to know. I'll see you at 6:30 and ride with you to Mona's house. After dinner, I'll take a cab back to the condo."

"That's a plan!" replied Mylowe.

That evening when Mona opened the door, she embraced both men at the same time.

"Come in. Mix a drink. Dinner will be later. We have pressing matters to discuss."

Mylowe was the first to raise his glass.

"Congratulations to two members of my stand-in family on their engagement. Have you set a date for the wedding?"

"August 5th," replied George.

Mylowe looked at them. "I can see you both look younger. Happiness outwits age."

George held Mona's hand. "We want to share our happiness with you and Rema. You're our family. How can we help Rema?"

Mylowe frowned. "If we look at the various situations around Rema, only the coroner's inquest would directly affect her."

"That's right!" said Mona. "John Swenson's revenge is over."

"And he is dead," Mylowe replied.

"Are we certain of that?" George asked.

"John willed his house in Dayton to Rema and she is the beneficiary of his life insurance."

"You're now managing her personal matters, aren't you Mylowe?" asked Mona.

"Yes."

"How will Rema react to your estrangement from Melody Ann?"

"She'll be sad. I'll be living at home and Ruthie May will also be there. Eve Porter plans to stay on until the end of the winter semester. With people around, Rema will be fine."

George stood up to fix another drink. "Eve told me Maggie has resigned. What are you going to do about that?"

"I'll hire someone else to do the cooking."

Mona looked at George. "You just have to talk to Dr. Patterson about the inquest."

"I suppose you want me to influence him not to call for a coroner's inquest."

"Do you think you have enough influence?"

"I could try."

"You know that getting the inquest dropped would change Rema's future."

"Maggie is also a suspect," George said.

Mylowe stared at George. "Maggie's not guilty."

"Right!"

"The one thing we should guard against is bad publicity," said Mylowe. "Cira is a small town. If the media should pick up the gossip about the inquest, it could ruin Rema's reputation."

Mona went into the kitchen. She returned twenty minutes later and announced that dinner was ready.

During dinner, Mylowe agreed to tell Rema about Melody Ann's pregnancy. It was also decided that Drench Martin should tell Rema he could not find any records on Emille's drowning. And, if George can stop the coroner's inquest, there would be no need to mention it to Rema.

Mona looked at Mylowe. "You must call Rema."

"I'll call tonight and tell her I'm coming tomorrow. I'll take Ruthie May with me."

"Rema's expecting to hear from me today," Mona said.

Mylowe nodded. "Okay, I'll call her after dinner."

Rema had been working at the desk in the den for most of the afternoon. Henry Daly, the accountant who kept the records for the Libra Center, met with her earlier in the day. After they reviewed her financial status, Henry had suggested she consider selling the Libra Center. The market was good and the public's acceptance of a metaphysical learning center was at its highest peak. The business was profitable. It was a perfect time to put the center up for sale.

Earlier in the week, Rema and Eve had arrived at the same conclusion. Rema mentioned she believed anything created has to first be imagined. She was certain to put the Libra Center on the market was the right thing to do and set about mentally visualizing the circumstances that would complete a sale. She decided not to set a selling price in her head. Setting that kind of mental constraint on the situation would probably delay the sale.

That evening, she was back in the den at her desk when Mylowe called.

"Hi!" he said, "Are you busy?"

"Just finishing some paper work."

"It's great news about Mona and George."

"Indeed, it is."

"I called to let you know I'll be arriving tomorrow for short visit. Ruthie might come with me."

"How wonderful! Have you talked to George today?"

"About the double wedding? Yes, I have."

"Are you and Melody Ann on the outs?"

"It's something like that. I'll tell you about it tomorrow."

57

REMEMBERANCES

Before eight o'clock the next morning, Mylowe approached Ruthie May's door in the nurses' building. After the previous night's telephone conversation with Rema, he decided to invite Ruthie May to go with him to Justin House.

His doubts were swept away when she accepted his invitation. The job in the laundry was her only concern. Mylowe understood her reluctance to ask for time off, but did not press her to arrange it. He went to his office and waited.

Within an hour, she was in his office.

"I didn't know what clothes to pack," she said. "So I packed all of the new clothes you bought me."

Mylowe, pleased that her confidence level had changed, knew she had begun to trust her instincts. The drive to the Miami Airport was the first time Ruthie May had been in a taxicab. Inside the terminal, she was exuberant as she watched the planes pull up to the boarding gates.

Aboard the flight to Dayton, Mylowe guided her to a window seat and helped buckle the seat belt. During takeoff, she gasped and closed her eyes. As the airplane leveled off, she relaxed.

"Are you comfortable?" Mylowe asked.

"Oh! Yes! What do we do now?"

"We talk, we eat or we sleep."

"I want to say something."

"Okay, go ahead."

"I've know why my father didn't love me."

"Why didn't he?"

351

"He didn't' know how to love."

"Many people aren't able to love."

"Are they always so nasty?"

"Maybe."

"My father was nasty."

"He was probably unhappy."

"Yes, being unhappy made him vicious."

Mylowe realized Ruthie May had been sidestepping a life of moral hazards. Her conversation about her father had opened a door.

"When children are born, they are emotionally unblemished," he said. "If they live where unstable emotions exist, it will affect them. It's possible they can become emotionally unbalanced."

"That's the word."

"What word?"

"Unbalanced. Don't you see? If I had talked when I was a child, I would have turned out to be more unbalanced than I am. Talking would have given my father more reason to abuse me."

"You're probably right. I'll bet you had conversations with an invisible friend."

"How did you know? Her name was Mary Frances."

"Most young children have invisible playmates. I was eleven years old when I discovered my invisible friend."

"What was your friend's name?"

"His name is Greylord. He's still with me."

"Do you trust what Greylord tells you?"

"Yes, I have learned that trust comes from the inside."

"When babies are born, do they trust?"

"Yes, but if they're mistreated, their trust is diminished. Sadly, when abused children reach adulthood, they do not recognize what trust is."

"I should learn to trust my intuition."

"I'll bet your intuition gives you a lot of direction."

"Yes, but my brain often tells me not to follow my intuition."

"That's because you're only using your brain to make decisions."

"Then my brain is not my decision-maker."

"When you only use the brain to make decisions, you are using the very lowest part of yourself. Following your intuition will help make better decisions."

"My intuition never lasts. It comes like a flash and goes away before I can think about it."

"Intuition is transported through short-lived high energy."

"How do I hold on to it?"

"First, think logically. Don't allow your brain to muddle up your intuitive thought."

"That's hard to do."

"I know. You need to trust your intuitive thought. Confirm what you know to be true and add some imagination."

"I have a lot of imagination."

"If you do it is because your parents didn't squelch it."

She leaned forward. "Squelch my imagination? How could they have done that?"

"It's not uncommon for parents to stop their children from imagining. After that happens, children only talk to themselves. In my line of work, persons who talk to themselves are considered either odd or psychotic. Many normal children self-talk. They often give themselves vocal commands like 'hurry up, stop that, or that's bad.'"

"When parents make fun of their children talking to themselves, the children's imaginations go underground deeper than before."

"How sad."

"Self-talk is common. We all have conversations in our heads. The question is, why do only a few of us let it out?"

"Oh!" said Ruthie May. "My ears are hurting."

"The plane is descending. It's getting ready to land."

"Oh! My ears ache."

"Swallow and keep swallowing. The pain will stop."

When the plane landed, Mylowe guided Ruthie May into the Dayton terminal. After retrieving their bags, they walked toward the rental car desk. Ruthie May stayed by his side. For her, everything was a new experience.

For the next two hours, Mylowe drove from Dayton to Wexlor. Ruthie May was amazed at the acres of farmland, the green lawns and the large areas of woods.

In Wexlor, Mylowe turned on Justin Lane and entered the brick gateway entrance to Justin House. Rema met them at the front door. She hugged Mylowe and turned toward Ruthie May.

"My dear, we've been waiting for you."

Ruthie May nodded. "I'm glad to be here."

Eve Porter stood behind Rema.

"This is Eve Porter," Rema said. "Eve is my friend and my left hand."

Eve led them into the den. "This is where we hang out," she said.

"How was the flight?" Rema asked.

"Ruthie May had pain in her ears when we were landing," Mylowe said.

Rema looked at Ruthie May. "Eve will help you get settled upstairs."

Ruthie May nodded and followed Eve into the foyer.

Alone in the den, while Mylowe poured a glass of water for himself, he became concerned as he watched Rema struggle to put a sweater over her shoulders.

He sat down in front of her. "I don't know whether to be honestly honest or dishonestly honest."

"I hope you came here to be the former."

He took a deep breath. "Melody Ann is going to marry her childhood sweetheart. She's pregnant. She's not certain who the father is, but she's made up her mind not to marry me. There's nothing I can do."

"I see."

"George is right. My obsessive behavior drove her away. Stupid, huh?"

"Sometimes there's a miracle in disaster."

"Do you think I should skip the post-mortems?"

"I do. Take the situation from where you are now and consider a solution to the entire problem, then only look as far as the next step. You would be wise to do some creative listening."

He heard himself yelling. "Creative listening at this juncture is crap. My mistakes are devouring me "

"Hear me out. A client of mine, a doctor, when steeped with doubt or facing a tough decision, would lead his horse through the pasture. Walking beside the horse, the doctor talked to the horse. He described his feelings, his fears, and his doubts. Before the walk ended, the doctor always knew the solution. It came from inside."

Mylowe dropped his tall frame onto the sofa.

"I'm sorry," he whispered. "I didn't mean to yell. Losing Melody Ann is not having a therapeutic effect on me. However, I've learned an important lesson. I've been self-absorbed, impatient and over-anxious."

Rema sat beside him. "You've suffered from a common human disease."

"What is that?"

"The disease of over-prodding."

"If that's what it was, I was nearly blown away by the antidote."

Rema held his hand and stroked his hair.

"I know you love Melody Ann."

Tears filled his eyes. "I hear her voice. I feel her beside me. I smell her sweetness."

His head lay against the back of the sofa. Rema patted his hand and wondered if she should mention that Dr. Patterson had called her. Or did Mylowe know the reason the coroner called the house? Had Mylowe come home just to tell her about his breakup with Melody Ann? What else was happening?

"Please forgive me for invading your life with my stupid actions," Mylowe said. "Right now, I think it's important for you and Ruthie May to get acquainted."

"I agree."

He got up and walked toward the desk. The account books from the Libra Center caught his eye. "I see you've been doing some bookkeeping," he said.

"I met with my accountant this afternoon. He thinks it's a good time to sell the Libra Center. In your medical world, is there some diagnostic test that will tell me when it is the best time to sell?"

Mylowe shrugged. "I think you'll know."

For a long moment, they were silent.

Eve and Ruthie May came into the den. "We've been on a tour of the house," Ruthie May said. "It's a beautiful house."

"Oh!" Eve exclaimed, "Before you arrived, a lady called. I wrote down the number."

Mylowe recognized the telephone number and seemed surprised. "Will you excuse me? I'll place the call from the tower."

He went toward the pantry. At the bottom of the stairs leading to the tower, he leaped on every other step until he reached the top. The iron gate and the door to Eben's Tower were open. He rushed inside.

In the den, the conversation between Rema, Eve and Ruthie May turned to the subject of Justin House. Ruthie May was curious about its history. Rema recounted her first visit and told of the deplorable condition of the house. "Mylowe was a toddler and had rushed into the garden," she said. "He almost sat on a bed of thistles. There were broken windows and falling plaster. Birds and mosquitoes were flying in the house. The kitchen appliances were barely working."

Eve and Ruthie May enjoyed Rema's description of the night she and Felic slept in the garden on lawn chairs. Before they settled in, they covered Mylowe's crib with mosquito netting. The next morning Mylowe was wrapped in the netting. After that episode, Felic announced they would never sleep in the garden again. From that moment, they slept inside even though the odor of fresh plaster and paint was overwhelming.

Amused at Rema's story, they did not see Mylowe in the doorway.

"I was looking for Maggie," he said.

"She was here earlier and prepared dinner," Rema replied. "She'll be back tomorrow."

"When do we eat?" he asked.

"In twenty minutes," replied Eve. "I need to warm the food in the oven."

"I'd love to see the kitchen," Ruthie May said.

As soon as they were gone, Mylowe leaned back in his chair. He noticed a glow in Rema's eyes. Her smile seemed more spontaneous. He wondered if Ruthie May's vitality energized Rema.

"Did you take care of your telephone call?" Rema asked.

"It was the Reverend Mother in Miami."

"Did she have good news?"

"She gave me the name of the adoptive family of baby boy Durston."

"Do they live in Miami?"

"Yes. They're elderly and are in poor health. The Reverend Mother is going to their home to speak to them."

"Does Ruthie May know about this?"

"No."

After dinner, Eve and Ruthie May washed the dishes and tidied up the kitchen. Eve warned Ruthie May that Maggie was fussy about the kitchen.

"The best thing to do," she said, "is to leave it the way you found it."

Ruthie May laughed at Eve's warning. "Maggie and I love to tell tales about each other," she said. "You'll soon learn not to play our little game."

"Where's Mylowe?" Ruthie May asked.

"He's in the garden. It's lovely there this time of the evening."

"Are there still mosquitoes out there?"

"Not any more."

Eve walked with Ruthie May to the French doors that led to the garden and pointed outside. Ruthie May walked into the garden. Mylowe was sitting on a wooden seat that surrounded a tree.

"When I was four," he said, "I knew this seat was meant to be sat on, but my greatest sport was to march around on it."

She sat beside him and looked at the sky. "Everywhere I look it is beautiful."

Mylowe touched her hand. "This is where I want to live for the rest of my life," he whispered. "I want you to live here with me. Do you think you could?"

"Rema and Eve are very nice. The house is wonderful."

"I want you to be happy in this house. Rema is frail. I don't know how long she will be able to manage the house. Eve will go back to her home next winter. Some day you'll be the first lady of Justin House."

"Oh! No! I couldn't be the first lady. I'm not prepared. I didn't learn how to use the correct fork until I was fourteen."

"At Justin House, you'll have the opportunity to be anyone you want to be. You could enroll in college, start a business or become a writer."

"What will you be doing?"

"I will be following my dream."

"What is that?"

"On the vacant land behind Justin House, I will construct buildings that will serve as a center to provide unique health care."

Inside the house, Eve walked up the stairs with Rema. When Rema was settled on the chaise lounge in her bedroom, Eve stood in the doorway.

"I'll leave the door ajar. Mylowe will know you're waiting for him."

Rema sat quietly. She realized she needed to take more chances, see more and feel more. She had come to a dangerous place in life. To turn back from it, although it may be right to do so, would depreciate her spirit. Though it might be foolish and dangerous in her current poor physical condition, she hoped in the end her frailty would make her a better person.

She wondered if Mylowe would call Ruthie May "mother." She scolded herself for not wanting to give up the title. It was foolish to consider such a question. Mylowe wouldn't spend the rest of his life not addressing Ruthie May as his mother. Embarrassed by her selfish thoughts, she shook her head and prayed they would go away.

Her bedroom door opened and Mylowe stood beside her. "I wanted to say goodnight," he whispered. "Were you asleep?"

"I was thinking that Ruthie May has a beautiful soul."

He laughed. "She also has a great sense of humor."

He bent over her and kissed her cheek. "Sleep well, mother."

58

CHANGE

According to word-of-mouth history, Justin House was built in the years when families of the middle class employed servants. Eben Justin didn't believe in doing what others expected of him. With open contempt for the fashion of the day, he would not permit quarters for servants to be included in the design of Justin House.

As Mylowe interviewed applicants to fill Maggie's position, he also searched for a full-time, live-in companion for Rema. In the winter, Eve Porter would graduate from Wexlor University and return to Michigan to teach. Still, the lack of servant bedrooms in the house was proving to be a hard-to-solve puzzle. Fortunately, the cleaning ladies employed by a company in Cira would continue to do the housekeeping chores.

Building the clinic on the hill behind Justin House would create additional household problems. The only facility in Wexlor for travelers was a small rooming house at the edge of town. During construction of the clinic, it was not possible to plan how many craftsmen might be required to remain overnight. The architect and construction manager would definitely live in Justin House during construction. Any additional workers staying in the house would put a burden on the household staff.

On this particular afternoon, Mylowe went upstairs and stood in Rema's doorway. She looked up from her book.

"Come sit by me. What have you been doing this afternoon?"

"I've been counting bedrooms."

"What great secrets are you hiding from me?"

"I'm not hiding secrets. I'm just handling the day-to-day stuff."

"How soon are you and Ruthie May returning to Miami?"

"On Monday. It's time for Ruthie to meet the Reverend Mother."

Rema's eyes sparkled mischievously. "Have you found a replacement for Maggie?"

"How did you know I was interviewing?"

"I have my ways."

"Yes, I've been talking to applicants for Maggie's job. I hope to find someone who will learn from Maggie and help Mona prepare for her wedding."

"The wedding is in six weeks. Will Ruthie May come back from Miami with you?"

"I think we can count on it."

"Mona will be here in two weeks to prepare for her wedding."

"We're short on bedrooms. Do you think we can fit everyone in?"

Rema patted his hand. "We'll manage," she replied.

On the return flight to Miami with Ruthie May, the confined seating was uncomfortable for Mylowe. His legs ached. Halfway into the flight, he noticed numbness in his fingers.

He knew moving his legs disturbed Ruthie May. She had touched his arm to quiet him. He stood up and winked at her.

"The space between these seats is too small for my long legs," he said. "I'm going to take a walk."

His legs nearly collapsed under his weight. Clutching the back of the aisle seats, he managed to wobble toward the bathroom.

In the bathroom, he sat on the toilet lid. Stretching forward to the basin, he put his hands in cold water.

Fearing he might not be able to stand again, he grabbed the basin and stood up. Strength had returned to his legs. Relieved, he went back to his seat.

Ruthie May looked up. "That was a long walk."

To distract her, Mylowe took her hand and said, "During the time when I was searching for you, I discovered some history about your family."

Perplexed, she asked, "I didn't know my family had a history."

"I have the death certificates of your mother and father. When I visited Sally and her son, they directed me to visit the Anchor Bar. At the bar, an elderly man called Grover told me that after your mother's death, your father sent you to live with Arnold and Margaret Tuttle. From county records, I learned Arnold Tuttle died in 1994 and Margaret lives on Miami Beach."

"Is Arnie dead?"

"Yes, Grover told me you were the second child born to Dave and Evelyn Durston. Your parents had a baby boy several years before you were born. The boy was put up for adoption."

She rolled her eyes. "Yes, I know."

"You knew you had a brother?"

"Yes, my mother told me the night she died. My mother was very sad about giving her baby up for adoption. She said my father made her sign papers. They took the baby to a convent in Miami."

She looked out the window.

"The Reverend Mother at St. Angeline Convent would like to meet you," Mylowe whispered. "She has contacted the family who adopted your brother."

"Will I see him?"

"Yes, of course. Are you willing to go with me to meet the Reverend Mother?"

"Yes! Yes!"

Mylowe sat back and relaxed. Ruthie May's enthusiasm was a good omen. She had lived through a series of moral hazards and had reached an intersection. It was now up to her to either recoil or go forward.

The plane landed and taxied toward the gate.

The following afternoon at the Sisters of St. Angeline Convent, a novice ushered Mylowe and Ruthie May into the Reverend Mother's office. The Reverend Mother was already at her desk. As she stood up, the soft rustling of her traditional sleek, long, black garb echoed throughout the scantly furnished room. Her head, covered with a starched white wimple, moved freely as she welcomed them. Mylowe guided Ruthie May toward her.

Tenderly, he said, "This is Ruthie May Durston."

The introduction was cut short when a burst of howling wind shook the glass panes in the office window. The Reverend Mother abruptly turned to secure the window latch. "There's a hurricane coming. It's early in the season."

Aware of the interruption, she turned toward Ruthie May. "My dear, I am so pleased to meet you." Ruthie May nodded.

Before they sat down Mylowe said, "Ruthie May has known for many years that her older brother was given up for adoption."

Surprised by Mylowe's uncharacteristic outburst, the Reverend Mother questioned Ruthie May.

"How did you know about your brother?"

"On the night my mother died, she told me to find my brother."

"How old were you?"

"Eleven. She told me to find him and he would take care of me." Ruthie May lowered her head. "I never tried to find him."

"All things happen as they should," replied the Reverend Mother.

Ruthie May raised her head.

The Reverend Mother untied the cord on a brown portfolio, took out papers and read aloud.

"Baby boy Durston born on November 9, 1953, was brought to St. Angeline's on January 4, 1954. Adoption occurred on March 12, 1954. The adoptive family was Mr. and Mrs. Gilbert Spar of 1428 West 14th Street, Miami, Florida.

"I've spoken to Mr. and Mrs. Spar. They are elderly and in poor health. Their adopted son, baby boy Durston, is now Father Xavier, a Jesuit priest. He's serving in Bolivia and is expected to return to the United States in December of this year."

"What do we do now?" Mylowe asked.

"Mr. and Mrs. Spar suggested a letter to Father Xavier would be appropriate."

"Would you write it?"

"Yes."

Ruthie May said, "My brother must be forty-two years old. I wonder if he resembles our father."

Driving back to the nurses' residence, Ruthie May was quiet. Mylowe escorted her to her room, but did not go inside. He kissed the top of her head and walked away knowing she needed time to process her reentry into life.

Going to his office, he found a message from Roy Farrell, the investigator he had hired to research Ruthie May's family. Dialing Farrell's number and hearing Farrell's voice, Mylowe asked, "What have you found?"

"On Dave Durston's service life insurance, Ruthie May Durston is the beneficiary. I'll fax you the info."

"Good work!"

"Is there anything else?"

"Yes. See what information you can find on a Jesuit priest. His name is Father Xavier. At the time of his adoption, his adoptive parents, Mr. and Mrs. Gilbert Spar, lived at 1428 West 14th Street in Miami. Maybe they still live there."

Roy Farrell replied. "I'll get back to you."

"Don't disturb the Spars. Call me when you have information."

The phone receiver fell on the desktop. Mylowe reached to replace it on the cradle, but couldn't pick it up. The numbness in his fingers had returned. He stood up and walked around the room testing the strength in his legs.

In his office at the far west end of the clinic building, George Whitetail placed a call to Melody Ann. For days, he had considered the merits of talking to her and decided he had nothing to lose. When she heard his voice, her tone became cool.

"Don't hang up!" he begged. "I just want to make sure you're okay."

Her tone softened. "I'm moving ahead."

"Is there any way I can help?"

"I'm doing what is best."

"Are you going to marry your childhood sweetheart?"

"No, but I don't want to marry Mylowe either. You won't be a snitch, will you?"

"Of course not! Would you tell me if the child is Mylowe's?"

"I would if I knew, but I don't know."

"I assume you'll find out after the birth."

"Yes."

"How are you feeling?"

"I could be better."

"I have a college buddy living in Des Moines. He's a gynecologist. I'll give him a call. You'll be in excellent hands."

"Can I trust you—and your buddy?"

"It's our secret."

George hung up the telephone. He would not scold himself for going behind Mylowe's back. His offer to help Melody Ann was on Mylowe's behalf. If the baby is Mylowe's child, perhaps this intervention might help two people who belonged together and needed to reconcile their differences. He spun the desktop rolodex until he found Dr. Ben Riley's telephone number.

59

STATUS QUO

The cabby, hired by Dr. Drench Martin at the Dayton airport to drive him to Wexlor, stopped the taxi beside the Justin Lane street sign.

"Is this the place, Doc? Doesn't look like anybody lives on the street."

Drench leaned toward the cab's front seat. "The entrance to Justin House is a thousand feet ahead on the left."

"Oh! Yah! Is it inside those brick posts?"

"That's the main entrance. Drive up to the front door."

Coming to a full stop at the front of the house, the cabby jumped out and opened the taxi's rear door. "Here yuh are, Doc. I'll go find a service station. Pick you up in two hours."

Before Drench could push the doorbell, Eve Porter opened the door.

"Dr. Martin, please come in. Rema is in the den waiting for you."

"I hope my tardiness was not too disturbing. Hiring a cab at the airport for a period of six hours turned out to be a real project. I finally found a Dayton cabby who was willing to take a day away from the airport. To catch the return flight to Miami, I'll need to leave in two hours."

Eve nodded. Guiding Drench toward the den's doorway, she stood aside to let him pass.

"Dr. Martin has arrived," she said to Rema.

Rema looked up from the desk. "Drench, it is a pleasure to see you again. I know traveling here was an inconvenience."

"For me, traveling anywhere is inconvenient. I use a limo service at home. Airport cabbies don't like to be away from the airport on long trips. But I've said enough about my travel problems, how are you?"

"I'm regaining my strength. I've decided to put the Libra Center up for sale."

"Was it a prolonged decision?"

"Yes, I spent more of my energy deciding to sell than I realized."

"I didn't know about the center. Is it a clinic?"

"It's a place of tranquility. People come to the Libra Center to understand more about life. By various ways, they learn to manage their lives and solve most of their problems. Most discover a new understanding of their philosophical beliefs and spiritual needs."

"How is this accomplished?"

"The center employs a naturopathic physician, two psychologists, two astrologers, an herbalist, an acupuncturist and two preventive health counselors. One of the psychologists is a shaman and practices the ancient art of shamanic healing."

"What is shaman?"

"A shaman acts as an intermediary between the natural and supernatural worlds by embracing a belief in powerful spirits that can be influenced to cure illness. When the energy or the body's vibration levels are increased, healing is stimulated. "

"How many years have you owned the center?"

"Fourteen years. Each year, I've been inspired to keep the doors open. People from all areas of life come to study. A teacher comes to reflect and refresh her perspectives for the classroom. Parents, grieving the death of their sixteen-year-old son, are comforted. A distraught health professional seeks to dispel her thoughts of suicide. A computer programmer with liver cancer meditates and uses his own vibrations to prolong his life."

"I see you are ahead into the new trend toward alternative medicine. Today, I've come to offer you some healing."

"I'm very grateful. When my emotional and mental days are a challenge, I think of you. I've been looking forward to this day. I know you bring me information to quiet the roaring winds in my heart."

Her words caused Drench to shift uncomfortably in his chair. He dreaded this moment and sighed.

"There aren't any records in Cuba of Emille's drowning," he said. "Neither is there a record that John Swenson, your ex-husband, lived in Havana or anywhere else in Cuba."

Rema eyes blinked in the attempt to stay in control and defensively interrupted Drench before he could continue.

"John told me he was working undercover for the CIA. There might not be a record in Cuba."

"My investigator examining CIA archives confirmed that John Swenson was not connected to the CIA. Neither was he in Cuba for twenty years."

"Where was he? He had to be somewhere."

"He owned a small bar in Key West, Florida."

"Was Emille with him?"

Annoyed at his hesitancy, Drench tilted his head back and looked at the ceiling. "According to some incomplete sheriff records, a boy drowned in the waters off Key West, Florida, at the age of ten," he said. "The body was not recovered. When I researched the burial site records in South Florida, there was not a burial site for Emille Swenson."

Rema's body language displayed her anxiety. "Emille must be buried somewhere. John Swenson is buried in a Dayton, Ohio, cemetery. Could Emille be buried there, too?"

Drench shifted his weight, raised his fleshy hips out of the chair and walked to the fireplace.

Earlier in the week when he talked to George Whitetail about his discoveries and his upcoming visit to Rema, he had expressed a certain level of concern. He feared, as did George, the absence of records and a gravesite for Emille would not bring closure for Rema.

"We did find John Swenson's burial site in Dayton," he said. "It's a single plot. After checking all the cemetery records throughout Montgomery County in Ohio, and in South Florida, a grave site for Emille was not found."

Rema looked away. After several minutes, she murmured.

"It's so strange. My memories of the son I gave birth to are all mixed up with the impostor who lived with me in this house for eight years. Each boy lived with me for eight years. How coincidental is that?"

Drench nodded. "I know."

Rema clasped her hands together and held them tightly on her lap. Her voice was calm.

"What did you learn about Paul Moore?" she asked.

Sifting through the contents of his briefcase, Drench pulled open a yellow file folder. "Paul Moore was born on March 21, 1963, in Dunnellon, Florida. From the age of twelve, he was continually expelled from school for numerous violations. His family life was non-existent. Mother was a whore. Father was her pimp."

Rema gasped. "That poor boy."

"Somehow Paul finagled his way into college. The record shows he paid his tuition from the proceeds of selling stolen articles acquired by burglarizing homes and small businesses. He graduated from the University of Florida in Gainesville summa cum laude with a degree in International Languages."

"Did you find how Paul Moore got connected with John Swenson?"

"John Swenson returned to Miami from Key West in 1990. Presenting falsified documents, he was hired as a parole officer in Dade County."

Rema interrupted Drench.

"I know the rest of the story. On his deathbed, John Swenson cheerfully confessed to me that Paul Moore was one of his parolees. John hired Paul to impersonate Emille."

Drench shuffled through his papers. "I also have Paul Moore's arrest record."

"Read it to me."

"His first arrest for burglary was in 1977 when he was fifteen. He was found guilty of larceny in 1979 and served a year in a correctional institution. In 1981, 1983, 1989 and 1990 he was convicted of drug dealing. On those various charges, he spent from one to seven months in county jails."

Rema shook her head.

"According to Pinchey Wilson, the bail bondsman I knew in Miami, Pedro Swenson, alias Paul Moore, was bailed out of a Miami jail by a member of the mafia. This was the beginning of the fraudulent scheme John Swenson planned against me."

Drench was surprised by Rema's quiet complacency and her knowledge of the details of John Swenson's vendetta against her.

While Drench checked his watch, Rema asked, "Do you know why the county coroner would want to question me about Paul Moore's death?"

Drench's jaw dropped. He grunted, cleared his throat and shoved the files into his briefcase to maintain his composure.

"Routine," he mumbled, "The coroner's just being thorough."

"I hope that's all it is."

"Are you concerned about meeting with the coroner?" Drench asked.

"There's something going on behind my back. I think it's about Paul Moore's death," Rema replied.

"Is the coroner coming here to see you?"

"Yes."

"Is it soon?"

"Next Tuesday."

Drench reached for his briefcase and fumbled with the latch. He wanted to detour the subject of the coroner's visit. Turning away from the briefcase, he exhibited his most professional smile.

"Well, my dear, you seem to be coping very well. Do you want to ask questions about any part of my research?"

"No."

"You're not going to fret that the information about Emille is inconclusive?"

"It's too late and I'm too old. I believe my reoccurring dream of Emille drowning in the ocean was predictive. When I couldn't accept his death, I left my emotional door wide open for John Swenson to instigate his evil plan."

Again, Drench looked at his watch. His only thought was to hurry to the nearest telephone to tell George Whitetail that the county coroner was visiting Rema on Tuesday.

"I must be going," he said. "My cab is waiting."

"Come back soon," she whispered.

Eve appeared in the doorway. "Dr. Martin, your taxi is here."

Drench reached for his briefcase and hurried to the front door. Inside the taxicab, he asked the driver to stop at a telephone booth. Within three city blocks the driver stopped the taxi. From the rear seat, Drench pushed forward and struggled to find an address book in his briefcase. The cabby opened the rear door and helped Drench from the cab. "I'll not be long," he said. "Keep the meter running."

After making the collect call to George Whitetail's office number, Drench waited impatiently. When he heard Dr. Whitetail's voice, he said, "George, I've just come from Justin House."

"How did Rema react to the information?"

"She was calm. I feel so guilty for leaving her alone after delivering such distressing information. Did you know the county coroner has scheduled a meeting with Rema on Tuesday morning?"

"No, I didn't know. When I spoke to the coroner about the indictment against Rema and Maggie, he gave no indication of his intent of holding a coroner's inquest. I think he's a man on a mission."

"I'm on my way to the Dayton Airport. Let me know if I can help."

George Whitetail hung up from Drench Martin's telephone call and angrily punched in the telephone number of his condo. When Mylowe answered, he resisted the urge to sound upset, and spoke slowly.

"Drench Martin was at Justin House today. Rema accepted his news rather well. She told Drench Dr. Patterson was coming to see her on Tuesday."

"Why?"

"Evidently I didn't change Patterson's mind about holding an inquest."

"Dr. Patterson may have a personal plan. Is he up for re-election?"

"Would indicting two aging women on shallow evidence get him re-elected?"

George pounded the desktop.

"Damn it! This has happened because I gave Dr. Patterson Felic's autopsy report."

"Do you suppose Dr. Patterson believes Rema discovered Paul Moore was an impostor and she administered the poison?"

"That notion would make a hell of a novel."

"Look at it from Dr. Patterson's point of view. A man called Emille Swenson was admitted to the hospital and died there, but Dr. Patterson learns the body was not Emille Swenson. The body he autopsied was Paul Moore."

"Dr. Patterson couldn't have known anything about Paul Moore."

"Why not?"

"Because Paul Moore's body was cremated weeks before Rema went to Dayton and learned from John Swenson that Paul Moore was an impostor."

"But John Swenson is dead. We only have Rema's word that she didn't know Paul Moore was imitating Emille."

"You're forgetting that Eve Porter witnessed the entire meeting in Dayton between John and Rema."

Mylowe paused. "That's our defense! Rema didn't know Paul Moore was an impostor."

"I assume you will be with Rema for the Tuesday meeting with Dr. Patterson."

"Yes, I may not come back to Miami if Ruthie May agrees to go with me to Justin House. There's nothing more we can do for three months until Ruthie's brother returns from Bolivia."

"Right now, you must deal with Dr. Patterson."

"I know. Right now, everything else is taking priority over raising the funds to build my clinic. But if I'm to establish a clinic when the time is right, the financing will be in place."

"That's being optimistic."

"Yes, but I'm not doing another thing toward the clinic until I find out what Dr. Patterson is going to do."

Mylowe and Ruthie May arrived at Justin House on Sunday afternoon, two days before Dr. Patterson's scheduled visit. After a light dinner, Eve went upstairs to help Ruthie May unpack.

Opening the dresser drawers to show her the space available, Eve sat on the edge of the bed while Ruthie May transferred her things from the suitcases to the drawers.

"You'll love it here," Eve said.

"I'm a little nervous. I've always lived alone."

"Are you apprehensive?"

"Yes."

Eve took empty hangers from closet and passed them on to Ruthie May. As Ruthie May began putting her garments on the hangers, she paused. "Why are you staring?"

"I was looking at your clothes. They're new."

"Yes, Mylowe took me shopping."

"You'll use seasonal clothes in Ohio."

Ruthie May bowed her head. "I should have realized that."

"Of course, you'll gradually add to your wardrobe until you have clothes suitable for cold weather."

"I have not lived in any place except Miami."

Eve put her hand on Ruthie May's. "You'll like the change of seasons in Ohio."

60

THE INVESTIGATOR

On Tuesday morning before the county coroner's visit, Mylowe waited with Rema in the den. Looking up from papers on her desk, she stared at him. "You look concerned," she said.

Rather than respond, he closed his eyes.

"Was that a groan?" she whispered. "Is the secret you're guarding so shocking you can't speak about it?"

"My secret?"

"You know. The reason Dr. Patterson is coming here today."

"Truthfully, I don't know for certain why he's coming."

"For certain? Then you do know something. Is it about Paul Moore?"

Eve appeared in the doorway.

"Dr. Patterson and Dr. Nearson are in the living room."

Rema stood up. With her right hand, she lifted her left arm across her mid-section and laid it against her body. She walked into the foyer and on into the living room. Mylowe walked behind her.

Dr. Patterson stood by the window and turned around when he heard footsteps.

"Mrs. Swenson," he said stiffly, "I am Dr. Patterson. This is my associate, Dr. Nearson."

Rema nodded and sat down on one corner of the white brocade sofa. Dr. Patterson acknowledged Mylowe, but didn't extend his hand. Instead, he waved toward his associate. "This is my assistant, Dr. Nearson."

Exhibiting a high degree of awkwardness, Dr. Nearson lowered his eyes. Mylowe sat beside Rema.

Dr. Patterson walked across the room and grasped the back of a mahogany Chippendale chair and cleared his throat.

"My office is investigating two men who lived in Justin House at different periods of time and died from an unclassified poison."

Rema looked shocked. "Poison?" she asked. "Unclassified? What does unclassified mean?"

Dr. Patterson ignored her question. "Do you employ a woman named Maggie Finch?"

"Yes, Maggie's been in our household since Mylowe was two years old."

"Do you think Maggie Finch would have reasons to harm Felic Ort or Paul Moore?"

"No sir!"

"Before Felic Ort's death, you and Dr. Ort were estranged. Is that true?"

"Yes, but we reconciled before he died."

"For what length of time before his death had you reconciled?"

"Shortly before."

"A month, a week, a day?"

"A day before. We spent the night together."

"Tell me about Paul Moore. When did you discover he was impersonating your son, Emille Swenson?"

"My husband told me."

"Was that before Paul Moore's death?"

"No, after Paul had been cremated."

"Is there a witness who can verify your husband's statement?"

"Yes, Eve Porter was in the room with me when I learned about Paul Moore's impersonation."

"Would Mrs. Porter be able to testify that your husband was sound of mind?"

"Yes."

"Mrs. Swenson, it is important that you understand why I ask these questions. Until we identify the poison that killed these two men, you and Maggie Finch are under suspicion."

Mylowe closed his fingers over Rema's trembling hand and directed his question to Dr. Patterson.

"How did this unclassified poison enter the bodies?" Mylowe asked.

"Through inhalation. A very, very slow and deliberate process of inhalation."

"A slow process?"

"Yes, possibly over a period of years."

Mylowe shook his head. Until this moment, Dr. Patterson had not defined the unclassified poison as an inhalant. "How many years was the poison inhaled?"

"Three to five years."

"How might the poison have been administered?"

"We've theorized it could be the smoke of burning candles, a poisonous herb placed inside bed pillows or sprinkled on bed sheets and blankets, washcloths and towels."

"Not very conclusive evidence. Do you have anything more solid to work on?"

"We would like permission to examine the house, the basement, attic and garage."

Mylowe squeezed Rema's hand. "You have our permission. When would you like to begin?"

"Immediately."

The meeting ended quickly. Dr. Nearson stuffed his notes into a leather folder and followed Dr. Patterson to the front door. Eve, who had been waiting in the foyer, hurried to open the door.

After Drs. Patterson and Nearson had gone, Mylowe turned to Rema.

"Not a friendly fellow."

"What happens if the search fails to find a poison? Maggie and I are already under suspicion," she said.

Mylowe replied. "The evidence is weak and Patterson knows it. We will be cooperative. The investigators should be out of the house before Mona arrives to help with the wedding. I'll explain the situation to Maggie, Eve and Ruthie May. You tell Mona."

"Should I be worried?"

"Not at this point."

Mylowe walked with her into the kitchen. He kissed her on the cheek and hurried through the pantry to the stairway leading to Eben's Tower. Bounding up the stairs, he hurried into the tower, slumped into a chair and closed his eyes. He knew he was the only one to solve this dilemma. Rema had nurtured him in a past life. Her role had been confirmed when he was regressed back to one of his past lives. The deeds from their past lives together were coming back and forcing him to find the solution to help her.

Was it time to admit this was a lesson to learn? His eyes popped open when he remembered that Rema had told him about the 13-degree Aries ascendant in his natal astrology chart. She said it made him an 'I come first' personality. He did not take advice from others. How many times had she explained that life is only an illusion with no beginning and no end? Our human senses deceive us so skillfully that we are tricked into believing that life is real when it is only a dream that moves with us from one life to the next life.

If that were the case, what lessons would he learn from the coroner's inquest? Perhaps, he was to feel more compassion toward others and let go of his selfish attitude. He wondered if he should feel her pain.

He bowed his head and whispered. "I haven't yet learned to do that!"

The next day, Dr. Patterson's rubber-gloved investigators examined every part of Justin House. They scraped bits of paint from the walls, took dust and dirt samples from the furnace, the heat runs and registers, drained the water heaters and sampled the residue. A thorough inspection of the house foundation, the underground cellar, the flowering shrubs, the kitchen spices and cooking utensils, bed and bath linens, mattresses, carpets, medicine bottles, drawers, closets and plumbing.

If Maggie had been in the house, she would have been watching the horn-rimmed investigators dismantle the house. But Mylowe sent Maggie home saying the house was being examined for termites.

Two weeks later, when the investigation was complete, only Dr. Nearson met with Rema and Mylowe. Unable to meet their searching eyes, he lowered his head and rustled through papers from his briefcase.

"The investigation of the house is complete," he said. "Although this is an old house, we have concluded that the unclassified poison did not stem from any part of the house. There is no reason to suspect the poison was administered from the heating, ventilating or plumbing systems."

He stood up quickly and walked from the room. Mylowe followed him. "Is that all? What is the decision? Will there be an inquest?"

Dr. Nearson's small, oval, pinched face became more twisted and gnarled.

"You'll receive a letter from the coroner's office," he murmured.

"Will the letter give the results of the investigation?"

"It will be about the date of the inquest."

"Is the inquest already scheduled?"

Dr. Nearson's idiotic gaze did not stop Mylowe from asking more questions. "If nothing was found in the house, what kind of evidence for an inquest do you have?"

"I'm not at liberty to say."

Mylowe grabbed Dr. Nearson's shoulder.

"You little mealy-mouth pipsqueak," Mylowe muttered. "Give your boss this message. If I do not have a detailed report of this investigation by four o'clock tomorrow afternoon, my lawyers will sue your office for harassment and invasion of privacy. Now get out!"

Eve, who had been standing by, opened the front door. The disheveled Dr. Nearson exited through it.

"Damn!" Mylowe shouted as he turned and walked back to the living room where Rema was still sitting. "The problem with these small town creeps," he roared, "is they try to wear too many hats."

"Too many hats, what do you mean?"

"Dr. Patterson is a medical examiner. He's trained in pathology and forensics. That should be his only job. But he's also the county coroner, a bureaucratic appointee."

"So, isn't it a good thing to have a coroner with medical training?"

"In most instances, I suppose it's okay, but not in this case."

"Why?"

"The county coroner has lost his perspective and is hinging a case on perfunctory evidence. He enjoys the excitement of the inquest. He's probably never called for one before. Unless we can come up with a solution or find the poison, he'll call for an inquest."

Mylowe charged around the room waving his arms and slammed his fist on the top of the grand piano.

Rema bowed her head knowing that the progression of the planets in her current chart had already revealed she would be involved in a legal conflict. She decided not to tell Mylowe.

61

THE WEDDING

In her wedding dress, Mona Pierce stood in Rema's bedroom before the mahogany-framed, full-length mirror. Her petite figure, curvaceous despite her short stature, was draped in filigree lace that lay over the sculptured ivory satin bodice and skirt of the Chanel original. She turned from side to side making certain the hem was straight. A light tapping on the door made her turn around. "Come in."

Eve Porter pushed the door open just far enough to peek around the edge.

"The flowers arrived and are all arranged," Eve whispered. "Do you want to come down and see them?"

"No, I want to be surprised."

"The foyer is decorated beautifully. What a great place to have the wedding ceremony."

"Initially, I wanted the ceremony in front of the great stone fireplace in the den, but this hot August weather is not conducive to a burning fireplace."

Eve closed the door and went downstairs. Mona turned back toward the mirror. She wanted this day to be a glorious experience. Dr. George Whitetail was her soul mate, the person she had waited for all of her life.

Remembering the day of her first wedding was a dream that floated in and out of her memory. It was long ago. Most of the memories had faded. She had married Will Pierce out of desperation. Both knew the daughter born eight months later was not Will's child. Years later, when their biological son was born, they blundered and stumbled with him through his childhood and his youth. They were relieved when he joined the Marines at eighteen. Neither of their children was endeared. After Will died, the daughter, Marianne, was married with children of her own, and Charles, home from the service and in college, had drifted away.

Mona raised her head to look again into the mirror determined that today's joyous union would not be stained because Marianne and Charles had turned down her invitation to attend her wedding. She uttered a deep sigh knowing she had cut off the last connection to her children when she announced her upcoming marriage to George. Although she had let them know she would always be there for them, it did little to allay their strong aversions to the marriage.

Mona tilted her head and nodded agreeably at her reflection. A melodious strain of Eve's piano prelude wafted up the winding stairs and into the upper hallway.

The bedroom door opened. Rema entered holding two bouquets. One of bluebells and baby breath and the other was identical except for the addition of yellow roses.

"Are you ready?" Rema asked, handing the rose bouquet to Mona.

"Yes," replied Mona. "Is everyone here?" She turned and walked through the open door. Mylowe, looking extremely handsome in a white linen jacket and black trousers, was waiting in the upper hallway and extended his arm. Mona looked up at him thinking Mylowe was more of a son to her than her own son had been.

Sweeping the thought aside, she grasped his arm. Rema moved ahead and made her way down the staircase. Her pink silk voile dress floated around her with each step until she reached the altar.

At that moment, the melody of Mendelssohn's Wedding March filled the foyer. Mona and Mylowe stepped rhythmic downward on each step of the winding staircase. The guests, seated in semi-circle rows around the foyer's center, stood and remained standing until Mona and Mylowe reached the floral decorated center of the foyer. George smiled at her.

Pastor Morris Diltz, robed in brown with a white stole draped around his shoulders, stepped forward. The music stopped.

"Today," said Pastor Diltz waving his arm toward the guests, "I, too, am here to observe this celebration." He stepped backward nodding to George, who was resplendently clad in a white suit and wearing a multi-colored, feathered, full-length warrior headdress. George turned toward Mona and took her hand.

"It is the custom of my people," he said, "to unite man and woman by joining their blood."

Mona replied. "It is the custom of my people to unite man and woman by placing a ring on the fourth left-hand finger that will remain forever as a symbol of togetherness."

Pastor Diltz stepped forward.

"I have been requested to instruct this man and woman with these words. Give of yourself to me for I can ask for nothing less than I can give. And if I ask for anything that is less, because I am always in want, know from this day forward that only in you do I have everything."

Rema stepped forward holding a small open box on her palm. Mylowe did likewise. From Rema's box, Mona took a gold wedding band. George took a narrow gold band from Mylowe's box.

Pastor Diltz announced, "These rings have been anointed with the combined blood of Mona and George and signify the exchange of the energy between them. As they place the rings simultaneously on the finger of the other, as an officer of the court of God, I pronounce them to be husband and wife."

He raised his arms and announced, "I am pleased to present to all those in attendance, Dr. and Mrs. George Whitetail."

Eve began softly playing <u>Barcarolle</u> from Les Contes D'Hoffman. George bent down and kissed Mona. The guests stood. The bride and groom casually walked among them shaking hands and acknowledging their congratulations.

Rema thought Mylowe was walking behind her, but realized he was still standing at the altar. She made her way toward him.

"Why aren't you joining us?" she asked. "Are you ill? You look strange."

Mylowe nodded. "I'm not feeling quite myself, but please don't draw any attention to me. I'm going to sit down. Just stand by me and continue to talk, maybe no one will notice."

"I can tell this is not the first time you have felt this way. Do you know what it is?"

"No, but it will go away in a few minutes."

"You'd best sit up and look alive. George is coming this way."

"Oh! No!"

George arrived quickly. "What is wrong with Mylowe?" he asked.

Rema quickly replied. "He has a bit of indigestion. We're going to the kitchen for some baking soda."

George stared at Mylowe. "Are you sure it's just indigestion?"

"Yes," Mylowe replied, "too much acid."

George walked away.

"I think I can move now," Mylowe said. "Go back to your guests. I'll go into the kitchen."

Rema reluctantly walked across the room and began talking to friends. Mylowe waited several minutes before standing up. The numbness in his fingers had already subsided. It was a sign that his legs could now hold his weight. Supporting himself on the back of a chair, he stood up and went into the kitchen. Minutes later and feeling stronger, he returned to the foyer and talked with the guests. When it was time, he toasted the bride and groom. Mona kissed him tenderly on the cheek.

"You're working too hard," she whispered. "Spend more time with Ruthie May and Rema. They could use your attention. I'm worried about the coroner's inquest. Rema has only mentioned it once, but I can tell she's concerned."

"I tried to stop it. So did our lawyer."

"George said the inquest could lead to a trial."

"There's not enough evidence for a trial. I wish I could dig up something that would show how flimsy the coroner's case really is."

Mylowe hugged her. "Have a wonderful honeymoon. I'll take care of everything here."

She smiled and walked toward George who was talking to Dr. Matthews and his wife.

When the bridal couple was preparing to leave the house, Eve released hundreds of bubbles into the air. The bubbles floated to the foyer ceiling, many burst in mid-air. A large portion of bubbles went whirling against the grandfather's clock when the front door was opened.

Later after all the guests had departed and the caterer had driven away, Mylowe quietly went to his room. Rema retired to her suite leaving Eve and Ruthie May to turn out the lights.

Within the next two weeks, Mylowe hired a toxicologist to help him find the type of poison Felic and Paul Moore had inhaled and to find its source. He decided to arrange a toxicology survey of Paul Moore's office at Wexlor University.

On Tuesday afternoon at three o'clock, Mrs. Quincy, the administrative assistant to President Matthews, ushered Mylowe into the president's office. Dr. Matthews walked from behind the oversized mahogany desk to shake Mylowe's hand.

"You look fit," he said. "I haven't seen you since the wedding."

"I'm on a mission."

"What kind of a mission?"

"To find something that will exonerate Rema from suspicion of poisoning Felic and Paul Moore."

"Ah! Yes! I heard. It's nasty business. Have you had any success?"

"No, I wonder if there might be a clue in Paul Moore's office."

"I wouldn't know what that might be."

"Perhaps, some type of inhalant placed inside a book."

Shocked at Mylowe's words, Dr. Matthews paused.

"You're getting ahead of me," he stammered. "Was the poison an inhalant?"

"Yes, a slow acting type taking two to five years to kill someone."

Dr. Matthews leaned away from his desk. "Do you think someone in the university might be responsible?"

"I'm grasping at straws."

"I realize that. How could it be found within the university? You should realize there have been no other deaths in the academic staff other than Felic and Paul Moore."

Mylowe bowed his head then slowly raised his eyes up to face Dr. Matthews.

"I was hoping you might permit a toxicologist to look in Paul Moore's office."

"You do realize someone else is currently using that office. I could arrange to have it emptied, but only for a few days."

"No one need know the man is a toxicologist."

"Good God! I hope not. The university doesn't need a scandal."

"When you've made the arrangements, my toxicologist will be ready."

Mylowe stood up and embraced Dr. Matthews. "Thank you," Mylowe whispered.

On the same Tuesday afternoon while Mylowe was away from Justin House, Ruthie May and Eve decided to tidy up Eben's Tower. They knew Mylowe had not emptied the wastebasket in weeks and a good aerosol spraying was in order.

"Should we take dust cloths?" Ruthie May asked.

"Good idea," exclaimed Eve, "but we have to hurry. Mylowe will be coming back soon."

"How do you know that?"

"He doesn't go away for more than an hour. Do you worry that he is still longing for Melody Ann?"

"I do, but he doesn't speak her name."

"I know. It's strange somehow, but I believe he thinks about her."

Ruthie May shook her head. "It's so sad."

"Come along," whispered Eve, "the time window for us to get in and out of Eben's tower is narrowing."

Hurrying up the stairs to the tower, the women emptied the wastebasket into a plastic bag, dusted the desk and bookshelves and damp-mopped the board floor. They finished and stood in the doorway surveying their work.

"What is locked in that big old safe?" asked Ruthie May.

"Once there were valuable rare books. They're gone now. I guess there still might be some family archives still in there."

"Family archives?"

"Old journals and diaries."

"How interesting. I wonder if Mylowe has read them."

Eve shook her head and walked down the stairs urging Ruthie May to follow. In the pantry, they stopped to hang up the mop and toss the wastebasket contents into a larger receptacle. They were about to leave when Mylowe appeared in the doorway.

"Hey! What's up?"

"We just tidied up the tower for you."

"You take such good care of me."

"We know," replied Ruthie May.

Mylowe moved past them and went up to the tower. He sat down and dialed Dr. Whitetail's private number. George answered immediately.

"George, I received permission from Dr. Matthews for the toxicologist to examine Paul Moore's office. It's an outside chance that anything will be found, but I have to cover all the bases."

"Have you considered having Felic's body exhumed?" asked Dr. Whitetail.

"Should I?"

"In the last decade, forensic medicine has made terrific advancements. Maybe the new technology would give an in-depth report. Felic's autopsy was not performed at a high-tech lab."

"I wonder if Rema would object to exhuming Felic's body."

"You could ask her. Exhuming Felic's body might save her the trauma of a trial. By the way, how is Maggie Finch handling all this?"

"She doesn't understand it, but she hears the gossip."

"She could be guilty."

"I don't think so."

"I hope you're right."

Mylowe hung up the phone, leaned back and closed his eyes. Until now, exhuming Felic's body had been a last resort. He was nearly out of options, but, more importantly, he was running out of time.

He knew at this time of the day Rema would be in the den. Walking through the kitchen, he waved his hand to Ruthie May and Eve, who were polishing silver serving dishes.

"Good work, up there," he said referring to their work inside the tower. "It smells like a rose garden."

He walked across the foyer and stopped in the doorway to the den. "May I interrupt?" he asked.

Rema looked up from the papers on the desk. "Yes, but what are you doing away from the tower in the middle of the day?"

"I'm talking to you."

"Something important?"

"I hope you'll think it is."

"Well, let's have it."

"To save you from going to trial, we need to exhume Felic's body."

Her face paled.

"I know it's a shock, but hear me out. We need to take advantage of the new forensic technology and have Felic's body examined more scientifically. At the time of his death, only a coroner's autopsy was performed."

"Do you think the poison that killed him will still be in his remains?"

"I don't know, but we're running out of options and time. I know it's a drastic move."

"No." she whispered. "It's a smart move."

"Then you approve?"

"Yes."

"Since you approve, I'll make the arrangements."

"I have one stipulation."

"What is that?"

"Don't tell me when the exhumation occurs."

"Agreed," said Mylowe.

62

THE TOXICOLOGIST

On Monday morning, Mylowe rushed to the office Paul Moore had occupied during the eight years he taught languages at Wexlor University. Dr. Matthews had arranged to have the office vacated for the day to allow toxicologist, Dr. Harvey Trowbridge, to search for the unknown poison that caused the deaths of Paul Moore and Felic Ort.

Inside the office, Dr. Trowbridge was inserting small glass pipettes into a special padded carrying case.

"Dr. Trowbridge," Mylowe said, "I'm Dr. Ort."

"Yes, yes," Dr. Trowbridge replied with a chilling crackle in his voice. "I'm finished here. I won't have a report for a day or two."

Mylowe nodded. "A swift appraisal is really needed."

"Ohio is a long way to travel."

"I know Wexlor is an out-of-the-way place."

Dr. Trowbridge closed the carrying case. Without regard to Mylowe's presence, he shoved a matchstick from his pocket into his right ear.

"Damn!" he muttered. "My ears are still clogged. The flight from Los Angeles was a killer."

Dr. Trowbridge was a dweeby fellow wearing trousers a size too large. The length of the pant legs ended in a four-inch fold over his cumbersome black and silver cowboy boots. At first glance, his lower body seemed much too large for a small man. His thin, craggy face, littered with deep pockmarks, led Mylowe to believe the renowned toxicologist had shied away from any kind of life outside of his laboratory.

Mylowe watched as Dr. Trowbridge broke off a piece of the matchstick and scraped built-up dirt from under his fingernails. With the unused end, he nonchalantly picked food particles from between his gold-filled, protruding, front teeth.

Momentarily stunned by the doctor's self-absorbed actions, Mylowe turned away and looked out of the window. Although Dr. Trowbridge had been highly recommended and enjoyed an impeccable reputation, Mylowe was feeling a bit uncomfortable. Putting Dr. Trowbridge's personal hygiene methods aside, Mylowe was convinced that this talented toxicologist would undoubtedly be the only person on the planet to find the unclassified poison.

Since the arrangements for exhuming Felic's body were set for the next morning, Mylowe had rented a fully equipped laboratory on the campus of Focale Junior College for Dr. Trowbridge. The mortuary where Felic's remains would be held was a city block to the west.

Mylowe turned from the office window. "If you're ready to go," he said, "I'll take you to the lab."

"Yes, of course. I'll need the rest of the day to set up. Will I be able to sleep in the lab?"

Noticing Mylowe's reaction, Dr. Trowbridge hurriedly explained. "When I get into a project, I don't like to leave my work."

"I'll have a cot delivered to the lab."

"How close is the mortuary to the lab?"

"It is less than a city block. You will have access to the body at all times. The numbers where I can be reached are by the telephone in the lab."

Dr. Trowbridge held the pipette case against his body as if he were transporting valuable gems. Mylowe escorted him to the car and drove to the rented lab in Cira. After Mylowe made certain the eminent toxicologist was comfortably settled, he drove back to Justin House.

It was late. In the upstairs hallway, a strip of light gleamed from beneath Rema's bedroom door. Mylowe raised his hand to knock, but slowly pulled it away. He felt Rema had already sensed the exhumation of Felic's body would take place in the morning. He decided not to disturb her.

He went to bed, but didn't sleep. There were overwhelming thoughts bouncing around in his head. He hadn't begun to calculate the cost of bringing Dr. Trowbridge from Irvine, California, to Wexlor, Ohio. Under the circumstances, money wasn't a consideration. The source of the poison had to be found or life at Justin House would never be the same.

From the first day Rema stepped through the front door of the old mansion, she had given the house a special kind of energy. A new life. Rema had also provided him a wonderfully fulfilled life. He could not fail her.

At some time during the restless night, he went to sleep. He was awakened by the alarm on his nightstand. It was 5:30. He would not worry about a shower until the exhumation was complete and Felic's body was safely delivered to the mortuary.

He moved quietly in the hallway outside Rema's bedroom. Once in the car, he guided the vehicle away from the house without turning on the headlights. At the gatepost entrance, he turned and drove toward Woodlawn Cemetery. Ten minutes later, he parked near Felic's gravesite.

The early morning air in the cemetery was filled with a light mist that dropped noiselessly on the limestone tombstones. The serenity was soon disrupted by the grinding noise of the yellow backhoe digging into the ground. The casket was lifted from the vault and placed on a gurney and loaded into the hearse. Back in the car, Mylowe followed the hearse from the cemetery road to the highway.

Mylowe waited in his car under the mortuary's canopy as the mortician and his aides moved Felic's remains inside. The casket, although now covered with a tarpaulin, was in excellent condition. Mylowe turned the car around and drove to the lab. Dr. Trowbridge unlocked the door and let him inside.

"The remains are at the mortuary," Mylowe said. "We need to be discreet. Dr. Patterson does not know about the exhumation."

"How did you manage to keep it quiet? In California, an exhumation requires the consent of the coroner."

"Just say, I got a special court order."

"That may not be enough to keep the coroner out of this."

"I hope it's enough to give us time to let you do your work."

"I understand."

Mylowe went to the door. "Keep this locked," he said.

Dr. Trowbridge, polishing the lens of a microscope, nodded.

Mylowe stood by the door surveying the benches lined with the special equipment Dr. Trowbridge had ordered to be installed. He drew a deep breath hoping the answer would be found in this lab.

"Do you need anything?" he asked.

"Only a little time," replied Dr. Trowbridge.

That evening, Mylowe worked in Eben's Tower until after midnight. At one o'clock, he went to bed.

In the morning, Eve Porter's tapping on his bedroom door awakened him. He squinted at the bedside clock. It was ten o'clock.

"Just a minute," he yelled scrambling into a robe. "What's up?" he asked.

"Rema and Maggie received notices this morning. There will be a coroner's inquest," she said.

"When is it scheduled?"

"November 26th."

"Where's Rema?"

"In the den."

"I'll be right down. You'd better drive over to Maggie's house and sit with her. Tell her I'll be there as soon as I talk to Rema."

He shut the door. While he had expected the inquest notice, the realization that a date was scheduled made his heart race.

He leaned against the door, breathed deeply and exhaled slowly. If he had discovered anything about resilience, it was during his teenage years. After he shot Felic's gun at railroad cars and was put on probation, Felic did not speak to him again. As the recipient of Felic's angry stares, he learned to bounce back on the theory that he would not let Felic see him sweat.

He dressed hurriedly and stood in front of the mirror. He must be calm. Rema and Maggie needed to see his strength.

He entered the den, dropped casually down on the sofa and looked at Rema.

"Eve tells me you and Maggie received notices of the inquest."

"Eve's more upset about the notice than I am. You should go talk to Maggie."

"I'll go in a moment. I asked Eve to drive over and sit with Maggie until I arrive."

"This will be the end of Maggie."

"What do you mean the end?"

"She won't come here to work anymore. She's not well."

"Let's wait and see how she reacts. I've offered to replace her. She doesn't want to leave."

Rema's tone changed. "Are you as busy today as you were yesterday?"

He looked away knowing she was asking if Felic's remains had been exhumed. He did not reply.

"Then you'll you be home for dinner?"

"I'll let you know about dinner." Mylowe leaned over the desk and kissed her. "Tell Ruthie May I'll try to be home."

Walking across the foyer, Mylowe was reminded of his stupid, empty-headed, teen-age compulsions and remembered how calmly Rema had reacted to them. Although she had not always exhibited the anguish she felt during his compulsive moods, this morning he saw the same stern position of her jaw.

At Maggie's house, Mylowe sat at the table in her kitchen. Eve had hurried away saying she had errands to run before eleven o'clock. Mylowe dipped a tea bag up and down in the cup of hot water. "This inquest is just an inquiry," he announced. "The coroner needs to give the county prosecutor evidence that a crime has been committed."

"With poison?"

"Yes."

"Lordy! Lordy! I never bought rat poison. I don't know a thing about poisons."

"The coroner has to present his suspicions. If there is not enough evidence there will be no trial."

"I'm so worried. My son-in-law says I can go to jail for the rest of my life."

Mylowe took her hand. "I'll find a solution. You have to believe that."

She looked at him through her tears. All she could see was the little boy who wanted to be a policeman.

"Mister Mylowe, are you not feeling well? You're pale."

"Just indigestion," he replied. However, it was more than that. His hands were numb and the strength had gone from his legs.

"I could use more tea and another cookie."

In his Miami office, Dr. Whitetail waited for Dr. Ben Riley to come to the phone. After a series of annoying sharp clicks, Ben Riley said, "Hello, George. I delivered Melody Ann Thame's baby last Thursday. It was a boy."

"Everyone healthy?" asked George.

"Yes, quite. Melody Ann is fine. She went home two days after delivery."

"On the birth certificate, do you know who she named as the baby's father?"

"She declined to name the father pending some genetic blood tests."

"Did you take a sample of the baby's blood?"

"Yes, she requested it. I sent it to the lab along with Dr. Ort's blood sample you sent to me. And I included a blood specimen from her companion."

"Her companion?"

"Yes, I believe his name is Knowles——Bart Knowles."

"When will the report come back?"

"In three weeks."

"Thanks, I'll call you in three weeks." George flipped the pages of his appointment book forward three weeks and made a note to call Ben Riley. He was tempted to call Melody Ann and congratulate her, but suppressed the idea.

Sitting quietly at Maggie's kitchen table, Mylowe regained strength in his legs. Before departing, he put his arms around Maggie's plump, buxomly body and helped her sit in her favorite chair.

"You rest," he whispered. "Don't you come to work until this matter is resolved."

Maggie murmured, "I trust you."

Driving to Cira to see Dr. Trowbridge, Mylowe's fingers were numb. He parked beside the highway until partial sensation returned.

Dr. Trowbridge unlocked the lab door when he heard Mylowe's voice and hurried back to the microscope. He spoke without raising his head. "I've found nothing in the university office that would lead me to investigate it further."

Mylowe sat on a lab stool and leaned over the bench holding his head in his hands.

"There's something wrong with me," he whispered.

"Got a bug?"

"No, it's more. My fingers go numb and I lose the use of my legs."

Dr. Trowbridge straightened up from the scope. "How long have you been experiencing these episodes?"

"Four months, but more frequently in the last week."

Dr. Trowbridge slid off the lab stool and moved toward Mylowe. He did not hide his concern. "Have you lived in the family home all your life?"

"Yes, except for the seven years I was in medical school."

"What have you been doing since your residency?"

"I lived in Miami for a while. I returned to the house last year."

Dr. Trowbridge pulled a scalpel from one of the glass shelves.

"What are you doing?" Mylowe asked.

"Roll up your sleeve. I'm just going to scrape the surface of your arm and take a look at the debris under the microscope."

"What are you thinking?"

"I'm thinking you're ingesting poison from somewhere in the house. Think, man, think! Do you use the same areas of the house that the other two men used?"

Mylowe shot him a frozen look and spoke slowly. "I use the tower as my office."

"The tower?"

"Yes, we call it Eben's Tower. Felic Ort's great grandfather, Eben Justin, added it to the roof on the back side of the house."

"Did Dr. Patterson's crew examine the tower?"

"No."

"Why not?"

"I don't know. I never thought to show them the tower room. The access to it is through a panel in the pantry."

"A concealed panel?"

"Yes, the access is one of Eben Justin's eccentricities."

Preparing the particles from Mylowe's arm onto a slide and peering into the microscope for several minutes, Dr. Trowbridge pulled another slide onto the platform and adjusted the scope.

"Ahhum! Ahhum! Hummmmm! Hummmmm!" he muttered.

"What is it?" asked Mylowe.

Dr. Trowbridge's tough facial expression changed before Mylowe realized what was happening. The toxicologist was actually grinning. "Tomorrow," he said, "I will examine the tower room."

"Do you have a theory? You were comparing my dermatological scrapings with another slide."

"I was comparing your scraping with bone debris from the deceased."

"Is there compatibility?"

"Indeed! Now, go and let me get on with my work. Pick me up in the morning—the earlier, the better! By the way, is there any possibility of obtaining the autopsy report on the other man who died after living in Justin House?"

"It would be a neat trick with a coroner's inquest scheduled for later. The records are sealed."

Mylowe wanted to ask more questions, but realized Dr. Harvey Trowbridge was not a man to disclose information until he was certain it was valid.

Mylowe drove to Justin House. He dared to believe Dr. Trowbridge had latched onto a new, positive step in his investigation. At Justin House, Mylowe found Rema, Ruthie May and Eve sitting in the den.

"You said you would call," Rema said.

"There's a ray of light in the investigation Dr. Trowbridge is conducting. Mind you, it's just a small ray. I shouldn't be speaking about it, but we all could use some good news."

"We could use some good news," Rema said.

"In the morning, Dr. Trowbridge is coming here to examine Eben's Tower. He questioned me today about Dr. Patterson's investigation of Justin House. Do you realize Eben's Tower was not examined by Dr. Patterson's crew?"

"Why not?"

"The wall panel was closed. The examiners didn't know about the tower. Today, Dr. Trowbridge took a scraping of my skin and compared it with another sample he had gathered. There was compatibility."

"Isn't he grasping at straws?" asked Rema.

"Grasping or not, he asked a very, very important question. He asked what common area in Justin House I used that was also used by Felic and Paul Moore."

The women's voices rang throughout the house.

"Eben's Tower!" they shouted.

Rema held her left arm close against her body and stood up.

"Maggie Finch hated that tower. She always said it was spooky. She closed the wall panel every time she went into the pantry and found it open. I'll wager Maggie's the one who closed the panel before we sent her away before the investigation."

"Praise to Maggie," Eve said. "And bless her. She's so frightened."

During dinner that evening, the conversions were positive. For the first time in months, there was hope. Mylowe called Maggie and told her of Dr. Trowbridge's discovery and praised her for closing the wall panel in the pantry.

"Oh! Mister Mylowe, that terrible tower was always the death of me. Now, it may save my life."

63

APPREHENSION

After an evening of positive dinner conversation, the next morning Rema, Ruthie May and Eve hustled through the daily chores. Each was holding her thoughts in check. Any discussion of finding the poison was pointless until Dr. Trowbridge examined Eben's Tower.

Mylowe awoke at five-thirty and arrived at the laboratory before seven o'clock. When he knocked on the laboratory door, Dr. Trowbridge promptly turned off the equipment and clutched the leather case that held the glass pipettes to his chest. He motioned toward the microscope.

"You carry the scope," he said.

During the ride to Justin House, Dr. Trowbridge was silent except for momentary ahemmm's and mutterings under his breath. Mylowe had determined the doctor's noises and mutterings were a physical release of tension when approaching a difficult task. Mylowe decided not to interrupt the process.

At Justin House, Mylowe ushered Dr. Trowbridge into the pantry and stopped at the west wall. Dr. Trowbridge nodded and motioned for Mylowe to open the panel. Once the panel was open, Dr. Trowbridge examined the hand-hewn wood pulleys that operated the door, turned and followed Mylowe up the narrow staircase. At the top, Mylowe pulled the iron gate aside, opened the wood door, stepped inside the tower room, turned on the battery-operated lamp and set the microscope case on the desk.

Inside the tower, Dr. Trowbridge stood under the overhead transom looking upward.

"Titillating and curious," he exclaimed.

"Why do you say that?" Mylowe asked.

"The building inspectors of today would condemn this tower."

"Why?"

"No air, no ventilation system, no electricity. My, my, my, I would have not believed such a place existed where intelligent men did their work."

Mylowe walked toward the door. "Is there anything I can get for you?"

"No, but can you tell me if anything has been removed from this room."

"Some rare books that were in the safe have been put in storage."

Dr. Trowbridge stood near the bookshelves leaning forward to read the book titles.

"There are still some valuable volumes here. Are the books accessible?"

"Yes, they're in a bank vault."

Dr. Trowbridge carefully opened the leather case. The glass pipettes with plastic caps in the ends were secured with leather straps. On the opposite side of the case in slotted places were miniature tools similar to surgical instruments—scalpels, probes, clamps and forceps.

Dr. Trowbridge, noticing Mylowe's interest in the tools, grimaced. "These are my own design," he muttered.

"Very unusual," Mylowe remarked.

"I do unusual work."

"Indeed, you do. I'll let you get to it. Do you want to break for lunch?"

"No."

"Okay, I'll come up at seven."

Dr. Trowbridge gloved his hands and studied the transom. "When you come back, bring a stepladder."

"I'll take care of it. See you at seven."

At the bottom of the stairs, Mylowe pulled the wall panel shut and went into the kitchen. He was met with a barrage of questions.

"What's Dr. Trowbridge doing?" asked Rema. "We're so anxious, we can't wait."

"I'm too excited to work," whispered Ruthie May.

"The doctor is taking samples of everything. I'm not to bother him until seven tonight. When I go up, he wants me to bring a ladder. He will not come down until he gathers everything he wants."

"Why a ladder?" Rema asked.

"To examine the transom."

"He must be an obsessive compulsive character," Eve said.

To everyone's amazement, Mylowe put three teaspoons of sugar in the tea Eve brewed for him. He noticed their surprise. He smiled.

"I need the energy. The next few days are going to be stressful."

"You're right about that," said Ruthie May.

Mylowe bent down to pet Angel rubbing against his trouser leg. He picked her up and held her.

"Angel is the calm one. She's the only member of this household not affected by Dr. Trowbridge's work in the tower."

He stood up and set the cat down on her four paws. "I've an appointment," he said. "I'll see you ladies at dinner."

They nodded and watched him disappear through the kitchen door.

"What's so important with him?" asked Eve.

"There are doings at the cemetery he doesn't want us to know about," Rema said.

"The cemetery?" asked Ruthie May.

"They exhumed Felic's body so Dr. Trowbridge could examine it. I would guess they're putting Felic back in the ground so Dr. Patterson doesn't find out."

"Do you know that for sure?" asked Eve.

Rema sighed. "I'd bet the farm on it."

Driving to Woodlawn Cemetery, Mylowe worried that since his actions surrounding the exhumation were obvious to Rema, he wondered how soon it would be before Dr. Patterson was aware of it. While he had managed through the court to legally exhume Felic's body, Dr. Trowbridge's assertion that coroners are usually a part of an exhumation was accurate.

He entered the cemetery just as the hearse carrying Felic's remains arrived. The backhoe's engine made a loud grunting sound. When there were no other vehicles in the cemetery, Mylowe began to relax.

The mortician's assistant approached him. "Should I have asked a minister to be here to say a prayer or benediction?"

"I don't know. What is protocol?"

"Some do, some don't. Anyway, we're ready."

Mylowe stepped forward as the casket was lowered into the vault. He stood close enough to see the workers seal the vault lid, then turned and walked toward his car. The sound of the dirt falling on the top of the vault resounded throughout the quiet grounds.

64

THE MALADY

The morning of the third day in Eben's Tower, Dr. Trowbridge emerged and began a one-man investigation of the foundation, cellar and internal walls of Justin House. "He's like a spider monkey," Eve whispered to Rema during breakfast. "He's all over the place."

"I believe Dr. Trowbridge will find something," Rema said in a low tone. "But, you're right. He's an obsessive compulsive character."

"When will he tell us what he's found?" asked Ruthie May.

"Have you asked Mylowe that question?"

"No, but someone should. The tension around here is building more each day."

The conversation ceased when Mylowe walked into the kitchen.

"Who's going to ask me the big question?" he teased.

"I am," said Ruthie May. "When does Dr. Trowbridge share his discovery with us?"

"What makes you think he's made a discovery?"

Ruthie May winked and grinned. "You know something. I can tell by the gleam in your eyes."

"Am I that transparent?"

"You are to me."

"Me too!" exclaimed Rema.

"Well, ladies, it goes like this. Remember that fragmented stub of a tree sitting beside the safe in Eben's Tower?"

"The dead stick of wood potted in volcanic lava?" asked Eve.

"Yes."

399

"What about it?"

"Strangely enough, the resin on the wood contains an exotic poison. At four o'clock tomorrow afternoon, Dr. Trowbridge will meet with us in the den and tell us about his discovery."

"Will the discovery exonerate Rema and Maggie?" Ruthie May asked.

"I believe it will. We still won't beat the deadline for the coroner's inquest, but I assure you there will not be a trial."

"Whoopee!" yelled Eve. "Whoopee! Whoopee! And Whoopee!"

Rema smiled bravely. "It's been a long process," she murmured.

"I agree," Eve replied. "It's been too much stress on Rema and Maggie. Although Rema was prepared to face it, I'm not sure she or Maggie could have made it all the way through a trial."

The Next Afternoon

Mylowe had driven to Maggie's house to bring Maggie and her husband, Clyde, to the meeting with Dr. Trowbridge.

In the den at Justin House, Rema, Ruthie May and Eve had placed chairs around the desk so Dr. Trowbridge could sit at the desk.

In the foyer, Eben Justin's giant clock with its kingly booming chimes had just finished striking four o'clock. At the kitchen door, Mylowe held it open for Maggie and Clyde Finch and ushered them into the den.

Returning through the foyer, Mylowe rushed up to Eben's Tower to escort Dr. Trowbridge to the den. At the same moment, Eve opened the front door and welcomed Martin Walsh, the family attorney.

Everyone was seated when Mylowe and Dr. Trowbridge entered the den. Since the family had already met Dr. Trowbridge, Mylowe introduced Martin Walsh to Dr. Trowbridge and steered Dr. Trowbridge to sit behind the desk.

Rema clutched her left arm close to her body and draped a shawl over it to ward off the early November chill. Ruthie May sat quietly at one end of the sofa with her hands clasped together on her lap. Eve sat at the other end of the sofa with her right fingers touching her left wrist as she counted each beat of her heart.

Mylowe, standing beside the desk, was the first to speak.

"As you know we have all gathered to hear the result of the toxicology investigation conducted by Dr. Harvey Trowbridge." Mylowe nodded to Dr. Trowbridge and sat down on a nearby chair.

"In the examining process," said Dr. Trowbridge, "the resin from the fragment of a piece from a tree sitting in volcanic ash in Eben's Tower contains a deadly inhalant—a poison. My colleague, who is an authority on exotic poisons, has studied the tree fragment. He is prepared to testify that residue from the tree's residue was found in the lung tissue of Dr. Felic Ort and Paul Moore.

"In the laboratory, we are still working to break down the poison's chemical components. It is an exogenous poison. It is one that comes from outside the body and enters by way of the lungs. It is a severe irritant and causes inflammation of the lungs, collapse of the extremities, feeble pulse and rapid respiration. Such extreme changes in the lungs and brain result in death from the collapse of vital organs."

Rema gasped and bowed her head.

Aware that Dr. Trowbridge's announcement had caused an invoked silence, Mylowe stood up. Before he could speak, Dr. Trowbridge continued.

"There is a disturbing element attached to this discovery that those present in this meeting should thoroughly understand. From the autopsy reports of Dr. Felic Ort and Mr. Paul Moore, and the lab tests conducted on Dr. Mylowe Ort's current physical condition, it has been determined that Dr. Mylowe Ort is experiencing physical signs similar to the intermediate cycle of inhaling this unclassified poison. It is therefore imperative that the lab technicians break down the components and immediately prepare an antidote. I have recommended to Dr. Ort that he stay away from Eben's Tower."

The room became quiet. Maggie moaned, but no one moved until Mylowe again stood up.

"I had not anticipated that my physical complaints would be aired, but since they have, let me say that Dr. Trowbridge has assured me that an antidote will be forthcoming."

Rema leaned forward in her chair. "Are we to believe all this turmoil in our family has occurred over a stick of wood in Eben's Tower? This is a nightmare. Although finding the poison will exonerate Maggie and me, we now learn that the poison is slowly killing Mylowe." She stared at Dr. Trowbridge. "Did you know, Dr. Trowbridge, that all the men who lived in Justin House spent hours and hours in Eben's Tower?"

"No, I didn't know. Are there any old medical documents available that would give some history of the health of those men?"

"No," replied Mylowe.

"Eve said she saw diaries in the safe in Eben's tower," Ruthie May said.

"Yes, I was in the room when Eve found them," exclaimed Rema.

Dr. Trowbridge stood up and gathered his papers from the desktop. He glared at Rema and Ruthie May.

"I suggest you read those journals. I'll be in my laboratory, should you require my help." He turned toward Mylowe. "Are you ready, doctor? Let's be on our way."

The two men hurried across the foyer. Mylowe grabbed his overcoat at the back door, but raced back into the den and looked at Eve.

"Eve, will you take Maggie and Clyde back to their house. I'll be gone several hours. Don't wait dinner."

When he disappeared through the den's doorway into the foyer, no one had moved. Martin Walsh, the abrupt, self-centered lawyer, sat motionless. Clyde Finch's hand clung to Maggie's arm hoping she would not moan again. Everyone in the room was in shock.

Ruthie May broke the silence.

"Eve," she said, "when you come back from Maggie's house, let's go to the tower and bring the diaries down into the den."

Eve nodded agreeably and ushered Maggie and Clyde toward the back door.

During Dr. Trowbridge's announcement of Mylowe's illness, Martin Walsh's brusqueness had notably disappeared. He moved his chair closer to Rema.

"What a state of affairs," he whispered. "If you need anything, anything at all, I'll come right over."

Rema was surprised by Martin's kindness. She shook his hand.

"Thank you for coming," she whispered.

* * * * *

In his Miami office, George Whitetail hung up the phone. It was the third call this week to Dr. Trowbridge.

George had asked Dr. Trowbridge if the designation of the antidote for the poison was forthcoming from a laboratory in California. Dr. Trowbridge's reply was hazy. He felt it was too early to commit to a positive answer.

George was worried. According to Dr. Trowbridge, the episodes of numbness in Mylowe's hands and the weakness in his legs were increasing. George grabbed the phone and called Mona.

"Hi! Would you call Rema and invite us to visit Justin House? Mylowe's strange condition is deteriorating and I need to be there if he is hospitalized."

"I'll call right away."

"Good, in the meantime, I'll get us on the night flight from Miami to Dayton. I've taken that flight before. We can either stay in the airport hotel in Dayton, or drive to Wexlor."

Mona dialed Rema's business telephone. When Rema answered, Mona said, "Would you like company?"

"Indeed, I would," said Rema.

"George has a meeting in Cleveland on Tuesday. He's driving me to Wexlor and going on to his meeting. I don't have his schedule. Can we come?"

"Oh! Please come. I need your cheerful energy. In the last week, Mylowe has had seven episodes of losing strength in his extremities. He's so tired."

Mona pretended to ignore Rema's concerned tone and spoke hurriedly to avoid more conversation about Mylowe. "If I'm to board a night flight in four hours," Mona said glibly, "I've got to start packing. See you tomorrow. Bye."

George Whitetail drummed the top of his green, monogrammed, ballpoint pen against the desk-top. Inwardly, he was thinking of calling Melody Ann to tell her about Mylowe's illness. He thumbed backwards three weeks through the desk calendar. He stopped on the page he had noted about his call to Dr. Ben Riley about the arrangements for a paternal blood test for Melody Ann's baby and Mylowe.

Turning the calendar pages forward, he counted twenty-two days. Perhaps, the result of the test was back from the lab. He dialed Ben Riley's office and waited.

"Hello, Ben," he shouted as the Des Moines gynecologist answered his page. "Has the report on Melody Ann's baby come back yet?"

"Yes, this morning. Bart Knowles is not the infant's father."

"Does Melody Ann know?"

"Yes, I called her two hours ago."

"Thanks for all your help. I'll be in touch."

Dr. Whitetail leaned back in his chair and sat quietly before dialing Melody Ann's number in Des Moines.

When she answered, he said, "I know about the test results. I'm calling to tell you about Mylowe. Now, don't hang up until you hear what I have to say. Mylowe is very sick," he whispered. "He is being poisoned by the same poison that killed Felic and Paul Moore. A lab in California is working night and day to make an antidote. I'm flying to Justin House tonight to be with him."

"Is he dying?"

"Yes, unless they are able to make an antidote."

"Are you asking me to go to him?"

"Would you?"

"And take the baby?"

"Yes."

"Freddy is not a month old. I'm not sure I should travel. Will you ask Mylowe if he wants to see us? If he does, I'll come."

Dr. Whitetail smiled and pumped his fist into the air. "I'll call you tomorrow afternoon. Will you be at home?"

Her reply, filled with emotion, was barely audible.

"Yes," she whispered, "I'll be waiting."

* * * * *

Inside Mylowe's bedroom in Justin House, Eve Porter plugged a telephone cord into the jack near Mylowe's bed. "It's all set," she said raising the phone to her ear. "There's a dial tone."

Mylowe, fully dressed, was recovering from a recent episode of weakness in his legs. He rested in a wide comfortable chair. "Please don't bother," he said.

"No bother. You can take your calls in your room instead of going to Rema's room. I don't understand why you don't have a telephone in your room."

"I've always worked in Eben's Tower. I miss going up there."

"Did you know George and Mona are coming tomorrow? Rema said George has a medical convention in Cleveland and Mona is staying with us."

"I could use a good doctor."

"Good! Meantime, you can conduct business from your room."

Eve hurried through the door and was gone before Mylowe could say more. He leaned back and closed his eyes. Psychiatric training had taught him not to panic when changes in his life occur. Clinging to old ways inhibit new opportunities from appearing. This was a time to let go of the old. He felt his body was shutting down.

The most positive thing from all of this was that Rema now understood why Felic and Paul Moore had died. It was his destiny to help her. He had to stay alive. His dying would not lighten her burden. He reread a letter he had written to George Whitetail dated November 1, 1996.

Dear George:

Today, I'm sending you all my journals. Throughout my life, I have written daily in these journals and recorded happenings along with my innermost feelings.

These records also portray the lives of the people who have been an integral part of my life. I know you will keep these writings and, in time, appoint a suitable resting place for them.

The malady that has overtaken my body has all the medical people scratching their heads. Perhaps, the fault is in me. I may have made assumptions based on my own neurosis, but in my heart, I am forever trying to continue life, such as it is.

Dr. Mylowe F. Ort

Mylowe creased the letter and returned it to the file. For now, he would not send it. He struggled to his feet and stood up. His legs were strong again. The episode had passed. When he turned around, Ruthie May was standing in the doorway.

"I'm okay," he murmured. "I'm embarrassed the entire household is put on emergency status when my legs give out."

Ruthie May came into the room.

"I was hoping you could come down. Eve and I have just begun to read one of the old diaries locked in the tower safe. It's family history. We wondered if Dr. Felic had read them."

"He never mentioned the journals. I would like to know what's in them."

"Then you'll come down? Are you sure?"

"Yes, give me a moment to change my shirt."

"You're so handsome when you smile," Ruthie May whispered. "See you downstairs."

As he was changing his shirt, Mylowe looked into the mirror. There was something different about his face. A softness that agreed with the responsible choice he had recently made about this degrading illness. His choice was to follow the pure thoughts sent into his head from his spirit. The spirit always presents thoughts to be acted upon. It is a pure message and should not be muddled by the brain. Mylowe smiled. He was remembering the times he had let his brain shred his pure thoughts into unworkable situations.

As a boy, he had taken Felic's gun and shot at railroad freight cars. Subsequently, he was put on court-ordered probation. During the days that followed shooting at the freight cars when he needed courage to withstand Felic's anger, he learned the best way to survive was to follow his spirit-driven thoughts.

His attention was diverted from his thoughts when the telephone rang. He reached for the phone. "Hello, this is Mylowe Ort."

"Dr. Ort, this is the Reverend Mother at St. Angeline's Convent. Ruthie May's brother, Father Xaiver arrived in Miami several days ago and was in my office this morning for two hours. He's anxious to see his sister. Could you bring her to Miami?"

Mylowe dropped into the nearby chair.

"I'm sorry, it's not possible. I'm not able to travel. Would Father Xavier be willing to come to Justin House?"

"I'll ask him. He's in the chapel."

Mylowe's heart was racing. The excitement made it difficult for him to breathe. His palms, sweaty and weak, held the phone to his ear until he heard the deep tone of a male voice.

"Hello Mylowe, this is Father Xavier. Am I speaking to my nephew?"

"Indeed, you are."

"I've traveled a long way to hear your voice. Is my sister there?"

"Yes, she's downstairs."

"We have much catching up to do. The Reverend Mother tells me you're not able to travel. She suggested I come to Wexlor."

"Is that possible?"

"Yes. Could I speak to Ruthie May?"

"I'll ask Ruthie May to come to the phone."

Buttoning his shirt and hurrying down the stairs, Mylowe walked into the den where Eve was reading aloud from one of the diaries.

"Ruthie May, you have a phone call."

"Who is it?"

"Father Xavier."

"My brother?"

"Yes, he's in Miami at the convent with the Reverend Mother."

Ruthie May ran to Mylowe's room.

"She's so excited," said Rema. "I was hoping the first meeting with her brother would be face to face."

Mylowe grinned. "It has worked out the way it is to be. Someone said that coincidences are God's way of performing miracles anonymously."

65

FAMILY

Ruthie May hurried to Mylowe's bedroom and paused before picking up the telephone.

"Hello," she said, "this is Ruthie May Durston."

"Ruthie May, I am your brother, Edward Michael Spar. I believe our lives have been twisted by fate. Without details, the Reverend Mother briefly outlined your early life. I was raised by adoptive parents and grew up as an only child. The church has been my life since I was twenty. In the church, I am called Father Xavier. As my sister, would you call me Eddie? My mother calls me Eddie. Will you tell me about my biological parents? Was my mother kind and loving?"

Ruthie May brushed tears from her cheeks. "This is so wonderful," she whispered.

"I agree. When I received a letter in Bolivia from the Reverend Mother telling me I had a sister, I decided to come back home so I could meet you and also attend to my aging parents." He paused. "It may be too soon for me to consider retirement, but I do want to stay in the states."

Ruthie May's knees began to shake. She backed into a chair and sat down.

"Are you still on the line?" he said.

"Yes."

"From the Reverend Mother, I learned your son found you in Miami. You had been living alone for over twenty years."

"Did Mylowe tell you he is very ill?"

"No, he just said he was unable to travel."

"Mylowe is waiting for a medicine to be developed to counteract a poison that has entered his body. If the laboratory isn't able to find an effective antidote, he will die."

Father Xavier heard the desperation in her. "I'll be on the next flight from Miami."

"Thank you, Eddie. Mylowe and I will be waiting."

Ruthie May leaned back in the chair. Until this moment, she had not wanted to display her deep concern about Mylowe's illness. Like Rema and Eve, she had tried to keep her emotions controlled, but as each day went by, she was finding it harder to do. She realized she had a far different role to play than before. Mylowe was her son and he was dying.

Mylowe, Ruthie May and Eve were in the den when she went downstairs. She sat beside Mylowe.

"Do you realize you and I are about to be united with a member of our family. Through the blood of our mother and father, we now have each other."

"Is my uncle coming to Justin House?" asked Mylowe.

"Yes, he will be here tomorrow."

Rema smiled and pulled a shawl over her shoulders.

"I'm very happy for both of you. I grew up with three brothers. It's comforting to have a real family."

"I didn't know you had brothers," said Ruthie May.

"Yes. When I came to Ohio with Felic, my brothers did not approve of the arrangement because Felic and I did not marry. Over the years, I've lost touch with them."

"I'm sorry."

Rema shivered and looked at Mylowe. "Would you put more wood on the fire? I can't seem to get warm today."

Mylowe stoked the fire and added two small logs. "Would you be more comfortable in your room? You could rest there and have dinner."

She nodded and turned to Ruthie May and Eve. "If you'll excuse me, I'll see you in the morning."

"I'll be in later to say goodnight," Mylowe said.

Later in the evening before going upstairs, Mylowe ate dinner with Eve and Ruthie May. Once in his room, Father Xavier's call reminded him of the day he and Melody Ann met with Grover at the Anchor Bar in Miami. Grover's memories of the Durston family had provided him valuable information.

Grabbing the Miami telephone directory, Mylowe dialed the number of the Anchor Bar.

A muffled voice answered.

"Is this the Anchor Bar?" Mylowe asked.

"Yep!"

"Is Grover there?"

"Who wants to know?"

"Tell him Dr. Mylowe Ort is calling from Ohio."

"Okay."

Mylowe could hear the bartender yelling.

"Hey! Grover, a Dr. Ort wants to talk to yuh."

The bartender yelled into the phone, "He's comin'."

There was a long pause. Finally, Mylowe heard Grover's voice.

"Hello, this is Grover."

"Grover, how good to hear your voice. I'm not in Miami, but I'm calling to tell you how grateful I am."

"Grateful to me?"

"Your memory helped me find Ruthie Durston. She's my mother."

"Well, I'll be damned. You really found her?"

"Yes. And we located her brother."

"The baby boy Dave Durston gave away to a Miami convent?"

"Yes. Her brother is a Jesuit priest."

"Double damn. How about that!"

"I owe you a lot."

"That's okay, Doc. Glad to do it."

"Do you need anything? A place to stay or money?"

Grover shook his head. "Nope, got all I need."

"How about some beer money?"

"Beer is my weakness."

"I'll make some arrangements with the bartender. Thanks again, Grover. I'll call again."

After speaking to the bartender and adding money Grover's beer fund, Mylowe hung up the phone. Around nine o'clock, he checked on Rema and told her to sleep well. The next morning when he awakened, George Whitetail was standing by his bed.

"Did you just arrive?"

"Yes, Eve made breakfast. Do you feel like coming downstairs?"

George walked toward the door, but turned around and quietly said, "Melody Ann had the baby. It's a boy. She told me Bart Knowles is not the father. Melody Ann did not marry him. If you'd wish to see her, she'll come here and bring your son."

Mylowe sat up in bed. "For God's sake, George, why wouldn't I want to see her? But why would she want to see me again? I let her go without a fight."

"That's not important now. I wouldn't be telling you this if it she hadn't already agreed to come to Justin House."

"Are all the parental reports in from the laboratory? Am I the baby's father?"

"Yes!"

"You know something, George? You're a real friend."

"I'm also a member of this family. Although the six family members are not related by blood, our ties are strong yet tender."

Mylowe grinned and rested on one elbow. "Those ties are also tenderly tied," he murmured.

"Go on down to breakfast so I can call Melody Ann," George said. "I'll need to use your phone."

Mylowe stood up and leaned against the bedroom door. "Ask her if I can call her."

George waved his hand motioning Mylowe to leave the room. "I'll ask. I'll ask."

At the top of the stairs, Mylowe discovered his legs barely supported him. He shuffled across the foyer into the dining room and found Rema, Ruthie May and Mona sitting at the table.

Ruthie May spoke first. "You have to eat in a hurry," said Ruthie May.

"Why?"

"We're reading Albert Justin's diary."

"Wasn't Albert Justin the son of Eben Justin?"

"Yes, Albert was Felic's grandfather."

Ruthie May moved her chair next to Mylowe and opened the diary.

"On this page, Albert says he was brought up by two women. Both were Eben's wives."

"Felic always said that Eben Justin had two wives. Does Albert Justin say that Eben had fourteen children?"

"Albert wrote he was an only child. He was the only heir to Justin House."

Mylowe shook his head. "I wonder how the story began about Eben having fourteen children."

"On another page, Albert said Eben Justin was a recluse and very much misunderstood by his neighbors. He did say that one of Eben's wives was from India."

"Was she Albert's mother?"

"He doesn't say."

Mona stood up and began gathering the plates into a stack. She walked into the kitchen juggling silverware pieces on the top plate and talking above the clatter.

"I can't wait until we read the rest of Albert's diary."

"Where's Eve this morning?" asked Mylowe.

"She's at the university taking final exams," replied Rema.

"When does she graduate?"

"In three weeks. After graduation, she's going back to Michigan. She's been a real companion. I'll miss her."

Grinning impishly, Mylowe spread his arms over the table and touched Rema with one hand and Ruthie May on the other. "We're going to have a lot of excitement to keep you company. Melody Ann and I are parents of a baby boy. She's bringing our son to Justin House."

"Oh! Glory!" whispered Rema. "Is that true?"

"Yes, if we trust the lab reports, we have a son."

"When will Melody Ann arrive?"

"Soon, very soon."

Mona returned to the dining room. "What have I missed?"

Rema replied, "Melody Ann and the baby are coming to Justin House."

"I know."

"Why are you keeping it secret?"

"George threatened to send me back to Miami if I breathed a word about the baby. If Mylowe was agreeable, I knew Melody Ann would come and bring little Freddy."

A brilliant blush of embarrassment moved over Mylowe's face. "What's wrong?" Mona asked. "What did I say?"

Mylowe swallowed causing deep pain in his throat. "Until this moment," he whispered, "I didn't know my baby's name."

Mona stood up and patted Mylowe on his shoulders. "For now, you have a lot to be concerned about. I wonder why she named the baby Freddy."

"My middle name is Frederick. Why are you smiling?"

"I'm as guilty with names as you are. I never knew your middle name."

"I knew it," said Ruthie May shyly. "Mylowe told me when Dr. Felic Ort found him in Dead Man's Alley; he named him Mylowe Frederick Ort."

For a moment, no one spoke. Each woman, enveloped in her own concerned, prayerful thoughts, was on a timeless tour to glimpse into the future. Mylowe, now physically ill, biologically was Ruthie May's son, but he was also Rema's son—and, in a different way, he was Mona's son, too. Everyone wanted his life to go on.

Out of more of the need to act than from any sensible plan, Mona slid her chair closer to Ruthie May and Mylowe.

"Okay," she whispered, "I want to hear more from Albert Justin's diary."

Ruthie May nodded and read aloud for the next thirty minutes. During that time, George joined them and sat at the end of the table. Finally, she stopped reading, sipped some water and read from the top of the next page.

"August, 15, 1870. A large wooden box was delivered to our back door via of a horse-drawn wagon. When my father was called into the back yard, the wagon driver said he had driven for four days from a river freight depot in Cincinnati. The box had been shipped from the Limborg Rubber Estate in East Java, south of Malang, in the Netherlands, East India. The final stage of its journey was down the Ohio River on a river steamer.

"When the box was opened with a crowbar, my father found a letter inside from his friend, Clifford Haines, a research chemist for Charles Goodyear's brother, Nelson, in Java. Clifford Haines had been living on the Goodyear rubber estate for five years.

"The letter said the box held a piece of the Kalabee tree. Clifford gave explicit instructions that the wood piece be placed upright in a bed of lava. The wood from the Kalabee tree was a symbol of good fortune and the wood would survive forever without water."

George leaped to his feet. "Great Jehoshaphat! Did you hear what she just read? That dead stick of wood in the tower is from a Kalabee tree. How do I reach Dr. Trowbridge's lab?"

"The telephone number is on my rolodex in my bedroom," replied Mylowe as he started to stand up but fell back into the chair.

George turned to Ruthie May. "Tell me again. From what part of the Netherlands, East India was the wood shipped?"

"East Java, south of Malang."

George ran from the room as Ruthie May and Mona rushed to help Mylowe.

"You're going to be well again," whispered Ruthie May. "Just hold on a little longer."

Mylowe looked at her. He had lost all control of his legs and hands and had fallen to the floor.

Rema rushed to the phone in the kitchen to call an ambulance.

Upstairs in Mylowe's bedroom, George dialed the Savannah Laboratories in California.

"Hello, hello," he shouted. "This is a long-distance emergency call. I must speak to Dr. Harvey Trowbridge."

There was a long pause. Finally, he heard Dr. Trowbridge pick up a telephone.

"This is George Whitetail. I'm calling from Justin House. We've just learned the piece of wood in Eben's Tower is from the Kalabee tree and was sent from the Limborg Rubber Estate in East Java in Netherlands, East India, south of Malang, in 1870."

"Would you spell Kalabee?" asked Dr. Trowbridge.

"K-a-l-a-b-e-e," said George Whitetail.

"Malang is in Java in Indonesia on the Indian Ocean. I've been there," exclaimed Dr. Trowbridge.

"Keep me informed about any progress you make with this information. We're transporting Mylowe to the hospital in Cira, Ohio. You can reach me through the hospital switchboard."

In his office inside the Savanna Laboratories near Los Angeles, California, Dr. Trowbridge pressed the intercom key and called all the scientists and lab workers to his office.

When they had assembled, Dr. Trowbridge spoke. "Ladies and gentlemen, I have just been informed that the piece of wood we are dissecting in the lab is from Java. It is from the Kalabee tree."

Steve Hardy, a forensic investigator, stepped forward.

"It's a long shot, but I know something about the Kalabee tree. When I was in Indonesia looking for the chemical that had killed twenty-five natives while they were working in the rubber tree groves, I had a long discussion with a colleague who lived there.

"What struck me as odd was there was only one Kalabee tree in all of Java. I remember the first time I saw it. It was a monstrosity. The trunk was as large as a California Redwood. The branches extended over an area of a hundred feet. The natives touched it for good fortune.

"My colleague said the wood was poison. At one time, he had worked with a group or scientists to break down the chemical components of the Kalabee wood. While they couldn't be certain if they were correct, they named the poison dichloromethate."

"Hell!" yelled Dr. Trowbridge, "that's just a conglomeration of chemical components."

Steve Hardy replied, "Even if that's so, the measured amounts made up of the components could save Dr. Ort's life. Does everyone in this room agree?"

The "ayes" came from six of the ten people in the room.

"Okay!" said Dr. Trowbridge, "You've got thirty-six hours to make the antidote."

At Justin House, the medics placed Mylowe on a gurney and were moving him through the foyer when George came down the stairs. He rushed to Mylowe's side and turned toward one of the medics.

"I'm Dr. Whitetail," he said. "How are his vital signs?"

"His respiration is unstable."

George looked at Mylowe.

"This is just a small bump in the road. I gave Dr. Trowbridge the information about the Kalabee tree. He'll call me at the hospital as soon as he has the antidote."

Mylowe, too weak to speak, blinked his eyes. "You're welcome!" replied George.

After Mylowe was placed in the ambulance, Rema and Ruthie May went back inside the house. George met them near the front the door.

"Mylowe will be stronger when he is on oxygen," he said firmly. "Dr. Trowbridge has the name of the tree and its location. He'll call me at Cira Memorial when his lab has the antidote."

"The coroner's inquest is Tuesday morning," said Rema. "Will Dr. Trowbridge testify in our defense?"

"Making the antidote is more important. Dr. Patterson will not postpone the inquest on the information we have just uncovered."

Ruthie May tugged at George's arm. "We'd like to go to the hospital with you."

"I should go alone. In a couple of hours, Eve will drive you to the hospital."

Mona gave George a parting kiss. "I'll stay in the house," she said.

"If Mylowe's bedroom telephone rings, it could be Dr. Trowbridge. Be prepared to give him the hospital's number."

George hurried to his rental car. The women walked pensively into the den. Ruthie May sat in one of the blue velvet Queen Anne chairs. To keep everyone occupied, she opened Albert Justin's diary.

"According to Albert, he was seven years old when the box from Limborg Rubber Estate was delivered to Justin House. The next pages tell about his schooling. He became a tradesman and made fine furniture. The desk in Eben's Tower is one of the pieces he created.

"On a page dated January, 1914, Albert discusses Eben's health. He states that Eben has difficulty walking and breathing. A notation at the bottom of the page on May 4, 1914, states that Eben no longer can walk up to the tower. On December 31, 1914, Albert writes that his father, Eben Justin, passed away at the age of 81 years."

"I find it strange that Albert never mentioned his mother in his diary," Mona said.

Ruthie May turned several pages. "In the next pages, Albert speaks of his marriage to Sarah Webb. They had one daughter, Anne."

Rema stared at Ruthie May. "Don't you think it is interesting that before his death Eben Justin had difficulty walking and was experiencing respiratory problems?"

"Yes, those are identical to Mylowe's symptoms," said Eve. "But, Eben Justin was 81 when he died. Mylowe is 27."

Ruthie May, intent on keeping everyone's emotions balanced, continued to read from Albert's diary. "On May 3, 1930, Albert writes that his daughter, Anne Ort, gave birth to a son at 6:26 p.m. His first grandchild was named Felic Frederick Ort.

"The next entry is on August 5, 1930," said Ruthie May. "Today is the saddest day of our lives. Anne, our only child, passed away this morning due to complications she experienced when our grandson was born. Sarah and I, along with Manuel Ort, Anne's loving husband, will care for the baby. Although I have constant pain in my legs, I will do what I can for the child. At times, my legs become so weak I cannot stand. I fear the burden of caring for little Felic is falling on my wife, Sara."

"Listen to that," Rema chanted. "Albert writes of the same symptoms as Mylowe and Paul Moore experienced."

Ruthie May pointed to another page in the diary. "On September 4, 1931, Albert writes that Manuel Ort, Felic's father, was killed in a railroad accident."

"Holy Moly!" Mona exclaimed. "The entire family was dead except Sarah Justin."

Ruthie May turned the page.

"This page is in a different handwriting. It's dated November 12, 1933."

"My Albert passed away, on the fourth of this month. He had been bed-ridden for three months. We spent many happy years in this house. We loved it very much. There are memories here. Felic is three years old. A beautiful child. Sweet like his mother. Stubborn like his father. Bless us all. Sara Justin."

"Sarah Justin died in 1939," Rema said.

"How do know that?" asked Mona.

"Felic was nine years old when his grandmother died. He was put in foster homes until he was eighteen."

When Rema's business phone rang, she picked it up quickly and motioned to Ruthie May.

"It's Eddie, your brother."

66

THE ANTIDOTE

For the last three hours, Dr. Harvey Trowbridge had been asleep on a cot in the corner of the main lab at Savannah Laboratories. Everyone working on the antidote for the poison of the Kalabee tree had gone home by midnight the day before.

Earlier in the evening, Steve Hardy was able to speak to his colleague he knew in Java years ago. During the phone conversation, Steve did not learn anything new about the Kalabee tree. However, through a concentrated group effort, the lab people discovered the chemical components had deterred some of the poisonous action on Mylowe's blood specimen. Dr. Trowbridge had jokingly named the components "Pig Latin chemicals."

The lab scientists were working on the modern conception that a poisonous action is essentially a physio-chemical one. The distinction between a molecular physical action and a molecular chemical action is difficult to make. But, for all forms of poisons, a distinct alteration in the character of the colloids of the body takes place, as well as a change in the chemical composition of the poisonous substance.

It is rare that the reaction between the body cells and the poison is purely of a physical nature, yet this frequently happens in many poisons that act on the blood. The anilines, for example: the blood undergoes changes, not so much due to new chemical compounds formed, but due to physical changes in the tension of the blood serum and the blood-corpuscles whereby the blood coloring matters stream out into the plasma and the oxygen carrying functions of the blood are lost.

Harvey Trowbridge looked at his watch. Twenty-four hours of the thirty-six hours he had scheduled for making the antidote were already gone. Jumping from the cot, he woke himself up by running tap water over his head. It was certain he would not have sufficient data available on the discovery of the Kalabee poison to testify at the coroner's inquest in Cira, Ohio, on the following Tuesday. The inquest would have to proceed without him.

At 6:00 a.m., he had made coffee and drank it while reviewing yesterday's lab notes.

On the same morning in Wexlor, Ohio, while Dr. Trowbridge was reading lab reports in the Savannah Laboratories, everyone living at Justin House had come downstairs by 9:00 a.m.

Yesterday afternoon, Eve had driven Rema and Ruthie May to Cira Memorial to visit Mylowe. They returned home feeling that Mylowe's condition had improved slightly. George arrived at Justin House several hours later. They all had dinner together.

Earlier this morning, Ruthie May put the finishing touches on the smallest bedroom in Justin House. While the room was small, it was quiet. Rema had suggested the room would be perfect for Ruthie May's brother, Father Xavier.

Satisfied that the bedroom and bath were in perfect order, Ruthie May returned to the first floor level to wait near a window in the living room. Before she was settled, a yellow cab turned into the Justin House entrance. The cab stopped at the front door.

Ruthie May watched the man get out of the taxi. She uttered, "Oh! No! It can't be."

She continued to stare at him. He was an exact duplicate of her father except he was dressed as a priest. Finally, she hunched her shoulders and straightened her blouse. Self-criticism was a hang-around trait she had not conquered. So was judging. "Judge not," she mumbled.

At the sound of the doorbell, she quieted her self-recrimination and opened the door. She knew there was no magic in nightmares. The man standing before her, with a strong, horsey-face, grizzled, short dark hair and brown eyes that darted from side-to-side like a hawk brought back unpleasant memories.

He smiled. She relaxed. Unlike her father's smile that had been sadistic and calculating, Eddie's smile was kind, bright and shiny.

"Are you Ruthie May?"

"Yes."

"I'm Ed Spar."

Although her feet felt like she was wearing lead boots, she managed to step away from the door.

"Please come in."

"You look like my father," she blurted. "He was a sailor."

She hung his coat in the foyer closet and guided him into the living room.

"This is an old mansion. Have you lived here long?"

"I've been here for a short time. I lived in Miami my entire life."

"We have much to talk about. You said I resemble my father?"

"Yes, in many ways."

"Is that good?"

She shook her head. "Our father was not a pleasant person."

"What about our mother?"

"Sickly most of her life. She was dominated by our father. He made her give you away for adoption. Since you've just been in Miami with the Reverend Mother, you know the whole story."

"Yes, I'm aware of most of the family secrets."

"My son, Mylowe, is gravely ill."

"I've come at a stressful time."

"Rema, the woman who raised my son, told me that brothers are very comforting. I'm glad you're here."

The warmth of Ed's smile filled her heart.

"Come with me. I want you to meet the family."

Ruthie May entered the den ahead of Father Xavier. Inside the room, she guided him toward Rema and Mona who were each seated in the blue Queen Anne chairs by the fireplace.

"Rema," she said, "this is my brother, Father Xavier."

Turning toward Mona, her introduction was similar. "Mona, this is my brother."

Both Rema and Mona stood as he walked toward them.

"Ladies, please, be seated," he said.

Ruthie May motioned for him to sit by her on the sofa.

"Three members of our household are not present," Rema said. "Mylowe's in the hospital and Eve Porter is attending classes at the university. George Whitetail, Mona's husband, is with Mylowe at the hospital."

Father Xavier smiled. "I can feel the love and devotion all around me. I'll wager this house serves each family member in a different way."

"That's correct," Mona replied. "We all come to Justin House to be in its energy."

"Ruthie May told me about the terrible illness that has taken over my nephew."

"We're in shock. But Mylowe's illness has provided answers to many unexplained happenings in this house. The past has been revealed."

Ruthie May turned toward her brother. "You and I have a lot of catching up to do."

Rema leaned toward Father Xavier. "We welcome you to our family. Please consider Justin House your home. Ruthie May is looking forward to your visit."

Upstairs in the room Ruthie May prepared for her brother's visit, two strangers with the same bloodline sat down to learn about each other. After thirty minutes of conversation, Ed Spar looked wistfully at Ruthie May. "The Reverend Mother told me all she knew about your life before Mylowe found you. I sense you may have much more to share with me. In the short time we'll have together, I hope you will tell me."

Ruthie May nodded. "I was eleven when our mother died. I've only told Mylowe a small portion of what happened. I was thirteen when my son was born. That night, I was in the bathroom of room #218 in the old Green Palms Hotel. Lying face-up in rusty toilet water was my newborn baby. In the hall outside the room was my hired caretaker, Arnie Tuttle. He was returning from his nightly visit to the Anchor Bar. He had fallen on the floor and was kicking the door and yelling.

"I picked up a man's shirt from the tub, draped it over my open hands and scooped the baby from the water. I laid him down. He was quiet. Not crying. I don't know why, but I tied the torn cord on his naval with a rubber band. I just wanted to do the right thing. His eyes were closed. He wasn't breathing. He was dead. I wrapped him in newspaper, tied it shut with my hair ribbon and looked around for some place to put him. Arnie was still kicking the door. I was scared. I threw the bundle out the open window."

"Did you let Arnie in the room? Was he the father of your son?"

"Yes. Later that night while Arnie slept, I went to the place where the homeless people lived. The women there took care of me."

"How did you happen to be with Arnie Tuttle?"

"After my mother died, my father left me with Arnie Tuttle and his wife. Three months later, Arnie's wife ran away. That's when he raped me."

Ruthie May bowed her head and quickly raised it. She was smiling. "It was wonderful when Mylowe found me. I'm very happy and content."

"I'm pleased that you are," he said.

* * * * * *

In Cira Memorial Hospital, Martin Walsh who had been summoned to Mylowe's hospital room, stood at Mylowe's bedside.

"What can I do for you, Mylowe?"

"You can change my will? I have a son and I want him to inherit Justin House."

Mylowe ignored Martin's raised eyebrows.

"My son's name is Frederick Ort."

"Middle initial?"

"I don't have that information."

"If I remember correctly, you recently named your mother, Ruthie May Durston, as the heiress."

"Justin House will always be her home."

"I see."

"When will you have the papers ready to sign?"

"Tomorrow."

"I hope I'm still alive."

Martin Walsh shook his head and walked toward the door. Mylowe called out to him. "Tomorrow is the coroner's inquest. Will you get all the inside information? Squeeze it out of your buddy, Dr. Nearson, and let me know the verdict."

Dr. Whitetail met Martin Walsh in the doorway. "Martin didn't appear to be happy," he said.

"Martin doesn't like change," Mylowe said. "He prefers the status quo."

"Do you remember that your uncle, Father Xavier, is due to arrive at Justin House this morning?"

"Good! Ruthie May needs his support. Lately, I've not been there for her."

"You should rest."

"Is there any word from Trowbridge?"

"No, not since I gave him the name of the poisonous tree."

"Did you call Melody Ann?"

"Yes, she will be in Dayton tomorrow afternoon. Eve is going to meet her at the airport."

"She's probably nursing the baby."

"I believe she is."

"Will I see her tomorrow?"

"I'll try to arrange it."

George was concerned because he had not heard from Dr. Trowbridge. He hunched over in the chair as Mylowe closed his eyes.

"Please," he prayed. "Give Mylowe the energy to live. And could you give the lab guys some help? Amen."

Although Mylowe's eyes were closed, his thoughts were of Melody Ann. He was taking a grand tour of himself and realized he had ambushed his connection to her. There was a lot of damage to be repaired. A blur of blackness crossed over him. He wondered if he was dying. The telephone on the table rang.

George grabbed the phone. "Hello, this is Dr. Whitetail."

"Harvey Trowbridge here. We have a serum that is working on the blood specimen. We've decided to use it. Steve Hardy and I will catch a night flight and be at the hospital by noon tomorrow."

"That's good news! We'll be waiting."

He turned to Mylowe. "Trowbridge has the antidote. He's bringing it tomorrow. Get some rest. I'm going back to Justin House. See you in the a.m."

Mylowe closed his eyes. The oxygen cannula made his breathing easier. He wondered if Dr. Trowbridge had actually put together the correct antidote. What if it didn't work?

67

STRANGE CIRCUMSTANCES

The coroner's inquest had been in session for thirty minutes when Martin Walsh arrived at the Hancock County Justice Center in Cira. He stood in the hallway outside the courtroom where he knew Dr. Patterson was holding a coroner's inquest

After fifteen minutes, the door opened. Four men came out of the room. Martin Walsh recognized Dr. Patterson, the county coroner, and assumed the other gentlemen were the expert witnesses. Shortly thereafter, a lady court reporter, carrying steno equipment and a briefcase pushed through the half-open door. Dr. Jeff Nearson was the last to come out.

"How did it go in there today?" asked Martin Walsh. Jeff Nearson walked by him.

"It went as expected. Why do you ask?"

"I was just curious. The Swenson woman's inquest was well advertised in the media. Did you know the media compared Rema Swenson and Maggie Finch to the old dames in the stage play, Arsenic and Old Lace?"

"Ha! I didn't think of them in that way."

"So, will the prosecutor indict?"

"I'm not sure," said Dr. Nearson. "Let's talk about it over lunch. I'm starved."

"Good! Is the Cedar Room Inn okay? I've a meeting back here at one o'clock," said Martin Walsh.

Jeff Nearson nodded. "The Cedar Room is fine with me. I'll meet you there in ten minutes."

* * * * *

The same morning at Cira Memorial Hospital, George Whitetail had entered Mylowe's room to find Steve Hardy and Dr. Trowbridge from the Savannah Laboratories setting set up an IV unit above Mylowe's bed.

Dr. Trowbridge grinned half-heartily.

"Thanks for prearranging our arrival with the hospital medical staff. We're set up and ready when you are," he said.

"Let it go," George whispered. "Let it begin."

Dr. Trowbridge adjusted the drip sequence in the IV. When he was satisfied, he turned toward George and motioned to Steve.

"George, this is Steve Hardy. He's been the guiding force in making the antidote."

George shook Steve's hand and asked, "When will we know if the antidote is working?"

"There should be a dramatic improvement in Dr. Ort's respiration and muscle strength in forty-eight hours. It will take three to four weeks before he's able to move around."

Mylowe smiled weakly. "Not falling down will be a big improvement."

Dr. Trowbridge motioned to George to follow him into the hall.

"Is there something else going on?" asked George.

"Yes, the house Dr. Ort lives in might need to be condemned."

"What are you saying?"

"At the outset, that tower room on the second floor has to be destroyed. The poison from the Kalabee tree may have spread between the walls throughout the house."

"No one other than Mylowe is sick. Do you think it possible that the poison has reached other parts of the house?"

Harvey Trowbridge shrugged.

"I can't say. If the poison has spread, it will take three months for a special crew from California to sanitize the house and one more month before the house can be inhabited."

"This is a shock! I've never thought of the entire house being contaminated. Is the rest of the family in danger of inhaling the poison?"

"If it were my house, I'd burn it to the ground."

"The family will not allow it. With the proper cleaning, do you believe someone else could get sick?"

"There's a way that might permit the family to stay in the house."

"What is that?"

"You could ask my assistant, Steve Hardy, to meet with the local fire chief."

"Why?"

"The fire department could examine the house. Firefighters are quite knowledgeable about poisons and chemicals. Plus, Steve can give them all of our information."

Dr. Whitetail was noticeably upset.

"You do understand that Justin House is the center of this put-together-family. It's the pillar that binds us. By 4:00 p.m. today, Mylowe's twenty-two-day old son will arrive. Mylowe has yet to see him. Do we keep the baby out of Justin House?"

"I don't know."

George Whitetail turned, walked back into the hospital room and stood beside Mylowe. He looked toward the ceiling and prayed.

I implore the spirits of my ancestors to come forth and remove the poison from this young man's body. Lighten his burden. As a newborn, he never knew the contentment of suckling his mother's breast. He has courage, fortitude and great generosity of spirit. With a brave heart, he has walked alone to reach his destination wanting to turn back but always going forward. He has challenged destiny and destiny has summoned him to a duel with death.

George studied Mylowe's body. The sunken cheeks, the emaciated, wasted, thin neck and the limp, skeletal fingers attached to the carpus clearly indicated death was deliberately stalking nearby.

George shook the tears from his eyes and hurried to the parking garage. In the rental car, he sat quietly and wondered how he would tell Rema that Justin House had to be evacuated.

He drove to Justin House and was parking his car at the rear door as Eve Porter drove in the driveway. She had picked up Melody Ann at the Dayton airport. He hurried to greet them. Melody Ann was sitting in the rear seat beside baby Freddy, who was strapped safely in a car seat.

Opening the door for Melody Ann, George waited as she took Freddy from the safety of the infant car seat. She covered the infant's face with the tip of a lightweight blanket as she lifted him out of the car into the brisk afternoon air.

"Come out of the cold," George said pointing toward the house. "The back door is ajar."

Ruthie May met them in the kitchen.

"Here we are," George whispered. "Allow me to hold Freddy while you take off your coat."

When George lifted the blanket from Freddy face, the great warrior's eyes again filled with tears. "He's wonderful!" he exclaimed. "You're to be commended on a marvelous job."

George gave Freddy to Melody Ann and laid his hand on Ruthie May's shoulder. "Melody Ann," he said, "this is Ruthie May Durston."

Melody Ann held Freddy for Ruthie to see him. "This is your grandson," she whispered.

Ruthie May looked at Freddy. Slowly, she nodded her head. "Welcome. I'm so happy you've come."

George guided Melody Ann toward the den where Rema and Mona were sitting. Both women jumped on their feet and rushed toward her. They exchanged hugs. Rema stepped closer to look at Freddy.

"Oh!" she cried. "He's a beautiful baby."

"He's also a good baby," said Melody Ann.

Mona, standing beside George and wiping tears from her eyes, realized from George's demeanor that he had disturbing news. She backed away from the welcoming group, and quietly sat down on the sofa. George walked toward the fireplace and stood on the hearth.

Eve came into the den and also sensed George's awkward stance meant he was carrying a grim message about the effectiveness of the antidote.

At the same moment, Rema looked at George as she guided Melody Ann toward a chair.

"What is it, George?" she asked. "Is the antidote not working?"

"When I left Mylowe's hospital room an hour ago, the antidote was being administered. Dr. Trowbridge and one of his scientists, Steve Hardy, were with Mylowe. It's too early to tell."

"Is there another problem? You seem so disturbed."

"Have you heard any news about the coroner's inquest?"

"Not a word. Do you suppose the sheriff will bring a subpoena from the district attorney?"

"I doubt it. There wasn't much convicting evidence. Dr. Patterson was just trying to show his power. And Mylowe's ushering of Patterson's puppet, Dr. Nearson, out of the house didn't help the situation."

"I knew Mylowe's angry reaction to Dr. Nearson would cause trouble. Dr. Patterson is a vindictive man."

George bowed his head and shuffled his feet on the hearth. "There's something else that needs to be told. It's about Justin House. The house could be condemned."

Melody Ann drew Freddy close to her. "Is the poison still in the house?"

"No one knows, but the firefighters from the Cira Fire Department will examine the house within the next few days to determine if the poison has moved into the interior walls."

"I'm frightened," whispered Melody Ann. "Freddy shouldn't be here."

"So far, the poison has only been found in Eben's Tower," Rema replied. "Death occurred to the men of Justin House after they had spent years in the tower. Although Mylowe has only spent months up there, if the poison is throughout the house, we'd all be sick."

George realized it wasn't the time to mention that Dr. Trowbridge had recommended the house be burned to the ground. Rema caught him staring at her.

"What are you thinking, George?"

"I was going to suggest that Mona and I take Melody Ann and Freddy to Cira. I'll get a suite of rooms at the hotel. Melody Ann can visit Mylowe at the hospital tomorrow while Mona and I care for Freddy."

Melody Ann was visibly upset. "I should go home immediately after I see Mylowe."

Rema looked toward George. "You didn't say what the firefighters would do if they found the poison between the walls."

"Dr. Trowbridge suggested engaging a company from California to sanitize the house after Eben's Tower is torn down."

"Can't Eben's Tower be sealed shut forever?"

"That will depend on the fire department's examination."

"How long would the sanitizing take?"

"Three months of cleaning and a month's wait before anyone could move in."

Everyone was silent. It was Eve who broke the silence. "President Matthews and his wife are leaving for Africa. He asked me to housesit while they were gone. I'm certain he would welcome Rema and Ruthie May to housesit the president's home."

"But what will you do?" asked Rema.

"I'll stay with you and Ruthie May at the president's home until I graduate. After graduation, I had already planned to return to Michigan."

"Is there room at Dr. Matthews' home for Mylowe, too? He'll need a place to convalesce."

"Is Father Xavier in the house?" asked Dr. Whitetail.

"Yes," replied Ruthie May. "He's talking on the phone in Mylowe's bedroom."

"Do you know when he is going back to Miami?"

"On Saturday."

"Good! He'll have time to visit Mylowe."

Rema looked at Melody Ann.

"I would like you to stay here, but I understand your concerns about Freddy."

Melody Ann nodded. "I'll come back and bring Freddy after the house has been sanitized. I think Dr. Whitetail's plan is best for now."

"I'm so disappointed. We've not been able to visit."

"I know, but there'll be many, many other times, I promise."

Father Xavier was standing in the doorway and was ushered into the den by Ruthie May.

"Melody Ann," she said, "this is my brother, Father Xavier."

Father Xavier crossed the room and stood in front of Melody Ann. "The Reverend Mother at St. Angeline's Convent told me you were deeply involved in the search to find Ruthie May. I'm very grateful to you."

"If it weren't for Mylowe's obsessive nature, he would have not found Ruthie May," replied Melody Ann.

"I understand vital information was unavailable."

"That's correct, but fate has a way of opening doors." Melody Ann smiled mischievously. "And closing others."

Everyone in the room smiled at her remark. If any one of them thought of an appropriate reply, they did not say it.

"We best be on our way," said George. "We've had disturbing news about the condition of Justin House. Ruthie May will tell you about it. I hope you'll be able to see Mylowe tomorrow."

George hustled Melody Ann and Freddy through the kitchen into his parked car. Returning inside the house, he helped Mona and Eve carry Melody Ann's luggage to the back door. He started the car, turned on the heater, put the luggage in the trunk and waited while Mona packed an overnight bag.

* * * * * *

By 3:30 p.m. the following afternoon, George drove Melody Ann from the Goodfellow Hotel in Cira to Memorial Hospital. At the hospital entrance he warned her about the weakness in Mylowe's extremities.

"Does he know I'm here?"

"Yes."

"Should I go in alone?"

"Yes, he's waiting."

She took a deep breath. "You know, he's like a wad of gum stuck to my shoe."

"I know," he whispered.

At the hospital's front door, she looked back at the car and watched George drive away. Reaching room 123, she peeked inside. Mylowe opened his eyes before she reached his bedside.

"Hi!" he whispered.

"Hello yourself," she mimicked.

She took his hand and felt the coolness of his skin. Tears slipped down her cheeks. She used her free hand to wipe her eyes and nose.

"I don't want to cry," she whispered. "I've cried enough for one lifetime."

He felt her hand trembling. "I'm sorry I didn't fight for you," he said.

"I didn't offer you a choice. Don't you know that a woman's biological structure does not listen to her mind?"

"I guess my immune system was not strong enough to reject the poison."

If she thought his answer was strange, she didn't show it. There wasn't time to ask questions. Her vulnerability had taken over. She leaned over and kissed him on the lips.

"Do you know that the poison may have spread throughout Justin House?" he said. "I heard Dr. Trowbridge say the house should be burned to the ground."

She felt a shock wave move through her body. "No one mentioned burning the house down," she said calmly. "The plan is to sanitize it."

"How long will that take?"

"Three or four months."

"Where will we live?"

"I believe Rema and Ruthie May plan to housesit President Matthews' home. Eve is going back to Michigan. I want you to come to Des Moines and stay with me and Freddy."

"Have you told anyone about your invitation?"

"No, the decision is ours."

Mylowe squeezed her hand. "That's easy enough to arrange," he said. "We'll just do it!"

She smiled.

"You're so beautiful," he said. "I know being near you again will heal my body."

"Aren't you trashing your own philosophy? You've always maintained that we should not depend on others to make our lives better."

He grinned, and reached for her. Midway in the air, his arms fell down to his side.

"I'm a little weak."

A wide smile brightened her face. "Yes, I can see that."

"When will I see Freddy?"

"I decided not to bring him into the hospital."

"That's wise."

"I brought you pictures."

A light tapping on the open door interrupted the moment. A friendly voice said, "Hello, I'm Father Xavier. I'm sorry to break in."

"Come in," said Melody Ann. "Mylowe has been looking forward to your visit."

"On that note, I'll say I am also pleased to meet my nephew." Father Xavier stood beside Mylowe's bed. "Well, young man, you're having quite a battle. It's a nasty situation."

Mylowe extended his hand to Father Xavier. Again, it fell to his side. "Sorry, Father. I don't have much muscle strength."

"I'd like you to call me Uncle Ed. For me, the term of uncle has a family ring to it. My adoptive parents named me Edward Michael Spar. I didn't know until recently that my last name was Durston.

"Ruthie May tells me I resemble our father, Dave Durston. Did she tell you?"

"Yes, she did."

Melody Ann laid the packet of Freddy's photos under Mylowe's fingers.

"I must be going," she whispered. "It's time to feed Freddy." She leaned over him. "You will come to Des Moines, won't you?"

"Yes, as soon as I'm able to travel."

She kissed him longingly and walked out of the room.

Father Xavier stood quietly by.

"You should rest," he said to Mylowe.

"I need to ask you a favor and to keep a secret."

"What is it?"

"When Melody Ann and I settle in Des Moines, will you come and marry us?"

"It would be my pleasure."

Mylowe smiled. "I haven't asked her to marry me."

"I'm certain she'll be willing."

Mylowe closed his eyes and whispered, "You and Ruthie May are my closest relatives."

"Yes, and now you also have a son." Father Xavier bowed his head and whispered a prayer and walked away. Outside Mylowe's room, he met Dr. Whitetail.

"You're Dr. George Whitetail," he said. "I am Ruthie May's brother, Father Xavier."

George Whitetail smiled. "Father Xavier, this is an awkward meeting. I hoped it would have been at a better time."

"These are unusual circumstances. What is Mylowe's prognosis?"

"Grave, at the moment, but we are positive he will improve."

"I understand your wife and Melody Ann are staying at the Goodfellow Hotel. Would a visit from me be welcome?"

"Indeed, it would be. They need your spiritual support. We all do."

68

LIGHT IN A HARSH WORLD

While driving Melody Ann and Father Xavier from the hospital to the Goodfellow Hotel, George asked Melody Ann to stay in Cira one more day.

"I'll make first class flight reservations for you for Tuesday morning and Eve Porter will drive you to the airport."

"Why should I stay?" she asked.

"Mylowe is not out of the woods."

"Why haven't you said this before?"

"I want to keep a positive thought. Talking about my concerns changes everyone's emotional levels."

"Is Mylowe going to die?"

"I don't know. He's at a critical juncture."

"What can I do to help?"

"Be with him."

"Does Mona know about his condition?"

"Yes, tonight I'm staying with him. Would you consider taking Freddy to the hospital tomorrow?"

"If you think it's necessary, I would."

"Good!"

At the hotel entrance, Father Xavier helped Melody Ann from the car. George parked the car. They all rode the elevator to the fourth floor. George opened the door to the suite with his key card

As they walked into the room, Mona stood up from her chair.

"Freddy's sleeping," she whispered. "How is Mylowe?"

"Weak, very weak," George replied.

433

Father Xavier laid his coat over the back of a chair and looked at Mona.

"It's comforting to have you with us," she said. "Mylowe's illness has stirred a lot of emotions."

"Why is this happening to Mylowe? He's not a bad person."

"Good people also have lessons to learn in life. Many times a lesson is a penalty intended to teach us to live better. Lessons are very difficult to learn. It takes a long time to finally realize our penalties are really tests. When we don't recognize we're being tested, we fail the test. The next test becomes more complicated and more difficult to pass."

"Is there any end to the tests?" asked Melody Ann.

"Yes, after we recognize we're being tested," Mona said.

Father Xavier nodded. "That's a good point."

"But what is the next step?" asked Melody Ann.

"After we ask if we are being tested, we begin to manage the problem differently. We take time to plan a strategy in order to pass the test."

"Does this work?"

"It does if you are ready to face the lessons you're scheduled to learn."

Sitting beside Mona, George held her hand.

"Darling, I'm going to the hospital."

"Will you be there through the night?"

"Yes."

George turned toward Father Xavier.

"Father, Eve Porter is driving Ruthie May to the hospital tonight. When they are ready to go to Justin House, Eve will call you and make arrangements for you to return with them. In the meantime, Mona has ordered dinner to be served in the room. Thank you for being here."

At 8:00 a.m. the next morning, George went from Mylowe's room to the doctor's lounge to take a shower. Earlier at 4:30 a.m., he had summoned Dr. Trowbridge and Steve Hardy to the room. They examined Mylowe and agreed that the antidote was working, but much slower than anticipated.

"Steve, are we certain the dosage is sufficient?" asked George.

Steve Hardy hurried to the hospital lab to run a test on the reaction time to determine if the dosage should be increased. By 6:00 a.m. with the lab results complete, Dr. Trowbridge and George decided to increase the dosage.

After a shower, George returned to Mylowe's room. Steve Hardy was continually testing Mylowe's blood reaction every fifteen minutes. Each test result was showing improvement. By noon, Mylowe was alert.

At 1:00 p.m., the family attorney, Martin Walsh, stood in the doorway of Mylowe's room. Dr. Whitetail ushered Martin into the hallway.

"Mylowe's condition is improved," said Dr. Whitetail.

"I have legal papers that require Mylowe's signature."

"They will have to wait," Dr. Whitetail replied.

"Is Mylowe going to live?"

For all of his life, Martin Walsh had suppressed his emotions. As a child, he never cried nor displayed anger, jealousy, or hurt feelings. When he reached adulthood, he expressed himself less. Fumbling nervously through documents in his briefcase, he began to walk away, but turned around.

"Mylowe wanted to sign these documents today," he said. "Also at his request, I was able to get information about the outcome of the coroner's inquest."

George guided Martin Walsh toward a conference room. Safely inside the room, Martin spoke hurriedly. "The assistant to the coroner, Dr. Nearson, and I are school chums. We grew up in the same neighborhood."

"Did Dr. Nearson attend the coroner's inquest?"

"Yes. I spoke to him immediately after the inquest."

"Will there be a trial?"

"No, the charges against Rema Swenson and Maggie Finch will be dropped."

"Thank God."

"He did indicate that the coroner knew about the poison and the antidote on the day before the inquest. Dr. Patterson convened the inquest out of spite and a petty desire to humiliate Dr. Ort's family. The prosecutor chewed Patterson's ass for costing the county money and threatened to fire him as the medical examiner."

"That's the best news I've heard in weeks. If you don't mind, I'd like to tell Rema and Maggie. This family could use good news."

By 2:30 p.m., Mylowe opened his eyes. Dr. Whitetail leaned over him and whispered. "Melody Ann is waiting to be with you. She wants you to meet your son."

Dr. Whitetail guided Melody Ann into the room. He exited the room and stood outside. Standing by Mylowe's bedside, Melody Ann unfolded the blanket from the baby's face and held him close to Mylowe.

Freddy began to cry. Mylowe grinned at Freddy's outburst. Melody Ann leaned over Mylowe. "You will be strong again," she said. "Freddy and I need you. I wish I didn't need to return to Des Moines, but Freddy can't live in Justin House until it is repaired."

She touched his thin face and kissed him passionately. "There," she said, "that should make you want to get well." She gathered Freddy close to her. "Remember us in your dreams and come to us soon."

Two Weeks Later

Mylowe stood at the window of his hospital room. His hands and arms were strong enough to use a walker. His legs were still weak and needed more rehabilitation before they could fully support his body.

At 1:00 p.m., Ruthie May entered the room and tossed her coat over a chair. Mylowe stared at her. "I insist someone tell me the status of the problems in Justin House. George says he hasn't had a final report."

Ruthie May stood beside him. "The Cira firefighters completed the search for additional poison in Justin House. The deadly poison was confined to Eben's Tower. However, there is black Stachybotrys mold between the interior walls of the six bathrooms."

"What do they recommend?"

"Tear down Eben's Tower and have a qualified company do a mold remediation on the bathroom and kitchen walls. Fortunately, Rema has not been affected by the mold. She feels lucky."

"When are you and Rema moving to President Matthews' house?"

"The firemen said we could stay in the house until after the Christmas holidays. Before you go to Des Moines, would you come to dinner with the family?"

Mylowe sighed. "If George agrees, I'd like nothing better. Is Maggie still working at the house?"

"She's there every day and will continue to work for Rema at President Matthews' house."

Mylowe stared at Ruthie May. "Now that life seems to be on a more even keel, what are you going to do?"

Ruthie May bowed her head. "I received a check from my father's government service insurance. I've decided to study philosophy at Wexlor University. I also want to learn the social graces and be able to take Rema's place as the matron of Justin House should it become necessary."

Mylowe held her hand. "Someday you'll be first lady of Justin House."

"Shouldn't Melody Ann be first lady?"

"Only if you aren't able."

"Oh! I almost forgot. Eve hired a companion to be with Rema."

"Good! I was concerned you'd feel obligated to stay with her. You need to be doing other things with your life."

"I have a question. Will you and Melody Ann come back from Des Moines and live in Justin House? What would you do if it turns out the house is not inhabitable?"

"I'll tear it down and build an exact duplicate."

"And what about building your clinic?"

"I'm still planning to build it on the hill behind the Justin House. Why are you asking all these questions?"

"I want to tell Rema your plans."

"Does she think I'm deserting her?"

"I'm not certain. I know she lives life as best she can without feeling guilty for failing the people around her."

"She hasn't failed anyone. If anything, she's guilty of love in the first degree."

"She's lonely. Mona lives in Miami, and Eve Porter returned to Michigan. I hope you won't stay away too long."

"I've done things in my life I wish I could undo. But for now, going to Des Moines is the right choice."

69

REFLECTION

A week later

In her bedroom, Rema felt the morning's momentum come to a halt. She finished gathering the robes and slippers she would use for the next three months while she and Ruthie May were living in the university president's mansion. She breathed a rebellious sigh and sat down. Her lifeless arm dropped into her lap and tears welled in her eyes. She realized she was living on sheer will power and had used up all her joy. Day by day, the joy of helping others had fallen away. How did it happen? She wasn't prepared to die and couldn't leave this life without finding Emille.

She went to the closet. Shoving the hangers back and forth, she selected a blouse and skirt and dressed quickly. She was putting on sandals when she heard a tap on the door.

"Come in," she said.

"It's only me," said Mona dragging a piece of luggage. "I'm here to help you pack." She dropped the luggage and gasped. "Good Lord! Look at you. You're wearing your Gypsy clothes. You have knitting needles stuck in your hair. It's been ten years since you've dressed like that."

"You're right. I need to feel 40 again. What are dragging?"

"Your luggage! I'm here to help you pack." Standing by the bed, Mona yelled. "What is this? Are you packing only robes and slippers?"

"I'm not putting much effort in moving."

"Do you realize a move from Justin House could change your life? It's the 90's. There's great interest in astrology these days. You should teach astrology at the university."

"At this point of my life, I've some new concepts about astrology."

"What are you saying?"

"Behavior in past lives that was caused by the movement and magnetism of the planets also produced karma."

"Was it John's vendetta or Paul Moore's impersonation of Emille that changed your thinking?"

"The planets foretold that I would be prey to some underhanded scheme. John's vendetta against me was an accumulation of karma that was created during our many past lives together."

"So-o-o-o-o?"

"Karma, good or bad, comes back threefold."

"I know. I still remember what you told me the first time you explained karma to me."

"What did I say?"

"You said if parents abuse their children in one life, in the next life those parents could be reborn as children and return to the same family unit where the former children had returned as parents. The parents would abuse the children. It's karmic payback."

Mona grinned. "I envision Felic coming back as a female and you as a male. Wouldn't that be a great payback?"

Rema smiled. "I suppose it would be. That is not likely to happen because fate and destiny radiate a distinct authority. It affects what we do."

"How?"

"Life provides the stage and gives us the tools for living. We're the actors. We carry the reckoning from lifetime to lifetime of what happened in previous lives. From those accounts, our fate is designed for the current life."

"What does destiny do?"

"Destiny is the outcome of how we handle the tools fate gives us. If we were schooled to understand karma, reincarnation would have a different meaning. Until we understand karma, we continue from one life to the next acting out old behavioral patterns."

"What does astrology do?"

"In astrology, the birth chart is destiny. It shows personality and character, natural abilities and psychological makeup. The progressed chart, usually interpreted for the upcoming twelve months, indicates opportunities, upheaval and lessons. It works for many people and satisfies their need to relate to the stars and the cosmos. In times of major lifestyle changes and global unrest, astrology helps people navigate through change."

Mona pleaded. "Please reconsider teaching at the university."

Rema choked. "I cannot."

"Why?"

"Julia Farnsworth is the current Dean of Girls at Wexlor University."

"Why should she concern you?"

"She had an affair with Felic for five years."

"How do you know about the affair?"

"I read her love notes to Felic."

"When?"

"It was on the day I found Felic's old briefcase in my closet."

Mona slumped down on the bed. "Holy Toledo! Why have you kept Felic's love affairs a secret?"

"I was embarrassed for him. His colleagues thought so well of him, I didn't want to ruin his good name."

"You may have saved his good name, but you gave away something every woman gives away when her man cheats."

"What is that?"

"Her self worth."

Rema nodded. "Maybe that's true."

The conversation between the long-time friends ended when Maggie stood in the doorway.

"Yes, Maggie," Rema said.

"Will there be five for dinner? Dr. George is bringing Mylowe from the hospital for dinner."

"Set the table for six."

"Six?" Maggie queried. "There's only five."

"Father Xavier will be coming."

Maggie shook her head and hurried away.

By five o'clock, when Rema and Mona came downstairs, George and Mylowe were already sitting in the den by the fireplace.

Mylowe stood and hugged Rema. "If it's only for tonight, it's good to be home," he whispered.

Mona reached over and gave him a kindly, yet firm bear hug.

"Are Ruthie May and Father Xavier coming?" George asked.

"Ruthie's in the kitchen helping Maggie," replied Mona. "Father Xavier will be here shortly." She pointed toward the small table behind the sofa. "Have a drink. Dinner is almost ready."

"Good," George murmured. "I'll have one."

At that moment Ruthie May entered the room. Smiling, she said, "The early dinner requested by the attending physician in charge of our patient is ready."

Rema nodded and led them into the dining room. The muted light from the ornate gold wall sconces reflected off of the crystal wine glasses on the linen-clothed table. Each found their place as Father Xavier arrived. Mylowe stood behind the red velvet chair at the end of the table and motioned Father Xavier toward the empty chair at his right. Ruthie May stood at Mylowe's left. Mona was next to her. Rema was positioned at the other end of the table. George stood next to Father Xavier. Rema nodded and they all sat down.

After dinner, during dessert, Rema asked, "Have you noticed?"

"Noticed what?" asked Mylowe.

"We're a real family."

"I've felt that for many years," said George.

"Until recently, we did not have blood-related members," said Mona. "Rema says being together is fate and we have a lot to learn from each other."

"Well, this family began with Rema," Mylowe said. "When Felic found me in Dead Man's Alley, he took me to Rema and the family began with three members. Mona joined the family when Rema and Mona became friends. George entered the family because he wanted to help me. That made five members."

Mona looked at Mylowe. "You found Ruthie May. She was number six."

Excitedly, Ruthie May said, "My brother, Father Xavier, made seven. Mylowe, my brother and I are the blood-related members."

Rema nodded. "I think we all realize we are together to learn from each other and grow spiritually."

Mona tapped a spoon against her wine glass. "If regular families sense they had been together in past lives and know they are now together to learn from each other, does that change the way they act toward each other?"

"It makes a difference," Rema replied. "But it won't happen to all families until all societies believe in the reincarnated life."

"Can each of us in this family define what we have learned from each other?" asked Mona. "Since six of us were together in one particular past life, do the problems and experiences in China behind the moon gate make us more compatible?"

Mylowe nodded. "The knowledge we carry from one life to another is helpful. It's not just one past life that advances the level of our soul."

Rema nodded. "Felic wanted to be able to choose reincarnation. He said he felt shackled. He felt it unfair that the decision to come back into life was not his to make."

"Shackled?" Mona blurted in a raised tone. "Felic put the handcuffs on himself this lifetime." She shrugged. "I'd be curious to know what happened in my other past lives. Maybe I'd learn why I always talk out of turn and cause myself so much trouble."

"How many lifetimes have we all been together?" asked Ruthie May.

"I would guess it has been more than one," replied George.

Rema agreed and said, "We carry forward into each life our most important characteristic that defines our personality and makes us who we are. Being surrounded by the same souls helps up reach that level quicker."

Mylowe raised his glass. "May we return from destiny and be together again without end."

"Is now and ever shall be," whispered Father Xavier. "Amen."

70

THE
LOST and the FOUND

1998
Three years later

By dusk on the final day of construction, Mylowe's new medical clinic behind Justin House was ready for occupancy. As the tradesmen removed the last of the construction debris, Mylowe decided he couldn't let someone else figure out how to separate the half acre of ground between the clinic and the house. He despised the original plan of a high wire enclosure around the clinic. Frustrated by the set back, he unrolled the architect's plans and spread them across the top of his desk.

Sensing the answer was in front of him, but he was too tired to see it, he slouched in the chair, looked through a pile of yesterday's mail and wondered if it was a mistake to build his home office on the west side of Justin House with the only access through the kitchen.

Three years ago, the old mansion survived an internal sanitary cleansing to kill the mold caused by the Kalabee tree in Eben's tower. That same year in Des Moines, after he and Melody Ann were married, he returned to Boston and finished his medical internship.

After a year of being apart, they were now together. Despite his work in the clinic, he wanted to be a part of the everyday life in Justin House and added the office to the house to be near his family. Maybe a tunnel between the clinic and house was the answer.

He smiled at the thought but the reverie was short-lived when he realized he tossed an envelope in the waste basket addressed to Rema Swenson from Berrywood Psychiatric Home Center in Florida. Thinking he needed to stay focused, he shoved it in his jacket pocket.

The following morning before Ruthie May, went to her class at Wexlor University, she walked through the kitchen and stood in the doorway of Mylowe's office. He looked up from the set of building plans.

"Good morning," he said. "What class do you have today?"

"Psychology 101."

"Aren't you late?"

"I wanted you to know there's a message for Rema on the house phone from Dr. Terrence Mayfield."

"Where is Rema this morning?"

"Adele drove her to therapy."

"Ok, I'll take the message."

An hour later in the kitchen, Mylowe listened to Dr. Mayfield's message.

"Mrs. Swenson, this is Dr. Terrence Mayfield, Director of Berrywood Home Center. I sent you a letter regarding your relative who is one of our residents. Please call me."

After listening to the message, Mylowe shook his head and thought the call was a unique method of soliciting money. He redialed the number shown on the message board.

After four rings, a female voice said, "Berrywood Home Center, may I direct your call?"

"Dr. Mayfield, please."

"Thank you."

When Dr. Mayfield answered, Mylowe explained he was Rema Swenson's son and found Rema's letter mixed in with his office mail.

That evening after dinner, Mylowe and Melody Ann put Freddy to bed. Before eight o'clock, he tapped on Rema's bedroom. "May I come in?"

Rema was reclining on the divan.

"While you were at therapy today, there was a phone message for you from a Dr. Mayfield. I returned his call. He is the director of Berrywood Psychiatric Home Center in Florida."

"Did he want a contribution?"

"No, he said he sent you this letter."

Mylowe took the envelope from his jacket pocket, opened it and gave her the letter to read.

She gasped. "This doctor says a resident in his home center is a close relative of mine."

"Could it be one of your brothers?"

"No, it's all a mistake."

"Don't give it another thought. I'll call Dr. Mayfield in the morning."

During the morning call to Dr. Mayfield, Mylowe explained that Rema did not have a living relative and her health was fragile.

"How can this situation be resolved?" he asked.

"You could meet with the private investigators."

"Investigators?"

"We use qualified, professional investigators when we believe knowledge of a resident's personal family background will be beneficial to his future. The investigators work on a volunteer basis. Therefore, their progress on behalf of a resident is frequently very slow."

"Under what criteria is a resident afforded a private investigation?"

"A resident must live in our home center for a period of five years, continue to advance mentally and be qualified to live in a group home. If a family member is not listed on the resident's record, we are reluctant to transfer him to a group home."

"What are your reasons?"

"It's not our policy to throw one of our resident's into the water without evaluating the depth. At some time, he may be able to live on his own. Should he need assistance, there would be no one responsible for his welfare."

Although at the moment, Mylowe's main concern was to correct the assumption that Rema had a relative living at the home center, he was intrigued with the center's operational policies and wanted to learn more. He told Dr. Mayfield he was planning to be in Miami the next week and made an appointment to meet with the investigators.

Five days later on Saturday morning, Mylowe arrived at Berrywood Home Center. Although the home center was not contiguous to Berrywood Psychiatric Hospital, it was less than a mile away.

Coming from his office Dr. Mayfield exclaimed, "Dr. Ort, I'm pleased you would come. As I explained, we are located in the boonies."

"Until today, I'd not been in the panhandle part of Florida."

"Come into my office. I'll share some preliminary information about our resident before the investigators arrive."

Seated at a boardroom table, Dr. Mayfield read aloud from a patient file.

"A male patient, called Tim, was transferred from a small state mental institution to Berrywood Psychiatric Hospital. In 1993, his original medical records had been destroyed in the institution's fire. Without records, the institution's staff evaluated his age as thirty. They said as a young lad, Tim had sustained damage to a portion of his brain. It is unclear how the damage occurred."

Dr. Mayfield stopped reading and closed the patient file. "Our staff assigned Tim menial chores. He worked in the kitchen where Sam Chung, our chef, gave him special care. With staff supervision, Sam made soups and teas for Tim using Chinese herbs that might stimulate electrical activity in his brain. Over the next two years, our staff was astounded by Tim's progress. His memory was returning. He was able to speak haltingly. In one therapy session, he said he took rides in the ocean on a large boat called the Mi Toi."

Dr. Mayfield stood up as two men entered the room.

"Gentlemen," he said, "this is Dr. Ort. He is Rema Swenson's son."

Mylowe stood and shook hands with the investigators. "Rema Swenson raised me. I am not her biological son."

Dr. Mayfield turned to one of the men. "Dr. Ort is aware of Tim's early background. Charlie, will you continue?"

Charlie Watson sat down and opened his portfolio. "Tim's scant memory was a real challenge," he said. "Our only clue was a boat called the Mi Toi.

"The Florida archives of boat registrations revealed the Mi Toi was registered in 1968. The owner was John Swenson. I visited the Miami home address listed on the registration and talked to the current resident. He did not know the Swenson's.

"On a hunch, we searched newspaper archives for the word, Mi Toi, and found it had appeared on December 10, 1969, in the Miami Herald. The byline stated that an oceanographer, John Swenson, and his son, Emille, drowned in the Atlantic. The damaged boat, the Mi Toi, was recovered by the Coast Guard.

"Checking Dade County birth records, we did not find a record for John Swenson, but Emille Swenson was born May 11, 1962, in Miami, Florida. His parents were John and Rema Perez Swenson."

Mylowe gasped, pulled himself forward in his chair and leaned over the table. "How did you find Rema Swenson?"

Charlie Watson nodded toward Andy Smith. "Andy volunteered to find Rema," he said.

Andy opened his portfolio. "In a subsequent group session," he said, "Tim remembered his mother went to college. When queried in a later session, Tim said his mother found homes for little orphans.

"We knew it was a long shot when we made the decision to check with various welfare agencies in the Miami area rather than search through college records in every part of the country."

Andy wiped a thin trickle of sweat from his face. "It was a slow process and a disappointment when we decided Rema Swenson's trail was cold.

"A month later, we placed ads in Florida newspapers requesting information about Rema Perez Swenson."

Andy smiled and turned to the notes. "On Tuesday morning, February, 1997, I received a call from Dennis Wilson. He worked at Wilson's Bail Bonds in Miami. He said his uncle, Pinchey Wilson, knew a woman called Rema Perez Swenson. The nephew was cautious about providing information over the phone.

"On my next trip to Miami, I made an appointment and went to Wilson's office. After both men learned the purpose of my mission, Pinchey gave me the information we had been seeking.

"He said he met Rema after her husband and son drowned. She worked as night supervisor at a half-way house in Miami and gave astrology readings as a sideline. She lived in a trailer park across the street from the homeless shelter on the west side of the city.

"He knew she agreed to raise an abandoned infant and move to Ohio. Over the years, during conversations with her best friend, he learned Rema's husband and son were not dead. They had come back and stole from her. After Emille died from drug use, Rema learned from John that Emille was Paul Moore, an imposter he had hired to get revenge. John Swenson died weeks later. Pinchey copied Rema's Ohio address from the rolodex and give it to me. That's how we found Rema."

There was a long pause before Mylowe could speak.

"Your information is correct," he whispered. "I believe Tim is Emille Swenson. As you know, Rema has mourned three times for Emille. To tell her he is alive will be a chore. I'll need documented proof.

"In time, perhaps Emille might be able to solve the mystery of what happened to him. There have been several versions. John said they lived in Cuba for twenty years. Dr. Drench Martin's research indicated John actually operated a bar in Key West, Florida, and a young boy, possibly Emille, drowned while swimming.

"I wonder how Emille arrived at the mental institution. Was it John who placed him there? Did he ever visit him?"

Dr. Mayfield nodded. "I believe with the care you will give him in your clinic, Emille will be able to solve the mystery."

"Would you like to meet Tim?" asked Dr. Mayfield.

"Yes."

The next afternoon, Mylowe tapped on Rema's bedroom door.

"What happened in Florida?" she asked.

Mylowe held her hand as he told her about Tim.

She read all of the investigator's documentation and looked at Mylowe. "Are you really sure?"

"Yes."

"I hope you told them to bring him here," she whispered.

"Yes, Dr. Mayfield will bring him."

"When?"

"Within the next month. For a time, he will be more comfortable to stay in my clinic but you can visit every day."

"Will he remember me? Have you told the family? Do George and Mona know?"

"Yes."

As Mylowe moved to sit beside her, Angel, a fluffy ball of white fur, jumped off the divan.

"You know, when Emille died and his spirit didn't come to me, I felt he might still be alive. Could he have been the little boy in my past life regression when all our family members were in China?"

"It's possible. I brought a recent picture. Would you like to see him?"

When she took the photo from him, her soul released prolonged agony and expressed overwhelming joy. In her hand was the manly image of the boy in her heart.

In the years following, with care and love, Emille's physical condition stabilized while living at Justin House. His childhood memories remain indistinct. Still lingering is his haunting vision of rising to the surface of the ocean and seeing the stoical face of his father.

About the Author

The author, an octogenarian and a third generation metaphysician, has provided personal growth counsel nationwide for half of her life. She lives with her husband and cat, Missy, in Mayfield Heights, Ohio.

Printed in the United States
105262LV00001B/121/A